D1201219

ALSO BY SILVIA MORENO-GARCIA

Certain Dark Things

Signal to Noise

Love & Other Poisons

This Strange Way of Dying

The Beautiful Ones

SILVIA MORENO-GARCIA

THOMAS DUNNE BOOKS
ST. MARTIN'S PRESS
NEW YORK

THOMAS DUNNE BOOKS.

An imprint of St. Martin's Press.

THE BEAUTIFUL ONES. Copyright © 2017 by Silvia Moreno-Garcia.
All rights reserved. Printed in the United States of America.
For information, address St. Martin's Press, 175 Fifth Avenue, New York, N.Y. 10010.

www.thomasdunnebooks.com
www.stmartins.com

Designed by Devan Norman

Library of Congress Cataloging-in-Publication Data

Names: Moreno-Garcia, Silvia, author.
Title: The beautiful ones / Silvia Moreno-Garcia.
Description: New York : Thomas Dunne Books/St. Martin's Press, 2017.
Identifiers: LCCN 2017021477 | ISBN 978-1-250-09906-8 (hardcover) | ISBN 978-1-250-09907-5 (ebook)
Subjects: LCSH: Psychic ability—Fiction. | Socialites—Fiction. | Paranormal romance stories. | GSAFD: Fantasy fiction. | Love stories.
Classification: LCC PR9199.4.M656174 B43 2017 | DDC 813/.6—dc23
LC record available at https://lccn.loc.gov/2017021477

Our books may be purchased in bulk for promotional, educational, or business use. Please contact your local bookseller or the Macmillan Corporate and Premium Sales Department at 1-800-221-7945, extension 5442, or by email at MacmillanSpecialMarkets@macmillan.com.

First Edition: October 2017

10 9 8 7 6 5 4 3 2 1

Para mi abuela

PART ONE

Chapter 1

HECTOR WAS LIKE A CASTAWAY who had washed up on a room of velvet curtains and marble floors. The revelers might as well have been wild animals ready to tear off a chunk of his flesh.

He felt utterly lost, alien and alone.

As Hector watched from a corner of the room, ladies and gentlemen partnered to dance, women fanned themselves and smiled, and men greeted each other with a tilt of the head.

He had attended many glittering balls, but none in this city. He knew no one here except for Étienne and Luc, and he was waiting with breathless expectation for the arrival of Valérie Beaulieu.

The first thing he'd done upon disembarking was to make discreet inquiries about the whereabouts of the lady. He was glad to discover she was in Loisail and, moreover, that she would be at the ball thrown by the De Villiers. He had no direct connection to the De Villiers—or hardly anyone else in Loisail, for that matter, having spent the past ten years abroad—but he did know Étienne Lémy, who was able to secure him an invitation.

Hector had dressed according to the weight of the occasion in a new double-breasted black dress coat, white shirt, and a white bow tie. White gloves and mother-of-pearl studs completed the ensemble. In his excitement, he arrived unfashionably early, not wishing to miss Valérie, and after greeting his host had positioned himself strategically so that he could watch every elegant guest who entered the vast ballroom. But Hector had not been long at his post when he heard a couple of ladies commenting that Mrs. Beaulieu had been taken ill and would not be in attendance, which came as a shock to the women since Valérie Beaulieu's missing the opening of the season seemed unthinkable.

All his plans in tatters, the whole reason for his attendance at the ball suddenly vanishing, Hector did not know what to do with himself. Unable to stand the music and the noise, he escaped to the library, which was gloriously empty, its furniture decorated with a profusion of brass inlays, the bookcases primly protected with glass doors. The only reasonable course of action at this point was to wait there until he could perform a proper exit without seeming rude. He could not possibly retire until nine o'clock.

Hector consulted his watch, and after deliberating, he decided he'd brush up on his history. He wound up flipping through the pages of a book without touching them, having dragged a chair closer to him with a motion of his left hand, his talent at work. He did not read a single line, too troubled by thoughts of Valérie Beaulieu to make heads or tails of the words.

When they last saw each other, they'd both been nineteen, nothing but children, really. But he'd loved her. She had been beautiful, sophisticated, captivating. A perverse part of him hoped that time had somewhat washed away the colors from her face, but in his heart he knew this was impossible and that Valérie Beaulieu must remain as he remembered her: the most devastating woman in the room.

And he would not be seeing her that night.

The clock on the wall struck nine and the door opened. In walked a young woman in a blue pastel silk and velvet dress with appliquéd flowers along the bodice and skirt, the sleeves rather puffed out, as was in vogue.

She closed the door, taking several steps into the room before she raised her head and caught sight of him. "Sir," she said. "I'm sorry, I didn't realize there was anybody here."

"It's no matter," he replied, closing the book with his hands rather than with his mind; he reserved displays of his talent for the stage. He did not add anything else. He was hardly in the mood for polite conversation. The De Villiers prided themselves on attracting the cream of the crop to their functions—the Beautiful Ones, rather than the New People. The barons of barely minted empires of telegraph wires and fresh steel could socialize elsewhere. Hector had been offered an invitation, proof of Étienne's charm and his connections, but he knew he was, at best, a novelty for these aristocrats; at worst, an intruder. He did not wish to befriend any of them and threw the young woman a frosty look. The girl did not take his cue.

She looked at him carefully, her lips curving into a smile as she moved closer. "I know you. You are Hector Auvray."

"Pardon me, were we introduced?" he asked, frowning. He was sure he had not seen this girl before. He had been presented to the hosts, and Étienne had pointed out a few people, but not her.

"I recognize your face from the posters around town. You are performing at the Royal. *Phantasmagoric: Feats of Wonder,* isn't it? I was hoping to meet you," she said.

"Oh?" he replied, a noncommittal sound, even if his interest had been piqued. Few aristocrats would admit to knowing the name of a vulgar entertainer. Instead, they nodded their heads politely and either assumed or pretended he was a slightly more elevated type of person.

"What were you reading?" she asked, pointing at the book he was clutching between his hands.

"History. Miss—"

"Nina," she said, stretching out her hand. "Antonina, really, but I rather hate it. I'm named after a witch of a great-aunt, the most awful wretch who ever lived. Well, not quite, but I resent the association, and therefore it is Nina."

"Hector, though you already know that part." He shook her hand. "It's probably best if we exit this room now. A bachelor such as myself, a young lady such as yourself—we wouldn't want to cause a scandal."

Truly, he wanted only to get rid of her and could not have cared what anyone thought. If the girl wished to walk around the house without an escort, then let it be. He had come to speak to one woman and one woman alone. If she was not there, then Hector would wallow in his velvet misery.

"I can't possibly leave now," she replied.

"Why not?" he asked, annoyed.

She did not notice his tone of voice or did not care. Instead, she took off the dance card dangling by her wrist and held it up for him to look at.

"If I go out there now, Didier Dompierre is going to ask me for a dance, and if you'd ever danced with Didier, you would know he is the most terrible dancer. I have been told he'll put his name down for two dances, and you must be aware a lady cannot refuse a dance from a gentleman. It would be uncivil."

Hector did not understand why a man might want to corral this particular girl for two dances in a row. She was not an enviable beauty— somewhat run-of-the-mill, to be frank—and her square jaw, black hair, and thin lips were rather unstylish. She possessed eyes of a pretty shade of hazel, though, and her dress was very fine; perhaps that was enough for a young chap with poor dance skills such as this Didier Dompierre.

"Then your thought is to spend the rest of the evening here, avoiding him?"

"Not the rest of the evening, but, say, a half an hour, and by then he will have found some other girl he can stomp on," she replied, sitting in the chair in front of him and stretching her legs.

"This does not seem the best-conceived plan."

"It is a plan, which is what matters. Whom are *you* hiding from?" she asked. If she were another woman, this might have been mistaken for an attempt at flirting. Valérie would have taken the opportunity to lace her voice with honey, but the girl was plain and spoke plainly.

"I am not hiding from anyone," he said.

"Do you make it a habit to go to balls, then, and creep into the library to brush up on your history?"

"Do you talk to all men in this manner?" he replied, growing more curious than irritated.

She toyed with her dance card, putting it again on her wrist, and gave him a mortified look. "I apologize. This is only the second dance I've attended, and I can see it will end catastrophically already."

"This is the second party of the De Villiers' you've attended?" he asked.

"The second party in the city I've ever attended, and this is the beginning of the Grand Season, the true test of a lady's mettle. You must not think me a complete fool. I went to a couple of dances in Montipouret, but it was different. Small affairs. Loisail is large and there are many people and the rules are different."

He was talking to a country girl, for clearly the designation of "woman" would have been misplaced on her. Worse than that, a country rube. But Hector could not help but feel more sympathy than distaste. He had, after all, been a country nothing at one time and less polished than this girl.

He smiled despite himself, to assuage her. "No doubt you'll learn them soon. You seem quick-witted."

"Thank you," she replied, appearing rather pleased with his words.

She looked at him curiously and another smile crossed her face. "I must confess, I know more about you than your name from looking at the posters. I read about you in *The Gazette for Physical Research*. Alexander Nicolay has been investigating your telekinetic abilities."

"Are you a fan of *The Gazette*?" he asked, surprised that she'd be informed about Nicolay's research. He'd bumped into the man a couple of years back. He was attempting to measure and classify all psychokinetic talents and convinced Hector to let him take his pulse while he manipulated objects with the force of his mind. It was the sort of thing people did not think to bring up in casual conversation.

"Not particularly. But I am interested in the phenomena. They say you are one of the great psychokinetics of our era."

"I'm a decent performer," he replied.

"Modest, too."

She was a curious girl, and now he reassessed her again. Not an aristocrat and not a country rube and—what exactly? He didn't like it when he couldn't classify people.

He gestured toward the door. "Shall I escort you to the ballroom?"

She looked down at her dance card, carefully running her fingers around its edge. "Yes. If you feel inclined, you might partner with me for a dance. I would be really thankful. I was not exaggerating when I said Didier Dompierre is the worst dancer you've ever seen. Is that a terrible request? It's not, is it?"

He was somewhat amused by the question and her tone of voice, and though the girl's nervous energy at first did not sit too well with him, he had to admit he felt a bit relieved by her intrusion. He was full to bursting with thoughts of Valérie and could do with a few minutes more of light chatter. It would also satisfy the practical necessity of actually show-ing himself at the ball, which he ought to do at one point. He could not spend every single minute in the library. He could wallow later, in the privacy of his apartment.

"One dance."

She took his arm before he offered it to her as they exited the library, which was presumptuous.

The owners of the house had placed mirrors on the walls of the cor-ridor that led to the ballroom, an ostentatious touch, but this was a new trend that was sweeping the capital and soon the nation. Whatever took the fancy of Loisail would take the fancy of the whole of Levrene; this was a known fact.

The ballroom was huge, with tall gilded mirrors reflecting the attend-ees, magnifying the space: the party seemed to go on forever. Above them hung monstrous chandeliers that sparkled with all their might, and all around them there were ladies with their shoulders bare, in their fine silks, while the gentlemen stood sober and proud, creating a glorious rain-bow of colors, from the restrained browns of the matriarchs to the pale pinks of the unmarried women.

Hector carefully took hold of Antonina's hand and they joined the dance. He did not consider himself an excellent dancer, though he could manage. His partner fared poorly, but gave the feeling of being enter-tained.

"Do you know Loisail well, Mr. Auvray? Or is this your first time here? It wouldn't be, would it?"

"I don't know it well, no. I've spent only a few days in Loisail before my move here."

"How do you find it? Is it different from the cities where you've lived?" she asked.

He thought of the myriad countries and stages where he'd toured. To be back in his country of birth, in Levrene, was to be back home, though not due to a quirk of geography but because this was where Valérie resided. Here, in Loisail, even if she was hidden away at this moment. She existed and colored the city for him, lit it brighter than the elegant iron lampposts.

"Interesting. I have yet to form a strong opinion of it," he said po-litely.

"Then you intend to remain for a while?"

"I will be performing for a few months here, yes. As to whether I intend to make it my permanent base of operations, we shall see. And you?"

He did not expect her to launch into a complete and honest answer. A touch of coquetry, the outline of a smile, those would have been suitable. This had been Valérie's way.

The girl clutched his hand excitedly. "I'll most definitely be here until the summer. I am spending all of the spring with my cousin. My mother thinks a time in the city would do me good. Where are you lodging? My cousin's house is in Saint Illare."

"I think you've asked another bold question," he informed her.

"Is it, really?"

Her words were candid and he found himself amused by the naivety. Rather than schooling her with a scowl and a clipped yes, which normally suited him magnificently, he gave her a proper answer.

"To the east. Boniface. Not as smart as your cousin's house, I would wager," he said.

"Boniface. Is that so you can remain near the theater?"

"Indeed."

"I'm sure it's smart enough. Boniface."

As the dance ended, a young man moved in their direction, his eyes on Antonina. Hector was going to incline his head and release the girl, but on contemplating the look of pure panic that crossed her face, he did his best to suppress a chuckle and instead asked her for a second dance. She accepted and told him the man who had been moving toward them was poor Didier. In the end, he danced a total of three dances with Nina, but since two of the three were lively stevkas, they did not speak more than a few words.

After he had thanked her for the dances and strolled away, Étienne Lémy and his little brother, Luc, wandered over. Étienne was Hector's age and Luc a handful of years younger, though looking at them, people always swore they were twins, so alike were they, both possessing the same blond hair and stylish mustache. They furthered the illusion that evening by wearing matching gray vests.

"There you are, you devil. I couldn't find you anywhere," Étienne said, clasping his shoulder. "For a moment I thought you'd left."

"Not at all. I was dancing," Hector said.

"We saw. With Miss Beaulieu," Luc replied.

Hector did not realize until then that the girl had given him only her first name. He had not bothered to inquire further.

"Beaulieu?" he managed to say.

"Surely you've heard of them. Gaetan Beaulieu. She is his cousin," Luc said. "You have not met Gaetan?"

"I haven't had the pleasure."

"You must. He has the most magnificent wife imaginable, the most beautiful woman in all of the city, Va—"

"Valérie," Hector said, interrupting him.

"Yes. You do know them, then?"

"We both had the chance to meet Valérie before she was married to Gaetan, when she was in Frotnac," Étienne said, maneuvering Luc by his elbow and turning him around. "Luc, why don't you dance with Mari? She's our cousin and looks quite alone."

Luc glanced at a young woman standing by a mirror, the picture of a wallflower. The youngest Lémy made a face as though he had swallowed a lemon. "For good reason."

"Go on, Luc. It is your burden as a gentleman."

"She is a third cousin, and you know Mother keeps buzzing in my ear about her, driving me to madness," Luc protested.

"The more reason to dance with her," Étienne pressed on with a voice that allowed no further reproach.

The younger man let out an exasperated sigh but went in search of the lady.

As soon as his brother was at a prudent distance, Étienne spoke, his voice low. "You should not consider it. Not even for a moment."

"Consider what?" Hector asked. Antonina Beaulieu hovered not too far from them, milling about a small circle of people. He wondered if Gaetan resembled her. He'd not seen a picture of the man. Did he sport that dark hair and the long fingers that might have belonged to a pianist? Beaulieu! A thrice-damned Beaulieu.

"Don't act the fool. Valérie Beaulieu. You lost your head for her," Étienne said.

"Ten years ago," Hector said coolly, attempting to conceal any emotion in his voice.

"Ten, but I still recognize that look," Étienne assured him.

Hector did not reply, his eyes following the movements of Miss Antonina Beaulieu across the room. He made up both an excuse and his exit after that.

Chapter 2

NINA COULD NOT SAY THAT she was truly taken with Loisail. The possibilities the city offered were exciting and it was a lively place, but there were many rules she did not understand, many people whose names she could not remember, all the protocols and details only the seasoned resident could grasp. Furthermore, she missed her mother and her sister. She missed her home, which was not as elegant as her cousin's but which struck her as more inviting. She missed her beetles and her butterflies and was horrified when she considered all the species she would not be able to collect that spring.

But despite her homesickness, Nina understood that this was a great opportunity. The time spent in Loisail would allow her to refine her ways—there was no place as sophisticated and modern as Loisail, they said in books and newspapers—and it would permit her to make valuable connections. Most of all, the city might yield a suitable husband.

She knew well the kind of man her mother expected her to marry. A fellow from a decent family, with an excellent reputation and a generous amount of money at his disposal. It was all good and proper to marry a viscount, but when he came with a withered estate in dire need of repair, the coat of arms lost its luster. Nina's sister, Madelena, had wed a respectable physician and a member of the neighboring Évariste family.

It had pleased their mother, but Nina thought their tale lacked romance. Madelena and her husband had played together since they were children. Everyone assumed they would wed. Madelena's husband hardly even really courted her, knowing the answer even before he asked.

Nina dreamed a different outcome. The romantic novels she had read imprinted on her the notion of a dashing suitor. She'd read of men who inspired women to blush prettily, who made their hearts hammer in their chests, who could cause a girl to swoon. She'd read, yes, but never experienced it. Montipouret offered her only the well-intentioned neighboring boys from the Évariste estate and the serious, subdued Delafois. Boys who neither caught her attention nor were keen to court her. The city, though. The city could yield the chance of romance. While her mother was expecting only a suitable match, Nina was hoping for the romance of a lifetime followed by the grandest wedding imaginable.

She'd had no luck. Young, cosseted, she wished for someone dapper, like the men in her books. Didier Dompierre was the only boy who had made any serious attempt to pursue her, and Nina could not possibly picture him in a romantic light.

But that morning, as Nina dressed with the assistance of Lisette, the lady's maid Valérie had assigned her, she thought maybe her luck had changed: she could not get Hector Auvray out of her head.

He'd danced three dances with her. Three! Surely that meant something. She might have asked Lisette for reassurance on this matter, but the maid was prickly and resented being pressed into service of the youngest Beaulieu on account of Nina's restlessness, which often manifested with the levitation of objects across a room. In particular, Nina misplaced shoes. A single shoe would wind up on a side table, the mantelpiece, or some other place. Nina didn't intend to do any of this, it was a tic, but that did not mean Valérie screamed any less at Lisette, taking it out on the poor maid.

Lisette adjusted the collar of Nina's dress and made sure her hair was impeccable—Cousin Valérie was particular about her hair. Nina was running late, what with her daydreaming, and the maid huffed. Valérie was also keen on punctuality. Nina quickly made her way to Valérie's room, knocking twice.

"Come in," Valérie said. She was still in bed, her hair undone, and in a robe, but she looked practically perfect, as was always the case. Her room, too, was all for show, resembling the displays at the department stores downtown.

"Good morning," Nina said. "Lisette said you're not feeling well."

"It's another one of those dreadful migraines."

Valérie had just had a migraine the week before, the night before the De Villiers' ball. Secretly Nina had been pleased that Valérie decided to stay home. Valérie's attention to detail, her rules and demands, was stifling. When they went out in public, Valérie expected the world of Nina.

"Should I head to the park on my own, then?"

This was one of those city customs that Nina did not understand even though Valérie had explained it to her. It was of the utmost importance that twice a week between the hours of nine and ten they walk or ride around the nearby White Park, which was one of the largest parks in the city. The point, Valérie said, was to be seen. All the notable women in the city would—at least once a week—take a leisurely excursion through one of the popular green areas. Valérie scheduled her visits with rigor and chose the mornings because to stroll in a park in the evening, she confided, would be invariably crude. In the evenings a lady should be attending a party or a dinner, heading to the theater or the opera, not walking around in the semidarkness. Nina, who caught fireflies in the twilight hours during the summer, could only nod.

"I think you should be able to manage without me," Valérie said.

"Are you certain? I could stay and read to you."

Valérie pressed a slender, graceful hand against her forehead. "It would do no good. Go on and be sure to return by noon."

"I will."

Nina kissed Valérie on the cheek to mark her departure, a gesture the older woman did not seem to enjoy. Five minutes later she arrived at White Park, Lisette in tow. Nina might have walked it but took the carriage, as Valérie would have. It was fine to walk in the park, but a lady should reach it by carriage. It struck Nina as a bit ridiculous. She had walked to visit the estates of the Évaristes and the Delafois a number of times, and even walked into the village. Why, it practically took longer to get into the carriage and out of it than to reach the park by foot. But once again, Valérie had laid down the rules for her.

By carriage it was, then. Rather than walking the perimeter of the park, which was what Valérie did in an effort to be seen, Nina decided to rebel in the absence of the older woman. In the center of White Park, there was a pond. One could rent a wooden boat and row from one side of the pond to the other, or else sit on a bench. That was where Nina went, circling the pond and tossing crumbs to the ducks, sometimes without even touching them. When she ran out of them, she asked Lisette to purchase another bag of crumbs from the boys who sold them around the park.

The maid rolled her eyes at Nina. "That is for the country folk visiting Loisail for the first time," Lisette said. She had been born and raised in the city, and now reminded the young girl of this with her huffy tone.

"I don't care who does what and who doesn't. Fetch me a bag of crumbs," Nina said, trying to imitate Valérie's imperious voice. She did not succeed. Instead, Lisette took off murmuring under her breath.

Valérie paid careful attention to the people around her, but Nina would often grow distracted. It was no surprise that, alone and without her maid to swat her arm, she did not see Hector Auvray until he was but a couple of paces from her. She had been occupied following a duck and raised her head too late.

"Miss Beaulieu," he said.

"You are here!" she exclaimed, which was a terrible thing to say, and panicked by this mistake, she could think to add nothing else, staring at him in mute horror.

"How do you do?" he asked.

"Fine. I am fine. Very fine."

Dear Lord, he'd think her daft. Nina composed herself as best she could.

"I apologize. I thought you lived in Boniface and did not expect to run into you again this soon," she said.

"I do reside in Boniface. I am wasting time before I meet my friend who lives nearby. Are you by yourself?" he asked.

"Yes. My cousin had a migraine. I'm, ah, here on my own. My maid is about, somewhere."

"May I walk with you?"

"By all means."

Nina felt much improved once she was actually moving and comforted herself with the thought that her gaffes had not been witnessed by Valérie, who surely would have had recriminations to share, perhaps even pinched her.

"Did you have an enjoyable time at the De Villiers' ball?" she asked, and prided herself on how proper her voice sounded when she spoke this time.

"Most enjoyable," he said seriously, as if he were making an oath. It made her chuckle.

"You are fibbing. You left early," she replied, lightly slapping his arm, which would have earned her a double pinching from Valérie, but Valérie wasn't there and Lisette had also disappeared, which meant no tattletales.

"And how would you know that?"

"You mustn't think I was spying on you," she said quickly, and blushed.

She looked horrid when she blushed. Other girls blushed prettily, daintily even, but in Nina's case it was a series of angry crimson blotches.

"Do not be mortified, Miss Beaulieu, I meant nothing by it. Yes, I left early. I am a newcomer to the city and knew few people there. It was, to be honest, not most enjoyable."

"I understand. I didn't know the people there either and when I'm introduced to someone, I invariably say something dreadful. I wasn't dreadful to you, was I?" she asked.

"You didn't tell me your name," he pointed out.

"I did tell you my name. Antonina, Nina," she protested.

"Not your family name. I had to ask others who you were."

Rather than blushing this time, she found herself smiling because he had asked about her. It felt like an important detail. They walked in silence around the lake and she looked at him discreetly—or as discreetly as she could manage.

His hair was longer than was fashionable, brown and with a slight curl. He also eschewed the mustache that was obligatory for all men, thus branding himself as utterly foreign, though she rather liked that he did not know or did not care about the trends the others followed. She thought him noble looking, even if he also struck her as overly serious; a man who was not used to mirth, his handsomeness marred by a vague whiff of melancholia.

"Your friend lives nearby?" she asked.

"Étienne's house is on Jusserand Avenue. Étienne Lémy. I don't know if that means anything to you."

"Lémy? My cousin might know him. And Valérie, his wife, knows everyone. Maybe you've met. He is Gaetan Beaulieu."

"I haven't had the pleasure."

"He's well esteemed here," Nina said, unable to feign modesty. She was proud of Gaetan. He was not only the head of the family, but she thought him a wonderful man besides.

"You sound fond of him," Hector said.

Nina nodded. "We practically grew up together. He used to come to visit us every other summer when I was little. He was like an elder brother to us, though to be fair, his playmate was my sister, Madelena. He is her elder by only a year and I was a small girl. Do you have any siblings?"

"None."

"That seems odd. I have so many cousins, you'd need twice the fingers on your hands to count them all," she said, and raised her hands as if counting them. "Most of us summered together and thus I had an unending pool of brothers and sisters. It is a rather noisy household. I suppose that's what bothers me most about Gaetan's home: It's awfully quiet. You could hear a pin fall in the hallway."

"A museum of a house."

"Yes!" she exclaimed, delighted with the comparison. It did seem like a museum.

"It sounds like you miss your home," he replied.

"I do. But my mother says the city will do me good. I cannot believe you hadn't lived in Loisail before. How is that possible?"

"Must everyone live in Loisail?" he asked, and his voice was tinged with this delightful sarcasm she found refreshing.

The crushing blackness of his suit gave him a tragic air, and all put together she was impressed by the flesh-and-blood version of this man whom she had spied in posters throughout the city, spending an inordinate amount of time staring at his face on one occasion.

She decided then and there that she liked him.

"They tell me anyone who is anyone should," she said.

"I'm afraid I haven't been much of anyone."

"You jest! Why, you have no equal except maybe for Abel Rezo. Levitation of a horse? I'd like Reisz or Pressner to attempt that."

Hector frowned. "And you gleaned all this from *The Gazette for Physical Research*?"

"Not entirely. As I said, I'm interested in psychokinetics. Your name tends to pop up in that field. I've read a bit about you. More than a bit, perhaps," she said, and wished she'd brought a parasol. It would have given her something to hold on to. She feared any second now she was going to send pebbles splashing into the water with the sweep of her eyes.

Hector gave her a half smirk and took out his pocket watch, sliding the lid open. "Psychokinetics. You'll have to explain your interest in the subject when next we meet, but I should set off now if I want to make my appointment. It has been delightful speaking to you again."

"Delightful as your time at the ball or truly delightful?" she asked, spotting Lisette, who looked irritated. Their time was about to be cut short one way or another, and she wanted to know.

"Truly delightful," he replied.

"We may become friends, then."

He looked at Nina, seeming to take the measure of her. Valérie complained that Nina lacked tact, always talking too much or too little. She wondered if he agreed with the assessment and was about to make a quick escape.

"Without appearing to impose myself, Miss Beaulieu, would it be acceptable if I paid you a visit on an afternoon of your choice?" he asked.

A visit. A gentleman calling on her! People called all the time on Valérie and Gaetan, but not on her. To be the focus of attention delighted Nina.

"I would not mind at all. You could call on us on Tuesday after two."

"Though my psychokinetic powers may indeed be impressive, I have not yet grasped the art of reading minds. Where is this house that is a museum of yours?"

"At Lambal and Avil. It's the blue house. You'll recognize it rather quickly," she said, extending her gloved hand so he might shake it. He kissed it instead. Of course he did. This was the proper way to greet and bid good-bye to a lady. Nevertheless, it seemed to her a wonderful gesture and she wished she had misplaced the gloves, as also happened often. She might have felt his lips against her skin instead.

"Thank you. I shall see you Tuesday, then."

He gave her another one of those half smirks before turning around and walking away. Lisette arrived with a bag of crumbs and recriminations. Nina did not hear a single one of them.

Chapter 3

VALÉRIE WOKE EARLY NOT BY inclination but by force of habit. It was in her nature to remain languidly in bed until the sun rose high in the sky, but being a busy woman, she could not afford these luxuries on most days. There were always matters to attend to, and not only the amusements and diversions—shopping, eating, entertainment—a lady of her stature was expected to partake in, but also the myriad social gestures the wife of an important man must know. There was the running of the household, which should not be undertaken lightly, and as of late, the supervision of Antonina, Gaetan's little cousin.

That morning, though, Valérie had a chance to indulge herself, dozing in bed until it was late, and missed her walk in the park. Slowly she dressed, slowly she placed pins in her hair, slowly sifted through her jewelry box.

Readying herself was a long and elaborate process. Valérie was beautiful. She was blond and blue-eyed, and her skin was pale, unblemished by freckles or scars. She possessed a divine neck and the slender figure most favored by society. But nature's gifts may take a woman only a certain distance. It was not a matter of looks, but of picking the dresses that were the most flattering, the ornaments that drew the eye, in order to rise from mere beauty to perfection.

She was the kind of woman who started and ended trends, who made heads turn when she walked into a room, whose name dripped all over the society pages. She was a feature of Loisail, as imposing and dazzling as the new opera house. And so Valérie dressed slowly and took meticulous care in her appearance.

Once she was satisfied with the results, she went downstairs, to the conservatory. Valérie was proud of this feature of her home because, more than anything, it signaled the wealth and position she enjoyed. The city was as it had always been: rather crowded. Space was a luxury, homes rapidly shrinking in size. Important families had to do with reduced quarters, for example, renting the top flat of a building and stomaching a view of an alley. Thus, even though conservatories were all the rage, when a household could afford one, it was a modest affair, a piddling thing the size of a closet. Valérie's conservatory was massive, its walls rising high, iron and glass and greenery dazzling visitors. At one end of the structure stood a fountain with the figure of a kneeling stone boy next to it, a gigantic mirror placed behind it, reflecting the water. Baskets with plants dangled from the roof, and there was a bench where one might sit and contemplate the foliage.

Taste was the most important consideration in Valérie's conservatory, not practicality. There was no point in toiling with geraniums in this space. She had dedicated herself to the cultivation of striking plants. Ferns, palms, heliotropes, azaleas, these offered the refinement she sought. Lately she had been taken with the notion of orchids, but these might require the construction of an orchid house, an idea she was still mulling over.

For now, Valérie bent over her roses, running a finger over the delicate white petals. She employed a gardener who took care of her plants, but Valérie believed in the value of proper supervision, and since her new roses—a delightfully fragrant variety, highly ornamental—were the most precious flowers she owned, she thought it prudent to look after them carefully. These white ones had budded, opening to the onslaught of spring.

After Valérie was satisfied with the state of the conservatory, she went to her office. Valérie received an infinite number of invitations, thank-you missives, and letters, which must receive a response. Ordinarily she did not mind this activity, but there was a letter from Antonina's mother that had arrived two days prior and that she had been putting off.

With a sigh, Valérie sat down before the desk and opened the letter. It was, as she expected, the usual bit of nonsense from Camille Beaulieu. The woman worried endlessly about her daughter, asked how Antonina fared.

Valérie hardly knew how to answer. The truth of the matter was she considered Antonina half a savage, though her vulgarity was not truly her fault and must be laid at her mother's feet. The Beaulieus were an old and wealthy family, and their original home was in the south, in the region of Montipouret. Gaetan's father had been the eldest child, followed by another boy—Benedict—and two daughters. In an act that Valérie would never be able to comprehend, Benedict had married a nobody, the daughter of a local schoolteacher. As Benedict was the younger, sickly son, his possibilities were more reduced than those of his brother, but he ought to have done better than Camille.

At first glance, a casual observer might have questioned Valérie's distaste for the woman, since Valérie herself had come from an impoverished family. However, Valérie considered her situation to be utterly different. First of all, although her family had lost practically all their lands and money, they had kept their distinguished name. Valérie was born a Véries, and that alone was a form of currency. Second, Valérie was young, beautiful, and charming, qualities she thought made up for her financial shortcomings. The most charitable point one might make about Camille was that she was plain.

It was no wonder then that Antonina had grown to become a confusing girl. At nineteen she lacked all the skills a young lady making her entrance into society should possess. She could not sing, danced mediocrely, and displayed neither wit nor seductiveness. She was not particularly pretty, having inherited the tall forehead of the Beaulieus coupled with her mother's strong jaw and heavy-lidded eyes. But no matter, because Gaetan had decided his "darling" cousin deserved the excitement of Loisail and an engagement to a promising young man.

Gaetan was attached to Camille and her daughters, probably as a result of his mother's death when he was but a four-year-old. When his cousin Madelena had married, he sent the girl a most extravagant diamond-and-pearl necklace in addition to a lump sum of money to help the newlyweds establish their household, even though Madelena's father had already provided rather nicely for her. Gaetan's affection for his cousins was likely compounded by his sterility: they could not have children, this they had discovered a few years after their wedding. This biological fault spared Valérie from the presence of crying babies, creatures she did not cherish, but it also ensured that Gaetan's cousins acquired an even more crucial dimension. They would be his heirs.

Valérie therefore found herself in the uncomfortable position of having to introduce and cart around a girl who was not terribly fit for polite society. She, Valérie Beaulieu, chained to this lump of a child who at times proved annoyingly recalcitrant.

What to write, then? That after three weeks in Loisail, Antonina had not memorized the names, ranks, and particularities of the most important men and women of the city? That despite Valérie's best attempts, Antonina remained friendless? That she had done her utmost to antagonize Didier Dompierre and the other suitable young men Valérie had introduced to her?

No, Valérie wrote none of that. She clenched her teeth and replied with a brief, polite letter. Antonina was adapting to her new home. Now that the Grand Season had begun, there would be a chance for her to make new acquaintances and there would be the usual diversions that came with it: the opera, the races, the balls.

Afterward, Valérie tackled the rest of her pressing letters, and it was well after noon when she left the office. Antonina had returned by then. Valérie, carrying her thick address book between her hands, paused to look at Antonina, who was sitting at the foot of the stairs, absorbed in an idle thought. This was often the case with her. It was up to Valérie to organize advisable entertainment for the girl, to get her invited to the best parties, to choose the correct soirées, and grind through the name of every eligible bachelor she could think of. Antonina did nothing.

"We are expected at Ledaux's at two. You do remember, don't you?" she asked, perhaps more acidly than she intended, but then Valérie still had to come up with the name of a young man who would escort Nina to the races in two weeks. She had been counting on one of the Hamel boys to submit to that pleasure, but she'd heard from a good source that the two blasted young men were chasing after Jeannette Solé.

"I do. Yes," Antonina said, jumping to her feet and smoothing her dress. It was a dark blue, one of the stiff outfits Valérie had picked. If Nina had had her way, she might be walking around the city in a hideous calico print more fit to be made into a sack and filled with flour than to be worn by any woman.

"Good. Did you have a nice walk?" Valérie asked.

"It was lovely. I ran into someone, in fact."

"Oh?" Valérie said as she opened the address book, suddenly remembering that Esno had a son who was supposed to be visiting in the spring. Or was it a nephew? She must inquire about this, and quickly. "And who was that?"

"A gentleman I met at the ball thrown by the De Villiers. I've invited him to visit Tuesday evening. I hope that is not a problem."

"Antonina, you should not extend invitations without my approval," she said.

"But you told me I ought to make friends," the girl protested.

The right friends, not any friend, Valérie thought. Who knew whom this child had been speaking with. "That is not the same as having a caller. Has he sent his card?"

"No, but I don't think that should be an impediment. He's nice and he—"

"Really, Antonina. Inviting a stranger to our home who hasn't had the decency to introduce himself properly."

"I've asked you before to call me Nina. Nobody calls me Antonina," the girl muttered in that impertinent tone that irritated Valérie.

"Nina is not a name," Valérie replied. "Attempting to shorten your name is a horrid habit, one you should outgrow."

"I don't like being called Antonina."

"It is not a matter of what you like. As for this 'gentleman,' he has not sent a card and you should not have invited him," Valérie said. She started walking and hoped Antonina would leave it at that.

Instead, the girl followed her like a yappy dog. "My mother never demanded silly pieces of paper when people made visits, and the children of the Delafois would often appear unannounced to play with us."

"You are hardly a child to be playing at anything," Valérie said. She was truly exasperated now and wished nothing more than to hit the girl with the address book, knocking her senseless. "Who is this fellow, again?" she asked.

"His name is Hector Auvray."

Valérie had been ready to pounce on the chit, but when the name slipped from Antonina's lips, all the rage poured from her body. She felt weak, almost faint. She took a breath, clutching the address book tight.

Valérie spoke in a neat, sparse voice. "Consider this a singular exception. Ready yourself for Mrs. Ledaux's, the dress you are wearing is entirely too informal for a visit."

Antonina nodded before rushing up the stairs. Once the girl had disappeared, Valérie rested a trembling hand against the banister, needing the support. Yes, now she recalled. She had heard he was in the city. Had heard it and dismissed it, done her best to erase it from her mind. There was no point in knowing, though she had wickedly hoped she might catch a glimpse of him at one point.

He was now practically at her doorstep.

And Valérie had invited him in.

Chapter 4

AFTER HIS CASUAL MEETING WITH Nina in the park—which was not the least bit casual, he had been going there every morning after being told she could regularly be found in the area—and securing an invitation to the Beaulieu household, Hector found himself suddenly doubting his resolve. Long ago, he had established that his return to Loisail would entail an inevitable return to Valérie, which was perhaps why, paradoxically, he had stayed away for a long time. He desired both to see her and to thwart their reunion.

Hector looked across the street, at the Beaulieu house. Two stories high, its tall bay windows with their white shutters contrasted with the blue of the façade. It was an elegant, formal home, the initial B carved above the front door. There was also a side entrance emblazoned with a smaller B. He imagined this led to the carriage court. The structure proclaimed its noble roots and the wealth of its inhabitants.

He crossed the street and knocked. When a servant opened the door, Hector handed him his card. "Miss Nina Beaulieu is expecting me," he said.

The servant nodded, instructing Hector to wait in the foyer. Hector took off his hat, clutching it between his hands before finally daring to set it on the bench designed for visitors to deposit their coats and hats.

There was another B emblazoned on this piece of furniture. Very modern, the bench, boldly avoiding the old hat rack or the hall table.

For several panicked minutes, Hector thought he might not be allowed in. He was counting on Nina's eagerness to meet with him to pave the way for a visit, but there was always a risk that he might be turned away.

It was not the case. The servant returned and told him Miss Beaulieu would see him in the drawing room. This was a massive room of paneled walls painted with a multitude of lively birds of all sizes, but white birds only: swans mostly, along with doves and egrets. The décor was also white. White sofas, a white table against a window, white curtains. Accents of color were allowed here and there, for example, the vase of rich blues and yellows sitting in a corner, or the gilt furniture.

It was as he'd pictured it, this room, this house. Valérie's touch was evident all around him, almost heady, every artifact and decorative item proclaiming its provenance. There came the rustle of a skirt. He turned his head, too quickly, too eager to see her.

It was not Valérie. Nina stood at the door. Her black hair was pulled back, but a few tendrils hung loose, framing her face. The style did not especially become her, nor did the peach-colored dress.

"Hector!" she said, walking in with a big smile on her face.

"Miss Beaulieu," he said, giving the girl a slight bow of the head and kissing the back of her hand. "It's nice of you to receive me."

"I'm glad you came. It's nearly three o'clock. I thought you might have had other calls to make."

"There was other business I had to handle."

In reality he had spent half an hour circling the area in his carriage, doubting himself.

"What kind of business?"

"Antonina, you forget your manners," Valérie said as she walked in. "It's not polite to ask those questions."

She wore a cream-colored dress with a blue sash at the waist, her hair in a loose chignon, a string of pearls dangling from her neck. He was transported ten years back, to their first meeting, like opening a worn, beloved book you've memorized.

She had not changed. He knew she would not, she'd remain suspended in amber, for him and him alone.

Hector's youth had been a struggle. The grime of the fairs and a belly that was never full marked his first years. When his parents passed away, he'd endured, like a stubborn weed, growing tall and reed-thin. At fourteen he'd learned to escape most scuffles, or use his talent to protect himself, but he still ended up losing a tooth when three men pinned him down and beat him for his money. And then she'd come into his life like an angel from the heavens, and he constructed a completely different life for himself in his imagination. He'd always known he'd escape the narrow cots and stinking guesthouses where he lodged, and she was proof of this, a sign.

How he'd hated the world. Sometimes, when he glanced at men who slaked their thirst and appetites with impunity, he thought of throttling them. He had nothing. Then he had her, and the future was full of possibilities.

Just as quickly she was gone.

He looked at Valérie, stared at her, unable to bow or speak a greeting.

"Mr. Auvray," she said, extending her hand, her voice cool and composed while Hector felt himself quiver inside.

"Mrs. Beaulieu," he replied, raising her hand to his lips, but not kissing it, his breath upon her knuckles for a second before he released her. "Always a pleasure to see you."

Now that he looked more carefully, he realized she was not exactly the girl he'd known. Her face was thinner and had a firmness that had not been there. But she was as graceful as she'd ever been and had grown more exquisite, a feat he had not thought possible. It did not matter, whatever vague changes had taken hold of her physiognomy.

"You've met, then?" Nina asked, her voice unwanted, interrupting his reverie.

"I'm not entirely sure. Have we?" Valérie asked.

There was the hint of a dare when Valérie glanced at him. He took it.

"Ten years ago. You were in Frotnac at the time," he replied. "It was before your marriage."

Valérie frowned, a fleeting motion of her head. "I do remember you. You performed a trick or another."

"That was me."

"That is unfair, Valérie. You never told me you knew Hector! And after I've told you of my interest in psychokinetics," Nina said. She sounded like a doleful child who had been denied sweets.

Valérie's face was carved marble when she looked at the girl. "An unbecoming interest," she said.

"Hector, you must tell my cousin that psychokinetic feats are not a horrid crime," Nina said, playfully tugging at his hand. The gesture might befit a coquette, but he doubted she knew what she was doing.

"Does Mrs. Beaulieu truly think that?" he asked.

"Antonina has it in her head that it is fine for a young woman of her caliber to go around attempting to levitate decks of cards and shuffle them in the air as though she were a common street performer," Valérie said. "I strongly disagree."

"You disagree about everything," Nina replied, sitting on one of the sofas.

Hector smirked, amused by the tart answer, and sat across from her. "I didn't realize you had the ability, Miss Beaulieu."

"A little, perhaps. When I was five years old, my mother said I made it rain stones upon our house."

"Which is precisely why it's a poor idea to fixate upon such an activity," Valérie said.

"I don't intend to rain stones on your house, Cousin. Besides, what else am I supposed to do when you won't let me collect specimens while I'm here?"

"Specimens, Miss Beaulieu?"

"Pests," Valérie replied. She remained standing, her eyes fixing on a distant point instead of looking at either one of them.

"Beetles. And a few butterflies. You can't possibly consider a butterfly a pest," Nina protested.

"Now is not the time to discuss that. Would you fancy a drink, Mr. Auvray?" Valérie asked, her voice a knife that cut off the girl.

"You need not bother with me," Hector replied. He looked at Nina instead of Valérie.

Valérie, a marble column, spoke again. "I shan't have you telling my husband that I am a poor hostess, Mr. Auvray."

"I wouldn't dream of speaking such a thing to Mr. Beaulieu. Perhaps a glass of water," he said.

A servant brought the water and he sat back, admiring Valérie while

Nina spoke. He asked her questions he had memorized, questions that would seem both banal and polite: Would she be attending the races next month? Would she have her portrait painted by Herus—the painter of choice for all young ladies? They spent half an hour this way, Nina speaking, Valérie silent, Hector nodding. Finally he thought it enough, smiled, and bade the ladies good-bye.

"You must see me perform," he told them. "It might amuse you."

"Could we? Valérie, could we, please?" Nina asked.

"I'll consider it. Mr. Auvray, let me escort you to the door, and we can discuss this performance you speak of," Valérie said.

Valérie walked by his side, her head straight, her steps neither rushed nor too leaden. She walked as if he were not there, guiding him back to the entrance.

"I cannot believe you had the gall to come and see me," Valérie said, her voice low. Her tone betrayed her anger even if her face was impassive. "It is absolutely improper."

"I did not come to see you. I came to see Nina," he said, *his* tone scratching on insolence.

"What kind of fool do you take me for?"

Hector looked at her, with her spectacular disdain and her golden hair and the bluest eyes he'd ever seen. The insolence, he tucked it away, he could not wield it for long.

"I needed to speak to you," he said, admitting his weakness.

She responded with contempt. "You ought to have written a letter if you felt you had anything to say to me."

"I didn't think a letter would get your attention."

She stopped now, standing in front of a gilded mirror in profile, her hands pressed against her skirt. She was skillfully avoiding his gaze.

"You have my attention now. What do you want? Do you wish to somehow punish me for our hasty separation?" she asked.

"Hasty, yes. You wrote three lines informing me of your marriage. Three lines, Valérie," he said. He moved from her side to stand in front of her.

She looked up at him with a sigh. "Would you have enjoyed the details?" she asked.

Valérie had never been sweet or simple. Still, the retort cut deep and it must have shown, for her expression changed quickly, her voice softening.

"Hector, it was a long time ago and we were both silly to think we might wed. My family would not have allowed it."

"No. They needed Beaulieu's money."

"What does it matter?" Valérie said. "But you shall not . . . You will not tell Gaetan about our engagement, will you?"

It would have been a black mark against Valérie's character. An engagement was a serious matter, and breaking an engagement was poor form. Worse yet, Valérie had been secretly engaged when Gaetan courted her. It was enough to cause a great amount of strife if it became known.

"I'm not here to embarrass you."

"Why are you here, then?" she asked, sounding perplexed.

"I have not forgotten you, Valérie," he said quietly, and he tried to pour every inch of his soul into those few words, hoping she might see and feel and grasp how he'd loved her, how many nights he'd dreamt of her and tossed in his bed in despair, how many times he'd pictured her face. Now she was there, real and solid, and he wanted to die without her and wanted to live for her. As when they'd been young.

"Nonsense," she told him, and he realized, no, she did not see. *She* had not counted the days and nights. But, no, no, she had. Deep inside she must have.

"Nonsense? I made you a promise once, that I'd come back. Well, I've returned," he declared.

"What do you expect? That I shall get into your carriage this instant and abandon my husband?"

The only reason for his visit to this city was this woman. He could not spend another day away, pretending she did not exist. He had done nothing but pretend and failed miserably for ten years.

"Not this instant. I'm sure you've grown fond of the Beaulieu fortune," he said, matching her tone.

Valérie's face hardened again. Like a warrior, she quickly donned her armor, allowing him no access. "Fond of my husband, too," she said, looking at him firmly in the face.

"Truly? You seem bored out of your mind."

"Bored because I have to spend my days with his nitwit cousin. You'd be half-mad, too."

"I might be, since I intend to court her," he said, wishing to get a reaction from her, wishing for anything.

"How delightful! You have not forgotten me but now you turn your eyes to a silly girl who happens to have a pile of money beneath her feet," Valérie said, clapping her hands once.

"I have money aplenty. I am not looking to steal her fortune."

"Hector, don't be ridiculous." Valérie laughed merrily and the laughter dripped with undisguised scorn.

"It is about time I married," he said, pressing on.

"You'd marry her?"

"Why not?"

"You don't love her."

"There are plenty of shining examples in the world that demonstrate love need not be a condition of a successful marriage. You might agree on this point."

Valérie fixed her lofty eyes on him, anger coloring her cheeks. She began walking again, resolutely. "If you want to make a fool of yourself, then be my guest," she said. "For this is sheer foolishness."

Valérie was right. It was foolish, perhaps. But Nina would allow him to have access to this household. His love of Valérie was vicious. It gripped him utterly. He had to see her, had to speak to her, and if this was the way, then let it be. At turns he thought he might be able to spirit Valérie away if only they could share a little time together. Then he changed his mind; he decided that he could remain the chivalrous gentleman, merely loving her from afar. The latter appealed to his sense of romanticism.

Hector prepared to elucidate these notions and quickly gave up when he looked at Valérie.

He sighed and shook his head softly. "It would be good to have a friend. An accomplice, a partner. I've been traveling for a long time, Valérie. You cannot possibly understand how tiring it is," he whispered.

They had arrived at the door and he had fetched his hat and coat, so there was no reason to dally, but rather than ejecting him, Valérie simply stared at Hector. She reminded him of a lioness who has not decided if it will let itself be tamed or tear its master to shreds.

"I can understand," she said, her voice softening again.

Her hands were hidden in her skirts, but he reached out and grazed her fingers. He moved one step closer to her, pressing his lips against her hand, a gesture he had withheld in the drawing room for fear of betraying himself. But they were alone now, and the wild beating of his heart did not matter. When he released her, Valérie did not drift away, instead shifting closer to him, the space between them almost disappearing.

"Bring Nina to the Royal next Friday. You can both watch the show."

"I've no interest in the show."

"In some conversation after it, then."

"Not in any conversation with you," she replied, her voice honeyed.

He knew she was playing with him, as she'd done when they first met, masterfully teasing and flirting and driving him insane. He'd allow it. He was playing, too.

Hector inclined his head.

"Is there anything else you need, Mr. Auvray?" she asked, her hand upon the door.

"Nothing, for the time being. I'll send an invitation for the Royal. I trust you will be there."

He took his leave with that, not bothering to look back when he heard the door close behind him.

Chapter 5

VALÉRIE BEAULIEU OPENED HER JEWELRY box and riffled through its contents until she found the ring. Gold with a single pearl, a pattern of scallops decorating the band. It was not worth anything and it did not compare to the rest of Valérie's jewelry. She had gold-and-enamel earrings, a beautiful double-strand pearl necklace with a sapphire, a necklace of rich garnets, and a bracelet with the most dazzling diamonds. The ring, which she kept at the bottom of her jewelry box, was ugly in comparison to the other items she owned.

Yet she kept this ring because Hector had given it to her.

She had met him in Frotnac. It was the hottest spring in many years, and more than one distinguished family had fled the capital before the end of the Grand Season in search of a cooler locale. Frotnac, situated to the north, was the chosen destination for most of them. Valérie stayed with her friend Miranda Oclou, and Miranda's distracted mother.

Valérie's family was not what it had once been. The house, majestic at the height of the Véries' power, had become a tired relic. Jewelry, paintings, and even furniture were sold through the years to keep the family fed. Friends and relatives provided a measure of support, yet loans remained unpaid and everyone shook their heads sadly when they saw Valérie walk by. What could be expected of her? they prattled. A young lady of meager means would have a hard time attracting serious suitors. Picture her trousseau!

Despite everything, decorum must be maintained. Valérie's family was strict, and her grandmother demanded blind obedience to the old rules. She learned to play the piano and to sing, how to converse and dance, all the courtesies of a woman of her station even if her station was nebulous.

But Frotnac was far from that wretched gargoyle of a grandmother. Most important, it was more relaxed. A young city, it had grown significant in the past few decades, and it could not imagine the pomp of Loisail, its rules or ancient histories.

The feeling that summer was one of unending ebullience. Valérie and Miranda explored the city, shopped, and attended a number of soirées, dinners, and parties. One evening they went to a café where Hector was performing for the patrons. He levitated a chair, a couple of glasses, those sorts of tricks. She had seen similar performances around the city. Musicians, actors, even poets reciting their couplets for a few coins. Hector, however, struck her as a more impressive figure.

He was young and good-looking, and though his clothes were not the newest and most fashionable, he carried himself with an air of quiet grace and dignity that affected her. Nonetheless, she might not have spoken to him if it had not been for Étienne Lémy.

Étienne Lémy knew Miranda, and when he saw her he immediately walked to their table and sat down, inviting Hector to join him. Étienne was a wealthy young man who had decided to wander around the country and pay his way by playing the violin. He fancied himself an artist, and for the past four months he had been traveling with the troupe of a fellow named Derval. Hector was also a member of the troupe. They had, however, been left stranded in Frotnac after an inquiry concerning late wages with Derval ended in an angry confrontation.

Valérie was both disappointed and intrigued when she realized that Hector, unlike his friend, was not playing the role of the nonconformist. He was a genuinely humble young man with no money and no connections. But he was also intelligent, serious, and determined. While many wealthy fellows like Étienne Lémy were simply interested in wine and women, Hector was ambitious. He was saving money to buy passage to Iblevad. A previous member of Derval's troupe had gone there two years before. The troupe member said Hector's telekinetic skills were sure to attract no small amount of attention and had promised he'd recommend Hector to his employer.

Despite his admirable qualities, Valérie did not intend to become seriously involved with Hector. However, she found herself returning to the café, walking with him around the city, and suddenly she was seeing him every day.

It was summer. The hours in a day could stretch on forever, and she did not have to whirl back to the house where she was staying until night had fallen; night fell late. And sometimes they also met at nights in secret, Miranda and Étienne and Valérie and Hector navigating the alleys of the city, laughing and singing. The boys performed at the cafés and the girls watched, and then they went dancing.

"Are you my Valérie?" he would ask her.

"Who else's?" she would say.

It was summer and she was young. The heat made it difficult to think; the city made her careless. He kissed her, whispered in her ear, and she whispered back, tangled her fingers in his hair. She fell in love and when the summer ended, he told her he was heading to Iblevad to make his fortune. He'd come back for her. Would she wait?

She said yes.

The last time they met was at the docks in Loisail. Before he left, he gave her the ring. Valérie wept. He promised he would write and she promised the same. And never-ending love. She promised that, too.

She intended to keep her promise. The days grew cooler and snow fell upon the city. She wrote with ecstatic fervor. Ink and tears spilled upon the page. She missed him!

Grandmother complained she was not eating properly and looked pale. No one knew about Hector. She had not breathed a word about him.

That winter she met Gaetan Beaulieu. He was less dashing than Hector and terribly wealthy.

She wrote to Hector and he wrote to her, yet her letters were more paced now. It was a busy time. The Grand Season was starting and she was assured an invitation to the best parties, thanks to the attentive care of Gaetan.

Fall arrived and with it the rains. A year had passed. Hector assured her he was making progress. On the other hand, Gaetan had proposed. Her family pushed her forward. Here was their salvation!

She tried to stall. Grandmother summoned her. The woman sat in her favorite chair, which was more throne than chair, all in black with the ebony choker around her ancient neck. She had not donned a stitch of color since her husband died decades before. Valérie suspected the old cow enjoyed widowhood and the grim aura it gave her.

"What is this that you will not give Gaetan Beaulieu an answer?" she asked.

"I need time to think, Grandmother."

"Time! A woman does not have *time*. A man has turned his eyes toward you, but he might as quickly turn away and find a more tractable fiancée. Time and choice are not luxuries you can allow yourself. Do you know about your aunt Cibeline?"

"The Duke de Lammarck broke his engagement to her. It was a scandal."

"Yes, a scandal. He had to pay her father a sum for all the trouble, as one does in these cases, but then came an epidemic of smallpox. Her face was disfigured. She became such a nuisance, she had to be dragged off to the asylum at Rangel. Had she married him the previous spring, as I had suggested, this would not have happened. No woman needs a three-year engagement."

"But a long engagement, Grandmother, it gives one a chance to know the groom better."

"What must you know about Gaetan? That without him you will end up an old maid, penniless, living off the charity of friends?"

The withered woman reached forward and grabbed Valérie's hands.

"Soft, pretty hands. They won't be soft and pretty in a few years. You'll end up a governess for one of your old friends. How will you like to take care of Miranda Oclou's little ones? I won't live forever, and once I die the jackals will take what they can, this house, the bits of valuables left behind. You'll be cast out and alone. What will happen to your soft, pretty hands then, Valérie?"

She had not replied, trembling with rage, unable to speak. She wanted to spit at the hag's face. But she knew her grandmother spoke the truth.

Valérie did not demur after that.

She could never remember penning the actual letter, the moment lost to her, though years later she could recall the exact words.

> *Consider yourself relieved of your promise.*
> *I have wed someone else.*
> *Valérie.*

She kept the ring. She ought to have tossed it away. An idea held her back, silly as it might be, that if she kept it, she might keep a part of him. And there was a part of her in that ring, too. A younger, more carefree shard of Valérie.

Once in a while she would take the ring out and hold it for a minute or two before quickly putting it away. That night, however, Valérie held the ring for a long time.

"Nina informs me that she has a new admirer," Gaetan said.

She looked up at her mirror and her husband's reflection. He was a dull man with an air of satisfaction about him that she thought came from his wealth. The world, she thought, had been kind to Gaetan, and it had made him soft, undefined, placid. He paid for her bills, bought her expensive presents, yet she resented him for his lack of spirit and for his devotion to his family. She also thought ill of him for the things he refused to provide her: funds for the Véries, that post her cousin might have had in the army if only Gaetan had bought it.

The limits of Valérie's power and influence chafed her. She begrudged Antonina for this reason and also because she was by nature a jealous, possessive creature. She had to have every bit of everything, and that included every bit of everyone. Gaetan's love for others struck her as a personal insult, and if he could not love her absolutely with no room for another, she did not believe he could love her at all.

"I wouldn't call him an admirer. He did ask her to the theater," Valérie said. She placed the ring back in her jewelry box, straightened her shoulders, and reached for her hairbrush.

"I know. She told me yesterday and begged me to intercede in her favor," Gaetan replied.

The gossipy idiot. Valérie should have known she'd go running to Gaetan.

"That girl," Valérie muttered, "is trying to go behind my back. She knows full well you'll do whatever she wants. It's always like this with her."

Her brush caught in her hair and she pulled it down, sharply, to untangle it. It hurt.

"Valérie, you mustn't be angry. She's . . . excitable."

"I told her I would think about it. I have not made a decision."

"I understand. I must say I was a bit shocked. An entertainer new to the city talking to Nina?" Gaetan said, sounding surprised yet pleased. Likely he saw this as a mark of his cousin's attractiveness, the nonexistent Beaulieu charm. "But I spoke to René Rambulen this morning, and he assured me Hector Auvray's bank account is substantial and he is polite. Unlike other entertainers, he is not found frequenting cabarets and drinking establishments. They say he is, in truth, a bit too serious. Of course, that is not a complete assurance of his character."

"No, it's not," Valérie said. "But it is like Antonina to utterly lose perspective the first time a stranger says a word to her, and for you to go along with her in order to keep the girl happy."

Gaetan appeared contrite, but not contrite enough to stop pressing his point. "Valérie, it is . . . Nina is a sweet girl, but she is also somewhat misunderstood. When she was but a child, I remember how she used to make furniture move, pots clang. It scared the other children. They called her the Witch of Oldhouse. And now that she has grown up, even now they remember these things, and she's not had many suitors in Montipouret."

Any wonder why? Valérie thought. Antonina botched everything. When it was necessary that she speak, she grew quiet. When she must be modest, she was loud. When she must smile, she smiled, but too eagerly. She made a fool of herself when they visited the Deforniers, ensuring every young man in attendance quietly chuckled and thought *What a dolt!* and went in search of a more sophisticated young lady.

"She's not in Montipouret anymore. She has had many chances to socialize with people her age, to speak to charming young men."

"She's spoken to this one, at least. What did you think of him when he visited here?"

She held the silver brush in the air for a second, frozen, then slowly ran it down her hair. Her throat felt dry and she thought her tongue would not move, but she found herself forming words, her voice light.

"He seems an educated man, well groomed. It is difficult for me to say anything else, having met him but briefly."

"Yes, yes, of course," Gaetan said, pacing behind her in his favorite robe, the dark crimson one that suited him poorly. "I am torn, Valérie. I do not want to make her unhappy and rob Nina of the chance to make a new friend. On the other hand, who knows if he is a proper acquaintance. An entertainer, a performer. I do not wish to be closed-minded and fastidious. What do you think?"

Valérie bit her lip and set the brush down. Her fingers rested against the edge of her vanity for a minute as she considered what to say next. She could feel her heart beating fast in her chest, and she was afraid Gaetan might notice something was amiss even if he would not have noticed a conflagration in the room next door.

"Perhaps it wouldn't be bad if I accept his invitation to the theater. It would give us a chance to interact a bit more. We could make up our mind on him."

"That is excellent," Gaetan said. "Yes. You must go with Nina to the theater and converse with Mr. Auvray. And if you deem it prudent, we can invite him for dinner at a later date."

"Certainly."

Valérie turned around, feeling more confident. She looked fully at her husband, who was pleased with the result of their deliberations.

"However, I do wish you'd make it clear to Antonina that she must not be seeking you to adjudicate on these matters. Your aunt has entrusted her care to us, and I am merely looking out for her."

"I will speak to her. Do not worry," Gaetan said.

She felt wicked for a brief moment, for deceiving him. But she could not have told him the truth, that she'd met Hector years before and he was more than a performer she had once, casually, chanced upon. That was impossible. She could have steered Hector away from their household, though. She could still do it. She could convince Gaetan that the trip to the theater had been a disaster, make up a lie.

Valérie doubted she would. She felt irresistibly thrust forward. A force had been set in motion and she suspected she was helpless or unwilling to stop it.

Chapter 6

NINA WOKE UP EARLY THE day they were supposed to go to the Royal and spent an inordinate amount of time considering her hair. Valérie had picked her dress for this occasion, a dress that Nina did not like at all, but she did not want to jeopardize the invitation and she grudgingly obeyed the older woman's instructions.

The dress was white with long sleeves, three tiers of lace, and a pleated yellow satin sash. Valérie insisted it was the perfect dress for the evening. Nina thought it made her look washed out. She would have preferred the green dress she'd brought from home with the embroidered roses, but Valérie had imperiously declared it too gaudy.

White, then. But Valérie would not dictate her hair. It would have to be done up, but Nina decided it would be worn in an elaborate knot. This required the maid to part her hair into four sections, twist and gather it at the top of the head, and then place a back comb and hairpins to secure the hairdo in place.

She also picked her emerald necklace rather than the pearls Valérie had helpfully suggested.

They left the house close to seven o'clock. The carriage rolled down the wide boulevards, onto the Avenue of Ashes, named thus because the Temple of Our Lady of Ashes was located midway through it. The Convent of the Sisters of Solitude could still be glimpsed behind a tall wall and rows of poplars, but the avenue was not a place for holy thoughts anymore. It had morphed into one of the busiest arteries in the city, with many fine restaurants and entertainment venues. The Opera House rose on the area known as the Mound, but other establishments were also perched along the avenue. Key among these was the Royal.

The Royal, like its rival, the Pavilion, branded itself not as pure entertainment, but also as an enriching, educational experience. At the Royal, patrons could be treated to displays of the latest electromagnetic gadgets, optical illusions, or a plain old dance troupe. The eclectic mix required a wide range of performers, from makers of complex automatons to musicians. Of most interest were the "talents," those individuals who possessed strange abilities science was beginning to unravel. There were those who could make objects burst into flames and people who had mastery over animals, but Nina was most fascinated by the talents who could manipulate objects with their thoughts. Among these people, there was no doubt that Hector Auvray occupied a special place.

When Nina descended from the carriage, she looked up, wishing to take the time to admire the outlandish building. It was a large structure and looked far too excessive to really be called an attractive building, but its vastness inspired a certain reverence.

The arched doorways were flanked by two marble elephants, their trunks in the air. The main hall led to an imposing staircase. The floors were decorated with elaborate blue-and-white mosaics, the chandeliers dangling from the ceiling glittered, fairy-tale-like.

Nina and Valérie proceeded to the red-and-golden private box where they would watch the performance. Nina had not been to the Royal and she leaned forward, looking around with interest at the people beneath them and in the boxes around them, at the stage with its red velvet curtains, curious about every detail. Valérie, for her part, held her peacock fan in her lap and did not look at anything, her gaze fixed on a singular, invisible point.

The curtain rose. Music began to play and dancers streamed onto the stage. Nina felt impatient as they performed, the minutes ticking by. Finally the dance ended, the curtain fell again, and then rose for the main performance.

A man appeared and greeted the audience. The musicians assembled by the stage began playing a popular melody—"The Chestnuts"—and the man smiled, bowing.

"Welcome," said the gray-haired man. "Welcome, ladies and gentlemen. In a few minutes, you will be treated to a display of wonders. But first I must make it clear that everything that takes place on this stage is real: no parlor tricks, no sleight of hand."

The man gestured left and right, as if mapping the stage. "You are about to meet one of the most talented psychokinetics of our age. He has performed before queens and bishops, tantalizing audiences from Luquennay to Anuv. There is no feat that is too difficult, no manipulation of matter that evades him. And tonight he stands before you. I present Hector Auvray."

Another curtain rose and an elaborate backdrop was revealed, a view of Loisail from the air. Hector walked slowly onstage as everyone applauded. The posters showed him with a crimson cape, but he wore a double-breasted black dress coat, a burgundy waistcoat with details in gold thread, and a wide, matching cravat enhanced by a gold pin. When he reached the center of the stage, he bowed and took off his white gloves, handing them to an assistant.

"First, Mr. Auvray will demonstrate to you the basic nature of his talent," said the announcer. "Here we have but half a dozen ordinary chairs. Nothing to them, mere wood and a few nails."

As he spoke, Hector's assistants set down the chairs in a row. Hector stood in front of the row of chairs, without looking at them, his eyes fixed on the audience. Then he moved a hand and the chairs all moved in that direction, as if roped together. He moved his hand in the other direction and the chairs settled back in place. A flicker of his hands and the chairs stacked themselves on each other to the oohs and ahhs of the viewers, then unstacked themselves.

"Large objects are no concern for Mr. Auvray, but how about something smaller?" the announcer asked. "A deck of cards, perhaps."

An assistant approached Hector, and he took a deck of cards, letting it rest on the palm of his hand for a moment before he began shuffling the cards in the air. He made the cards dance around him, then whirl up and down the stage like a tornado, circling the announcer, who was reciting more lines about the deck, a common deck, and the finesse required to perform this kind of demonstration.

Next there was a change of backdrops, more music, and explanations before Hector emerged again and stood in the middle of the stage. They lit long white candles all around him. Thirty, forty, perhaps. The announcer continued with his speech, discussing the nature of fire and a divine spark, and Nina leaned forward in the dark, wishing she could be closer to the stage or that he might lift his head in their direction. He knew the box they occupied.

"Watch now, as even fire cannot evade the command of Mr. Auvray," the announcer said.

Hector raised his hands, the candle flames rising with them, and with one movement of his arms they merged into a prodigious ball of fire that he then snuffed out with a clap of his hands, causing several spectators to shriek because, for a moment, it seemed like he was about to scorch himself.

"What is the secret? It's all in the power of the mind, ladies and gentlemen," the announcer said as the assistants wheeled out a box. The announcer reached into the box and pulled out a handful of crystals, which sparkled under the lights of the stage.

Hector also reached into the box, and the crystals rose and coalesced into different shapes: a box, a sphere, even a flower.

When the moneyed people of Loisail entertained themselves, they were not supposed to display emotion. Neither glee nor passion colored their faces. This silliness was left to the common people. But Nina, candid, smiled widely and tried to speak to Valérie, sharing her thoughts about the performance. Valérie whacked her on the wrist with her fan and Nina bit her lip. She did not try to speak again, but she did not wash the excited smile from her face.

"Now, ladies and gentlemen, we must ask what seems like a silly question. Can Mr. Auvray dance? Yes? What do you think? We'd need music to find out."

There was chuckling as the musicians pressed their bows against the strings and murmurs that increased as the assistants dragged three extremely tall mirrors onstage. Hector traced a circle around a mirror, then another, then a third, and the mirror began to spin with him. Then a second mirror spun, and a third, all perfectly synchronized. He stood in the middle of a circle of whirling glass, the mirrors shifting with the music. They were "dancing," as the man had promised.

"Isn't it magnificent?" the announcer asked, but the wonders had not ceased. Hector gestured to one of the mirrors and it fell, resting above the floor. He stepped onto the mirror and with a flick of his hands moved another in front of him, stepping onto that one as well, as though he were climbing up a moving, ever-shifting staircase. Once he had ascended high above the stage, he stood still on top of a mirror, like a character from a children's book riding a magic carpet. The audience gasped as he drifted above their heads, around the theater.

He rose high; his hands brushed the monstrous chandelier dangling above the audience's head. He lost his grip and plummeted and everyone shrieked. Nina pressed a hand against her mouth, jumping up from her seat, the clangor of a cymbal punctuating the beating of her heart, but then he rose again, smiling, and everyone let out a breathless sigh as the music swelled and the announcer declared that this was Hector Auvray, ladies and gentlemen, the one and only.

"Please put your hands together for Mr. Auvray," said the announcer.

Nina obeyed and clapped as hard as she could. Valérie pulled her back down, onto her seat, with an angry scowl.

When the show ended, Nina and Valérie remained in their box. Valérie slowly fanning herself, Nina fiddling with her gloves—she'd taken them off and now struggled to put them on again. Hector arrived shortly after. He had changed into more casual wear, a gray dinner jacket, an overcoat under his arm. Tall, slim, and charged with a palpable magnetism that might have been the energy left from his performance, he stepped forward, and Nina dropped one of her gloves.

"Ladies," he said with a bow, kissing Valérie's hand, then Nina's. "I hope you enjoyed yourselves."

"It was amazing!" Nina said at once. "I've never seen the likes of it."

She might have told him a thousand things she had enjoyed, but he turned to Valérie politely.

"And you, what did you think?" he asked Valérie.

"It was a fine performance."

"Had you ever seen a show of this type?"

Valérie's mouth was grave. She shook her head. "Not on this scale," Valérie replied.

"You must tell me how you do it. Especially the process with the cards," Nina said.

"Don't be a bother, Nina. I'm sure he does not want to explain the finer details of his work."

"Perhaps in the future we can discuss it," he said.

She felt vindicated by his words. Valérie made it seem like it was horrid to be interested in telekinesis. Nina could not see the harm in it. It was not as if she could pretend she was not a talent of a sort herself. Ever since she was a girl, she'd made things move. She'd given the maids a bit of a fright at times—the rain of stones upon the house lingered heavy in everyone's memory—and she couldn't control it well, but Nina tried to consider it all in a scientific light. The universe was unveiling new wonders every day, the motorcar and the photographic camera, to name but a handful of the inventions dazzling the world. She preferred to classify herself as one of these new wonders.

On occasion her thoughts turned less jovial. There were taunts and misunderstandings, angry recriminations when her ability disturbed the household. Even Mama and Madelena had at times looked at her with worry.

"Would you like to go to Maximilian's?" Hector asked.

"Can we?" Nina asked, turning to Valérie.

"Only for a few minutes," Valérie replied.

Maximilian's was close by. They walked. At this point in the night, the restaurant was busy, but Hector had either secured a reservation or was deemed sufficiently important that they were quickly shown to their table.

The inside was brightly illuminated, gleaming silver and sparkling glass and lacquered tables dazzling the eye. Hector ordered champagne and ether-soaked strawberries. The combination was tangy, but not unpleasant.

When they socialized, Valérie invariably directed the conversation, but Nina was emboldened, either by the setting or the company, and she raised her voice and her glass.

"You must tell me what Iblevad is like," Nina said.

"It would be difficult to describe a whole continent," he said soberly.

"Do try," she said.

Nina had seen drawings in books, colorful plates that reproduced the flora and fauna of Iblevad, but she wanted him to speak of it, to make it more real. He seemed to give it a thought.

"The north is gruesomely cold in the winter. Sometimes when you take a breath, it hurts, that is how cold it is. But to the south there are jungles, and if you walk there in the summer, under the heat of the noon sun, you will truly believe you will be cooked alive even if you wear a straw hat."

"And armadillos roam all around?" she asked.

"There are armadillos, yes."

"Iridescent butterflies, too."

"Yes."

"It must be a sight, Port Anselm in the spring."

He had, until that moment, been distracted, but his eyes fixed on her then as if he had just noticed they were sharing a table, and there was mirth in his gaze. What she'd said had pleased him, and his words came more easily, regaling her with an exact description of the port, how it looked in the afternoon sun.

Valérie looked irritated. She hardly drank a sip and her eyes were hard. Nina guessed she wished to go home, but Nina would not move an inch. Hector spoke about Port Anselm, and Nina asked him many questions. How long had he been there? How had he arrived, by boat or train? She might have spoken to him all night long. But she was not a drinker—the champagne and strawberries had gone to her head—and despite her best efforts, she found herself yawning. This was her undoing.

Valérie uncoiled a smile. "Poor Antonina, we must get you to bed," Valérie said a little too loudly.

"Why?" Nina whispered. "Valérie, I took the trouble of doing my hair and wearing this dress and—"

"I am fearing you will spill champagne all over your pretty dress."

Nina thought her cousin sounded amused, even happy. Was Valérie mocking her?

"But we've hardly had a chance to talk," Nina complained.

"Here now, give me that," Valérie said, smiling again as she pried Nina's champagne flute from her fingers. "It's enough, dear girl."

Nina wanted to yell at Valérie and demand that she stop treating her like a child, especially when Hector was sitting right across from them, but she knew that if she did, Valérie would tell Gaetan that she had be- haved poorly.

"You must forgive me, Mr. Auvray. I am rather tired," Nina said with downcast eyes.

"No need to apologize. It's understandable. I myself should head home. I have an early morning tomorrow. Mrs. Beaulieu, I hope this is not the last time we meet. Miss Beaulieu, it was a pleasure seeing you," he declared, kissing their hands.

The evening was truncated, but at least Nina drew comfort from these words. A pleasure seeing her. This signaled more than polite chatter; she was sure of it.

"Valérie, we should invite him to dinner," she said once they sat in the carriage, her lids heavy. "Gaetan said we could if you thought it appropriate."

"I know."

"He is nice, isn't he? He was attentive."

"Maybe."

"You don't like him?" Nina asked, turning to look at Valérie.

Valérie's face was, as usual, cool and composed. She held her peacock fan between her beautiful hands, a finger brushing upon a feather. "I did not say that."

"What is wrong, then?"

Nina was not good with boys. She knew this. She would have thought Valérie might be pleased to see her talking with a man without tripping over her words.

Valérie let out an exasperated sigh. "Nothing is wrong," she declared. "He may sup with us next week."

Nina was so delighted, she gave Valérie a hug, remembering too late that the woman was not fond of any physical demonstrations of affection. Nina was used to hugging Mama and Madelena, used to their laughter.

"Nina, please," Valérie said.

Nina quickly moved away from the older woman. Valérie idly raised her fan and continued to run a finger along a feather, her attention now devoted to this object. Nina had ceased to exist for her. It did not matter. Because she had agreed. She had agreed and Nina could see Hector again.

Chapter 7

THE CRIMSON FOX WAS ÉTIENNE'S type of café. Well located, small, and with an eclectic clientele, actors mixing with painters, mixing with newly rich impresarios. It was the kind of place where one might bump into women like Nathalie de Peurli, the most famous artist's model in all the city, be robbed blind by ruffians, or share a cigarette with a duelist before he slipped out to meet his nemesis.

The café honored its namesake with the hue of its walls, painted a bright crimson, and the colored glass windows, which featured two pairs of foxes.

At six o'clock, the café was bursting at the seams, and Hector had a hard time finding Étienne among all the patrons. Finally he saw his friend, sipping his coffee and disinterestedly leafing through a newspaper, sitting at the back of the establishment. Hector had to elbow his way toward Étienne's table. There was no possible way to delicately move through the café; the tables and chairs were so close together, there was scarcely any space for the waiters to walk around.

"My apologies," Hector said. "Business bled into the evening."

"Do not worry," Étienne replied, folding the newspaper and putting it aside. "It's fine. What shall we be having? I have not ordered any food."

Hector sat down and took off his jacket. It was hot inside and the ambience was casual enough that one might get away with such a thing, whereas merely considering the act at certain other venues would have been a terrible faux pas.

"Shouldn't we wait for your brother?"

"Luc's abandoned us. He's off chasing a skirt. The traitor."

"Then he takes after you."

"My days of women and wine are over, my friend. My fiancée, the dearly beloved Celeste Faré, would not abide it. I am a model of faithful domesticity."

"I still think it's a minor miracle you were able to find yourself a bride."

"I'm not that horrid. Until recently I was one of the most eligible bachelors in town," he said, smiling his genial smile.

"If you say so," Hector said.

"But speaking of women and miracles," Étienne said, taking out his cigarette case and plucking a cigarette. "I heard you had dinner with Valérie Beaulieu."

The name robbed Hector of any mirth, his face growing serious in an instant. "Who told you?"

"It doesn't matter. She is one of the most well known women in the city. Every movement she makes is spoken about." Étienne lit his cigarette, giving Hector a measured look.

"She chaperoned her cousin, Antonina."

"Hector, you do not mean to tell me—"

"I intend to court Antonina Beaulieu," Hector replied brusquely, as if he meant to shock his friend.

Neither man said a thing. The laughter of the women at a nearby table rolled toward them, sounding almost like mockery.

Étienne shook his head. "Do you think that is a good idea? You and Valérie—"

"That was a long time ago. A single summer."

Étienne seemed hardly convinced. Not that Hector expected he would be. In fact, he had hoped they would not have this conversation. Étienne was one of the few persons who knew about his relationship with Valérie, and the kind of hold she'd had on him. Because it had not been a single summer. Valérie had shattered him. The intensity of emotion he felt in those days had vanished, and in its place there lodged a tepid, distant approach to everyone.

"You were mad about the woman. You risked everything for her."

"Indeed. It didn't get me far. Perhaps I'll have better luck this time."

With Valérie or with Nina? He did not specify and he realized the same question must have occurred to his friend because Étienne looked uncomfortable.

"I know you, Hector. And I know about Miss Beaulieu. You seem hardly well matched. She is neither sophisticated nor accomplished. I think she is a talent, too."

"And? Have you forgotten what I do for a living?" Hector asked, raising an eyebrow at Étienne.

Étienne turned his head, blowing a puff of smoke. "No. But a lady should not attempt it, you realize as much. She toyed with a teacup at a reunion at Defornier's house, making it float around, and smashed it against the floor. It was an accident, a tic, who knows, but in the end an embarrassing episode. The Beaulieus have money but everyone knows they have not been able to buy Antonina common sense or proper manners."

"I like her more already," Hector said, and thought of his early years spent juggling cups in the air for a few coins.

"She's young, Hector, and you are not."

"What, I'm a senile lecher?"

"You *are* an old man. Maybe not in years, but we both know you are ancient. You're tired inside."

"I told Valérie almost the exact same thing," Hector muttered.

Étienne gave Hector a questioning glance, but Hector raised his hand, waving away his friend's inquiry before he could begin to formulate it.

"I'm not trying to be young again. This is not a spiritual vampirism."

"Then what is it about?"

Revenge. No. Retribution. God, he couldn't even pick the right word. No. It was about Valérie. About a chance to be close to Valérie. Also a chance for something else. Fairness. Yes. Why was it that everyone else was allowed a chance at happiness and he was not? Why should

Valérie be married, sharing the warmth of her bed with her husband while Hector watched the days slip away in the loneliness of his apartment? He'd had plenty of that. It was enough.

"I like her. She's easy to talk to. And there is a pleasant sensation when being in the presence of someone who regards you with admiration. People look at me all the time, Étienne. I am onstage, they clap, and when we are introduced, they express their delight in my performance. But they don't admire me. I'm not esteemed."

"Hector, come."

"No, it is true. It is different to be a gentleman like you, born and bred, than to be a man of my ilk."

"You are hard on yourself."

"I am honest. But the point is, I do not think she would see any difference between the two of us. She might even hold me in higher esteem than you, even if you are a Lémy. Despite her provincial ways or whatever other faults she may possess, she is a Beaulieu and belongs to a category of ladies men like me are not allowed to pursue, yet I feel she does not see it that way. I am her equal."

Étienne nodded, putting out his cigarette in the dregs of his coffee. "What does Valérie think of this courtship of yours?"

"Why would you ask that?"

"You said you spoke to her."

"Briefly," Hector said. "Besides, I said I 'intend to court her.' Nina and I have conversed only a handful of times."

"My question remains the same. What does Valérie think?"

"She thinks I am a fool. As you do."

"I did not say that."

"You disapprove."

"Have you ever even courted a lady? Aside from Valérie? No."

He recalled his first terrifying year away from his native country. Immediately upon his arrival in Zhude, one of the largest ports in the north of Iblevad, when he lodged in a cramped, flea-infested lodging house for young men, his boots were stolen while he slept. He had to walk through the city in his formal shoes, which were not suitable for the cold. He could have either a lunch or a dinner, but not both. The other young men smoked cheap cigarettes to keep the hunger at bay, but

Hector could not even afford those and went around to cafés and shops and street corners to put on his shows. In the evenings, against the dimming light, he wrote to Valérie, pages filled with words of love, phrases he'd stolen from poets who declaimed at the same coffee shops where he juggled for his supper, and others composed from his own imagination.

When she abandoned him, he tore the paper to shreds with his thoughts, flung the inkpot out a window, determined never again to commit passion to the page.

He had not spent his life living in a monastery, but he had limited himself to more ephemeral relationships. No, he had not courted many, *any,* ladies since Valérie.

"I am not a green boy. As you mentioned, I am an old man," Hector said, irritated.

"If I were you, I would be trying to stay as far away from the Beaulieus as possible. As far from Valérie as possible. But I am not your father to tell you what to do or not. You know how to live your life. At least, I hope you do."

"Thank you."

"You are welcome," Étienne said, raising his arm, trying to attract the attention of a waiter.

The waiter arrived, notepad and pencil in hand.

"We need the finest wine you have. We are toasting to my friend, who is desperately in love and wishes to be married," Étienne declared.

Hector did not appreciate the joke and glared at Étienne.

His friend shrugged. "It has to be brought up, doesn't it?" Étienne said.

"What?"

"Love."

He thought of Valérie, her face like a poem, lifting her hands, laughing, the sun catching in her tresses. The arc of her arm in that instant, when she ran her fingers through her locks, then extended her hand to touch his cheek. "I love you," she had said. "I'll wait."

"Love is not a concern anymore," Hector said, his voice hoarse.

The waiter returned, placing a bottle and two glasses on the table. Hector drank deeply, feeling as though he'd swallowed a fish bone and it had lodged in his throat. But it was only phantom pain. A pain he knew well, which he'd nursed for a decade.

Étienne let out a sigh and raised his glass. "To you, my friend," he said.

Chapter 8

IT WAS A DAY FOR social calls, and Valérie had ordered Nina to don a suitable dress that she might drag her through the city, a process made most unpalatable due to the constricting, uncomfortable shoes the girl was required to wear. Valérie was particular about everything, from the buttons on Nina's gloves to the size of the heel she should sport, and poor Nina, accustomed to boots that would serve her well on her entomological expeditions in the countryside, tripped more than once as they moved down the boulevard.

"You must be the slowest girl in all of Loisail," Valérie scolded her. "We'll be late."

"It's not yet three o'clock," Nina said.

"Keep up," Valérie replied with a huff.

They reached a narrow, mustard-colored three-story building tucked away on a side street, a relic of primordial Loisail since it was made of wood instead of sturdy stone and time had warped the structure, making it lean to the left.

This was the domain of Mrs. Dompierre. Nina smiled and sat in a corner of the sitting room, which was too warm. The windows were always closed despite the stifling heat, and half a dozen women gathered there, sipping their chocolate—Mrs. Dompierre did not believe in modern teas or the occasional glass of wine.

Nina did not understand why she was summoned to these soirées. Valérie never let her speak. Young girls, she said, had best keep their lips closed and let the elders do the talking.

"And I'm given to understand you went to see a performance by that fellow, Hector Auvray?" Mrs. Dompierre asked.

"It was good," Nina piped up, but then Valérie stared at her with eyes as sharp as glass and Nina looked down.

"Yes, these days everyone is going to the Royal," Valérie said dismissively.

"Everyone thinks he's sensational, it's that aura of the foreigner he has about him. But I must say, my dear, I prefer the lure of the piano over these new sort of performances."

Nina sighed; she glanced at the chocolate pot sitting on a silver tray in the middle of a low table. Idly she made it slide slightly to the left with her mind, growing restless. By the window she could hear pigeons cooing and wished nothing more than to crack the shutters open, the chance to feel the breeze.

"I think he seemed somewhat distinguished in the posters we saw around town," declared Cecilia Gugeno. "Not exactly the rough man you might expect, although in person, who knows. Perhaps he has one of those dreadful provincial accents or the manners of a peasant, they tell me—"

"He is a perfect gentleman and very nice," Nina said angrily. "And he sounds as eloquent as anyone in this room."

Nobody interrupted Cecilia Gugeno, and as soon as Nina had spoken, she realized her grievous mistake. Not only did Valérie stare at her, but all the other women turned their heads in Nina's direction and pursed their lips besides. Nina twitched her fingers and without meaning it, she made the window pop open with a loud bang, the shutter clacking against the wall. At the same time, the chocolate pot and the silver tray slid across the table. Mrs. Dompierre let out a squeak and Cecilia jumped in her seat and a woman spilled her chocolate.

You'd think Nina had shot one of the attendants. The window was closed, the pot returned to its place, the spilled chocolate cleaned up by a solicitous servant; all these actions were conducted in a long, painful silence. Then followed a stilted conversation until Valérie said they must be on their way.

Once they were outside, the woman gripped Nina's arm. "Are you a complete dolt?"

"Valérie, I didn't mean—"

"What an embarrassment!"

"Valérie—"

"No!" Valérie said, moving in front of Nina and raising her index finger in the air, as if she could jab the clouds. "You will not come up with another one of your excuses. Every time I take you out, you do a thing like this."

"That is not true."

"Not another word."

Nina clutched her hands into fists and clamped her mouth shut, and she wanted to cry but it was best not to make a bigger mess of things. She doubted Valérie liked her on a good day, and right now she must loathe her. Her sister had assured her Valérie meant well, that she was simply strict, but Nina could not help the feeling she was constantly walking on thin ice with her.

When they returned home, Nina fell back upon the bed and pressed her hands against her face, making the paintings rattle against the wall for a moment. If Valérie heard that, she'd be even angrier, and Nina rubbed her hands together.

Gaetan stopped by later, cautiously sitting on the bed. "Valérie says you had a bad day."

"Just a mishap or two," Nina mumbled. Gaetan seldom chided her as Valérie did, but she hated disappointing him.

"Maybe it's too much," Gaetan suggested. "We could postpone the dinner with Mr. Auvray. I don't think we've sent out the invitation yet."

"No, don't do that," she said vehemently.

Gaetan raised an eyebrow at her.

Nina's face felt warm. She tried to school her expression and spoke in a lower tone. "I mean to say there is no need to postpone it."

"Nina, I know you want to make friends—"

"Then let me make friends. Everyone Valérie introduces me to despises me."

She strived to do the proper things, to be liked, to fit into the niche of normality and decorum demanded by the city. But Loisail was arrogant; it viewed strangers with a raised eyebrow. She was Gaetan's cousin, but also one of *those* people, the country folk who seek to ingratiate themselves with the Beautiful Ones and must be repelled. They might have been more accepting if, perhaps, she'd shown herself meek and solicitous, but Nina, despite a youthful malleability, troubled them. They saw a determined spark lurking behind those hazel eyes that they classified as insolence, a lack of artifice that struck them as boorish, a capacity to remain unimpressed by the bric-a-brac on display that they deemed stupidity. And there was the matter of her talent, which confirmed suspicions Nina was, at best, a "difficult" child.

"Don't be melodramatic, sweetheart," Gaetan said.

Nina had every desire to be melodramatic, to give free rein to thoughts and instincts, as in those books where people loved and lived and declared the most beautiful sentiments, but instead she nodded.

Gaetan patted her hand, as if to soften his words. He was indulgent with Nina. They shared a naive optimism, fixating on all that was admirable and pretty in the world, and like any two people whose natures intersect, this drew them close together.

"Now, how about you buy yourself a new dress and we'll forget anything bad happened today, hmm?" he said.

NINA HAD NOT VISITED BONIFACE and was astonished to find the streets narrow and unwieldy. It was a network of alleys and bridges, undisturbed by the avenues that cut through other parts of the city. There was no point in taking a carriage here; one must walk, and walk she did through this labyrinth, pausing to ask for directions half a dozen times before she found herself on a quiet street. It was a block from cafés and restaurants and the bustle of merchants, but all of a sudden the noise ceased, giving way to old buildings with pots of geraniums at the windows.

In the middle of the street there stood a statue of a girl holding a bowl in her hands; someone had deposited flowers in it for good luck. Hector's home was located a couple of paces from this statue, behind a tall, elaborately decorated iron door.

Nina pulled a string, which was connected to a bell. A long time

elapsed before an old woman came out. She was the building's superintendent and seemed suspicious of Nina, eyeing her up and down.

"I'm here to see Hector Auvray," Nina said. "I am a friend of his. Do
you know if he is in?"

"He should be. Upstairs. He has the top floor for himself."

The top floor was the fifth one, marking him as a man of wealth
though one not entirely concerned with fashion, since he lodged in the
older quarters.

She knocked twice. When he opened the door, he looked surprised.
He startled Nina, too. She had been expecting one of the servants to answer. Perhaps he had no live-in staff, which seemed odd to her. He was
dressed rather casually, too, a shirt and an unbuttoned vest. Gaetan never
looked this relaxed.

"Miss Beaulieu," he said. "You are . . . ah . . . here."

"My cousin has invited you to dinner Friday night," she said, extending her hand, holding a white envelope. "Valérie had intended a courier
would bring you the invitation, but I thought I could deliver it person-
ally."

"And Mrs. Beaulieu agreed with you?" he said, frowning.

"Not exactly," Nina replied. "She doesn't know I'm here."

There was a time when a chaperone was indispensable at any gathering of young people, but Loisail nowadays toyed with this convention.
It was generally believed that if a family approved of a young man and
he had been given permission to court a lady, he could take her for a
stroll around the city and engage in a few choice activities. They could
visit respectable, educational venues such as museums or walk around
the park without anyone frowning. It was also fine for a man to see a
lady home in a carriage if he had been her escort to a ball.

There were exceptions. No young girl could attend the theater or
the opera alone with a man. Nor could she have dinner with him at a
restaurant, although a light refreshment at a respectable tearoom, earlier
in the day, might be tolerable. In smaller towns, these conditions were
ignored, or others imposed, and the lower classes flouted these strictures.

But to wander onto a man's doorstep like this? This behavior was
not sanctioned. She trod on dangerous ground, the recklessness of youth
on display.

"Well. It's a thoughtful touch to bring the invitation all the way here, though you really shouldn't have bothered," he replied, taking the envelope carefully, as if it were made of porcelain and might break.

She vacillated, but only for a second. She'd spent most of the night rehearsing her words and it wasn't too difficult to repeat the phrases she had memorized.

"The truth of the matter, Mr. Auvray, is that I came because I wanted to speak to you in private. The other night, you said you would tell me the secret with the cards. You could tell me now."

"Now? In my home, Miss Beaulieu?"

"Valérie won't ever let us discuss it when she's around."

"That may be true, but, Miss Beaulieu . . . you do realize it is unseemly to have you in my home by yourself?"

Nina stood up straight and looked him in the eye. If she'd come this far, she might as well speak plainly, not blush and be embarrassed by his words. At any rate, now that she had started this line of conversation, the words threaded themselves together and would not be pulled apart.

"Mr. Auvray, I have been warned endlessly about the liberties men may try to take with young women, but I think I'm correct in saying you are a gentleman and therefore above reproach. Also, when last a lad tried to take liberties with me, I soundly slapped him and that solved that problem."

"You need not slap me, Miss Beaulieu. Come in, then. Voices carry and I'd rather not have the superintendent share every word we speak with the whole building, as she is apt to."

Nina walked in and was amazed to see he had no formal foyer, the apartment instead extending and opening all around them. Four enormous windows on the east side let in an abundant amount of light. Lustrous armoires and chests and bookcases were set against the west wall. The dominant piece in the room was a table long enough for a dozen people to dine together, though that was impossible at this time since it was covered with papers, boxes, and a myriad of other items.

Paintings hung from the west wall, but others had been left haphazardly piled against a table leg or a chair. A six-panel lacquered dressing screen stood on the other end of the room, dividing it. Beyond it she could glimpse a dark hallway.

It certainly was a large apartment.

"You brought all these things from abroad?" she asked.

"Most of the furniture, except for a couple of pieces. But, yes. A great number of things. You wanted to ask me about my card trick?"

"I wanted you to teach me your card tricks," Nina said, stopping in front of a wooden cabinet with the most darling hand-painted ceramic knobs.

"Whatever for?"

"I've tried it on my own, Mr. Auvray, but I cannot manage it."

"Yes, but why? A proper lady learns the steps of a dance, not how to spin cards in the air."

"You sound like Valérie," Nina said, running a hand along the cabinet. "I thought you might understand."

"I'm afraid not," he said.

"I've had the ability since I was a baby. The maids claim I'd push dishes off the table without touching them before I had even learned how to speak. In the countryside, they say this means the spirit is restless. Your soul is trying to escape your body. Other times, they say you are a witch."

She stopped to admire a still life depicting a vase with bright yellow flowers and kept her eyes on the painting as she spoke.

"My father was a modern, educated man. He put everyone in their place, informing them there was a rational and scientific explanation for my ability. But my father was not always around to correct people."

She turned toward him, her hands behind her back.

"You must not think I am attempting to portray myself as a victim. I do understand their dismay. At times, I have not been able to control it. Everyone remembers that occasion four years ago when I shoved Johaness Meinard off his horse and nearly got him trampled. I didn't mean it. It happened, though.

"But then I started reading about people like you. And I realized that there are those who have a better grasp on the ability than I do. The other night, you were completely in control. You made mirrors spin and cards fly through the air. It was effortless! I thought maybe you'd tell me how you do it."

Hector's face was serious. It reminded her of the statues lining the boulevards.

He digested every single word she had spoken, taking his time to think what he would say.

"It's not a matter of telling you what to do," he said. "You don't tell someone how to dance."

"You can't teach it?"

"I can teach it. But it's not a task you learn from one day to another."

"I'm a quick study when I put my heart into it. And I'm good with memorizing facts. I can identify hundreds of butterfly and moth species with absolute certainty. You can ask Gaetan or Valérie or anyone," she said, briskly moving to stand in front of him.

The suddenness of her movements jolted him, and he cleared his throat. "It's not about memorizing, Miss Beaulieu. The dance metaphor is more apt than you can imagine. I can tell you the steps of the dance and I can even practice the steps with you, but if you have two left feet, I'll never be able to make a dancer of you."

"I do not ask that I be able to juggle mirrors onstage. Only that I not shatter them or make pots clang at an inconvenient time," Nina said. "Besides, you don't even know *if* I have two left feet. For all you know, I am more naturally talented than you."

He quirked an eyebrow at her, looking skeptical.

"Let us see what you can do," he told her, walking toward the table and uncovering a pack of cards that lay hidden under a pile of books.

He grabbed a handful of cards and tossed them on the floor; then he stepped back. "Can you move those, send them in my direction?"

If he'd seemed serious before, now he was amused. Perhaps he expected her to fail in this demonstration. But she had not been called the Witch of Oldhouse for no reason.

Nina looked at the cards, concentrated, and sent them scattering in his direction, as if a strong gust of wind had blown them away.

"Not bad. Do it again."

She did. Three times. He was more amused than ever, a faint smile on his face.

"Not bad at all," he declared with a hearty nod. "And you were, what, two years old by the time you were manipulating objects?"

"I'd say so."

"Does anyone else in your family have the same ability?"

"If they did, they never said."

"Let's do it again, but this time I want you to move only the red card," he said, shifting the cards. There were six black ones upon the floor and a single red one.

Nina concentrated again, fixing the red card in her mind, and pushed it. Unfortunately, she also pushed three black cards. She tried again, shoving four cards across the floor. By the fifth time, she was growing frustrated and unintentionally scattered all the cards.

Nina took a deep breath and another, her fingers curling tight.

"It's fine, Miss Beaulieu, don't fret," Hector said, and as he spoke, the cards returned to their place on the floor in the same pattern they had been before she lost control of them.

"I'm sorry. It's hard to focus on a single one."

"I know. You need to use your hands."

"My hands?" she replied.

"Yes. Use your hands to direct the objects, a bit like a conductor with an orchestra," he said, making a motion with his right arm as he spoke. "The hands don't do anything per se. It's your mind. But they help you focus your actions. I don't always use my hands, because I've been doing this for a long time, but in your case it's different."

"How should I move my hands?"

He had been observing her, arms crossed, at a distance. Now he moved next to her and held her arm, lightly raising it in the direction of the red card.

"Point."

Nina extended her index finger. His hand was on her wrist. He moved it in a sweeping arc, left to right and back again, though it accomplished little. He paused, his hand still resting on her wrist.

"When you manipulate an object, what is it like? What do you feel?" he asked.

"It's strange. It's like a tug," she replied.

"The same feeling you get when you walk with your eyes closed and you are about to hit a wall."

"Or the feeling you have when someone is coming behind you," she said, turning her head slightly and looking up at him.

"It's almost like you touch the surface of a still glass of water and there is this slight resistance until your fingers sink in the liquid. But when you move an object, you don't break through the surface, you are gliding over it."

"Like the pond skaters, when they walk on water."

"The what?" he asked, looking down at her.

It was then Nina realized, abruptly, how close they were to each other. She felt an intense animation but did not dare move a muscle.

"You've not observed those bugs?" she asked, and managed not to stammer the words, although her nervousness must have been obvious. But he was busy looking at the cards now, which she was ruffling, unthinking.

"It's not one of my hobbies, no."

"They do glide on water," she continued, and she had to bite her tongue to stop herself from detailing their life cycle. When she was flustered, she tended to go on.

"It's like that, isn't it? You have to feel the tension, but you must glide. Too much pressure, you lose control. That is fine for the unexpected shoving of dishes off the table, but not for purposefully manipulating an object. Miss Beaulieu, let's trace the path you want that card to take and make it glide."

He moved her arm again, left to right, gently. Nina decided to focus on the task at hand; otherwise, she was going to break into giggles or blush a terrible crimson. She looked at the card, felt the weight of his fingers against her wrist, felt the tug and the pressure he had mentioned. The red card slid across the floor.

"Remember to breathe," he said.

She did. She breathed in and out, slowly, and the card continued to slide until it hit the frame of a painting left upon the floor. Hector stepped back and she dropped her arm.

"It works," she said, spinning around to look at him. "It really works."

She forgot for a split second that she'd been nervous, that he was close to her, that he'd touched her. She simply reveled in her triumph. Hector smiled, full of cheer; his gaze grew deeper. The remoteness he wore upon his shoulders like an ornate mantle had dissipated. He was truly there, not just physically, she thought, but absolutely. Then he appeared to recall something and ran a hand through his hair, glancing down at the floorboards.

"Yes, but the key is practice. You can start with one card, but you should move to two, three. Shuffle them without touching them, things like that," he said, bringing his hands up. The cards, following his motion, assembled themselves into a neat deck. He retrieved the box from which he'd taken the deck, placed the cards inside, and handed it to her.

"Here," he said. "You can keep this."

Nina held the deck tightly, nodding. She had not been nervous when she walked in, but now it was as if a fiery red spark had started burning in her, and he spoke with a voice that was cool, in contrast to her warmth.

"You also need to remain collected. I could see the tension in your body when you failed to do it properly. You need to breathe. You need to calm down. I'm sure your bug does not skate across the water by thrashing around," he said.

"No, it's graceful," she said, dearly wishing to stretch out a hand and touch his arm, but he was spinning around, looking for something on the table.

"You can be graceful, too, Miss Beaulieu," he said, but he was not looking at her.

She smiled, delighted by his words. Grace was not her strong point. Women like Valérie could glide across the room, as if they were swans, but not Nina.

"Thank you," she whispered.

A tall grandfather clock chimed, another echoing it somewhere in the vastness of Hector's home.

He nodded. "I have to head out soon. I have a business lunch."

"Yes," Nina said, feeling mortified now that she considered the whole situation. She had barged in on him without caring to ask if he had affairs to attend to. "I'm awful, intruding on you the way I did."

"Do not worry."

They walked back toward the entrance. Hector kissed her hand quickly, bidding her good-bye, and Nina turned toward the stairs. She stopped and turned back.

"You won't forget the invitation?" she asked, wishing to prolong their encounter.

"I'll remember."

"And I haven't upset you, have I? For asking about the card trick."

"No. It's not every day I meet a lady who could toss all my glassware onto the floor without touching it," he replied in a neutral voice.

"You are teasing me," Nina said, smiling. "I'll practice. I most definitely don't have two left feet."

"I don't think you do."

She thought, she hoped, he might edge closer to her. She felt dazed and giddy, and it was a miracle her talent had not manifested and sent a chair scampering across the floor. But it was there, she thought, this feeling, like the scent of the coming rain, all around them.

Hector did not step closer. He held firm by the door, insulated, far away. She guessed this was the gentlemanly, proper attitude a man should have and was disappointed.

"Good-bye, Miss Beaulieu," he said with a slight inclination of his head.

"Thank you," she said. "Good-bye."

He smiled at her, and her disappointment turned to joy because he looked pleased with her, happy.

When the door closed and Nina was alone, she took two steps down, then rested her back against the banister, the box with the cards pressed against her chest. She'd lost her train of thought and remained there for a bit, until she recalled that Valérie might notice her absence. She'd be flayed alive, boiled in hot oil, if Valérie knew she had gone out without a chaperone to visit a man. Nina hurried down the stairs.

Chapter 9

DINNER AT THE BEAULIEUS' WAS a carefully choreographed affair, everything from the beautiful white roses at the center of the table to the selection of each dish signaling Valérie's superb taste. She dominated the room with a trained certainty that made Nina seem drab in comparison.

As for Gaetan. Having spent many years trying to envision the man who had married Valérie, imagining his every gesture and feature, Hector found Gaetan's appearance almost anticlimactic. He had pictured Valérie's husband as somewhat older and more imposing. Gaetan Beaulieu, however, was a man who could never be called imposing. There was a distinctive banality about him. Hector almost felt sorry for him.

The conversation was stilted, and Hector felt that, if she had wanted, Valérie would have seamlessly made the whole dinner vivacious, but instead she sat, sphinxlike, conscious of her power, unwilling to lift a finger, smiling coolly as dish after dish was set down before Hector. Gaetan kept talking about people and places Hector did not know, with a petulant tone that made Hector stab the pale fish on display with his fork.

"But you must have met the Ludeydens," Gaetan said. "Isn't that right, Valérie? Everyone knows the Ludeydens."

"Yes," Valérie said. "Everyone does."

"I don't attend many parties," Hector replied. He had given a variation of this answer now thrice, and Gaetan was incapable of getting the point. Irritated, he kept himself from making the glass of wine jump into his hand, as he wanted to.

"Hector says there are many odd butterflies in Port Anselm," Nina said.

He'd almost forgotten she was there, at his side, and when she spoke, he was a little startled. He looked at the girl.

"Gaetan helped me catch a few when I was a child. He was a lepi-dopterist," Nina added.

"Hardly! My cousin exaggerates," Gaetan said. "But, say, you know about butterflies, too, Mr. Auvray?"

"I'm not a naturalist at all. But there was this occasion on which I had the chance to witness a moth drinking the blood of an ox. I'm told only the males do this and the females prefer to dine on fruits."

"Goodness," Gaetan declared.

Then the man began to explain his childhood hobby and how he'd pinned a series of fine moths, which decorated his room when he was a youth. The conversation was better after this.

Hector knew Nina had helped him out of an uncomfortable spot, and he wished he could have voiced his thanks, but since it was impossible at the moment, he looked at her again and smiled. She returned the smile. Sweet girl, he thought.

After dinner the men retired to the library, which, like the rest of the house, bore the imprint of Valérie's hand in the deftly placed silver ashtrays, the potted ferns in the corners of the room, the white sofa near the fireplace, the plush carpet.

He could picture Valérie walking around that room, her fingers brushing against the spines of books, touching the curtains. It was harder to imagine Nina in this room, in this house, even though she obviously lived here. Valérie occupied every inch of space. He thought of her as the pale, sweetly fragrant moonflower, which extends itself up and can surround and cover the whole of a structure, cocooning it.

"Would you like a brandy, Mr. Auvray?" Gaetan asked, opening a cabinet and removing a decanter.

"Yes, thank you."

"I am glad we could meet. Little Nina speaks highly of you."

"Undeservedly, I am sure," Hector replied.

Gaetan handed him a glass and smiled. Hector thought he had a stupid smile. A rather uncharitable rumination.

"As you may be aware, this is Nina's first season in the city. It is an important time in a young woman's life. Many people to meet and sights to see."

"I can imagine."

"Yes. I am glad she has made a new friend, and as I said, she speaks highly of you. Yet I must admit hesitation on my part when she mentioned your name. You see, you've been far afield for so long, you are almost like a . . . well, a foreigner. A bit of a mystery, which no doubt Nina finds interesting, but I myself must be cautious. A man's reputation is his calling card, and you have no card to speak of. I don't think I even know where your family is from."

"I am from Treman, Mr. Beaulieu. My family can't vouch for a name or estate," Hector said, his voice harder than he'd intended.

"What does your father do?"

"Both my parents are dead. I began performing when I was eight and have earned a wage that way for more than twenty years. I believe I've done well for myself in this time. I own the flat where I reside and two houses in the western countryside, plus many bonds, I have lost count of them. I have invested extensively in a number of ventures. I need not ever walk onstage again, though I enjoy it and therefore plan to continue performing."

It was all true, even an understatement. He was as wealthy as any of Beaulieu's friends. Perhaps not so wealthy as Beaulieu himself, though he was not fully aware of the man's finances, but wealthy enough to dine in the same establishments he did, join the same gentlemen's clubs, obtain invitations to the same parties. He'd soared to rare heights without the benefit of family or friends.

How he'd managed this in ten scant years was explained rather easily. Hector had been possessed. He'd felt it necessary to show Valérie he could achieve what he'd said he would do. To amass the fortune, the prestige they had dreamed about. Every step he took was inspired by the echo of that long-lost love. Even now, Hector knew he was still possessed. Perhaps even more than before.

What was he doing here, talking to this man, pretending cordiality? Étienne was right. It was a folly. But Hector did not make his way to the door. He sipped his brandy and held one hand behind his back, standing rather rigidly and looking at the numerous burgundy-leather-bound volumes lining the walls.

"Nina might have told you the name of our family's home. It's Oldhouse, for a reason. The Beaulieus have resided there for more than a century," Gaetan informed him. "This is nothing compared to my wife's family, but if you say 'the Beaulieus of Oldhouse' in Montipouret, everyone knows exactly of whom you speak. I gather it is not the case for the Auvrays of Treman."

"I like to think I am unique and therefore cannot speak of 'Auvrays.' There is only *one* Auvray," Hector replied.

"That I think you are. Let me clarify. Mr. Auvray, I admire a man as successful as you, a man who clearly has wit and determination. Wit and drive, however, do not equal impeccable manners," Gaetan said, pausing to take a sip of his brandy. "However, my wife seems to think you a perfect gentleman, and she is an excellent judge of character."

Hector was surprised to hear Valérie had vouched for him. He'd thought she might hinder his efforts to insinuate himself into her household. Could this mean she *wanted* him around? He looked down quickly at his drink.

"We would be happy to consider you a new friend, Mr. Auvray, and we most certainly welcome you into our home."

"I am glad to hear that."

"I do want to clarify one point. Nina is at an age to be courted. I can understand if you wish to be our friend, and Nina's friend, and would presume no other interest in her on your behalf. If you do, however, intend to court my cousin, I would like to know it now. For one, I appreciate formalities."

"I would not court Nina without your approval, Mr. Beaulieu," he said, glancing up at Gaetan. "She seems to me a kind young woman, and if you are willing, I would most avidly like to court her."

He could visit her all spring and all summer and well into the fall without an expectation of a marriage proposal, he thought. A whole year he might court her, and regardless he might gently retreat in the end. This he knew, though he understood little else. As Étienne had jested, he was rather green in this area. His courtship of Valérie had been a wild, quick affair. It had left him breathless and dizzy with love. This would be different. He would be expected to proceed cautiously.

Gaetan cleared his throat. "There is one detail I should mention. You have no doubt heard already about Nina's situation. She has a talent, similar to your own, I would think. I mention it because it has been a source of irritation to some people."

"She told me she can't always control it."

"It is not a constant clanging of objects, though it once was. When she was a child, it proved more vexing. It does, however, occur like an involuntary movement. A reflex, if you might allow the comparison. I thought I should mention it."

"As you said, it is a talent not unlike my own. She'll probably have complete control of it in a couple of years. Even if she didn't, it would not matter."

"I am pleased to hear that. My wife will be delighted, too, I am sure."

"I do not doubt it."

"Nina is bright and charming, but people sometimes have the most ridiculous ideas in their heads."

"She told me they called her a witch."

"The Witch of Oldhouse," Gaetan said, his face serious. "There was a boy in Montipouret who I thought might make a congenial match for her, but then I heard him using that name. I would not have allowed it."

The way he spoke made Hector realize that while Gaetan was a pompous, pretentious fool, he did care about his family. Well, he cared about Nina. Could the same be said about his feelings for Valérie? They were distant during dinner. There was no animosity between them, but he could feel no bond joining them. He wondered if he could expect the same if he married Nina, this clear separation, this gap to lie between them. Did it matter? He did not seek love in her arms. It surprised him how nonchalant he could be when it came to this girl when once he'd loved another with unadulterated abandon.

It was perhaps impossible to love in the same manner again, and he thanked the heavens for this mercy.

Chapter 10

THE CONSERVATORY WAS HER REFUGE. Iron and glass protected her, as they protected her roses.

Hector was due to arrive in an hour. Valérie sought the sanctum of the conservatory, where she could be alone with her thoughts. Or rather, where she need not think, instead fixing her eyes on petals and stems and thorns. She sat on the stone bench and let the silence of this space engulf her.

But then came footsteps, and Hector walked into the conservatory, eyes grave. He carried with him a bouquet of flowers. Prim white lilies for Antonina from one of the best florists in the city. He'd brought the same arrangement before, and Antonina had lost herself in praise for the flowers even though anyone might have told her it was roses or tulips that symbolized love.

Hector's presence made Valérie's heart beat faster, but she schooled her face and her voice, speaking in a neutral tone.

"You are here too early," she told him. "Antonina is in her room. I will call for her."

"No, not yet. I know I am far too early. I thought I'd have a word with you."

"With me? Whatever for?"

He stood in front of her, looked down at her, and she did not deign to look at him, instead glancing at a rose she had plucked on a whim, her fingers running along its stem, touching the thorns with care in order to avoid injury.

"We have not spoken, you and I, since that first day I visited your home. I want to make sure you are not upset by this courtship of mine," he said.

Her heart was racing, but honest anger overtook her, washing away what tender feelings she might have held. *How dare he,* she thought, how dare he imagine she would be hurt by his actions? Had he pictured her as a child, pining over her lost love?

Of course he had. He was a romantic. He always had been. Perhaps he thought she would break down in tears, like a weak fool, and he might hold her in his arms and speak a tender word to her ear.

"Upset? I? Would it please you if I were upset?"

"No, not—"

"It would," she said, interrupting him and rising to her feet. "That is why you have returned. To torture me. You will not have the satisfaction and I will not apologize to you. Yes, I did break our engagement and that was ten years ago. What of it?"

If his eyes had been grave, now they were incensed. She found satisfaction in the anger coloring his expression. Valérie had always known how to tease him, bend his hand, evoke strong emotions. She'd been thrust into the company of a husband who was like damp wood that could not be kindled, but Hector burned bright and fast; setting him aflame took but a gesture.

"What of it, Valérie? That first winter away I lived in a flophouse with no fireplace to warm me and a few ratty blankets to sleep underneath. Sometimes it was so cold, my fingers would bleed. I had little to eat, and opportunities for work were scarce, but every coin I managed to get my hands on, I'd save," he said, reciting his woes with a quiet, steely anger as he paced in front of her. "Because I was going to buy passage for the fair-haired girl I'd left behind, the one who said she'd wait for me. But she lied. She was a spoiled rich girl who did not give a damn about me."

"A spoiled rich girl?" she said. "Neither rich nor spoiled. A girl wearing yesterday's finery, having to live off the mercy of her father's old friends. You have no idea what it was to be me. All the family's expectations upon *my* shoulders."

She was not speaking idle words. Her family had invested in her. Whatever money they had was spent on dancing and music and etiquette lessons. Old heirlooms were dusted so she might wear a pretty necklace to impress young men, and other ones were pawned to buy her dresses and shoes that were not distressed. Because Valérie was their hope and their future. They all said it; they all knew it. Her grandmother eyed her as she would a goose being fattened for a feast, and the feast had come, and Valérie had bowed her neck in sacrifice.

She'd known no other answer.

Valérie tossed the rose away and pressed a hand against the bodice of her dress, her fingers flat against her stomach.

"Grandmother said I was the only one who could save us from ruin and then the engagement was over so quickly, I could hardly catch my breath. I could not object."

"Yes, you could have objected. You might have told them you were already engaged."

Valérie chuckled and looked up at Hector. Was he truly that naive? But then, she'd been seduced by this same innocence, this blindness of the heart.

"How do you think that might have gone?" she asked. "If I had told Gaetan, the scandal would have destroyed us all. Had I told my grandmother, she might have murdered me. I might be a pauper now, washing the flagstones you stepped on."

"Perhaps you should have thought of that before you said you'd marry me."

"We say a great many things when we are young. Eventually, we grow wiser."

She turned her back toward him.

They were both quiet, the murmur of the fountain the only sound inside the glass walls of the conservatory. The stone child, face upturned, appeared to be praying. Behind the fountain, in the mirror, she saw herself and Hector. He was staring at her reflection, his gaze burning her.

"Did you even love me, Valérie?" he asked.

She did not reply, her eyes fixed on the woman reflected in the glass, standing there in her dress of ivory chiffon, the purple satin belt around her waist, pearls dangling from her ears and neck.

He was asking about another Valérie, a Valérie she could only vaguely recall.

She saw him turn away from her in the mirror, his eyes now not on fire but cooling, filling with ashes, and the motion struck a panicked chord inside her chest. Valérie turned, too, grasping his sleeve.

"You know I did," she said. "You *know* I did."

She felt like crying now, like the fool she had told herself she would not be, and her fingers knotted with the fabric of his jacket, pulling him closer until he was appallingly near.

"Did you love him, too?" Hector asked.

"No," she said. "But my family did."

"What about now?"

Valérie thought of Gaetan. Her husband had disappointed her in a myriad of ways: his lack of passion, his blindness, his almost pathological devotion to his family, and his inability to provide Valérie with a family of her own as was expected—even if she might have resented him if he had given her children.

She could not muster more than a shrug.

"Gaetan is Gaetan. He is a busy man and a kind man, and often a weak man. I am as fond of him as I can possibly be."

"And us?"

He trapped her wrist with his hands, snagging her, until her fingers were pressed against his chest. She thought of when they'd been younger, his lips against hers, their hands knotted together. She knew they still fit well, she felt it; fit like Gaetan and Valérie did not fit, grossly mismatched.

"There's nothing to be done now."

"If you do not love him—"

"He is Gaetan Beaulieu and I am a Véries," she whispered, almost an automatic reflex.

"A Beaulieu of Montipouret, yes," Hector muttered, his hands sliding down, releasing her. "An important family, I've been told. God knows every girl in every town would want to be married into it, and ladies in yesterday's finery perhaps the most."

His voice was vicious, wanting to cut her, and she was surprised to discover it did. It hurt, the way he hurled the words at her. He did not say "whore" but he might as well have.

She colored with anger and could not sputter a single word. Then she looked down and noticed that he'd let go of the bouquet. Nina's flowers. Valérie picked them up, holding them with care.

"Men also wish to marry into families, hoping perhaps that they might rise above their station, though truth be told, I doubt such a feat could be accomplished."

"It's not her family's name that beckons me, hard as that might be to fathom."

"Remind me, what do lilies stand for?"

"Innocence," he said.

"She would be, wouldn't she?" Valérie held out the bouquet for him.

"There's something to be said for it," he replied.

"Indeed. Innocents do not question people's motives. You've come to hurt me, Hector. You've come to toy with us. Feel free to toy with her. But you'll find I am not a piece you can slide across your board."

He grabbed the bouquet with slow hands. A petal or two fell to the floor.

"Follow Antonina around and wed her and bed her and have a merry life. It is not my concern," Valérie said, her voice like nectar as she sat down on her stone bench once more.

"If you asked me now to leave and never come back, I would," he said.

She knew he was telling the truth. Because it would be akin to a noble deed, part of a martyrdom he might relish. But she did not want to give him that satisfaction, the knowledge that he disturbed her, that she could not bear to have him near her. To admit it would be defeat and Valérie would not be defeated.

"I'm not going to ask anything of you," she said.

"Very well," he replied tersely.

Hector left the conservatory with his lilies under his arm, his steps loud upon the stone floor. She sat in the solarium for a long while, finally rising and sweeping into the salon, where she found Hector and Antonina. She was putting the flowers into a white vase.

"Look, Cousin. Hector has brought me lilies again," the girl said, her smile wide.

"I know," Valérie said. "I saw them."

She patted Nina's hand, a dismissive gesture, glancing at Hector with detachment.

HE WAS NOW A REGULAR fixture, dropping by three days a week, and the zeal earned smiles from Gaetan, who thought his cousin had finally netted herself a sweetheart. Valérie had thought he'd end the charade after the third, fourth visit. She'd quietly bet on it. But there came the tinkle of the bell, which never failed to draw a shiver from Valérie, and then the sure steps of Hector upon her polished floors.

Most days, she ignored him, wearing a stoic mask. Seldom did she permit him to glimpse a stray glance of affection. But one day, well, it had been a long day. Last week, her cousin had stopped by to ask for money. It was the same old conversation. They had nothing, only the stones of Avelo, which had once been a great fortress and was now a ruin, and the house in Loisail where she'd grown up, which was falling to pieces with each passing year. Wouldn't Gaetan advance them money? They needed another loan.

Valérie despised this mendicant's dance. She had accounts at the best stores in the city, but her family didn't need gloves and hats and silver pins for their hair. She required cash, and that meant having to ask Gaetan. She put it as best she could, using her sweetest tone. Gaetan followed her lead in most things, but when it came to her family or his bank account, he was cautious.

"It's a little nothing of a loan," she said.

"Valérie, I have given him three loans in two years," Gaetan protested.

"You could have bought him that army post, and then it would be no concern. But since you refused—"

"Buying an army post. Valérie, what a thought. That would have been in poor form."

It was tradition that military officers who had not attained certain ranks at appropriate times were forced out of service, and this is what had happened to her cousin, who was rudely divested of his crimson uniform. It did not have to be like this. Merit was the usual coin in the army, men rising by skill and not due to their fortune alone, but although the system of commissions had been mostly abolished, it was not entirely gone: the king's personal corps maintained the practice. There had been a chance for the cousin to find himself in a comfortable position, but Gaetan had refused to provide the required sum of money for this purpose. Now Valérie's cousin faced the fate of all men like him: doomed to mingle at taverns frequented by soldiers, his clothes growing more threadbare, trading stories and drinking cheap wine.

"Besides, he is trouble, he got himself in all those scuffles," Gaetan said. "There was also that unpleasant business with a young woman."

When it came to the Véries, they should be a paragon of virtue and decorum. Valérie gave him a hard look, but she ceased in her protests. After walking around his office nervously, Gaetan finally agreed he would deposit the money in her cousin's account.

How she hated these performances! When they were over, she had to act the grateful wife and kiss her husband's cheek when she wished nothing more than to spit on him. Antonina was not forced to beg like this. A snap of the fingers, and she had whatever she wished, and Valérie seethed that afternoon as they waited for the brat to finish dressing and join them for a walk in the park.

Hector sat in the drawing room and Valérie stood, resting a hand upon the mantelshelf. She was more restless than usual, which he noticed, leaning forward.

"Is everything all right?" he asked.

She gave him a sarcastic laugh and a wave of her hand. What a silly question. There was no way to answer it. She let herself fall upon a chair in front of him, propping her head on her right hand, and glanced at him with her usual dismissal. She had a thought to say a cruel phrase, for the amusement of it. But as he sat there, looking rather earnest, Valérie let out a sigh.

"Do you remember what it was to be young?" she asked. "Every trouble would be solved by sundown, and every dawn you'd have a new chance to remake the world."

He paused for the longest interval, nodding. "Yes," he said.

"I'm tired," she said.

He stood up and she thought he might try to approach her. Quickly she shook her head and returned to her place by the mantelshelf.

"We might have a picnic, if you'd like it. It always lifted your spirits," he proposed.

"'Always,'" Valérie said with a chuckle. "We only went on two picnics."

"And it worked like a charm each one of those times."

Distant Frotnac. Thinking of it was like viewing a scene through frosted glass. She might have done anything back then, reckless with youth. Now she did nothing, encased in iron.

"Let us have a picnic, Valérie. I'll arrange for the food and drinks, and afterward we can go to the theater, watch a silly, light performance."

He had moved to her side and was smiling. Valérie, bewitched by his dark eyes, smiled back. "If you insist," she said in the tone of her girlhood, more a purr than proper words.

There came Nina's breathless voice as she walked into the room, her weightless laughter. "Mr. Auvray!" the girl said as she always did, while Valérie bit her lips.

Chapter 11

Hector planned for everything. He rose early, shaved, and dressed in a double-breasted waistcoat that was molded to his lean frame. He went to the market, fetching bread, cheese, and wine. He'd already bought a picnic basket the previous day. He stopped by the florist for a bouquet of pink roses rather than the white lilies he bought for Nina.

He planned for everything except the rain, which fell, sudden and aggressive, as soon as he stepped into the carriage. No spring shower, a full-blown downpour. By the time he reached the Beaulieu household, it was obvious there could be no picnic. He walked into the drawing room and set the picnic basket down on a table, along with the flowers. A few droplets of water had caught on the shoulders and sleeves of his coat.

Nina and Valérie were sitting in the drawing room. The younger woman had a book in her hands, while the older one lay on a divan, a hand resting on the back of it, the other upon her knee, submerged in deep thought. Valérie did not notice his entrance. Nina rose at once, as she tended to do. She either forgot or did not care that a gentleman was to approach her where she sat and then, after he kissed her hand, she might stand up.

"Mr. Auvray," she said with a chuckle. "Can you believe the rain? I think a thousand toadstools will sprout tomorrow morning."

"It is a bit of a downpour," Hector replied.

"I imagined you'd send word you were not coming," Valérie said casually, sitting sleek and still.

"My word is like iron. I keep my promises," he told her.

There was no secret meaning in the comment; the thought merely sprang to his head. But Valérie must have interpreted this as a veiled barb at her faithlessness because her face blanched and grew hard.

"You needn't have bothered. Clearly, we are not going anywhere," Valérie said.

"The theater is dry. We can sup at a restaurant instead," he replied, attempting to pacify her.

"The intention was to have a picnic, I thought. Not a restaurant."

"We could have a picnic inside," Nina suggested. "We did that when we were children back home. Lay down a blanket and eat here. We can make a game of it."

"I am not a child who plays games, unlike others," Valérie said, snappish. "If you will forgive me, I have more important things to do than to pretend I'm making mud pies."

Valérie made a motion to rise, to leave the room, and Hector, monumentally furious—at her dismissiveness, at himself for having spent the morning in a state of idiotic merriment at the thought of this outing, at the stupid rain—could not allow her to leave first. She always abandoned him, and now he meant to make his exit before she could.

"Good-bye," he said, and rudely stepped out without bothering to give her a second more of his time. He heard Nina gasp and hurried out of the house without a look over his shoulder, back to his apartment, where upon walking in, he threw all the windows open at the same time with a snap of his fingers, shutters banging in unison. He was boiling and he was lonely and outside it rained.

He let the water drip inside, form puddles by the windows.

During the night, he considered his idiocy, the way he milled around the Beaulieu household, searching for the crumbs of Valérie's affection. She must have a good laugh at him.

He should stop visiting. It had been a blasted idea since the beginning. There was nothing saying he had to go back, no need to knock on that door again. He thought Nina might find his disappearance confounding, but what of it? Yet he resolved to apologize to her for his uncouth getaway and to inform her, politely, that he might be scarce from now on.

Therefore, the next day he returned to the Beaulieu house, meaning to make a short trip of it. The maid told him Valérie was out and Nina was napping, but she'd go fetch the girl if it was important. Hector said it was, and he was pressed for time. The maid frowned, but went off to find her.

He waited by the foot of the stairs. Nina came down, not in an afternoon dress, but instead wearing a green lounging robe, her black hair falling freely to her shoulders. Worn slippers peeped beneath the robe, painting a bafflingly intimate picture. She noticed how he stared at her, and stared back at him in turn, standing three steps above Hector.

"Pardon me, but you said you had to speak to me quick," she told him as she clutched the collar of the robe with one hand.

He realized she'd headed downstairs in haste, for him, and the sweetness of the gesture struck him dumb.

"You said you need me?" she asked.

Hector nodded. He had not rid himself of his coat, nor his hat, which he held tight, running his hands around the rim of it.

"I was rude yesterday and wanted to apologize. I left like there were hounds chasing me. I am sorry."

Her grip on her collar relaxed. "I understand, Mr. Auvray. Don't feel guilty."

"You don't understand," he said. "I'm the worst of friends to you. You ought to spend more time with people who are more animated than me, younger and lively. I am like a rickety, haunted house, Miss Beaulieu. Best find a new abode. I won't be troubling you any longer."

Nina descended the remaining three steps, standing in front of Hector, and looked up at him. She was small, where Valérie was tall; he never failed to notice this difference. And, well, Valérie wouldn't have come down for him.

"Is it that you are annoyed at me?" she asked. "Or bored?"

"No. The opposite," he said, and rubbed a hand against his forehead. He sat down on the bottom step with a sigh, resting the hat on his lap. Cautiously, she sat down next to him. They were quiet.

"Hector, you can tell me," she said.

"Nothing, nothing, dear girl," he said, chuckling. "Nothing worth hearing."

He thought of his days in Loisail spent staring across the room at Valé-rie and the years before that spent conjuring the woman in his mind, and the misery that stamped his footsteps. He was unhappy; he could never be happy. And he liked Nina, she was good to him, but she was not Valérie.

Nina was smiling. "If you were not around, I'd be lonely," she said softly.

He thought to tell her something gallant, which might please her. Like "surely not for long" or another compliment that could be easily tossed and easily forgotten.

"I'd be lonely, too," he admitted instead. A deeper truth instead of shallow words.

Nina was silent. Her hair, falling down her back, curled a little, re-belliously, a detail that had been impossible to divine because each day she wore it up like all the other ladies in the city, pulled into dainty chignons.

"Everyone seems to think I'm an idiot or a child, but you don't treat me as either," she said. "I appreciate it and I appreciate the tricks you teach me, all the advice you give me. If you were to cease visiting, I would be sad—but I would not resent you, because you'd still be my friend. A good friend, Mr. Auvray."

She reached out to him, as if to grab his hand, which rested upon the hat, and instead he gripped her hand and pulled it up to his lips, kissing the back of it.

"You are too kind," he said.

They sat looking at each other and for a minute he was absolutely absorbed with her, a graceful quietness bracketing and protecting them. Wouldn't it be nice if they could remain like this? If the world grew smaller and everything else melted as easy as wax, his worries, his past, the whole lot of it. Then came sure footsteps and Hector turned to look at Valérie, who regarded them with a wintry glance.

"I see you are back," she told him. "And I see Nina forgot herself again. Go get into a proper dress, at once."

Nina hurried up the stairs with a hushed apology. Hector stood up, inclining his head at Valérie, while she rested a hand on the banister and turned her face to show him her profile. Her cheeks had some color to them, the slightest blush.

"You must not be angry at her," Hector said, thrusting his left hand into his pocket. He felt odd, like a thief who has been caught stealing a precious stone and is dragged before the magistrate. "I said I was in a rush, and rush she did, to speak to me."

"You did not seem in a rush," Valérie replied. "What were you discussing? The names you'll give all your children?"

"I was rude yesterday and came to apologize to her."

"And not to me. I see."

"I apologize to you, too, Valérie. I should not have snapped at you as I did," he said, pressing his hat against his chest and inclining his head again, signaling his departure.

He had not taken more than four steps when she spoke. Her voice did not crack, but it was strained, which was always odd when it came to Valérie. She modulated herself carefully.

"Do you ever pause to think about what you are doing, Hector?" she asked.

He turned around. She was looking at him with eyes that seemed transparent, the blue of them bled out and her golden hair like a halo. The hard look of a Madonna of unkindness, a blind stone idol who did not see him yet demanded sacrifice, worship, blood upon its altar. For a second those eyes parted, becoming the blue of her youth, filling with the desperate longing he had glimpsed a decade before, and which had drawn him in and drowned him.

"You are going to break one of us, and it will not be me," she said, and he almost caught her wrist, but she pulled away—she always pulled away—and left him alone.

Chapter 12

Nina stood by the door of the house, looking up at Hector Auvray, and he looked down at her in return.

It was the end of the Grand Season; one could feel the electric fervor of the city dying down into its summer slumber as the moneyed families made their yearly exodus to the countryside, a pilgrimage that had been in style since the days when Loisail was nothing but narrow cobblestone streets and mud splatters.

It was also her last chance to attend a lecture by the Entomological Society at the Natural History Museum, and she intended to do it.

"Are you certain Mrs. Beaulieu said that?"

"Yes. She has a dreadful headache and she told me if I was intent on going to the museum, then you should escort me."

"You and I out and about, and no chaperone," he mused.

At a public gathering of this sort in the daytime, and with him sanctioned as a proper suitor, this was not a concern, although they would not be able to sup together.

"Don't seem surprised. She knows you are a gentleman. Besides, I can show you that coin trick you taught me the other day. I've spent hours working on it."

"I warn you, I know nothing of entomology."

"It is no matter. Your one duty can be to look absolutely dashing by my side and nod your head charmingly," she told him.

Hector chuckled and gave her his arm, both moving toward his carriage, which was waiting for them.

He came by each week to see her with his lovely bouquets of lilies under his arm and that vague melancholic air of his. His eyes looked dented and wearied, but when he smiled, she thought it magnificent, and his laughter—though scarce certain days—was marvelous.

She sat in front of him as the carriage rolled down the avenue and took out from her purse a coin, holding it up for him to see.

Hector gave her a nod of encouragement and she tossed the coin in the air. It rose but never fell, Nina holding it in place with a movement of her hand, making it float between them.

"See?" she said, triumphant. "I've done it."

"Not quite. Make it be still."

"It is still."

"No."

The coin was not absolutely still—it trembled ever so slightly, it dipped and rose a tad—but it was the lightest movement.

"That does not count," she said.

"It does."

"It can't remain absolutely still, Hector."

"It can," he said. "Allow me."

She released the coin and he extended his hand. It floated between them, but this time it was absolutely still. Then he moved but two fingers, and the coin flew to his waiting palm.

"If you are going to perform a task, perform it properly, Nina. Do not cut corners or give it a halfhearted try," he said.

"I did try to do it properly. I spent hours practicing last night. I told you."

"It does not show."

Nina crossed her arms. She did not like him when he was like this, and truth be told, he was a rather exacting teacher. She thought he did it to scare her off and dissuade her from telekinetic tricks, but sometimes she thought he did it for another reason altogether, one she did not comprehend.

She tilted her chin up and looked out the window. It was a sunny spring day, and when they reached a wide avenue decorated with the bronze statues of notable citizens of Loisail, she looked at the beautiful flowers bordering the pavement, jasmines and tulips in darling colors.

They went by the fountain with its nymphs, all three holding their hands in the air, and stopped at the main entrance of the Natural History Museum, which she'd visited but once with Valérie, who had not liked it at all because it was an older building, rather cluttered. Nina thought it a fabulous place, a treasure trove. Most people marveled at the large animals: the impressive tiger about to attack or the bear frozen in its tracks, both wonders of taxidermy set against a painted backdrop. Nina preferred the smaller specimens. The insects like jewels upon black velvet.

They did not have time to pause and look at the pretty beetles or the delicate butterflies on this occasion, because the lecture was about to begin. They made their way to a room filled with many chairs and sat in the back.

The lecturer was Lise van Reenen, a naturalist who was noted as a butterfly collector. The talk that day was on the caddisfly, which lived near bodies of water and spun a cocoon of silk. Nina was impressed by Lise's delivery and the way she commanded the room.

When the lecture was over and they walked outside the museum, she remarked on this point.

"Some people, I think, are born to speak in public and know how to manage every word and gesture. As she did, as you do when you perform," she told Hector.

"It's not innate talent. It is practice, like dealing cards without touching them or making coins hover in midair."

"You make it seem easy."

"It's part of the trick. Do not reveal your inner thoughts, nor fears."

Men in black coats walked along the boulevard, and women held white parasols over their heads. It was suppertime and the restaurants were bursting with customers. He must take her home soon.

"We will leave for the summer in a couple of weeks," she said, because this thought had been darting inside her head since early in the day. "We are to go to Oldhouse, Valérie and I. Gaetan will join us at one point, as he likes to spend at least ten days in the countryside during the warm months."

"When will you return?"

"In three months' time and no sooner. My family misses me, and be-sides, Valérie says the city is not fit for living in the summer."

Nina did not understand how this could be, considering that Cousin Gaetan managed to stay in Loisail for many weeks during the summer, overseeing his business affairs, but it seemed that when one could man-age, one should abandon the metropolis, and none of the smart ladies would abide to be seen walking down the boulevards at that time of year.

"I was thinking you might visit us at Oldhouse," she said. "You could stay for as long as you like. We are hospitable and it is a pleasant place."

"I'm sure it is, but I will remain in the city for most of the summer."

"But not all of it?"

"My friend Étienne is going to Bosegnan, where his fiancée's sum-mer home is located, and I shall be going with him to meet the fiancée in question, who has been abroad for the better part of the year."

"That is perfect!" Nina exclaimed. "You must cross Montipouret in order to reach Bosegnan, and a few days in Oldhouse would not alter your course. Your friend is welcome to stay with us. We would all be jolly. I've grown accustomed to our talks and would miss you if I were not to see you for months on end."

"You may write to me."

"Bah. A letter is not the same at all. I'd have to write a dozen a day in order to keep you well informed. You know how I go on. Won't you join us at Oldhouse?"

"It's a serious request," he said, and his face was grim, as though she'd asked him to witness an execution with her. He was like this; a dark cloud would periodically blot out the sun and drain all mirth from his body. She did not understand it.

"'Serious'? It's a summer getaway in the countryside. Must you be gloomy about everything?" she asked. He was vexing her. She had thought he would be pleased at the idea and now found herself consider-ing that he might not want to spend an extensive number of days with her.

Hector did not reply and she glanced away, looking at the patrons who sat outside a café in the afternoon sun. Her lips trembled.

"I'll go," he said with a sigh, his hand resting upon her arm.

"No, you must not feel obligated to me," she murmured.

His hold on her tightened and he pulled her aside, under the awning of a hat shop. "Nina, I want to go with you," he said.

She knew by now he was the kind of man who, once he had made a choice, would follow the path set down unblinking, but as he looked down at her, she spoke.

"Are you sure?" she asked. He was close to her; if he but moved a step forward, the buttons of his coat would brush against her chest. She'd seen an illustration in a book where a man held a woman in his arms like this.

But he did not take that step. He smiled instead. "Yes," he said.

His smile was nearly shy, and she beamed at him in delight. "You will like it," she promised as they began walking again. "It's beautiful there."

"I haven't been anywhere near the countryside in ages."

"Where did you holiday when you were in Iblevad?"

He shrugged. "I seldom holiday anywhere. I've been busy working."

"Clearly I've come to save you from yourself."

"I wouldn't go as far as that."

"You'll see," she said, glancing at the street, the restaurants.

"Indeed. But for now, we should hail a carriage."

She sighed. "I wish we could keep talking and sup together. I wish we could go to Castet's. Wouldn't that be fun? Drinking champagne and eating oysters," she said.

"If you really want oysters, the place to go is the wooden stalls of the open market, early in the day."

"You wouldn't be breakfasting like that at the market, would you?" she asked.

"Why not?" he replied. "Does it sound too common?"

She shook her head. "Maybe. But also exciting. I envy you. I think you may do anything you want."

"Not *anything*," he said, and surely he meant little by it, but a deep note in his voice thrilled her. A promise, a secret, which made her reach out and touch his arm lightly as they crossed the street.

"There is a bird they call an oystercatcher and it is a mistake to call it thus, since it also dines on crabs, mussels, and echinoderms. Its eggs are darling, with the most handsome markings, but it has the nasty habit of leaving them in seagulls' nests for the other birds to care for," Nina said, because when she could not find proper words or gestures, she defaulted to the lines she'd read in books.

Though they had walked but a few paces, she realized she sounded breathless and likely this was why Hector paused to look down at her, curious, making her blush, which was what she'd been avoiding.

They stood motionless and then he leaned down, and she thought he meant to touch her, kiss her. Instead, Hector snapped up his head and spoke to a driver waiting by the curb. He helped Nina into the carriage, and when he released her hand, he smiled again, and in that fluttering second she knew she loved him, loved him true, and it wasn't the coy flirtation of a young woman.

Chapter 13

Montipouret was a region of rivers and lakes, its water mills constantly churning. It was also a place of forests, thickets, and marshes, which contrasted with the open fields and neatly divided parcels of the northern regions. Much of the travel in the area took place by boat. That was how the Beaulieus made their fortune a couple of centuries before: by ferrying wool upriver to be sold in other regions. Timber, coal, wool, and goats' milk were the staples of these lands.

The railway now cut through the region, but Montipouret remained less populous, more isolated, and rougher than the rest of the country. Reaching Oldhouse was still an odyssey. Valérie, used to her fine carriage and the macadam streets of Loisail, could not help but mutter to herself as they abandoned the train at Dijou and boarded a carriage that took them down a bumpy road that grew bumpier as the minutes went by. Soon it was not a road at all but a dirt path.

Eventually they arrived at Oldhouse, an estate lacking in grace. It was made of rough stones that had been piled upon one another in a manner that ensured it was sturdy, but nowhere near a delight to the eye.

Oldhouse was divided into two structures, the original Oldhouse having necessitated an annex at a point. A Beaulieu who had a modicum of artistic aspiration had ensured that the main structure and the annex were connected by a long, wide hallway with tall stained-glass windows. These were beautifully rendered but completely out of place, producing a grotesque contrast between the heavy building with small windows and the airy hallway.

Behind Oldhouse rose a tower, like a bony finger pointing at the sky. It preceded the house, marking the remains of another estate. These sights were not unusual in Montipouret, as the locals were fond of reusing whatever stones they could and building new homes with them. Debris and foundations were left here and there, smudges upon the land. The result was an anachronistic combination, one that only rendered Oldhouse uglier and more haphazard.

Valérie never relished the days she spent in Oldhouse, and she had loathed the previous summer when she had been forced to endure a month there in an effort to prepare Antonina for the Grand Season, an absolute waste of her time, since Antonina was often out looking for disgusting bugs or ignoring her advice. This year she'd had even less interest in visiting if it meant she'd have to stomach Hector and Antonina together for days on end, but when she had tried to extricate herself from Oldhouse, both her husband and Antonina's mother balked at the idea. They thought Antonina needed Valérie's guidance in this matter. An extended visit from a suitor was of the utmost importance and Valérie was a northerner, like Auvray. Who better to counsel the girl and watch over her best interests? Besides, Antonina's mother was busy running the household, while Antonina's sister was pregnant with her first child and did not live at Oldhouse anymore, though she had stopped by for a few days. Valérie was reckoned invaluable.

Valérie simply nodded her head as she always did, her face a pretty mask of porcelain, and declared she would accompany the girl.

Valérie and Antonina stepped out of the carriage and into Oldhouse. As soon as they entered the structure, four shaggy dogs rushed to greet them and Nina laughed and patted their heads while Valérie pursed her lips together.

Then came a coterie of aunts, uncles, and cousins. These, like the dogs, were a staple of Oldhouse. The place was always bursting with distant relations and associates of the family. The women clucked and hawed at them. Ordinarily Valérie would have been the center of attention, but they gathered around Antonina, exclaiming at her fine gown and finer looks.

They were dragged to the cavernous hall, with its ancient tapestries and its great fireplace, where most of the activity in Oldhouse occurred. Two gnarled women—twins, Lise and Linette—sat by the fire. Lise had the annoying habit of calling every woman "sweetheart," while Linette was almost deaf. They lived in Loisail, but like most of the Beaulieus they came to roost at Oldhouse in the summer.

Two younger women were also by the fire, in high-backed chairs of studded leather: Camille, Nina's mother; and Madelena, Nina's elder sister. Madelena took after her mother, with a trace of the Beaulieu in her. She had light brown hair, fine hands, and her mother's heavy-lidded eyes, which Nina had also acquired, though Nina's eyes were hazel instead of brown.

Camille and Madelena stood up and hugged Valérie and Antonina both, the sisters giggling when they saw each other.

"Madelena, you are as big as a ship," Nina declared, looking at her sister's belly. The woman was quite pregnant. Nevertheless, it was the height of bad manners to remark upon such a thing, and Valérie could not help but glare at Antonina, even if the girl was oblivious to her impropriety.

"And you look like a lady," Madelena replied. "Cousin Valérie, you have turned her into a woman fit for Loisail's society."

Valérie had to bite her tongue because all Nina could do was "look" the part.

"I have tried," Valérie said tactfully.

"We are happy to see you," Camille said. "We are also delighted to have you with us, Valérie. Do you know when Gaetan will be joining us?"

"Sometime next month. He sends his love."

"And when is Nina's friend going to come?" one of the younger cousins piped.

"He is her fiancé, silly goose," another cousin replied.

"Mr. Auvray will be here tomorrow," Nina said primly.

An animated discussion began, but Valérie raised her voice to interrupt the mutterings. "He is not her fiancé," she said. "Mr. Auvray is but a suitor. We must not get ahead of ourselves."

"Nina wrote that she expects to be married to him within the year," the cousin who had spoken before interjected.

Nina had the decency to blush and shake her head. "I said he might ask," she said. "I think he will."

More mutterings began. Valérie could feel the beginning of a headache. How irritating these people were!

She excused herself as quickly as she could, claiming she really should begin to unpack, but truly she could not stomach the commotion and the loud shrieks of Aunt Linette, who kept asking Lise what everyone was going on about.

Once safely in her room, which was located in the main house, Valérie sat on the massive bed, rubbing her temples with both hands.

This was the room where she always stayed whenever she visited the estate. It was crammed with heavy wooden furniture carved with patterns of intricate flowers. The bedspread was a sickening shade of green, with a carpet to match it. There was a fireplace with enameled tiles, the most attractive feature of the room because it meant she would not be cold; the house was eternally chilly.

This was one of the finest rooms in Oldhouse, they'd told her when she'd first arrived. It had been decorated to the taste of the northern wife of a certain Beaulieu and thus was reckoned most appropriate for Valérie, but it was still a sad chamber. The bathroom was better, all green marble with proper plumbing and plenty of towels. Nothing like Loisail, though.

She wondered what room they'd give to Hector and what he would think of this place. Perhaps he'd find some rustic charm in it, as he apparently found some rustic charm in Antonina. Valérie, grown jealously like a flower in a hothouse, could not see any prettiness in Antonina; her luxuriant qualities were to her an affront. It was like staring at a weed. Her upbringing made her want to stab it with a spade, stomp on it quick, lest it contaminate the garden.

Valérie began to unpack. She placed her dresses in the wardrobe, then carefully set her perfumes and her hairbrush upon the vanity. She had brought one of her jewelry boxes, though she did not think she'd have the occasion to wear this finery. She pulled idly at her necklaces, feeling the weight of her pearls.

Her hands found Hector's ring.

There was a knock on the door, and before Valérie could reply, Antonina breezed in.

"Valérie, did you bring that blue sash of yours? I'd love to borrow it for tomorrow."

Valérie placed the ring aside and shook her head. "I did not."

"That's a pity. I'll have to ask my sister if she has one."

The girl was ready to bolt again, but Valérie raised her voice. "Antonina, may I speak with you?"

"Always. What is it?"

Valérie had thought about her exact words and was satisfied with the speech she had concocted. "Antonina, I can understand how exciting it must be to have Mr. Auvray staying at Oldhouse. Yet I am afraid you are a bit *too* excitable when it comes to him. Today, for example, you said you expect him to ask for your hand in marriage though he has not made any formal inquiry of the sort."

"He brings me flowers every time he visits," Nina said wistfully, clasping her hands together, as if she were holding an invisible bouquet.

"Darling child, I am sure during his life he has had plenty of occasions to take flowers to a number of girls."

Antonina frowned. Her face was already looking stormy, though Valérie had spoken but a few words. The girl had a temper and wore her heart on her sleeve. "Are you saying he is a cad? He is a perfect gentleman, I can assure you that."

"A bachelor of his age—"

"Valérie, please, I said he was a perfect gentleman," Antonina said, raising her voice in a way that always made Valérie want to slap respect into her. She spoke when she pleased, she frowned and she cried and she was crude.

Valérie sat still, her haughty head high, and she looked carefully at the girl. "You must be cautious. A man may change his tune or never sing the tune you expect him to sing at all. You do not know him well enough. It is not advisable to fling yourself at a man simply because he brings you flowers. Be sensible and watch the words that come out of your mouth. You should not have spoken of an engagement without proper assurances."

"It was merely . . . I wrote a few letters to my sister and my cousins, and they asked—"

"You lack decorum," Valerie declared, a judge speaking a sentence.

"Of course you'd say that," Antonina told her. "You simply hate

Hector because he is not one of the boring boys you would have picked for me."

"All of them sensible young men."

"*I* do not want to be sensible." Antonina had begun pacing around the room.

Valérie gritted her teeth. "I was your age once and know how tempting it is to throw caution to the wind, but I—"

"I doubt it. I doubt you were ever young at all. Why, you act as though you are older than my great-aunts Lise and Linette combined. You reproach me everything and allow nothing. Why must you be so . . . so mean?"

Valérie was not one prone to kindness, though she had, on occasion, been known to be fair. She was attempting to be fair with Antonina, who was, after all, her cousin by marriage. What was she receiving? Nothing but awful words and terrible manners.

Valérie had viewed Antonina as a piece jostled between Hector and herself, a speck of guilt moving her to speak. Now the guilt was washed away by pure anger.

If Antonina defied her, then she was her enemy.

"Ignore my counsel as you always do, then," Valérie said. "I waste my breath on the likes of you. You'll end an old maid."

Antonina was contrite for a moment, but this was only a moment. Her eyes soon sparked again with that fire of hers. "He does intend to marry me. You shall see."

"I await news of his proposal with bated breath."

"You mock me," Antonina said, sounding affronted.

"You mock yourself."

Finally words failed the girl. She exited the room with a loud bang of the door, which made Valérie wince even if the theatrics were to be expected. She rubbed her temples again, wondering what the next day would bring and the day after that, Hector's presence surely blotting each sunrise like ink spilled upon a page. And Antonina with her inane twittering, making it worse.

Chapter 14

Étienne dozed for most of the train ride and Luc complained, a pattern that was reenacted once they boarded a carriage and set off for Oldhouse.

"I hope there is hunting here," Luc said. "I will absolutely die if there isn't even any hunting."

"I'm sure there's game enough," Hector said. He had not been this far south, but he'd had plenty of opportunity to survey the countryside as the train cut its path through the land, his eyes falling upon brooks and dense patches of trees.

"But would they have proper horses?" Luc wondered, shaking his blond head. He was as handsome as he was spoiled, a prime example of the Beautiful Ones. "There's nothing worse than a hunt with an old nag to ride. Why did you drag me here, again?"

"I did not drag you here," Étienne replied. He had placed his hat upon his face to try to sleep. "Father sent you with me because you were chasing after a dancer."

"As if you haven't chased dancers of your own."

"You were spending ridiculous amounts of money on her. *Borrowed* money, I may add."

"A bracelet here and there. Besides, haven't I been marvelous lately?

And I've been thinking about that hotel I told you of, a resort by the sea, if only I could gather the proper funds for—"

"You might as well ask for the moon."

"No, it makes perfect sense, Étienne, only you won't listen, but I—"

"Take it up with Father," Étienne said, crossing his arms.

Luc took out his cigarette case and shook his head. "I tell you, Hector, you had the right idea being an only child. Existing under the shadow of not one but *four* older brothers is exhausting. Especially when they won't stand up for you in front of Father."

Étienne let out a loud "hmfff" in a reply but did not bother to vocalize his thoughts any further. Hector for his part merely shrugged.

A little while later they arrived at Oldhouse and barely had enough time to rush to their rooms and change for supper. When they came down, they were ushered into a dining room that, despite its long table, hardly offered enough space for them.

Hector found himself a bit astonished by the number of people around him. He had grown used to solitude and silence, and this was a loud bunch. People were introduced to him, but he soon lost count of their names.

He was seated to the right of Camille, Nina's mother, and across from Nina. A bit farther to Nina's left sat Valérie, and they locked eyes a couple of times before she turned her head away. Étienne and Luc were seated apart, and Hector could not possibly speak to them.

For dinner there was a vegetable soup with plenty of cabbage, followed by rabbit and lamb in a condimented sauce, accompanied with carrots and bread. There were also cheeseboards and biscuits. It was simpler fare than what could be had in the city, but then, he had expected this and did not mind.

After dinner he attempted to catch hold of Valérie while everyone was exiting the dining hall. He had not had a chance to talk to her in private since their last disastrous encounter. He wanted to attempt a more civilized interaction.

It was not to be had. Nina intercepted him before he could stop Valérie, as he was preparing to climb the wide stone staircase that led to the second floor.

"Did you have a pleasant journey?" she asked.

"Yes."

"And your room? Do you like it? We can have you moved if it's not to your taste."

"No, it is fine," he said, his eyes following Valérie, who was walking up the staircase, pins with pearls decorating her hair, her dress the most blinding white.

"If there is any dish you'd rather have, you can let us know. We have a fine cook."

"Thank you," he said.

He could not see Valérie anymore. He'd lost his opportunity. Now he looked down at Nina, almost surprised to find her standing in front of him; he had been distracted by Valérie's presence and she'd quietly moved closer to him.

The girl looked different. Her thick black mane fell loosely down her shoulders, as it had near the staircase in Loisail. She was not the kind of woman men would stare at in admiration, attempting to secure a dance with her. She lacked style and grace. But there was a mysterious assertiveness in her eyes at times, which he enjoyed, and her hair was nice— it made him curious, he wished to touch it.

"I can show you and your friends the house tomorrow," Nina offered.

"We'll take you up on that offer," he replied.

There was no more to add, but she hovered in front of him and he did not dash up the stairs, stretching the seconds, until, blushing, she spoke an excuse and retreated from sight.

When Hector arrived in his room, he discovered it had been commandeered by the Lémy brothers, who were sitting at a table by the window, playing cards. Luc drank from a silver flask; Étienne was tilting his chair back and forth.

"Do you not have rooms of your own?" he asked.

"Yes. But they are tiny. You have the largest room of the three of us. I'm practically sleeping in a closet," Luc complained.

"I'm sure that's a lie."

"You should join our game," Étienne said.

"I'd lose my shirt."

"You can afford another one," Luc said. "Say, do you have any idea what Nina's dowry amounts to?"

"No idea and no interest," Hector said, crossing his arms and leaning against a bedpost, watching the men play.

"A romantic!" Luc said, chuckling.

"Don't bother him," Étienne said.

Hector glanced down. A romantic, no. A fool. What was he doing in this place, even? But she'd asked him to come, and he had not wanted to say no even if a dozen excuses might have been easily manufactured.

The next morning, Étienne, Luc, Nina, and Hector walked around Oldhouse, with the girl pointing out the library in the annex, the sitting room, the dining room, which they had already seen, and other areas of interest. They had stables and horses, but no courts for the modern sports preferred in the city. There was a music room with a piano and a harp, but no proper game room where the gentlemen might smoke and play billiards. No conservatory, instead an herb and vegetable garden. And so it went. Oldhouse was plainly an old-fashioned, simple country manor. Luc seemed deflated by this discovery, Étienne was slightly pleased at his brother's discomfort, and Hector accepted it without judgment.

After their tour, Nina offered to show them the river she said ran near the house, but Étienne and Luc wanted to go riding. Hector and Nina were left to themselves.

The river was close, as Nina had promised. It was wide but its waters were gentle. When they reached it, she picked up a flat stone and turned to him.

"Watch," she said.

The stone hovered above her hand and she tossed it away, making it skip across the water without laying a hand on it.

"Bravo," he said. "Nicely done. I'm impressed."

"You are not humoring me?"

"I would never."

She smiled at this and made another stone skip across the water. Hector imitated her and sent several stones skipping across the water behind her own.

"When did you know you were a talent?" she asked.

"Ever since I can recall."

"But who taught you? Someone must have taught you, as you have been teaching me."

"My parents were both performers of a sort—she played the violin and he could sing. We were part of a troupe. There was an old woman who performed with us. Grandmother Sandrine, they called her. She was a talent. She'd juggle objects in the air without touching them. I learned from watching her, and then the rest was me testing my limits. Once in a while I might catch sight of other performers and try to determine what they'd done. I made my professional debut at eight."

"Did you get to travel much?"

"Somewhat. All through the spring and the summer, but in the fall and the winter we'd head back to Treman to rest. There's no business at that time of the year in the small towns, and the roads are hard."

"What about Iblevad? Did you travel often?"

She flung two stones this time and they both skipped gracefully across the water.

"Yes, and far in the beginning. I went with small acts to obscure towns because those were the places where you'd be booked. But then, if you were good and you were lucky, you could claim better spots and remain in a significant city."

"It seems strange. To spend your life wandering from place to place."

"It was a living."

"And now? Have you fallen under the spell of Loisail and wish to remain there forever and ever?"

The mention of Loisail brought to him, unbidden, the memory of Valérie's face. He associated her with the city, her white dresses and pale face seemed to reflect the beautiful, clean lines of the metropolis.

"I'm not sure," he said.

"That is no answer," she reproached him.

"I am sorry if my words do not please you," he said, his voice harder than he had intended.

Nina quirked an eyebrow at him, perhaps trying to determine what was souring his mood. He stuffed his hands in the pockets of his trousers and stared at the water.

She, in turn, began humming to herself and walked a few steps from him, picking a twig, tossing it at the water first with her hands, then grabbing another and flinging it away without touching it. Nina was lighter on her feet now. More practiced, as if she was better suited to navigating slippery stones and muddy banks than dancing on glossy parquet floors.

Unlike Valérie, who had been made for elegant dances and the lights of the city, the whisper of a fan against her cheek, her smile sparkling under a glass chandelier. The most beautiful woman he'd ever met.

He tried to imagine what he might be like if he'd never laid eyes upon her, if they'd never spoken. Whether he might be happy or equally miserable. Perhaps he was predisposed to follies, the victim of a nervous ailment.

Hector looked across the water, at the trees on the other side of the riverbank, and he breathed in deeply.

Nina turned toward him, her smile full of mischief. Her eyes looked more green than brown under the shade of the trees. "I can make a stone skip farther than you," she proclaimed.

Hector looked at her and shrugged. The game had lost its appeal for him.

"Try me. If I win, I am mistress of this river and it shall bear my name. If you win, we can call it the Auvray."

"It is silly. The river already has a proper name, and no doubt you know it."

"What if it *is* silly," she said, standing on a rock, close to the water. "Are you afraid I'm better than you at this?"

"Surely you are not," he said.

"Toss a stone."

Hector decided to humor her, feeling that she would not cease if he did not concede. He sent a stone across the water and it skipped four, five times.

"I am better," she said as the stone disappeared into the river.

When she proceeded to demonstrate that this was the case with ease and panache—her stone skipped eight times—he chuckled and placed an arm around her shoulders in a gesture of gentle camaraderie.

"You are mistress of the river, Nina Beaulieu."

"You can borrow it once in a while if you like," she said. Nina glanced up at him, resting a palm against his chest, her fingers on the buttons of his coat.

He was scrupulously well behaved when it came to the girl, not even daring to kiss her cheek. He did not fancy himself a cad. He was cautious. There could be no harm this way, he reasoned. He was but a friend, he told himself. He had yet to make binding promises. He could have peace of mind this way.

Nina was a pleasant creature, and if her face was not as pretty as Valérie's, then her disposition was more amenable. Logic dictated he should cease any pursuit of Valérie and attempt a more solid and achievable relationship with Nina. In theory, he was willing to follow such logic.

In practice, he was paralyzed, and had been in this state for some time. His visit to Oldhouse only served to make this point more obvious.

Hector had spent so many years being the man who loved Valérie that he could not conceive of becoming anything else. She was a goddess at whose feet he worshipped, and to cease in his adoration of her would imply he had spent a decade following a false idol.

All his grand romantic passions and florid sentiments, each sigh and each ache, would amount to nothing. *He* might amount to nothing.

Hector gently stepped back, putting a certain distance between them. Nina gazed at him with questioning eyes. Innocent she might be, but not so innocent as to not realize something was amiss. Books and poems must have suffused her with notions of romance, of suitors and kisses, which now did not come.

But her suspicions were vague. Fervent passion had evaded her. Nina could only guess a void existed. Hector could keep her dancing to this tune for months. And yet.

Love, he'd told Étienne, was not a concern for him anymore. He could not assume it was the same for her. She'd want to be loved, and then what would he give her, except wan smiles, a tepid kiss upon the brow, a life of monotones?

He turned around to look at Oldhouse and slid his hands back in his pockets. "Shall we head back?" he asked, his tone light though his tongue felt leaden. "Étienne and Luc might have returned by now."

"Very well," she said, and her voice was also mock light.

He watched her walk ahead of him and shook his head.

The sublime pain of Valérie kept dragging him away, down, like the river dragged stones, twigs, and leaves in its path, brooking no compromise.

Chapter 15

THEY WENT BACK NOT TO the river but to a sluggish stream that ran farther away, specimen bottles in hand. Nina picked up pieces of bark, looking to see what insects lay beneath. She brushed her hands against the tall grasses and listened to the wind rustling in the trees. Red and blue dragonflies danced above the riverbanks. The caddisflies had not yet hatched, and rested upon the surface of the water in their cocoons of silk.

Hector brought her luck, nevertheless, and Nina found a beautiful water diving beetle that was the color of molten gold and looked like a lady's brooch that she might wear to the opera. In the process of catching it, Nina thoroughly soaked her shoes and skirt.

They sat atop a stone slab, the sun shining bright, and in a short amount of time her skirt was dry. It was nice outside, the silhouette of Oldhouse in the distance against the blue sky like out of a picture book.

When they reached the house, she guided him straight to the library. The bookshelves spanned from floor to ceiling, sagging under the weight of knowledge, decades of the family's books also piling on the floor and chairs. This was one of the finer rooms in the house, and Nina had spent many hours here, spinning the engraved terrestrial globe upon its cherry-wood base, reading at turns sentimental fiction and at others scientific texts. Anatomical drawings decorated the walls, and a long carpet, dimly faded and with an elaborate pattern of green and golden diamonds, ran at one end of the room.

The most eye-catching element in the library was a massive mahogany cabinet containing rows and rows of drawers, each one with a number painted on it. Next to it, there was a humbler cabinet that held pins, bottles, pillboxes, string, cork, brushes, ink, and all the other items one might need to mount beetles and butterflies, which she'd been doing since she was a child.

Nina set her specimen bottle upon a table and opened the mahogany cabinet for Hector to see. "This is what I was telling you," she said, holding up a tray. "All my specimens are kept here."

The tray contained diminutive yellow, red, and blue beetles in the brightest colors imaginable, glistening like fine-cut glass.

Hector looked at them curiously. "You must be able to fit many specimens in here."

"Hundreds," she said, taking out another tray and showing him the beetles there. They were all a brilliant blue and larger in size than the others she'd shown him. "The most exceptional specimens go in the upper drawers."

"Do you only collect insects?"

"Butterflies and beetles alone. There are an infinite variety of beetles, and you can find them nearly all year round. Do you know that perhaps one fifth of all living creatures are beetles?"

"I did not know that."

"They live everywhere. Near the water and in the bark of trees, in the sand or in the jungle. Besides, they are most beautiful. It is like owning a chest of six-legged jewels."

"In that event, I suppose instead of purchasing a necklace for you for your birthday, I ought to buy you a beetle."

"Perhaps you should," she said. "Though my birthday is not until the winter and still far off."

Hector walked around the room and leaned down to look at a few volumes and journals she had left scattered upon a circular center table.

"*The Gazette for Physical Research*," he said, holding up one of the journal copies.

"Where I met you," Nina replied, setting her tray down.

She stood next to him, watching him as his fingers touched the cover of a book. He opened another one at a random page.

"Are you the chief naturalist in your family, or does your sister share this passion?"

Nina shook her head. "Madelena and my mother's passion is words. If ever you need to know the meaning of an obscure word, Madelena will provide you with it. My aunts Lise and Linette were avid bird watchers and went to the islands of Souxe many times to see tropical ones, though they are far too old now to be chasing after them. They have rare illustrated monographs in their home. My cousin Gaetan enjoyed looking at moths, of course. And there was my father, though he was more interested in physiology, which seems reasonable considering his condition."

Hector gave her a questioning glance.

"He was born with a weak heart," she explained. "They said he wouldn't live into adulthood, which is why he was not sent to be schooled in Loisail as my uncle was. He stayed in Oldhouse all his life with his sisters."

"Hence the engravings."

"Yes, see here," she said, moving toward one engraving and pointing at it. "That is a human heart with all its veins and arteries. It was drawn by Georges Pizon—he is one of the best anatomical artists of our time. He was my father's friend and correspondent."

The drawing was in color, the ventricles rendered in shades of gray, but the veins and arteries highlighted with blue and crimson. The organ was shown in an anterior and posterior view.

"I saw a drawing once, it purported to show the regions of a woman's heart," Hector mused. "It mapped the lands of coquetry and sentiment."

"A poet's fancy."

"And you do not fancy poets?"

"I didn't say that, but one must admit a real heart as seen by the anatomist bears no resemblance to the heart the poets speak about, dainty in its shape."

He was amused by her words, quirking an eyebrow at her and placing his hands behind his back as he inspected the engraving.

After a while, he turned his head to look at her. "When did your father pass away?" he asked her.

"Four years ago this fall."

"I'm sorry."

"You shouldn't be. As I said, they expected him to die in childhood, and he grew to marry and become a father. He confided in me once that he was so frail, everyone let him do as he pleased while his brother had to do as the family said. He said sometimes being the runt of the litter has its benefits, which is excellent news for me, since I am also a runt."

"How is that?"

"I'm the Witch of Oldhouse, Mr. Auvray. Do you think there is a region of the heart where you can find our talent? Or of the brain? I have a porcelain model of the brain," she said.

She looked around, trying to remember where she'd put it. Nina was scrupulous about her insect collection and she did try to maintain a similar amount of order when it came to books and other items, but they were more slippery to handle. She picked them up and dropped them and left them, she pulled them down and promised herself she'd take them up again only to find three weeks later they were still resting against the chaise longue. Letters, letter openers, knickknacks, suffered a similar fate, scattered by her talent or her own hands.

"I do not know what makes me capable of manipulating objects with my mind alone, though learned men have tried to provide the answer and will continue to do it," Hector said.

"The tests they did, what were the machines like?"

"Measuring devices, for the pulse and respiration. A needle traces a line upon paper and they look at it."

"It's supposed to be a congenital condition, isn't it? Like being color-blind," Nina mused. "Did they tease you about it when you were a child? Or was it different for you?"

"I started performing when I was but a child, and there was not co-pious teasing. I was another act set between the pretty dancers and the man who could make dogs jump through a hoop. When I was older and we'd go into towns, sometimes the locals would give us trouble, but it amounted to naught for the most part."

"What kind of trouble?" she asked, drifting to the other side of the room and climbing on the tall stepladder to see if the porcelain brain might be hiding behind the atlases she had been inspecting the previous day.

"The trouble bored lads like to get into. They'd taunt us and try to pick fights, but they'd generally stop when they saw I could hurl a man across the room without setting a hand on him. They were rowdy young men looking for another type of performance."

Nina willed an atlas aside, and another. It was not there. She began stepping down. "Did they ever hurt you?"

"Someone cracked a bottle across my back one evening. But I was drunk and silly that time. And then, there were a couple of beatings. . . . I lost a tooth. I have a false one now. You'd never be able to tell, but it hurt like hell when it happened."

He lifted an arm to steady her as she climbed down the last two steps. "I'm sorry," she said gravely.

"I didn't play the best of venues when I was starting out. And for a while after that." He smirked, trying to make light of it. "You'll think me a rogue now."

"I would never. You know a gentleman by his deeds, my sister says."

"Wise of her."

Nina touched the ground and smiled at him. Their walk had left him in high spirits, and she was grateful for this. He'd been upset a few days before, when they'd skipped stones by the river. One moment he had been warm and near; the next he was a block of ice, impenetrable. In the love stories she'd read—books borrowed from this library—the men were always solicitous, sweet, and pledged their love in long, effusive speeches that ended with a tender kiss.

Hector said nothing of the sort and he did not try to hold her in his arms or kiss her like the polite gentlemen of those narratives. Neither was he like the highwayman or the pirate who appeared in yet another type of book, this one peppered with more adventure, which required that he kidnap her.

In short, she was not his sweetheart, and this confused Nina. If he was to marry her, shouldn't he spare a kiss for her and declare his love? She was certain they'd wed and had written practically as much when she corresponded with her cousins and her sister. The whole household watched them both with expectant eyes. It could not be her imagination, as Valérie implied. That day, when she invited him to Oldhouse, she'd thought he'd kiss her.

The answer, then, must be he was shy. She'd have to have enough boldness for the both of them. Should he remain aloof, she would put pen to paper and express her affections. She did like him, although she had not ever thought how a lady would go on about revealing this to a man.

As she was considering this, she saw a white object on the floor, half-hidden behind a curtain.

"There!" she exclaimed, and rushed to pick up the model she'd been looking for. It was heavy and Nina could not imagine how it had ended up there—though, when she was nervous or excited, she did have the tendency to move things around the room without touching them.

Nina held the model up between her hands.

"My brain, Mr. Auvray," she joked.

"A fine one it is," he said, grabbing the model and turning it around in his hands.

His finger traced the porcelain ridges and folds, the names of each region, which had been engraved upon the white surface.

"It's chipped," he said, showing the chunk missing.

"A tad of frontal lobe, gone," she said. "Do you know that the physiologist Bertrand Ariste has been studying this area?"

"I did not know." Hector set the porcelain brain upon a shelf and patted it before turning toward her. "You're an exceptional specimen yourself," he said. "Do not forget that point, ever."

Nina decided it was the best compliment anyone had paid her. But he gave her a curious look that was, she thought, half sadness.

She wanted to extend her hand and touch his face, to ask him what made him sorrowful, and then, to kiss his mouth, to lavish caresses upon him. She did not dare, not yet, but she knew well that the quivering feeling inside her could not be contained any longer. If he didn't, she would!

Chapter 16

HECTOR WAS NOT ONE FOR laxness. He'd spent his whole life climbing up the social ladder, running from place to place, jumping from task to task, asking his assistant, Mr. Dufren, to fetch him one prop or another. In fact, upon learning Hector was going to spend a few days resting in the countryside, Dufren had not believed Hector at first, thinking it was a practical joke.

Hector liked having markers in his life, elements that could guide him. Now when he opened his shutters in the morning, he did not know what he was supposed to do. A relaxing country stay baffled him, though it did not irritate him as it irritated Luc Lémy, who yearned for the city for entirely different reasons.

Hector quickly found a rhythm to Oldhouse. There was an early breakfast in his room, and then he'd venture down either to accompany Nina on one of her insect-hunting expeditions or for a walk around the house. Once this purpose had been accomplished, Hector tended to camp in the library. In the afternoon, there was supper to be had, everyone piling into the dining room. Afterward, several of them usually retreated to the great hall for conversation. There, or in the library, Nina and Hector put their talent to use.

In Loisail, Nina did not display her talent in public and they did not practice tricks in Valérie's presence. But upon his arrival at Oldhouse, Nina's mother had asked if he would not perform for them. Hector obliged, presenting the sort of act he might have executed in cafés or taverns in his youth: spinning two plates, opening a book onto a page, making a coin dance above his open hand. When he was done and they'd all clapped, Hector turned to Nina and asked her if she wouldn't show her family the trick with the coin. At first she had not wanted to, shy, but then she'd changed her mind and made the coin hover above her hand, blushing and glancing down when she was done.

Her family was surprised. He gathered that Nina's talent had been more about knocking down books from bookcases by accident or shuffling cutlery in the kitchen drawers without realizing it than any formalized application of the ability, but that was no longer the case. Thus, in the evenings, they generally settled together to practice in view of all.

That afternoon was no different. Luc stood by the fireplace, Valérie rested on an overstuffed chair, while Hector and Nina occupied opposite sides of an old divan. They played with a pack of cards in the dim, cool room.

He shuffled the cards and then inclined his head, indicating it was her turn. Nina moved her left hand, making three cards slide from his deck and float toward her waiting fingers. He shuffled the cards again and again inclined his head.

"Dear me, how many times are you two going to do that?" Luc asked, hovering over Hector's shoulder.

Luc was bored. He had been bored for the past half hour, fidgeting and circling them, frowning and stepping back. He was like a child, quick to pick up a toy and quick to forget it, always seeking a new, shiny amusement.

"We are practicing," Hector said. "It's important to get it right."

"Whatever for? It is not as if Miss Beaulieu is a performer at the Royal, as you are."

"It's not the point."

"What is the point? It's all incredibly odd, this business with the cards. Weren't you building a house with them yesterday? What shall that prove?"

"Physics," Hector said.

"I'll say, it's peculiar to see a woman doing this," Luc declared.

"Perhaps Nina means to reinforce her reputation as the Witch of Old-house," Valérie said.

Valérie sat half-reclined, her lips curved into a sneer, her pale skin contrasting with the darkness of the room and granting her a provocative air. She was alluring, but when Hector glanced at Nina and saw the way her eyes went wide with quiet pain, he felt desire wilting from him.

"That is a cruel taunt to repeat," he said, his voice hard.

Valérie leaned back haughtily. "Are you to reproach *me*? These idiotic parlor tricks are fit for rogues in gambling dens, not a proper lady. Not that Antonina behaves like a lady. Half the time she is close to a savage."

"Pardon me, but Antonina is a *true* lady, unlike some others who put on airs and merely pretend to be gentlewomen," he affirmed, his eyes firmly set on the older woman, the barb undeniable and as sharp as a saber.

Valérie stood up at once in a fury of pink damask and marched out of the room with such haste, several people stopped speaking. Hector sat in silence, letting the three cards that had been floating in front of him fall down upon the divan.

"Thank you," Nina said.

Hector looked up at her and saw she was smiling. "You've slain a dragon for me," she added.

"I've been crude and will no doubt pay dearly for it."

"She deserved it," Nina said, her voice low. "You don't know how it was when I was small, how they'd taunt me for it. I didn't mean to make the flour fly through the kitchen, I didn't mean to make the stones rain or the porcelain shatter. It happened and they'd frown or they'd laugh or they'd say, 'There goes the Witch of Oldhouse.'"

"It was like that, too, for me at times. I almost burned a guesthouse in Zhude—I knocked over a lantern. I did not mean it. They threw me out in the middle of a snowstorm."

"You were angry?" she asked. "When I'm angry . . . it's hard to keep a grip on it. I fear it will overcome me at times."

"I was," he said. This bit of their talent they had not discussed, both too afraid to voice the limits of their control. "But, the talent, you use it, it doesn't use you."

"That boy. I shoved him off a horse."

"Yes, you mentioned it."

"He was almost trampled. But I did mean it, I did," she said, her voice faint.

"We all make mistakes."

She looked at him, her eyes catching the light in the gloom of the large room, a winsome green shade in that instant. "Why were you angry, when the fire happened?" she asked.

"I'd had my heart broken."

It shocked him because it was an honest and deep answer. He had hardly ever told people about his troubles; he guarded them. His secrets were not for Nina.

He turned his head. If they continued in this vein, if she looked at him longer, he might tell her about the times he wished to die in his bed, the moment when he'd contemplated the never-ending sea. Hector excused himself.

The next day they sat outside, on the grass in front of the house. Étienne lay on his back, hands behind his head. Valérie sat under a white parasol, shielding herself from the sun's rays, although it was not a sunny day. A few of Nina's cousins and assorted relatives were nearby, chatting with each other.

He had stayed out of Valérie's way, but could not help frequently looking in her direction, magnetized.

"We should play a game," Luc declared. "Have some fun."

"What game would you like to play, Mr. Lémy?" Nina asked.

"Tag!" a younger cousin yelled.

Others agreed eagerly and Luc thought it a splendid idea. Even Étienne was roused to his feet by his brother.

Nina stood up, brushing bits of grass from her skirts, and looked down at Hector. "Are you joining us?" she asked.

"Not this time," he said.

She smiled at him before running off with the others, their shrieks and giggles soon sounding distant. Only Valérie and Hector were left behind.

He turned toward her. Valérie wore an embroidered, white silk dress with a smocked waistline and her ever-present pearls, her blond hair carefully coifed and pinned in place. She had a book with her, but was not reading it. Several times he had seen her grab it, open it to a page, then close it and place it at her side again as if she'd thought better of it.

Valérie's eyes were fixed on the sky, and when she spoke, her voice sounded relaxed, even languid. "You should have gone with her," Valérie said.

"Valérie, I—"

· "Good day," she declared with a chilling finality.

Without looking at him, her eyes still on the sky, Valérie stood up, then walked back into the house.

Hector watched her disappear inside Oldhouse and instead of following her, as he badly wanted to, he took a side path and walked away from the house, his head down.

Valérie had never been gentle or simple. But her passion, tucked under her perfect exterior, had echoed the passion within him. They were both creatures of tempestuous seas and stormy nights. But how it hurt sometimes!

He walked for a while, attempting to fill his head with the songs of birds instead of memories of this woman, and failing. Hector tried to satisfy himself thinking that Gaetan had not inflamed her heart. No, he could not picture the pleasant Mr. Beaulieu inspiring anything but the most insipid feelings. Neither the rolling anger nor the yearning of their days past, nor the tumultuous reconciliations when—after a day of scowls—Valérie suddenly turned toward Hector and declared breathlessly that, alas, she loved him. They always came apart suddenly and suddenly rejoined, as if nothing had ever been amiss, caught once again in their joy.

But now, now this meeting did not take place, the gap between them only growing by the day, and he stood at the edge of a chasm. It could not end like this.

The clouds had multiplied and he sensed the impending arrival of rain. Hector retraced his steps and returned to Oldhouse, walking past the strange, ancient tower that loomed behind the main building, as raindrops began to splash more forcefully upon the land. He felt old and tattered and wanted simply to lie down and lie still.

"Hector, here," a voice said.

He raised his head and saw Nina standing at the entrance of the tower, wrapped in its shadow.

"What are you doing?" he asked. "I thought no one goes in there."

She'd said so herself the day she took them on a tour of the grounds, though he ought to have known the rules did not apply to her.

"We are playing hide-and-seek. I'm hiding," she replied.

"I think you'll win. I did not see you standing there at all."

"Good," she replied. Even if he could not look at her properly—she stood in shadows—he could tell she was smiling. "You probably haven't seen the room in the tower. Come up. It's a gorgeous view."

It was raining harder, the summer drizzle threatening to become true rain.

"I'll break my neck. This does not look solid."

"It has stood for a few centuries, it can stand one more day for us. You'll get soaked if you stay there," Nina said, and disappeared inside.

He looked up at the tower, which was square in shape and rose five stories above the ground. One could almost hear the stones groaning with exhaustion. Atop its entrance was carved the image of a lamb and a word that had been smudged with time, perhaps her family's name? This must be a tower house, an independent structure and not a part of a manor in times past, though the ones he'd seen before were usually by the sea.

He wished to remain outside, with his melancholy.

Instead, Hector followed Nina up a spiral staircase.

"What is up there?" he asked, curious despite himself.

"You'll see."

"I can't see, that is the problem."

"Don't be afraid now, I'll catch you if you fall," she joked.

He was right to be cautious about entering the tower. The steps were narrow, it was dark, and there was no proper banister, but soon they reached the top floor.

The tower had been uninhabited for a great deal of time and the chamber they walked into did not have a stitch of cloth or furniture left. But there was a tall window—its shutters long crumbled into dust—on the east wall. The builders of the tower had carved stone seats to contemplate the scenery with ease. This was the prize.

"See," Nina said, rushing to the window and looking out.

The land spread beneath them, green and alive. Hector could see the river they had visited, its waters gleaming, and farther away, tall mountains. The ground was a chaos, sloping up here then down there; it was not neatly flat as in the north, and the air smelled of wet earth. Flocks of sheep grazed not far from the tower. Water and wood, this was her world, while he was forged in the city, on the road. He breathed in slowly, feeling better.

"Those are all ours. That's our flock," she told him, pointing down.

"There's a sheep carved above the entrance of the tower. Is that a heraldic symbol of some sort?"

"We've never been nobility, no," she said. "It's supposed to be lucky. I know a lot of rhymes about lambs—we learn them by the dozen when we are children."

"Appropriate, I suppose."

He had learned the bawdy songs of taverns; there was precious little time for rhymes. At the age she was being first fitted with corsets, he was making a living going from town to town, his voice thin as he announced himself and took off his cap, promising to show the audience miracles for a few coins.

"Do you like it here?" she asked.

"I do. It's peaceful."

"Have you ever been to Bosegnan?"

"No."

"It's by the sea. It's warmer there and the sun bakes the sands until they are white, whiter than any lady's linen. The fishermen have tiny boats, all painted red and lacquered as is tradition, and everything tastes like salt. You'll eat fish every day and drink sweet wine every evening with the Lémys."

She had a way of talking that he enjoyed because there was often merriment in her words.

"Will you write once you leave with your friends next week? I'll miss you if you don't," she told him.

Nina moved from the window, her right hand brushing the stone walls of the tower and looked at Hector.

"You won't miss me, not for a moment," he said, smiling.

"You could stop by on your way back."

She rested her back against the wall. It was cold, as if summer had been erased, the wind blowing and carrying droplets of rain into the tower.

"I don't think I can," he said.

She sighed.

Hector had not thought her beautiful in the city, under the light of large chandeliers with her hair up and gloves on her hands. But her loose black hair, thick and long, contrasted well with the rough stones behind her, and there was a charm about her hazel eyes, which never bore the same color in this land. She was looking at him now with eyes that were more golden than green, stung by his refusal, and he felt moved to place a cool, chaste kiss upon her forehead.

The girl seemed amazed and he himself was embarrassed by the gesture, but before he could apologize for it, he felt her hands slipping up and pulling him down for a kiss on the mouth. There was a comical element to it. A lady coaxing a man into a kiss, and she did not know how to do it properly, anyway.

Nina pressed her mouth to his, though, and he found his hands knotting in her hair, brushing down her side. And all of a sudden it wasn't funny and he was tipping his head forward, kissing her again, like a lover, not the delicate kiss she'd given him.

She grabbed the lapels of his waistcoat, drawing him near, until there was no space between them. Her hands were distressingly soft when they touched his face, sliding down between his chin and the collar of his shirt.

He stroked her hair and looked into her eyes. For once, there was no teasing in them; she was not playing. He'd thought the whole world was one unending game for Nina, chasing dragonflies and speaking her facts and attempting card tricks, but abruptly she'd grown serious and full of longing.

She was beautiful, her eyes brimming with intent. He pressed his face against her neck, his hands racing down her body, and he felt himself caught on the edge of something, as he had not been in a painfully long time.

The boom of thunder startled them both, making them jump, and the flash of lightning brought him back to his senses.

He was both mad and stupid.

Nina managed a tremulous smile and this sent him three steps back from her, though he ought to have put an ocean between them, the way he felt right that second.

She'd been, until that moment, an abstract concept, a bunch of jumbled lines that did not amount to a clean figure. She had been rendered flesh and blood, alive and supple.

Hector did not live the life of a monk. He understood desire. But desire was not passion and passion was not love. He might give himself to desire while keeping the vault of his passion and his love for Valérie intact. She was like a saint he venerated at her altar. There'd never been any space for another. But now he felt as though a thief had stolen into the vault, desecrating all the noble romantic dreams he'd built.

He'd allowed himself to feel passion for someone else.

This was a betrayal.

"That was not proper of me," he told Nina. He did not recognize his own voice, raspy with dread.

"I did not mind," she said.

"We should go."

He went quickly down the stairs and did not bother to slow when she called his name. Outside, Nina managed to catch up with him, pulling at his arm.

It was raining hard and he welcomed the cold water sliding under the collar of his shirt because the rain nested in her hair like minuscule jewels, it crowned her in summer glory, and he dearly wanted that desperately lovely girl. Thank heavens then for the rain, which cooled his spirit.

"Hector, we must speak," she told him.

He knew what she wanted to say, it was written clear on her face: she loved him. How stupid he had been, telling himself he was no cad yet being a cad all the same. He'd crossed the border he promised himself he would not cross with her, the shield of his polite distance disintegrating.

She loved him and it stung. Before, he could have neatly snapped his ties with her, stepped away, and let another fellow court her. She would have forgotten him in a fortnight. She was young.

Yet.

She loved him and he knew he'd done this, and he ought not to. He should have known better how easily the sentiments of a young woman could be swayed. He should have known she was not the experienced coquette who flutters her eyelashes at one fellow and another, nor the calculating rich merchant's daughter who measures the weight of a man in gold. He should have known that she loved him *already*.

He'd been selfish and ignored this truth. This more than anything dampened any ardor.

Nina tried to touch his face and he was forced to turn his head.

"I shall not use you in this way," he said.

"What?"

She was confused, but he could not explain. Not then and not there. Perhaps later, once he'd managed to unravel his thoughts, he'd calmly sit down and speak his mind. Or not. Hector could not tell her about Valérie, for one. He might be able to make her understand that he was entirely unworthy of her and that she would be better off setting her sights on a good man, someone who was not a fool longing after a woman he could not have.

He should have left long ago, should have abandoned her at the foot of the stairs that time back in the city.

"Forgive me," he muttered.

She looked terribly forlorn, her long hair now a wet mess and her dress soaked through. He felt the weight of guilt as he hurried into Old-house, but there was nothing more he could say.

Chapter 17

VALÉRIE LAY IN BED, STARING at the ceiling and trying to find a measure of sleep, which, as usual, eluded her. Her thoughts meandered and tangled together, like strange plants might tangle in the depths of the ocean.

She had not imagined the anxiety the constant presence of Hector would bring her, nor the wretched anger Antonina might evoke. Valérie saw them each morning, talking during breakfast or laughing with each other, as if caught inside a glass bauble, in a private space of their own making, and she hated them.

Antonina was young and carefree, and Hector was solicitous, kind to her.

It disgusted Valérie. And now they'd piled another injury on her.

How dare he speak to Valérie like that! And over whom? Over Antonina! Precious, stupid "Nina," gilded girl who could have anything she wanted and apparently that included anyone.

She closed her eyes. She opened them. She tossed a book she had been attempting to read at the window shutters.

Valérie rose from bed and decided she could not stay in that room one minute longer. She wrapped a shawl around her shoulders and walked toward the stairs, hoping she might find solace if her body were not at rest.

She had not gone far when she saw a figure move ahead of her and turn a corner. For one second she thought it a ghost, an apparition in white, but then she shook her head and recognized her. Antonina, barefoot in her nightgown. Was the girl sleepwalking?

Valérie followed her quietly and realized Antonina was headed toward the section of the house where the men slept. What was this wretched child doing?

She kept her distance and peeked around a corner, watching as Antonina stood before Hector's door and bent down, dropping something. The girl rushed away, a scared, wild animal.

Valérie waited for a few minutes before tracing Antonina's steps. She stood in front of Hector's door and bent down to retrieve whatever object Nina had left behind. It was a letter. In her haste, Antonina had not slid it completely under the door, and Valérie pocketed it.

Back in her room, Valérie lit two candles and sat at the desk. In the city, there was the wonder of gaslights and even electrified light fixtures, but in Oldhouse, wax and oil had to suffice.

Antonina's writing was more a scrawl than true words, but Valérie was able to read the letter all the same.

Dear Hector,
I find it hard to put my thoughts into sentences, but I must do it or I think I will go mad.

Hector, I love you. I count the hours when I cannot see you and treasure every word you speak to me.

I thought myself happy to simply bask in your presence, but when we embraced I knew the true extent of joy. I want nothing more than to be in your arms again and to kiss you. If what we did was improper, then I confess myself a wretched and foul creature, because I want nothing more than to touch you again.

Should you want me only for one hour or one day, I would gladly take it. I would gladly take whatever you offer. I am not ashamed to admit this.

And should you love me as I love you, then I would be the

happiest woman in the world. But for now, I dwell in uncertainty and hope your heart holds at least a fraction of the affection mine holds for you.

In the end, all I can say is: I am yours,

—*Nina*

When she was done reading, Valérie folded the letter back in place, her fingers tracing its creases carefully. If she did not scream right that second, it was only because she closed her hands into fists, her nails biting half moons into her palms.

Afterward, she lay in bed and pulled the covers up onto her chin. It was ridiculous pap, the letter, but it filled her with dread.

In the morning Valérie rose late, dressed with the utmost care, and quietly inquired as to the whereabouts of Mr. Auvray. A servant told her he'd seen him heading toward the library.

The servant was correct and she found Hector standing by a bookcase, perusing its contents. He was alone, which suited Valérie's purpose; she went directly toward him. Valérie had decided there was no point in being subtle, a solid approach was necessary.

"I will ask you this but once and ask that you answer truthfully. Have you had the audacity to seduce Antonina under this very roof?"

His shoulders had been relaxed, but he snapped up to attention, grave, glowering.

"What?" he said, sounding more than a little affronted. "I have not. What has she told you?"

Valérie did not reply. It was he who must speak, and she gave him ample time to furnish an answer, knowing he'd elaborate quickly enough.

"We kissed, nothing more has passed between us. You thought differently? Do I seem like the man who'd behave immodestly?"

He spoke the truth, she could tell, and he'd always had honor and noble intentions aplenty. Nevertheless, the answer did nothing to soothe her. There was a taste of bile in her mouth that she knew she could not wash away.

"It does not matter. If she has not ruined herself, she will soon enough. She has no shame," she exclaimed.

"In heaven's name, what are you talking about?" he asked.

"Be merry, Hector. You have won. I concede to you. I thought to grant you my indifference, but I cannot. You are hurting me. A nail in my heart each day you pursue that girl, and now I see this will not end until you have ruined us all. I beg you now, leave. You've wounded me, you've won. Take that as your badge."

Valérie had a mind to speak calmly, but tears stung her eyes, forcing her to turn her head and press her hands against her face. He tried to pry her hands from her face, but she would not allow it and turned from him in a fury, resting her back against a bookcase. She would not weep for him.

"Valérie, it was not my aim to hurt you," he said gently.

"It was. All along. Do not lie. I knew you'd return one day. I knew you'd return and punish me."

"I only wanted to see you, once."

"Oh, but you came back. Twice and thrice and all those other times for *her*."

She drew her hands from her face and looked at him. His eyes were not the same as they'd been in his youth, darker perhaps, drawn with pain. And his mouth, it was stiff and recriminating.

"There's comfort in being cherished by someone, even if it is not the person you want," he said. "If you loved me but for a moment, I would—"

"Do not dare to ask me to love you. I never stopped doing it," she said, and wished to roar the words but they came out in a whisper.

He took a shaky breath and stared at her. If only he had changed more. If only. But she could still see the boy he'd been in his face, hardships and anger unable to drown him completely. And it was this detail that drew her closer to him.

"Valérie, I told you once I'd take you away, and I can keep that promise. We can leave right this instant, you and I," he said with smothering sincerity; it made her shiver and she had to sit down on a sturdy chair.

He approached her slowly, as if he was afraid she'd bolt, kneeling by her side, holding her hands between his own.

"Why should we despair? The world is vaster than Loisail. We can board a ship and sail away. I shall buy you a house of your choice, wherever you want. We'll be lost in the crowds, we'll make a new life. We can be together as we planned all along."

"In a foreign land," she said. "Under an assumed name because I could not call myself by my family's name without dying of shame."

"You can have my name."

She could not make her hands be still, the fingers trembling, and she had to shove his hands away because his touch only made them tremble more.

What a pretty fantasy he spun, as only Hector might spin, but she knew at once it could not be. She could not vanquish the chains of reality, could she?

"I will always be a Véries," she said, but her words were almost tentative.

He rose then, cursing her under his breath. His anger gave her the fuel she needed to spark her own rage, and she was grateful. Engulfed with blazing fury, she felt she stood on firmer ground. The words, the reasons, everything came to her easily now.

"You think it is that simple? To bring dishonor to my family? You think I can throw away everything I have ever worked for? You have no understanding of the world. You are as you always were, with your head in the clouds. You do tricks for adoring crowds onstage and forget that it is not all artifice and sleight of hand when you step off. The pauper does not get the princess, Hector Auvray."

He was comely in his intensity and even comelier as her words struck him, making him lose his grip.

"Artifice, when you are the liar! God, of course you are a liar," he said.

He paced in front of her, all bitterness and spite. She rested her hands against the arms of the chair, holding tight to it. She wanted to reduce the room to ashes and had to content herself with biting her lips.

"You did not intend to run away with me," he said, turning to her with narrowed eyes. "You said the words but did not mean them. It was a silly affair for you. You would not have gone with me, would you? Even if I had returned with all the gold in the world, you would not have gone with me.

"You liar," he said, leaning down suddenly against her arms, against the chair, and looking down at her.

There was untold cruelty in those words, they sliced against her like scissors tearing through paper, and Valérie could not help herself—she spoke.

"I would have gone with you. If you had returned without a single coin in your pockets, I would have gone with you all the same. That is why I married Gaetan. Because I was ready to throw everything away for you. My name and my honor and my family. No one—no one, you hear me—can have that power over me."

He stared at her, disbelieving. She stared back. She knew he wanted to deny it, to blot out the truth, but it could not be denied, and he believed. He finally understood. She saw him crumble before her, his eyes bright with tears, his pain so clear she thought she might touch it. It was real, solid. His voice, when he spoke, was a murmur.

"You are a vicious, mad creature," he said.

She wanted to cry and could not. She wanted to weep for that proud girl who had broken her own heart and tossed it to the dogs, and she wanted to weep for the older woman who had been left behind with a gaping hole in her soul. But if she could do it again, she knew she'd still retrace her steps. She was not Antonina Beaulieu, who offered herself like a sacrificial lamb, who gave everything of herself to the world for the world to devour. She was Valérie Véries. She hated herself sometimes for it, but she was Valérie Véries.

"And I am a fool," he muttered. Perhaps he might cry for the both of them, dear Hector.

"Yes, you are," she said.

He yanked her to her feet and placed a harsh, desperate kiss on her mouth. It had been like this, too, when they were young. This desire, the stubbornness of her theatrical, calculated refusal, the pleas, until she broke against him and kissed him back.

A game they played.

But when they were young they were free, and afterward they could make vows that they intended to keep. Now there were no promises to be made, nor any measure of soothing tenderness.

Valérie kissed him nevertheless. Knowing the hopelessness of it all made her want to hold on tighter to him. She also wanted to hurt him, and she knew well enough that her caresses would wound more than any blows.

His mouth burned her and she knew he wanted to brand her, his fingers were digging too deep in her flesh, and she relished the touch. She thought of biting his tongue, drawing blood.

There came the loud thump of a book falling upon the floor.

They both turned their heads.

Antonina stood at the door. One of her books had slipped from her hands, but she still held on to the other one tight. Her lips were trembling.

Finally, she let go of the book she had been clutching, and at the same time several volumes jumped from the shelves and fell against the carpet, as if echoing her motions. Then the girl turned around and ran out of the library.

Hector meant to follow Antonina, but Valérie held on to his arm, forcing him to turn and look at her.

"It's all over," Valérie said.

Hector did not reply, rushing out, looking faintly ridiculous in his distress. She chuckled at this. She rubbed her fingers against her mouth and she chuckled, and then she bit her hand because tears were streaming down her face.

Chapter 18

IN THE SUMMER NINA LIKED to rise early, sometimes even before the dawn. She'd go to the river and take off her shoes, walking on blades of grass fresh with dew. She'd watch the fireflies and listen to the birds as they began to chirp in the trees. These things brought her joy.

She had been anxious and brittle the day before, unable to understand what had caused Hector to part quickly from her side after they kissed in the tower. He did not come down for dinner, which only added to her woes.

Wrapped in perfect misery, she questioned the stars for any secret answers they might give her, but they could not soothe her. The books talked about men set aflame, pursuing women, but it was she who was burning and knew not what course to take. The only thing the heroines in her books did was weep until a man rescued them. Or kidnapped them, if he was a pirate.

That spark that burned in her, that ember lodged in her heart, pushed her forward, emboldening her.

Close to midnight she grabbed a piece of paper and began scribbling. Her hands trembled at first, but as each word fell in place, she grew calmer. By the time she left the letter at his door, she had erased all doubts, and in the morning, when she woke and traced the margins of the river, she did so with a smile on her face. She was alive that morning, alive with hope and love. Each breath she took, each beat of her heart, every sigh, was meant for Hector. She existed for him alone and knew nothing but him.

Surely he loved her but was afraid to say the proper words! Cousin Gaetan had expressed reservations about him when Hector first began to visit them, unsure if he was a gentleman of high enough stature to deserve the attention of the Beaulieus. Perhaps Hector felt the same, and now faltered.

Whatever the reason for his shyness, Nina knew she'd done right and soon everything would be well. They would be together; this was clear. It was as if she could read the imminent signs in the water and the rustling of the trees. She pressed a hand against her lips and smiled.

Nina took her time walking back to Oldhouse, and when she went past the stables, she heard the dogs barking. Luc Lémy was attempting to shoo them away, but they only barked more.

"Here, now. Here, boys," she said, and the dogs immediately ran toward her, wagging their tails.

She bent down to pet them.

"Thank you for that," Luc told her. "I don't know how you do it. Every time these devilish creatures see me, they try to bite a chunk out of my leg."

The dogs were huge; they were meant for herding sheep, but gentle with children. She chuckled. "Mr. Lémy, they wouldn't bite you. They must simply like you."

"Believe me, Miss Beaulieu, they despise me."

"Maybe you are a cat person."

"Heavens, that sounds even worse. Horses, Miss Beaulieu, there's a reliable animal. Put a bridle on it and enjoy a ride, that's my kind of pet. Better yet, place them in front of a carriage and be done with it. Or a motorcar. That is a fine invention!"

He shook his head. Mr. Lémy and his brother Étienne were both brilliant creatures with their blond hair and their amicable smiles. Luc in particular was the portrait of the city dandy, his clothes always impeccable, looking as if he'd just shaved and gotten a haircut no matter what time of the day it was. He smoked tiny black cigarettes, which he carried in a silver case, and had a way of flattering every woman, no matter her age. Even her old aunts, reticent creatures, thought him a charming fellow.

"You can't ride a motorcar here, Mr. Lémy. It would get stuck in the mud within five minutes flat."

"You are correct about that," he said, as if surveying the road that led to Oldhouse. "That is precisely why Loisail is the best city in the world. Who heard of a land without motorcars?"

"There are plenty of places without motorcars. Besides, you are going to Bosegnan."

"Yes," Luc said with a roll of his eyes. "Land of shellfish."

"You, sir, are the worst man I've ever met. If you keep criticizing the countryside, I shan't invite you back. Why, look at the sun. It shines wonderfully today. You wouldn't deny it's a marvelous day for a stroll. Who'd want to be stuck inside a motorcar?"

Luc scoffed and kicked a pebble away. "A marvelous day, no thanks. Two days ago I forgot to wear my hat when I went for a ride, and now look at my face. I look like an overcooked shrimp."

"Nonsense," she said.

"It is true. We are not all as lucky as you, who seem to glow every time a stray bit of sun touches your face. No, summer in Montipouret does not suit me."

She almost felt like informing him that he'd have to stomach one more summer in the countryside, or at least a couple of summer days, since she believed the Lémys would be invited to her wedding the following year. The Beaulieus married in Oldhouse. Even Valérie had yielded to this custom. The civil ceremony had taken place in Loisail at the insistence of the bride, but the religious marriage had been outside, behind the house, with long tables covered with the whitest linen set for the wedding lunch. Nina recalled the excitement of that day and that she had been allowed to have a whole glass of wine for herself.

Valérie's dress had been a thing of wonder. White silk and satin, a bridal veil of antique lace, a bouquet of white flowers in her hands, and a diamond fringe necklace that was expensive and extravagant. The people of Montipouret spoke of it months after the wedding had concluded. How Nina wanted this, the pomp, the toasts, her picture in the papers.

"Don't despair, Mr. Lémy. Come now, come here," Nina said, calling to the dogs as she went inside to ensure they would not follow him.

She walked into the kitchen, where the cook immediately chided her for having brought the infernal pups in with her, but Nina shrugged and threw them a piece of sausage while she stole a piece of bread. Her mother insisted a proper breakfast consisted of a boiled egg a day, followed by a couple of slices of cheese, but Nina seldom complied with these instructions.

Nina went up to her room and fell upon the bed, stretching her arms above her head. She dozed for a while, and when she woke she went around the room, looking at the reading material piled by her bed. Her horrid habit of leaving books here and there was obvious to any casual observer, and the maids often complained they could not dust properly because Nina hoarded too many volumes and she grumbled if they took them back to their shelves.

Nina grabbed two books and decided she should return this pair to the library as a gesture of goodwill.

Soon enough she reached her destination and opened the door.

She saw Hector and Valérie standing in the middle of the library, but at first she thought it couldn't be them. They were kissing, his arms entwined around her, and Valérie's lips rose to meet him, like a flower turning toward the sun, and he held on to her tight.

Nina thought she had a fever dream, such as when she was seven and had spent a whole night writhing in pain. Why, that couldn't be Valérie. Why, that couldn't be Hector.

A book slipped from her hands, and when it crashed against the floor she realized, wide-eyed, this was real. This was happening.

They both looked at her.

She'd read about hearts breaking in books, and it had seemed a curious business to her because it was physiologically impossible for a heart to crack like a piece of porcelain. But now Nina felt pain, actual physical pain assaulting her as if someone had thrust a dagger into her flesh, and it hurt so badly, she did not know if she could remember how to breathe. This, too, was a physical impossibility. Breathe she must, and yet she stood like a woman drowning, her breath burning her throat, caught in her mouth.

Unwittingly, she sent several atlases and volumes of poetry flying against the floor.

Finally she was able to breathe, gulping, like a swimmer breaking through the surface of the water. Nina turned around and hurried out of the library.

She moved with rapid, almost noiseless steps, a hand pressed against her stomach.

"Antonina," Hector said behind her.

She lifted her skirts to move faster, though she did not run. She could not manage the proper functioning of her limbs. She *wished* she could run. She wished she could run forever.

She saw the faces of maidens and knights painted in the colored windows of the hallway, blazing greens, reds, and yellows upon the floor.

"Antonina, please stop."

Flowers and an apple tree sparkled, the sun shining bright through the glass. There was a lamb, too, in a long panel of opalescent glass. It grazed on a perfect meadow.

"Antonina, will you stop and speak to me, please."

"Nina!" she shrieked, turning toward him and flinging her hand down, opening it, her fingers splayed so wide, they almost hurt.

Panels of glass shattered. The docile sheep was turned into fine bits of crystal, the knight tumbled upon the floor, the maiden was destroyed. The glass fell and she willed it to crash again and again, wanting to grind it into the finest sand. A shard bit into her flesh, sinking into her palm, and she stopped. She felt spent, a flame that had guttered out.

He'd avoided or repelled any damage and stood in the middle of the hallway unscathed while her hand throbbed.

"Nina, for God's sake, you are injured," he said, moving toward her.

She raised her hand, stopping him in his tracks, then shoved him back, hard, with a motion of her fingers. "Don't come near me. Don't speak to me. Never, ever, speak to me."

She ran back to her room—she'd remembered how to run, could instruct her legs to do this once again—avoiding the startled servants who muttered and wondered what that infernal racket had been. The door locked, she went into her bathroom, staring at her injured hand.

Nina willed the glass shard to move and slid it out of her skin; she made it float before her eyes, examining it. It was a thin piece of green glass, now tinted crimson with her blood.

She opened the faucet. The cold water comforted her. She washed her hands and wrapped a towel around the wound.

Nina went to the bed and sat in the center of it. She cried, and then she wiped her tears with the towel, and she cried again. She thought she'd never stop weeping, but eventually her sobs ceased. She lay there, an empty vessel.

The bleeding had subsided.

She closed her eyes.

Then came a knock and she raised her head. Outside it was dark and the stars had come out. She'd slept for many hours, a dreamless, black sleep that did not quench her despair.

"Open up," Valérie said.

Chapter 19

VALÉRIE SHONE WHEN SHE WAS placed in a difficult situation. In a way, she relished the challenge. Even now as she stood trembling inside, she knew she would find a way out.

Antonina had caused a ruckus, smashing windows and running through Oldhouse. No one knew what had happened, and they gathered in the salon to sit together and gossip. Hector was there, looking as livid as could be, and so were Camille and Madelena, along with several older cousins.

"I am not sure what has occurred," Camille said. "Mr. Auvray, you said you were with her?"

"Antonina is upset because she was mistaken about Mr. Auvray's interactions with her. She assumed a marriage proposal was forthcoming, but he cares for her only as a dear friend," Valérie said quickly, priding herself on her choice of words.

"Is that true, Mr. Auvray?" Camille asked.

Hector nodded. Immediately came a wave of whispering.

Madelena, sitting on a couch, looked up at Valérie. "I cannot believe my sister would behave this way, even if disappointed," Madelena said.

"A few years ago, did she not shove that boy off his horse? I recall he was injured," Valérie replied.

Everyone clearly remembered that incident. They looked around at each other, nodding.

"That was four years ago. She was barely more than a child, and Johaness Meinard was an ill-mannered, cruel boy," Madelena protested.

"There was also the episode with the stones," Valérie said. "How did that come about? I don't recall."

An uncomfortable silence rested upon the room. Antonina's follies were tolerated at Oldhouse, but it could not be denied she did not have a commendable grip on her talent.

"I should speak to her," Hector said.

"Or I," Madelena said.

Madelena made a motion as if to rise, but Valérie spoke at once, aware she could not allow the sisters to talk at this point. Who knew what poisonous words Antonina could spill? She must ensure this snake's venom was drained before allowing it to roam freely around the house.

"You would only upset her more. Let her rest and dry her tears. In the morning she may have seen the senselessness of her actions," Valérie said, and extending her arms, she clutched Madelena's hands. "Come, dear cousin, Antonina is young, as you said. Barely more than a child."

"Nina can be temperamental," Camille conceded. "Valérie is correct, it might be best to let her rest."

Madelena nodded. It was thus agreed that Nina would not be coaxed out of her room until the next day. Supper was a grim affair. Camille and Madelena fretted, while Hector's eyes were glum—you would have thought he had witnessed an execution. Valérie was not in high spirits either, but she did not give in to despair. Having shed a few violent tears and lost a measure of control when they had been in the library, she now felt equipped to solve this situation with the aplomb it required.

Once night fell, she knocked at Antonina's door.

"Open up," she said, and when no reply came, Valérie spoke again. "I have your letter."

Antonina opened the door and stared at her with unmitigated fury in her eyes. Valérie imagined duelists gazed at each other in this manner before they pulled the trigger. But Valérie was not afraid; she almost wanted to say, "Don't make it too easy for me."

"Did he truly give my letter to you?" Antonina asked.

"Let me in and maybe you'll learn the answer."

The girl agreed, as she'd expected. Antonina was likely itching for a fight and a chance to pile as many hard words as she could at Valérie's feet.

Valérie walked in and looked around, finding an empty chair and sitting straight. Antonina followed her every movement. She saw the girl was clutching a towel between her hands, as if it were a talisman. How young she looked, though Valérie did not feel envious of this youth. She was a half-formed being, a creature with no edges.

"I have come because I can imagine what thoughts run through your head at this time. You must be eager to put pen to paper and inform my husband of what you think you saw," Valérie said.

"I know exactly what I saw. You've taken Hector as your lover."

"Dear girl, I have not."

"What do you call it, then? A friendly hello?"

"A kiss. We only ever shared kisses, even when we were in the thrall of youth."

Kisses and a few embraces, and one heated evening, it might have come to more but Hector was gallant and somewhat naive, a romantic with high ideals. Valérie—cautious, too—recognized that life had not given women many cards to play and one valuable one she possessed was the stamp of her virtue.

"What do you mean?" Antonina mumbled.

Antonina moved closer to Valérie, as if she were trying to get a better look at her. The towel she held, Valérie noticed, had red splotches upon it. Dried blood. The girl twisted the towel violently between her hands. Had she harmed herself during her fit? It could not have been too badly.

"You can't guess? Must I say it?" Valérie asked.

She realized that, yes, she must say it. Antonina could not understand implications; she must be shown in stark black-and-white the meaning of words. Not that Valérie minded instructing the young woman this one time.

"I met Mr. Auvray when I was your age. We fell in love and I promised him my hand in marriage. But he went away, to Iblevad, and I was pressured to marry your cousin Gaetan. Once Hector returned to the city, he sought me. He begged me to run away with him, saying that he still loved me and always had."

Antonina was trembling. Valérie watched her step back and raise her hands, digging her fingers through her hair. "He was chasing after you, wasn't he?" she whispered. "He wasn't after me, he wanted you all along."

She did understand now. Valérie leaned forward, and hearing how Antonina's voice cracked, she almost felt sorry for her and could have attempted one kind word, except then the girl spoke again in a high voice, which cut Valérie to the bone.

"And you, you . . . strumpet—"

"Don't you dare to judge me when you are the silly whore who is willing to rut with the first fool who knocks at her door," Valérie said, rising to her feet, tall and proud. "I gave him nothing, and still he returned until today he felt compelled to kiss me. I offered no comfort to him and I did not yield. But you there, practically offering yourself on a platter for the man. The passionate words in that letter, they almost made me cry."

Antonina swallowed and tossed away the towel she had been holding. "You will return the letter to me," the girl said.

"I shall do nothing of the sort."

"It's not yours!"

"It is now. Listen to me carefully, beloved cousin. If you even think to breathe a word of what you saw today or what I told you to *anyone,* I will immediately produce that letter and hand it to Gaetan. I will say you are accusing me out of spite and madness, to cover your indiscretions. I will prove that you have tossed away your virtue to a man who then decided he would not marry you, making a mockery of you."

Antonina looked like a wild creature from the forests she loved, her black hair gnarled and her teeth bared. "That is a lie," Antonina said.

"But those are your words on paper, Cousin Antonina! Your words don't lie."

"That is not . . . You are twisting the intent of my letter!"

"It could be read that way, could it not?" Valérie asked. "Gaetan will be terribly disappointed. And think of the scandal if the letter ended up in the wrong hands! Would you like to see your name emblazoned in one of the dailies? It has the right ingredients: daughter of prominent family and a world-famous performer, embroiled in a salacious tale. One way or another, I think you'd end up in a convent far away, in a place where you can't see your mother or your sister. I don't think you'd make a satisfying nun."

She watched Antonina waver as the full implication of the words she'd penned became obvious. A girl could be destroyed with half as much.

"Gaetan wouldn't send me away. He wouldn't believe your lies."

"After your performance?" Valérie asked, spreading her arms. "They are sweeping away all the shards of glass you left on the floor. Half of Oldhouse thinks you've gone mad."

"Gaetan cares about me," Antonina said, stubbornly gnashing her teeth.

"Shall we find out how much he cares? If you ruin me, believe me, Antonina Beaulieu, I will do everything in my power to ruin you, and I guarantee I will succeed. All a woman has is her reputation, and you won't have one shred of it once I'm done with you."

There was boiling rage in the girl's eyes. Valérie was afraid for a moment she might attempt to throttle her—though if she did, Valérie would use this to her advantage. Nothing would please her more than to yell for help and have the servants pry the girl off her. She could affirm the child had gone mad.

A book—no, two—fell to the floor as if scattered by an invisible wind, but that was all. Perhaps exhaustion had set in and Antonina could summon no more power, or else she was trying to control herself.

"I won't tell," the girl said at last, and gave Valérie a severe, proud look. "Know that I do it for my cousin. He does not deserve the pain this would cause him."

Valérie could not read Nina's words as anything but the marks of a weakling; she appreciated only one type of strength.

"I'm glad we understand each other," Valérie replied, satisfied, and thought her a dolt.

Antonina sat at the edge of her bed. Her eyes were weary and she clutched her bedsheets ferociously, but Valérie could tell her will to fight had evaporated. This was the still after a storm, and the girl was her own wreckage. She could do no harm now.

Valérie went to the door, her hand resting upon the handle when she heard Antonina speak.

"You said he loved you and always had," Antonina said in a low voice. "And do you love him?"

"That doesn't matter."

"It matters to me."

Valérie sighed and turned her head. In ruins, still, the girl tried to clasp a shred of tender feeling to her heart. It was not to be had.

"Dear, dear Antonina. Don't be silly. The point is he's never loved *you*. And he never will. Dry your tears and be a good girl; when they ask you tomorrow what happened, tell them you mistook his intentions and he will not marry you. It won't be too far off from the mark," she concluded.

She closed the door and she heard the loud scattering of books upon the floor. The girl had lost control, in the end. Valérie shrugged. There was a pang of regret in her heart for Hector, and perhaps a dull sympathy for Antonina, but she pushed both feelings away, knowing she could not afford to pay them heed.

Chapter 20

"IS EITHER ONE OF YOU going to tell me what happened back there?" Luc asked.

They were in the dining car because Luc wanted to eat, but Luc immediately took offense with the menu when he saw it. He was the kind of man who demanded lobster and truffles for lunch, changing his mind at the last second, deciding it ought to be veal and asparagus soup. The reduced offerings available did not please him. There was nothing to be done about it. Had they taken the Thursday train, they would have been able to travel aboard the more luxurious *Southern Express*. But they had left Oldhouse two days before their scheduled departure.

Hector could not bear to remain there a second longer.

He had attempted to speak to Nina before he left, knocking at her door and trying to coax her out, but she had not responded. Not a word. Her mother and her sister both were terribly embarrassed and spoke apologies. Hector could do nothing more than nod his head. He had no idea what to say.

Hector promised himself he would write to Nina later, once a sensible amount of distance remained between them. He'd write from Bosegnan, he'd atone.

"Eat your cake," Étienne said laconically.

"Truly, Brother, can you treat me more like a child?" Luc replied as he lit a cigarette and frowned, looking at Hector. "They were saying Nina Beaulieu barricaded herself in her room and has gone mad, all because you did not propose to her."

"Stop it," Étienne said. "You've asked thrice already and he is not answering."

"I ask because it seems extreme. No wonder I don't dare to propose to a girl."

"You don't propose to girls, because there is not one who would be willing to endure you."

"Again with the jabs, Étienne!"

Hector watched the men squabble, as they often did, and raised a glass of wine to his lips. The train was moving but Hector felt as though it were going nowhere. He saw flashes of green, trees and rocks and mountains, pass by. They blurred together and he turned the glass he was drinking from between his fingers, examining its facets.

He knew, sitting there in the dining car while others ate and smoked and chatted, that Valérie was correct. It was all over. Not merely his courtship of Nina, but his eternal pursuit of Valérie herself. He had been able to love her, hopelessly, for years and years. She was married, she was far from him, and when he saw her again she was cold. Yet his love did not diminish, his adoration of this woman did not cease. He was chained to her, to this brilliant ideal of a perfect love.

Because he had always known that if he could have Valérie in his arms again, all would be well. It would be as though the decade that separated them had never happened and they would return to the happy days of their youth when everything was possible. It was as if he could unwind the clock with her aid. And once this happened, there would be nothing but joy.

But then she had spoken and revealed the true reason why she had cast him aside, and Hector realized with horror that this perfect love he'd built in his heart was ugly and grim. Had he known Valérie was difficult? Yes. Had they fought before? Yes. He had, nevertheless, failed to understand her cruelty.

Had she been kinder in their youth? Sweeter, perhaps? Had the years made her harder? It did not matter. His had been a futile endeavor. He could not have Valérie back, because the Valérie he loved had died, or perhaps had never been.

It was his fault alone. Other men were happy enough, living with their feet firmly planted on the ground. Hector had wanted more. He wanted the thrill of passion, the feelings people sang about in operas. Theatrics, but then hadn't he made a career for himself on a stage?

The glass Hector was holding in his hands caught the rays of the sun, sparkling. He set it down against the table and frowned, watching the countryside.

He tried to recall what Valérie had been like when they met. He had vivid images of her, of the exact details that made her. The dimples in her cheeks and the white ribbon in her hair. She had been elegant, proud, exact in manners and words, quarrelsome at times and harsh far too often, spiteful and beautiful, passionate in her affections. But in the end, she had given nothing true to him. Despite her lovely words and her kisses, she had remained veiled and sealed off.

He'd been a heedless boy who had turned into a man full of rancor and discontent, sensing that life had betrayed him, stolen from him what he ought to have possessed. He had thought the missing piece was Valérie—and he had been right, but not in the manner he expected.

He crossed his arms and pressed his forehead against the window.

And then he saw the river flowing not far off and he thought of Nina Beaulieu, who had not wronged him in any way and whom he'd hurt nonetheless.

At that moment, Luc Lémy rose and excused himself, loudly proclaiming he was heading back to their compartment since everyone was terribly glum.

Once they were alone, Étienne folded the newspaper he had picked up at the station. "Now that he is gone, shall we talk or do you intend to travel to Bosegnan in absolute silence?" Étienne asked.

"Silence would be good."

"Silence when you are drunk is fine, but sober it chips at your mind. You had a row. How bad was it, truly?"

"Terrible. She saw me and Valérie kiss."

"Dear God, Hector."

"Hush," Hector said, raising a hand, palm open. "I realize how idiotic I was."

Étienne refilled his glass of wine and he grabbed Hector's glass and refilled that one, too. Hector needed stronger liquor, a drink that would burn his throat and blot his thoughts. It had been years and years since he'd been roaring drunk, not since the days when he would visit taverns with Étienne, but he dearly wished he could attempt this sport again for a single day.

"Does anyone else know about this? Aside from Valérie, Nina, and you."

"No. I imagine she would have told her mother already if she cared to tell—she had two days to speak her mind to her before we left. Not that it matters."

"Perhaps you are right and she's decided to be magnanimous. But, Hector, what a fine mess this is. And Valérie, you and she—"

"Nothing," Hector said. "There is no 'Valérie and I.'"

He had been riddled with the disease of love, but Valérie had operated on him and finally, brutally, cut out the putrefied flesh. Hector lifted his glass and did not drink. His hands, used to performing tricks and juggling objects in the air, seemed to fail him and had grown weak.

"I am sorry about that even if I could have predicted something like this would happen. I know the extent of your feelings for her," Étienne said. "I'm also sorry about the girl. You appeared to get along well enough."

"Yes."

Étienne waited for him to elaborate but instead Hector drank his wine. Étienne, understanding there would be no more conversation, slowly unfolded his paper and began reading it again. But then Hector changed his mind and spoke.

"I've never met anyone like her."

"Like Valérie? Ah, I admit she's easy on the eyes, but hard like a diamond," Étienne said, shaking his head.

"Like Antonina," Hector replied.

He recalled when she'd told him about Bosegnan and how, even though he did not really care to visit the city, he grew interested in it because she liked it. He had wanted to look at it so he could tell her about it later, sharing his impressions. He did not understand many of the other things she fancied, like her precious insects, but he did enjoy when she spoke about them. He missed her already.

"I think she wanted nothing from me," Hector added, "nothing at all but to let her love me."

Étienne raised his eyebrows at that, but as usual he had a perfect reply. "It's a damn tragedy. Now, drink up. Let us not mention any women for the remainder of the trip," Étienne said. "Once we reach Bosegnan, we can have champagne and ask Luc to take us to meet his friends. He'll find a party somewhere, he always knows someone no matter where he goes. We shall be merry and we shall be young again."

Hector nodded but he knew it was a lie, that they'd never be young. He couldn't be like Luc, he'd never been like Luc in the first place. But it was fine, he'd be fine. He'd press the memory of Valérie away, like a precious, dry flower. In time perhaps he might even be able to make amends to Antonina Beaulieu.

But then he thought of her face when he'd last seen her, her eyes pained. And he knew that despite whatever he might want to tell himself, he could not heal her shattered heart.

Chapter 21

SHE TOOK HER MEALS IN her room and did not venture outside, despite her mother's pleas. Gaetan arrived in Oldhouse for his annual summer visit, but even he could not persuade her to come out. When Gaetan and Valérie left, she was relieved.

At first, when Nina lay upon her bed and curled up under the covers, she could summon no proper thoughts. She made the books tumble from the bookcases many times over, the unintentional expression of her anger. One evening the box of cards Hector had gifted her fell upon the floor, the cards scattering all around her, and Nina thought she was about to cry again.

She'd cried far too often.

But she did not weep, instead gathering the cards with her thoughts and shuffling them. He'd taught her this, at least the principles of it. She shuffled the cards once and muttered his name, then she shuffled them again, and again she said his name.

She was struck with the idea that if she did this enough times, if she said his name out loud, it would eventually lose its meaning. She sat on the floor, in her nightgown with her arms wrapped around her knees, and she said "Hector Auvray" half a dozen times while she attempted to shuffle the cards without making a mistake.

She did it every day from then on. Sometimes she lost control of the cards and she had to start again, and she did not shuffle them well at first. But every evening she worked on this trick.

When she felt she had mastered it, she began to work on another.

Slowly she sought the books that until then she had forgotten, content only to dash them across the room. She ran her hands over the pictures of the butterflies, which had given her pleasure, their colors bright upon the page.

He did not write to her, not one single letter. It pained her, but what was one more hurt atop other lacerations?

At the end of summer, Madelena had her baby, and three days later Nina made the trek to her sister's house. It was the first time she had ventured outside her room, and she felt strange, sure everyone stared at her when she came downstairs with a hat in her hands.

Her mother, however, gave her a warm embrace and declared in a neutral voice that they would travel to Madelena's after lunch.

Madelena's baby was a darling thing. It already had hair, and when Nina held it in her arms she saw that the baby's eyes were gray.

"Will they stay like this forever?" she asked Madelena.

"Martin says they'll change and turn their true color in due time," her sister said.

Madelena lay on a huge four-poster bed with crimson covers. The Évaristes had always taken red as their symbol, ever since they'd made their fortune importing precious dyes that would be used to turn plain wool into beautiful, colorful garments. Even Martin's hair was red, and Nina had teased Madelena about this.

Nina handed the baby back and her sister cooed at the child, smiling down at her daughter.

"What will you name her?"

"I was thinking Viridiana, but Martin might call that a betrayal."

Nina chuckled at that and Madelena smiled once more. Nina sat on the chair that had been placed by the bed, her hands in her lap.

"How are you, truly, Nina?" Madelena asked softly.

"Mother told you I'm fine."

"Mother is not here now."

Nina held her hands together. She did not reply.

"Nina, you can talk to me and I will always listen," Madelena said.

Nina had a look of perfect misery, which she tried to disguise by speaking calmly. "I loved him and he didn't love me back. That is all there is to it," she said.

"Ah, Nina."

"Please don't be sorry for me," Nina said, looking up at her sister, eyes sharp. "All of Oldhouse already pities me—I cannot abide your pity, too."

Madelena gently shushed her baby, which had begun to stir. She rocked the child.

"I remember when you broke your arm," Madelena said once the baby calmed down. "You were seven. It was when we went to the Devil's Throne."

The Devil's Throne was a rock outcropping that had a funny shape. In a part of it, one could sit as if upon a chair. They said this had been a sacred spot at one point and that a statue of Ione, goddess of the forest and the hunt, had stood there in the days when pagan customs were the norm, before the fort at Dijou was built. But not a speck of the statue was left now, though in these parts, people might still pray to Ione and honored saints alike. Certain habits did not die.

"It was my left arm," Nina said. "I remember. Mother was furious at us."

"The next summer we were playing there again, and again you jumped atop those blasted rocks. As if falling once wasn't enough."

"I didn't fall the second time."

"I know," Madelena said. "And you were not afraid to climb a second time."

Afterward, Madelena spoke of other things. She concentrated on talk of the baby, news concerning the Évaristes, she even told Nina the cat had a new litter, six tabby kittens. On the way back to Oldhouse the next day, Nina thought again about the outcropping.

The leaves were changing color by the time she ventured to the Devil's Throne, from green to reds and yellows. She knotted her gray shawl around her shoulders and left early. By then there were fewer comments from her relatives.

The Devil's Throne was far from Oldhouse, but it was good to be outside again, following the familiar paths. She was surprised to see the world had not changed while she was sequestered inside her home. The trees remained rooted to their spots, the mushrooms were popping up in the patches where they could normally be found, the sheep roamed the fields they always roamed. The world remained and there was something remarkably comforting about this thought, since heartbreak often invoked images of cataclysms that would devour every speck of ground beneath one's feet.

Montipouret could exist without Hector Auvray, and so could Nina.

When she reached the outcropping, she took off her shoes, as she did when she was a girl, and climbed to the top until she rested her back against the smooth rock and looked up at the sky. She had missed all summer and with it the evening flights of beetles, their metallic green carapaces catching the ebbing light.

The rains came fully to Oldhouse a week later, drenching the land. It was the season of storms, when lightning streaked the sky.

Nina no longer ate her meals in her bedroom, joining her family in the dining room each day instead. The mass of the Beaulieus had returned to their homes with the coming of the rains, and now only the core members of the tribe remained. Nina felt more at ease with fewer people staring at her.

Her great-aunts Lise and Linette wrote to her when fall was ending and frost decorated the ground, the earth grown hard. They invited Nina to visit them in the spring. It would be a welcome distraction for all of them, they said. Nina had not thought about Loisail, she had pushed it from her mind, and she did not reply when her mother read her the letter.

The morning when the first snow of the season fell was the same morning Nina practiced a complex card trick, assembling all the cards into a fan that would then be reassembled in the shape of a sphere. When she was done working with the cards, she went to the window and opened it, breathing in the cold air. Snowflakes began to accumulate on her windowsill.

She realized, as she stood there with her head bowed, looking at the flakes, that she had utterly forgotten to say Hector's name that day. She had forgotten to say it for several days.

Nina went back to the Devil's Throne. This time she took her heavy coat, her gloves, scarf, and boots. The rocks were tinted white and the snow crunched beneath her feet as she climbed the outcropping and surveyed the sky. She had an odd sensation, as if she were an insect newly emerged from its silk cocoon that must dry its wings in the morning sun.

With the coming of winter, Oldhouse grew even more quiet and sedate. Nina and her mother went to the Évaristes' household for a party, and all should have been merriment and excitement, but a few of the younger Évariste boys, who had returned home during their winter break, must have heard the stories going around about Nina because they gaped. She was used to such things: the tale of how she'd shoved Johaness Meinard with her talent had been popular a few years before. Still, it hurt to know she was the object of blatant gossip. Everyone from Vertville to Dijou would likely spare a joke or two about the Witch of Oldhouse this winter.

Nina's mother, sensing her discomfort, asked again about Loisail. Her great-aunts had written a second letter and said the girl ought to stay with them for a couple of weeks.

"Or perhaps you'd rather stay with Gaetan and Valérie?" her mother asked.

"No," Nina said quickly. "My aunts have certain natural history materials that Gaetan does not trouble himself with."

This was an excuse, but it was also true. The old ladies maintained an impressive assortment of books and monographs on birds, which Nina found interesting. It was not her passion, but it would be better to spend her time reading about species of fowl than to have to endure living under the same roof as Valérie.

"What do you think? You could take off for a week."

"Perhaps I should go for the whole Grand Season," Nina said.

Her mother seemed surprised at this. "Nina, you do not have to."

"I want to."

She had climbed back atop the Devil's Throne even after she'd broken her arm, and Nina had decided Loisail would be a similar feat. She would not spend her life eternally avoiding the city. She wouldn't give anyone more reasons to talk about her or look at her sadly.

They had likely expected her to die of heartbreak, to wither and grow gray, but Nina thought she would not give them the satisfaction. Not to the silly folk who made jokes about her, nor to Valérie and Hector.

She still grew sad when she thought about him. But the feeling washed away quickly enough: she willed it to wash away as she willed the cards to turn.

It was more difficult certain mornings when, in the semidarkness of her room, she forgot to raise her defenses and Hector would intrude, unbidden, into her mind. She'd recall the exact way his mouth curved when he smiled, and this memory was utterly painful, drawing forth the wretched longing she'd hidden away. She could not wash this so easily, and the memory remained in the dawn; it stained her heart, like the sap of trees, which clings to clothes, to skin, to everything.

Nina buried her face in her pillow and squeezed her eyes shut.

A sea roared inside her and made demands, but she waded it, she bobbed up, took a breath, and opened her eyes to the cold winter morning. Then she rose because the day was there, the world was there, and she wanted to be part of it.

PART TWO

Chapter 1

THE BEST BOOKSHOPS IN ALL of Loisail were located two blocks from the Square of the Plague. Its formal name was the Plaza Varnier, named after a war hero long dead, but most people remembered it because in the Year of the Plague, many centuries before, this had been one of the spots where pyres were set up to burn the dead. There was a legend that a house across the square, with distinctive yellow tiles decorating its façade, had been spared disease because the owners were pious. Thus, for a time, this had been an informal peregrination spot for the sickly who wished to be cured of impossible maladies.

Nina walked by the bronze statue of General Varnier and peered at his resolute face, arm stretched out toward the heavens, sword in hand. A pigeon sat atop the statue, unaware that it was lounging on the head of a historical figure who had helped topple cities.

"Miss Beaulieu, how do you do?" a male voice asked, and she turned her head.

It was Luc Lémy, dressed in a blue jacket that brought out his eyes. He took off his silk hat and pressed it against his chest. Nina extended her hand in greeting, and he kissed it.

"Mr. Lémy," she said. "It's good to see you again."

"Likewise. What are you doing in Loisail? Have you come for a few days of shopping?" he asked.

"I'm staying with my great-aunts this spring."

"Not with your cousins? I was thinking of paying your cousin Gaetan a visit this week."

"No," Nina said simply, and focused her eyes on the pigeons milling about the square, looking for crumbs.

"I understand completely," he replied, smiling at her, a conspirator. "It is easier to give the elderly relatives the slip and seek excitement, is it not? Drinks and billiard games kept me entertained when I visited with my grandfather two summers ago. Have you been going to a good many parties?"

Nina had to admit her great-aunts were more lax than Valérie and Gaetan ever were. They did not go out often, most of the social functions Nina had been subjected to last spring were out of the question, and though in theory they were supposed to accompany her as she went around the city, her great-aunts both complained of aches and pains and had let Nina do as she willed. There were also no reproaches about Nina's clothing and shoes, which was how she was walking around Loisail in a simple cotton dress without the ruffles, flounces, and pearls Valérie adored.

"I'm sure I do not seek the same excitement as you do, Mr. Lémy. No, I haven't gone to parties," she said, but her voice was pleasant. She did not think she had any business chiding him, and Luc had a sunny disposition—it would have been difficult to chastise him even if one wanted to.

"No parties? During the Grand Season?" he said, frowning, as though this were an alien concept.

"I've been in the city only for a couple of weeks."

"That's plenty of time to go to parties. Do not tell me you are one of those women who spends her days at sewing circles and organizing charity bazaars? I detest such things, and you are far too young for that nonsense."

A pigeon approached Nina's foot, bobbing its head up and down, but a dog, let loose from its leash, began chasing it and sent it flying off. The pigeons atop the statue ignored the ruckus and stayed in their place.

"I sew poorly," she said, watching as a heavyset matron in a heavy pink hat picked up the dog and shushed it.

"Good!" he exclaimed. "You ought to be dancing."

Nina couldn't help but laugh at that. He seemed to take games and balls rather seriously, Mr. Lémy. It was endearing.

"Where are you headed?" he asked.

"To look at books."

"By the gods, surely not on a pretty day. Are there books around here, anyway?"

"Past the street of the perfume-sellers," she said, glancing in the appropriate direction. "There are a dozen shops. You haven't noticed?"

"No. I am headed to the Philosophers Club and I should warn you, despite the name, there are no philosophers there. It's a drinking den."

"Where?"

"Up there," he said, pointing at a faded building, four stories high, its windows impenetrable behind burgundy velvet.

"Why do they call it the Philosophers Club?"

"After a few drinks, all men become philosophers."

Nina nodded, and though she knew nothing of the Philosophers Club, she imagined it would be populated with men as bright and cheery as Luc Lémy, all in their finest jackets, drinking and smoking and laughing for hours on end.

Luc took out his pocket watch and slid the cover to the side, then looked at her. "I won't be needed for another half hour. Do you want me to escort you to your bookstore? This is not the best quarter in the city."

"It's not the worst either. I've been here before."

"Let me be gallant. It makes me feel better," he said, offering her his arm. "I'm sure your great-aunts would approve."

Nina draped her hand over his arm. "If you insist. But there are no drinks inside a bookstore."

"How dreadful."

They walked the scant two blocks necessary to reach their destination. The bookstores were all small and crowded. They occupied the first floor of each building, but the second and third floors either served as living quarters for the owners or housed restaurants. One could pick a favorite volume and then have an economical lunch.

Nina went into the Dandelion. It was not the best bookstore on this street, but it catered to geographers, nature aficionados, and those with scientific inclinations. It sold copies of the leading scientific gazettes and popular books, but also more obscure volumes.

The aisles were narrow and the books piled high. The trick at the Dandelion was that you needed to have been there before or you wouldn't find a thing. Nina stood on her tiptoes and brushed her fingers along the spines.

"What are you looking for?" Luc asked.

"Coronel Oudevai has been publishing drawings of the species he has seen during his travels in the Ammunok peninsula. I'm looking for the third volume. It should be out now. Here it is."

Nina grabbed the slim volume and opened it, turning the pages. She paused at a fine watercolor that showed an armadillo against a blue sky. It was the representative animal of Iblevad, found throughout most of the southern portion of the continent and therefore not so rare as other species, but she thought it a most delightful creature despite its being common.

"There are armadillos large enough, they might carry you on their back, did you know that?" she told Luc.

"I'm not even sure what I'm looking at, and you are saying it's as big as a horse?" he replied.

"Not so large, perhaps a pony. And there are big turtles, too. I saw a photograph showing a man riding a turtle. I'm not sure if anyone would attempt to ride an armadillo."

He peered over her shoulder at the book. The shop was stuffy and a bead of sweat slid down Nina's throat. It was an uncommonly warm spring, her great-aunts had told her. She'd forgotten her fan at home and made a mental note to ensure she carried it at all times.

As if echoing her, Luc raised a hand and tugged at his collar, loosening his tie. "We'll be cooked alive if we remain here, Miss Beaulieau," he whispered. "How about we pay for this?"

Nina could have stomached an hour inside the bookshop no matter if it felt like resting inside an oven, but she decided to be merciful, and they headed to the front, where an attendant wrapped the book in brown paper and tied it with a string. Luc said he'd buy it for her, and even though she protested, he ended up paying for it.

"It's the least I can do for being a nuisance," he said, handing her the book.

"You are not a nuisance," she replied.

"Don't encourage me. I could believe you."

When they stepped out, they both turned their heads, hearing the clock of nearby Saint Cecily strike three.

"Your club," she said. "I've kept you for a long time. You'll be late."

"Who ever heard of a man being late for drinks? The later is always the better," he said with a shrug.

"How kind of you to say that. Thank you for keeping me company," she said, and extended her hand to bid him good-bye.

Luc Lémy, however, did not seem ready to go. He held her hand in the polite city fashion but did not release it, instead moving a step closer to Nina and giving her a mischievous look.

"Did I mention that my eldest brother has acquired a motorcar?"

"No. I think not."

"He has. I've been learning how to drive it. I think I ought to take you for a ride in it. It's entirely safe, I assure you."

"Doubtlessly there are motorcar enthusiasts more suited for such pursuits than I," she said.

"Well, you see," he said, leaning down to speak in her ear, "I can't think of a single one I'd rather have with me."

"Mr. Lémy, I can't imagine you don't have a dozen names of a dozen other girls scribbled in your pocket book," she whispered back, mocking him a smidgen.

Luc laughed and kissed her hand, finally releasing her. He reached into his jacket and produced a mother-of-pearl pocket book, the initials LL engraved on the front.

"Write your address in my awful pocket book, and I shall pick you up Thursday morning for a ride," he said, also handing her a tiny black pencil.

Nina held the pencil between her fingers but did not scribble anything, aware that it was probably not the best idea to agree to the venture. Valérie would have had a fit and declared it improper on a number of levels, and she would have been correct. However, Nina had a hard time adhering to proper behavior, always keen to make exceptions for herself.

What held her back mostly was that Luc was part of Hector's social circle. She did not think them the best of companions—she'd had the impression that Luc was included in the trip to Oldhouse because of his brother, and not because Hector was particularly friendly with him—but they knew each other. She was sure they talked and dined on occasion.

But what if they did? She was nothing to Hector, and Hector was nothing to her. True, Hector had said Luc Lémy was a ladies' man, a scoundrel in fine clothes, but she could have deduced that herself.

She scribbled her address.

"There, Mr. Lémy," she said, returning the pocket book.

"I'm not 'Mr. Lémy.' If I have your address in my pocket book, you are bound to call me Luc now."

Luc Lémy could probably get a bear to remove its own fur so he could make himself a coat, and she smiled, indulging him.

"Luc, then."

"Thursday, Miss Beaulieu," he said, doffing his hat and bowing low. The sun glinted in his hair, making it look golden, and she thought wryly that Luc Lémy was the kind of man who might never have known a sad day in his life.

"Nina," she said, shaking her head, refusing to allow her thoughts to turn dark. "If you have my address in your pocket book, you are bound to call me Nina."

"Thursday early in the day, after breakfast, Nina Beaulieu," he said.

He was walking backward, facing her with his hat between his hands, with the result that he almost collided with a couple of people. That did not stop him, and he kept walking backward until the end of the block, when he promptly turned away from her, placed his hat on his head, and rushed off.

When she cut back through the square, she stopped to glance in the direction of the building where he'd said he'd be, and Nina waved at it even though she was sure he could not see her. She took a carriage nearby and headed back to her great-aunts' home. The old ladies greeted her with a kiss on the cheek and immediately began to talk about the heat, how there had not been a spring this warm in ten years.

Nina removed her shoes and sat next to them, her book on her lap. She rested her palms on the cover for a minute, smiling to herself, before she opened it and showed it to her great-aunts.

Chapter 2

THERE WAS, ALL AROUND THEM, the murmur of the theater, the groan of pul-
leys and chains as they walked behind the stage, the rustle of costumes
wheeled down corridors, and the talk of stagehands, milling about like
bees. It was Friday and Hector had two performances. It was not a day
to entertain a friend.

"It's nearly two o'clock," he told Étienne. "That's not nearly enough
time to go out. You ought to have told me you would be visiting."

He walked with quick, purposeful steps, and Étienne had trouble
keeping up and evading the people walking by them.

"If I'd told you I was coming, you wouldn't have seen me. You spend
your days locked up either here or in your home. I'm surprised you even
deigned to appear at my wedding."

Étienne had been married five months before. Most brides preferred
a spring wedding, which would allow them to travel in the summer, but
Étienne's new bride knew her name would stand out in the papers if she
wed in the winter or fall. She was a tactician, Étienne's wife.

"Nonsense," Hector muttered.

"Come, now, let us go eat."

"I can ask for food to be brought to my dressing room for the both
of us. Is that not enough?"

"No. It's a ghastly idea. It's already annoying that you must eat your meals at that desk of yours, but I won't do it. You can't possibly be needed here every single moment of the day."

"I am rehearsing a new routine," Hector said. "A spinning glass box, and I wouldn't want to drop it."

"As if you've dropped a prop in your life."

"It's filled with water, and even a moderately sized shark. The weight of the device is not inconsiderable."

"Hector, come along and forget about the shark for one minute."

Hector sighed. He turned to a man with steely gray hair who was at that moment instructing two young women carrying cutouts of giant anemones, part of the scenery that needed to be set up.

"Mr. Dufren," he said, "I am thinking of stepping out for an hour. Are there any pressing matters?"

"I think we can manage, Mr. Auvray," Dufren replied.

Hector nodded and ducked beneath a cutout, heading toward one of the side exits. The painted backdrops and silver moons of the Royal gave way to the bright day outside as he opened a door. However, the vision of the boulevard, full of carriages and passersby, did not fill him with joy. Truth be told, he was most comfortable in the confines of artifice, in the perfect world created by the stage.

"Where would you like to go?" Hector asked. "Anywhere nearby. I can't spare more than an hour."

"How about the Golden Egg? There should be a table available at this time of the day."

Hector nodded and they walked three blocks to the ostentatious restaurant known as the Golden Egg because the owner had decked every wall with a gilded mirror wider than two men. Any surface that was not covered by a mirror had wood paneling with inlaid paintings.

The food there was excellent and the service appalling, which was a requirement at any chic restaurant. Anyone who was somebody, or on the way to becoming somebody, was supposed to make an appearance at the Golden Egg. Hector had already made a requisite visit to the place and resented having to make another, but he decided to bite his tongue, lest he make Étienne cross. He realized that he was being insufferable and he did not want to be if he could help it, not when it came to an old friend.

They sat in chairs of plum-colored velvet, and the waiter handed them a menu. Hector ordered the soup before even glancing at the offerings, hoping it might be faster than another dish. Étienne and the waiter both frowned since it was bad manners to pick an item quickly, one must fret at the offerings and ask for advice, but Hector did not care what anyone thought when it came to his lunch.

"Tell me, then, how have you been?" Étienne asked.

"Busy," Hector said.

"You look fatigued. It's not that business with Valérie, is it?"

He'd let his hair grow even longer than usual, and the dark circles under his eyes testified to nights spent staring at the walls in his room. "The business with Valérie is done," he said.

It was not the exact truth. He did not pursue Valérie any longer and had accepted that whatever they'd once had ended long ago, but this did not mitigate the heartbreak. The bruise he'd suffered, however, had faded from black to a faint yellow.

"To tell you the truth, I worry about Nina mostly," he added.

I should have written to her, he thought while he unfolded his napkin and placed it on his lap. The waiter arrived with the wine and poured them each a glass.

Étienne made his selection for a main course and then turned toward Hector, an eyebrow quirked. "I don't know if what I am about to say will make it better or worse, but I suppose I should tell you before you hear Luc babbling on about it. Nina Beaulieu is in the city and I believe she is fine."

"Is she with her cousin?" Hector asked.

"No, she's staying with those great-aunts of hers, I forget their names."

Hector had not thought she'd return to the city. The notion left him speechless. Was she spending the whole spring there? The Grand Season, yes. He had not imagined her attempting it. He recalled, dimly, that her birthday was in the winter. He had jested he would buy her an insect.

He had missed that birthday.

She was now twenty.

"How did Luc come upon this information?" he asked.

"He ran into her the other day. I think she was buying books. She looked in good spirits, he said. That's all I was told. He spent most of an hour chewing my ear off about a card game he lost."

Hector shifted a saltshaker without touching it, making it slide across the table, an annoying mark of restlessness. He checked himself immediately and stopped the motion.

"I'm happy to hear that."

"All is well, you see," Étienne proclaimed. "Now, if you'd only have lunch with me more often, you wouldn't be looking this damn tired all the time."

"I like to work hard. Nobody ever made anything of himself by lying around all day."

"Share that philosophy with my youngest brother when you can. All he does is beg me for money. Father doesn't give him a cent and Jérôme wouldn't mind if he perished in a ditch, but I'm far too generous and he drains me every month."

Étienne launched into an impassioned speech about the negative aspects of all his brothers' characters, beginning with the eldest, Alaric, and ending with Luc, the baby of the family. Hector listened to him, and although normally this talk would have distracted him, even amused him, he could not be amused now.

When they parted, Étienne reminded Hector that he must come by for supper one day, now that he and his wife were installed in an abode of their own.

"We have one of the best cooks in town," Étienne said. "I'll be overly plump within a year."

"You'll be fine," Hector replied.

Étienne patted Hector's shoulder. Their long friendship must have clued Étienne about Hector's ruminations, or else he was exceedingly simple to read that day. "Hector, you could always *try* to make amends to her."

"To Nina?"

"Why not? Do you want me to ask Luc if he knows her address?"

"No," Hector said quickly.

"Take care, then," Étienne said with a shrug.

Hector went to his dressing room, his spirits curiously doused, and sat behind his desk. It was not a large dressing room, rather cramped for an important performer. A painted screen hid the area where he kept a couple of changes of clothes. Not all his costumes—he had too many, though a stray one sometimes ended up there—but a dining jacket and a couple of shirts in case he was required to attend a function after work. Behind the screen there was also a full-length mirror and an area where he kept ties, shoes, and a comb.

There were shelves piled with books and props, sheets of paper upon his desk, in a corner a potted plant. A wall showed a poster with his name emblazoned on it, the first big engagement he'd ever played. HECTOR AUVRAY, MARVEL OF OUR TIMES, the large letters read.

He sat upon a couch, brushing aside the newspaper he'd left there.

He had in fact written to Nina. He had not been able to mail the letters, pausing when he had only one paragraph down, then tossing his efforts in the wastebasket. Pages suffused with horrid guilt and imprinted with another, ghastly feeling he couldn't even name, but which caused him to count the days since he'd last seen her and to rip the letters to shreds. Six letters, and the sixth he did finish but it was terrible, so lacking in every sense that he'd given up and decided that his first instinct, never to write to her, had been correct. Now she was in the city and he thought, *I should have written to her.* The thought circled his mind, refusing to leave.

He performed that evening and the bit with the shark went well, the applause rising like a wave from the crowd. He bowed low, a hand pressed against his chest. When he was leaving the theater, he caught sight of Mr. Dufren.

"Mr. Dufren," he said, "I have a novel request for you. Do you think you can find me someone who sells beetles in the city?"

"Beetles?" Dufren asked, looking baffled. "For a new act?"

"No. I need pinned specimens."

"I suppose I can manage that."

Hector nodded. He hoped it wouldn't be too difficult. There must be a market for collectors, and anything you could imagine could be purchased in Loisail. He grabbed the door, ready to open it, and paused.

"Mr. Dufren, not mere beetles. Get me precious specimens, pretty ones."

"Pretty. Why . . . yes, Mr. Auvray. When do you want it?"

"As soon as you can. And I'll need something else. The address for Lise and Linette Beaulieu," he said.

"Very well."

Two days later, Mr. Dufren ushered an old man into Hector's dressing room. He came accompanied by an assistant who carried a large box, which they set on Hector's desk. They opened the box and showed Hector the contents: a multicolored collection of beetles, carefully preserved and mounted. Azure, yellow, red specimens.

"Green," he told them.

The men nodded and laid out green beetles until Hector paused over one that had a delicate metallic shimmer.

"I'll purchase this," he said.

The men nodded and began putting their specimens back in the box. Mr. Dufren waited patiently to escort them back outside. Hector, behind his desk, tapped his fingers against its surface, frowning.

"Twenty of them," he said.

The men looked at Hector in confusion.

"I don't need one beetle. I need twenty."

"Twenty beetles like that?" the assistant asked.

"No. Nineteen more. The rarest specimens you have, if you must go back to your shop to get them, do so. Twenty total. Mr. Dufren, do you have that address I asked for? I want you to send this one beetle there. Find a box for it, will you?"

"Yes, of course. Gentlemen," Dufren said, and motioned to the men.

A while later, Dufren returned and stood in front of Hector's desk. He placed a box on the desk. Hector raised his head and nodded at his assistant, handing him his calling card.

"Please send it," Hector said. "Tell the messenger it should be delivered into the hands of Nina Beaulieu."

"Sir, shouldn't you attach a note to this?"

"The card will be all. Please make sure those men bring me the beetles I need."

"If you don't mind me asking, what do you need twenty beetles for?"

The question caught him by surprise. He had not considered *what* he meant to do; it was all knitting itself together, a wild amalgam of thoughts coalescing into a single thread.

He wanted to make amends. He had no idea if it could be done but he wanted to *try*. She deserved it.

He'd been frozen in listlessness and self-pity for a long time now, and he finally felt himself thawing, as if the spring and her presence had spurred him into action.

How strange, he thought.

"I forgot a lady's birthday," he said.

"You do realize it would be more appropriate to send flowers for a birthday, don't you?" Dufren said with a sigh.

"She will like this better."

Hector turned his attention back to his papers. *It's done,* he thought. *It's done and nothing may come of it, but I hope something does.*

Chapter 3

LISE AND LINETTE LIVED IN Three Bridges Quarter, a section of the city where the river flowed beneath the eponymous three bridges, and tiny houses, all painted white, rose three stories high. The color was traditional in the quarter. Once, twenty years before, the mistress of a famous composer had attempted to paint her home a pale shade of blue, but this had been met with such ardent opposition that she had to refrain.

Each house in the quarter was a century old and had a garden at the front of it, with an iron fence bordering it and a path that led three steps up to the door. For the homes on the easternmost side of the quarter, the back door of the house led five steps down to a canal. Once upon a time barges had sailed there, following the current, though most of the traffic had now been diverted and went down the Erzene.

Lise and Linette's house was humdrum; the only detail setting it apart was the profusion of crocheted items inside. Lise had a passion for it, and she had made tablecloths and many doilies. There were doilies under cups and glasses, doilies on the sofa, doilies on the bookshelves. If Lise could have wrapped their cat in crocheted dresses, she might have done it.

Lise and Linette welcomed Luc Lémy into their crochet museum, wondering at the sight of him. He was outfitted in a plaid jacket, a jaunty cap angled on his head, as befitted a man engaged in a sport.

"Which is this one? Is this the Lémy who was married last fall?" Lise asked, taking out her spectacles. "Let me see you, young man."

"No, Great-aunt, this is Luc," Nina replied.

"Bah, if they bothered to look different, I might tell them apart."

"What?" Linette yelled.

Nina could not help but giggle. Luc, however, was the picture of courtesy. He greatly flattered both women and he was as charming as he had been at Oldhouse, which meant it took them nearly an hour to leave since her great-aunts kept chattering with the young man.

Once outside, Nina surveyed the promised motorcar. She'd seen a couple from afar, but they were rarities and carriages dominated Loisail. Etiquette said a lady could ride with a man in these contraptions, the same as a man could escort a woman home in a carriage after a ball, but driving one was another story. The devices were the toys of city boys who, like Luc, might drive them around the block to impress their friends with the apparatus.

The motorcar was a two-seater, finely constructed and painted a glossy black. Luc held the door open for her, and she admired the up-holstery. It suited Luc well, she thought, being as new and ostentatious as he was.

The streets nearby were empty and Luc was able to maneuver the motorcar with ease, humming to himself as they went around. At length they stopped by an area of greenery bordered by more of the white houses that characterized the quarter. It was not a park proper, merely a plot of land where the locals had once cultivated vegetables in an impromptu communal garden, now abandoned and growing wild with weeds. Some-one would build more tiny houses there one day, but for now it was forgotten.

Luc helped her out and they strolled through the grass until they reached a stone bench, solitary and weathered, that stood in the center of the plot. Nina sat down, surveying the plants and the yellow flowers that grew all around them. She could hear insects buzzing, everything around them teeming with life.

"How do you like the motorcar, then?" he asked, sitting by her side.

"I like it, though you should let me take a turn at it. I've seen how you drive and can imitate you."

"No, that's impossible."

"It's not. I'm sure I could drive it without even using my hands," she said, and as if to prove it, she cut a flower that grew by the bench using her talent and lifted it in the air, offering it to Luc.

He held the flower, examining the petals. "I think you would kill me with fright if I let you drive the motorcar with the powers of your mind."

"I can open a lock without touching it," she said. "That takes more effort than spinning a wheel."

"I'm sure—still it is not my motorcar, I've only borrowed it from my brother. And why were you lock-picking, anyway?"

"It helped me pass the time."

She did not specify that it had helped her pass the time during the winter months when she had needed to think of things that did not concern Hector Auvray, but Luc must have divined it because he eyed her with caution.

"Can I ask you what happened with you and Hector last summer?"

She had received in the past five days five boxes, each one containing a delicate beetle. A calling card came with every box, Hector's name printed on it. When she had been handed the first two boxes, she had not opened them, but at the third, driven by her natural curiosity, she'd finally unveiled their contents and remained mutely staring at the creatures.

Nina did not know what they meant and did not attempt to interpret them. The specimens now rested in their boxes, stuffed in the back of a desk.

She wondered if Hector had sent Luc for this reason, or if the arrival of the beetles had nothing to do with him. Was he spying on her?

"We were not a favorable match," she said, and her voice was beautifully calm and collected. If this was an attempt to gauge her state of mind, Hector would obtain nothing.

"I am sorry," Luc said.

"It was a child's fancy, anyway." Nina raised a hand and pressed it against her chest. She lowered her lashes so that he might not take the measure of her gaze.

Luc nodded and lifted her free hand, pressing a kiss against it. "I am in luck, then, since I can cast my net and see if I may catch the prettiest girl in the city."

She raised her eyes, frowning. Her hand rested firm and slender between his, yet she did not understand. "Are you jesting? I like your jokes, but this one would not be in good taste," she said.

"It's no joke. How could I joke about this? I don't think there's anyone fairer than you."

Perhaps she'd grown wiser or maybe it was the heat of the day that irritated her, but she was not enraptured by his words as he might have expected.

"Hush," she said, rising quickly to her feet. "I am sure you meet many beautiful girls."

Her heart, which had been placid, resting on dark velvet like the insects she collected, now began to beat wildly, though not for the young man next to her. Her thoughts, traitorous, flew toward another man, one who had never spoken words of flattery or love to her. And she was angered, thinking that he had not done it and now another would.

"What?" he asked, looking baffled.

"Exactly that. I'm naive, but not so naive that I cannot tell when a phrase has been said a thousand times before to others. Whatever game this is, I will not grow flustered and melt in your arms," she told him.

It seemed to her that indeed it must be a game, a ridiculous prank that had been set in motion by them all, and she went toward the motorcar.

"Wait, wait," he said, rushing to her side. "I do not know what you are going on about. I was trying to be charming, but I mean no harm. Come, now, don't be angry at me."

She crossed her arms upon her chest, staring down at the grass. Her ears were roaring as if she were standing by the seashore.

"Nina, are you all right?" he asked.

"I'm sick of people lying to me," she blurted. "People keep lying to me, and if what you want is to toy with me for an hour or two, please pick someone else. I thought you might be a friend."

"I am a friend. Please. I say silly things sometimes, but I don't think it was that bad. I'll tell you that you are the ugliest lady in Loisail from now on. Happy?" he asked, and his voice was cheery.

She looked at him. He was all sunny disposition and blue eyes.

"I'm sorry," she said. "I shouldn't be cross with you."

"No, you are right, I am a bit of a lout at times. Maybe Hector told you a few stories, but I can be gallant," he said.

At the mention of Hector's name, she swallowed and shook her head. The sun had hidden its face, shrouded suddenly in clouds.

"I don't think it was a child's fancy, was it?" Luc asked gravely.

"I mistook politeness for affection," she said. "I saw things that were not there, and do not wish to deceive myself again."

He grabbed both her hands this time and he graciously bent his head over them, placing another kiss on the back of them and giving her an earnest look. "There's something here, Miss Beaulieu."

Flustered after all, she dipped her chin. A butterfly flitted by and perched itself on Luc Lémy's head, white upon his dark cap. The sight made her smile.

"Don't move, there's a butterfly on your head."

"Oh dear," he said, and he did move. The butterfly flew away.

"It was a cabbage butterfly," she told him. "It's one of the first butterflies that emerge in the spring. They fly around during spring and summer, even into the fall until the hard freeze."

"Ah, bugs," Luc said, taking off the cap and running a hand through his hair. "No, can't say I like them."

"It's not a bug, Mr. Lémy. It's a butterfly."

"It has tiny legs and crawls around," he said, making motions with his fingers in imitation of a crawling insect.

"It does not."

"I said you should call me Luc."

Nina bit her lower lip before nodding. "I said you should call me Nina."

"Come. Let us drive around a bit more," he told her, and it was as if he could will clouds to be gone, the sun to shine again.

They walked back to the motorcar arm in arm, and when the time came to bid him good-bye, he said he'd return the next week with a carriage this time and they might go to Koster's for tea.

When she went inside, she saw a box resting atop a doily on a table by the entrance. Another package had arrived with the crisp white card and the name HECTOR AUVRAY emblazoned on its front. The fury that had assaulted her earlier returned and she rushed up to her room, jamming the box in the desk and locking it. She flung the key away and it slid under the bed.

She sat on the floor, in front of the bed, and stared at the desk, eyebrows furrowed. After a while she sighed and turned the lock with a twist of her wrist, using her talent, not even bothering to search for the key. The drawer slid open and she reached inside.

Nina opened the box that had arrived that day and gazed at the beetle inside. It was beautiful.

Had he recalled what she'd told him once, that she'd rather have beetles than a new necklace? Why should it matter? Each box came only with the damnable card and nothing else. It was like trying to read auguries in the dregs of coffee.

She had meant what she'd told Luc, that she could not afford to see things that were not there anymore. And here, with Hector, there lay nothing.

Nina watched the light fall upon the beetle; its blue body was iridescent, changing color depending on the angle.

Chapter 4

Valérie Beaulieu's roses were blooming well that year and she spent hours sitting behind glass walls, in the company of her flowers. Once in a while, however, the memory of Hector would suddenly come back to her. She would recall how he had stood in the library and how dark his eyes had looked when he leaned down to kiss her. It was as if a phantom fraction of him had followed her and lingered in this space, haunting her when he had the opportunity.

On the days when this occurred, Valérie would bark orders to the servants, demanding that all the linens be washed and pressed, the silver polished, every corner of the house dusted as if she could exorcise him with these gestures.

Then she returned to her daily calls, her walks in the park, the management of the house, and the tending of the flowers.

The afternoon Luc Lémy stopped by was one of those calm days after the storm. The young man had not sent word that he wanted to be received, but Valérie allowed him to meet with her, feeling magnanimous.

They sat in the drawing room, Valérie in a mauve silk reception gown with golden buttons running up the front, ribbon edges at the neckline, and ivory lace bordering her wrists.

"You are radiant as always, Mrs. Beaulieu," Luc Lémy said, bowing low, pearl gray gloves in hand.

"How kind of you to say so. Please sit," she said.

He did and smiled at her. "I hope you'll forgive me for dropping in unexpectedly," but his tone indicated he was not sorry at all, the young man was self-centered, spoiled. "However, I believe you will find the visit pleasant. I've come to talk business with you, and I'm sure you'll be interested in my words."

"Then you must be mistaken and want to speak with my husband."

"No. Not today, at least. The business concerns an estate of yours." Luc Lémy took out a silver cigarette case and lit a tiny cigarette. He held it between his fingers but did not smoke it, as if he were merely toying with it.

"I have no estates."

"Avelo Keep in Treviste. From what I understand, the king granted it to the Véries five hundred years ago."

"Six hundred," Valérie said, correcting him. "Not that I can imagine why it would interest you."

Avelo had once been an important fortification, defending the Northeast from incursions, but that was centuries before. The Unification Act had brought a peace that did not necessitate Avelo. The lands there were infertile, yielding no prizes. This, coupled with the slow descent of the Véries, had left the place a ruin that they did not maintain and seldom remembered.

"I realize it is not much to look at. But it does have a wonderful view of the sea. If I remember correctly, when the king granted your family that keep and surrounding lands, he specified it could never be sold."

Had they been able to sell it, they would have, instead of having to dispose of crockery and silks. Luc Lémy must know that and also the extent of the financial limitations of the Véries. Valérie's marriage to Gaetan had saved the family from absolute ruin but had not restored it to its former glory, and their coffers were woefully low.

"What do you have in mind, Mr. Lémy? Best be quick about it since I do not have all day," she said, her generosity rapidly dissipating.

He had the smug smile of a boy who has performed a naughty prank. "Forgive me, Mrs. Beaulieu, I do not mean to steal all the minutes in the hour from you. What I have in mind is business, as I said. Business that will enrich us both. The stones of Avelo are worth nothing, but the land, that land is valuable. Do you know that outside Ygress they are building a hotel? The Panorama, it is to be called."

"What of it?"

"Avelo has a better view of the sea. The railway line is being extended three towns north, connecting with Apluri. If the Véries lease that land to me, Mrs. Beaulieu, they will profit handsomely. I will build a hotel, dazzling in its luxury. I can promise your family an annual fee and a bonus in exchange for the use of the land, secured in a long-term lease of a hundred years."

"A hotel? At Avelo? Who would go there?"

"Anyone who seeks a superb time. Hotels are mushrooming up the whole region. Everyone wishes to gamble, drink, and be merry."

Valérie frowned. It was not a terrible idea. The only thing Avelo could boast of were its blue waters, but if a blasted town like Ygress could inspire an upscale hotel . . . no, it was not a terrible idea.

"What do you know of hotels, Mr. Lémy?" she asked. "Your family makes school uniforms, doesn't it?"

He frowned as if remembering an unpleasant detail and waved his hand. "By the hundreds. But a boy must find his own way in the world. My eldest brother controls our business, the second-eldest is his right hand, and once it comes to me . . . I think Father is leaving me a button-making enterprise, acutely small."

"And what, you expect to sell your buttons so you can finance this hotel? I don't imagine you can build it on dreams and sand. Will your father back the venture?"

"There are two or three parties who might be interested in joining me. I expect my father might contribute to it, too, when he sees I have grown serious and mature."

Valérie stared at Luc Lémy. She did not know exactly how old he was. Perhaps twenty-four or twenty-five, but with his mustache and the look of a careless, fair-haired dandy who spent the evening drinking cocktails at Saserei's, he did not inspire any vision of maturity whatsoever.

"It might take you some time to manage this," she said dryly.

"Not nearly that long. I want to marry, which should help prove my mettle, and begin preparations for the construction of the hotel, before a year has passed. And here again is where I think we might assist each other. I want to marry Nina."

Antonina. Back in the city, with her great-aunts, and somehow she'd attracted the eye of this hungry fox, innocent lamb that she was.

"I see where you expect to get the bulk of your financing from, Mr. Lémy."

Luc, perhaps not used to direct talk, almost dropped his cigarette, but Valérie did not feel like being coy in that moment and she relished the startled look on his face.

"Don't look alarmed. You've done your research. I imagine you have an idea the amount of money her father left her? Not only the land, but the trust as well. And my husband would surely contribute to your bank account generously. Why, you might build yourself two hotels!"

"Mrs. Beaulieu," he began, but Valérie silenced him, raising her hand and shaking her head.

"I won't chastise you for having a solid head upon your shoulders, and the venture does interest me. However, my husband will no doubt notice you are a fifth son with little to offer to his bride."

"Last summer Nina was being courted by Hector Auvray," the boy said, sounding mildly offended. "He is a pleasant enough fellow, but he also spins mirrors in the air for a living."

"His account is worth more than the contents of a modest button-making business. Gaetan would not have invited him into our home if that were not the case."

Luc opened his mouth and exhaled loudly. He was sitting forward, an arm resting against his leg, the cigarette dangling from his fingers. His shoes shone brightly and he wore a nicely tailored blue suit, but Valérie could spot a man without a fortune of his own with practiced ease. She had been the same as he, concealing behind her beautiful smile the slim chances she possessed.

Luc had more opportunities than she'd had. What she would not have given for a silly business that sold buttons, or the generosity of older siblings. Yet there could be no denying Nina would enter this marriage with greater coffers than her husband.

It was not, however, an inelegant proposition. The lease of the land might liberate the Véries of the mendicant yoke they lived under, having to take whatever crumbs Gaetan threw to them. And if the venture went well, Luc would rise in esteem and position, and Nina with him.

"I admit you have a good name, though," Valérie said, smiling. "Your family is well liked."

At that Luc raised his head and straightened up a fraction.

"Good breeding, good manners, they are important. You move in the right circles and I wager you move competently. And you are clever, Mr. Lémy."

"Thank you."

"You dress sharply, and I am sure you could catch the eye of a young lady."

Now that his triumph was near, Luc allowed himself to smile back. But a triumph was not what Valérie was intending. She spoke sweetly, but her words were serious.

"A lease and a bonus are welcome, Mr. Lémy, but I would insist on an initial . . . shall we call it 'deposit'?" she said, savoring the surprised look on his face. "A sum showing your goodwill. Your hotel could sink into the sea, and my family would not see a cent. Don't worry. The payment can wait until you have wed and secured Nina's dowry. In exchange for a promise of your generosity, I believe I could breathe a positive word about you into my husband's ear. Your shortcomings need not be shortcomings at all."

This was what he had expected to hear, but not put in this way. He did not hesitate and nodded enthusiastically. "Thank you, Mrs. Beaulieu," Luc said. "You must not imagine that I care only for Nina's fortune, though. I intend to be a proper husband to her."

Valérie thought she knew exactly what Luc Lémy meant by "a proper husband." He'd give Nina half a dozen brats to tend to, kiss her gently on the cheek, and keep only discreet mistresses, ensuring that his affairs were not publicized. Nina, in her idiocy, would likely mistake all this for happiness.

Valérie smiled indulgently at the young man. "I know you will be. Tell me, since we are being candid, does Nina welcome your attention?"

"I've spent time with her and I believe she likes me."

"You should spend more time with her, then, until you *know* she likes you enough to be married to you. Gaetan is reluctant on the matter of arranged marriages. He'll ask for her opinion, and mine, and you do not want a lukewarm response from that child."

It was one of the most irritating bits of Antonina, the knowledge that her cousin would not force her into a marriage, like a parcel to be sold at the market. Valérie had been given no choice, but Antonina was allowed to have her heart's desire.

"I will definitely woo her. I wouldn't think not to. She is pretty and animated; it is the matter of Hector Auvray. I think she had her heart set on him," he said.

Hector Auvray. That was long past, though. Wasn't it? Surely she would have forgotten about him, and he had no doubt gone his own merry way.

She surveyed Luc Lémy critically. With his youth and light hair, and that air of sophisticated ease he had, could a girl of twenty ignore him? No, she wouldn't. She would notice him. She would beam at him. Give him a week, perhaps two, she'd be devoted to him.

Yet the sharp edge of dread stabbed at Valérie's heart as she recalled Nina's letter and the emotion poured upon the paper.

"Young man, listen to me carefully," Valérie said. "If you truly want Antonina, then you must erase any traces of that man from her mind. This Grand Season is an opportunity for us both, but you must do your part."

Valérie pressed a hand against her gown, feeling the golden buttons underneath her palm.

Chapter 5

HECTOR WORKED ON THE WEEKENDS, doing two shows every night. Thursdays he also performed, but only once in the evening. Mondays and Tuesdays he rested, staying away from the theater. He began his day with a cup of coffee and a piece of toast for breakfast, reading a book by the window.

Around lunchtime he headed to the outdoor market that stretched behind the former convent of Saint Ilse. There he purchased vegetables and fruits, meats and fish, and all manner of other foods. He paused at the bakery on the way back home for a fresh loaf of bread and bought a newspaper at the newsstand. Then he proceeded to cook himself lunch. Hector learned how to make his own meals out of necessity, when he had been penniless and young, but he had grown to enjoy the process and though he did not reject the notion of restaurants, he preferred home-cooked meals when he could manage them. He also took pride in his self-sufficiency.

When he was done eating, Hector read the paper, then went out for a stroll. He liked Boniface because of its narrow streets and alleys that led nowhere. It was easy to get lost there, and every block offered a strange new treasure. There was a store that sold only music boxes next to a per-fumer's shop, but take one turn, and you'd come to an oddly quiet alley that ended in a cemetery. There were sedate, hidden gardens and boisterous establishments. Places for contemplation and spaces for noise and life.

In the evenings, Hector stopped at a coffee shop and regularly patronized the Pearl and the Swine, where all manner of musicians performed. On occasion he visited one of the playhouses at the Green District.

That day the sun shone brightly. Hector thought he might depart for his walk earlier than usual, so he could take advantage of the wonderful weather. He sat by the window in his leather chair, about ready to put away his book and prepare himself, when a knock made him raise his head.

He stood up and walked toward the entrance. He was in his old, collarless lounging robe. He had not expected any visitors.

"Yes? Who is it?" he asked.

The silence made him move quickly, telling him he should hurry, and he flung the door open.

Nina looked at him, her eyes cool and her face composed. He was somewhat sad to see she was perfectly coiffed, her hair gathered at her nape. He'd liked her hair loose, a bit unkempt, as if the wind had been toying with it all day.

She looked like a lady now, and he thought perhaps her fashionable dress and prim hair were supposed to serve as a type of shield.

He stepped aside, allowing her in without a word.

When he closed the door, Nina spoke, her voice brusque. "What do you think you are doing, sending me beetles for many days now?" she asked.

"I thought you might like them," he replied.

"Why would I want anything from you?"

"I forgot your birthday. I purchased twenty beetles, thinking—"

"That you might buy my forgiveness with a few presents? That perhaps you can assuage your guilty conscience?"

"I do not ask you to forgive me," he said, "but I want to try to make amends."

Nina turned toward him and stared at him with utter ferocity. "How dare you say that, when you gave Valérie my letter, when you played me for a fool, when you did not even bother sending word for almost a whole year."

"What letter?" he asked, frowning.

"Don't pretend you don't know. The letter I wrote to you."

"I don't know what you are talking about."

"You lie."

"I would not."

She looked surprised, her anger perhaps retreating back a tad, yet only a tad. She shook her head in exasperation. "Fine. That does not invalidate my other points."

"Nina, I am sorry. For everything. I want—"

She brushed past him and he noticed the way she was moving her fingers, frustrated and angry. He could tell she wanted to dash objects about his home, her nervous energy palpable, those fingers of hers almost electric.

"No, you don't get to want anything," she replied. "You tricked me. Both of you. You were not pursuing me, you were chasing after her. I thought you liked me. I thought you were my friend. You should have told me the truth."

"How could I tell you?"

"I don't know how!" she shouted.

She sat on the chair by the window, where he'd been lounging, looking outside. On his table, papers rustled under the influence of her thoughts, and he feared she might send them scattering about the room.

But no.

She held her hands together tight, as if to keep herself from tearing his house apart.

"I do like you, Nina," he muttered.

She did not look at him. Her eyes were on the sky.

"I thought, sometimes . . . I'm not sure exactly what I thought. Valérie, she was like a stubborn splinter under my skin you can't remove no matter how hard you try. But then, at times . . . it was pleasant spending time with you. I thought, if I took a chance—"

"You thought you could make her jealous. Maybe you decided you could settle for second best. Never once did you think about me," she said.

How to answer her? He could not deny it. He pressed a hand against the windowpane, staring at the same clouds she was staring at.

"How can you think to make amends? How can you send me presents, as if to purchase your peace of mind?"

"I don't know, Nina."

Truly, he did not. The beetles had been a bout of madness. He had wanted to cheer her up; selfishly perhaps, he had thought to summon her.

There were spells, superstitions of the troupe. Herbs for love and for good fortune and for summoning, and though he never quite believed the folktales, he had *wished* to believe them in this case. Wished her there, in his home, for it was impossible.

But she'd come and her pain was raw, and he could not think how to say any of the things he'd thought he'd tell her if he ever had the chance.

The extent of his regret.

The explanation for his grievous actions.

"I did write to you. I wrote several times. If I didn't send the letters, it is because it is as you say. How could I ask you to forgive me in a single letter?" he asked.

She offered him no answer.

"I am sorry," he said.

He turned to look at her. Her hands were trembling and he saw the way she swallowed. Would she weep? What had he done, coaxing her to him? He ought to have left well enough alone.

"I do like you. You must not think . . . What you must understand is that I truly cherished the moments we had together," he told her. "There were many times when I would be amazed at how easily you could make me smile. You do not realize how difficult a task that is. I am not good with others."

He was growing desperate, anxious, and all he wanted was for her to believe the truth in his words. All he wanted was for her to somehow understand. As if, if she understood, some of the monstrous misery he shouldered might melt away.

"You do not know what it is like to want something for so long, you forget why you even wanted it in the first place, until the only thing left is a gnawing need and there is nothing that can fill it. And even though everything in your body tells you that you are killing yourself wanting it, you cannot stop."

Nina stood up, her movements casual. Her face was distant. He wasn't sure she had heard him. Perhaps she did not care. She hardened with every second that passed, and he found this alarming.

He did not want to see her grow this weary.

"You said you wrote me a letter," he told her. "What did it say?"

"Nothing important."

"Nina, please," he said knowing instinctively that it was important.

And there was a coolness to her eyes, which had been gentle and honest. There were the seeds of disappointment in the curve of her mouth, melancholy in her movements when before he'd only ever found a vibrant joy of the world.

Hector knew what she'd written. Not the words but the meaning. It was engraved in the space between them.

He took a step toward her. A painting fell down, knocked off the wall by her power. It was but a reflex; he recognized the untamed expression of her talents. But it stopped him in his tracks, and if he'd thought for a second that he might move closer to her, now he realized this was impossible.

He had no right.

Hector sighed. "If there was anything in my power that I could give you, if there was anything I could do to make you happy, I would do it. You must believe that. And if you ever would ask anything of me, know that I would answer affirmatively," he told her.

"I don't need anything from you," she said.

He could feel around them, all around the room, her restless energy burning the edges of everything in sight.

"I sent the beetles because I am a silly man who understands nothing. But I also thought you might take pleasure in them. I want you to be happy, I want . . . to *know* that you are happy, to know you are well."

Nina looked at him blankly, as though he'd spoken in a language she did not understand.

"You were my friend," he said. "I was a fool."

"You pretended to like me," she replied.

"No, no, don't return to that," he said sternly. "I liked you. I like you still. You can believe anything you wish about me, but not that my affection was false. I've liked you since I met you—more than that, I admire you—that's the truth."

She conveyed a wordless wonder. The conviction in his voice drew her toward him. She took a tentative step, then another, but she stopped at the third as if she'd remembered an important point.

Nina bit her lip and there was a girlish quality about the gesture, but then she fixed her eyes on him, steady and calm. "I thought I could never forgive you, but I realize that is not the case. I stand here before you, and I do not hate you as I thought I would. But I cannot forget either," she said.

They were quiet. Her talent, which had been perceptible a few moments before, simmered and died.

"Please send no more gifts, Mr. Auvray. Send nothing more," she said. She was trying to keep emotion out of her voice and could not manage it, but when she walked out, she did it with composure. She'd broken the colored glass windows in Oldhouse, might have broken the world in half in that moment, but she'd learned to rein herself in.

He'd taught her card tricks, but he hadn't taught her that.

He went to the window and looked down, scanning the street below, until he saw her marching out into the street. She turned a corner and she was gone.

The sun, as if mocking him, had shrouded itself behind a cloud.

It was he, then, who sent papers and writing instruments scattering across the table with a flicker of his eyes, happy to hear the noise of them landing against the floor and filling the silence she'd left behind.

Chapter 6

SHE WISHED GAETAN WOULD GO away and let her be, but he kept buzzing around her, stubborn. He never sensed anything about her, too obtuse to notice her moods.

"But, darling, you cannot possibly stay home," Gaetan said. "It's the Haduier party."

"Why not?" Valérie replied. "Make an excuse for me."

He was standing behind her, and she could see his sour face in the mirror. Agnes Haduier was a gossipy, wrinkled wretch. Lucian Haduier was a boor, the kind of fellow who in his cups would loudly bellow the most indecent words. Besides, the Grand Season was brimming with parties. They had already been to the De Villiers' and the Gannels', which were the more important balls of the early season.

Valérie adjusted the sash around her waist and stretched out a hand, running her fingers along the bottles filled with oils and perfumes, settling upon a jar containing a new face cream she'd purchased at Ambre. It smelled like almonds; it would be delicious against her skin.

If she'd been alone, she could have enjoyed trying it on. But he was standing there, eyeing her without truly seeing her.

Gaetan didn't see anything.

"Go by yourself."

"I cannot go without my wife. And after I bought you that new dress! And the brooch! Twenty perfect seed pearls. You were supposed to wear my brooch tonight."

"I'll wear it another time."

"When a man goes through a monumental expense for a party, he does not expect this response," Gaetan said.

He had not heard her or did not care. It was all about him. *His* wife who would not wear *his* dress and *his* brooch.

"Besides, Nina will be there. We haven't seen her in a long time," he added.

As if that would induce Valérie to go. She watched as Gaetan took off his jacket, muttering to himself. Was he really going to stay in? She hated him when he acted like this.

"With this migraine, I can't do anything but go to bed. Head off on your own," she said, hoping the prospect might induce him to simply leave her be.

"No, it's fine. I am tired and could use the rest. I'll miss seeing her, though."

She really did have a migraine, and this development was not going to improve it. Valérie decided to make the best of it since he had offered her an opportune opening.

"Take Antonina to dinner sometime," she replied, making a vague motion with her hand. "Speaking of Antonina, did you meet with Luc Lémy?"

"As a matter of fact, I did."

"He is a pleasant man."

"Pleasant enough. I don't think he knows how to do anything but have fun and drink."

"He's young. Besides, he told you about his business idea, didn't he?"

"Yes." Gaetan nodded as he undid his necktie. "It's not a bad one, and I think he said he has a fellow interested in providing a portion of the financing, Longder might be the name. Though more backers are needed."

"Then what is the trouble?"

Valérie turned around, fixing her husband with her gaze. He sighed and shrugged and did not answer, which made Valérie frown.

"Well?" she repeated.

"He seems boyish."

"As if Antonina is the pinnacle of maturity. He is what, twenty-four? About time he settled down and married, and since Nina ruined her first Grand Season by focusing her sights foolishly on a single man, who knows how she might fare this spring? It is one thing to be the new face at all the balls and another to be returning without an escort, milling around the edges."

"Valérie, don't be harsh."

"I am being honest. She followed none of my advice, did not pursue any of the young men I introduced her to."

Valérie had tried. She'd honestly tried to pour some sense into the empty-headed girl, but Antonina could not remember names and faces, would not make an effort. Antonina did as she pleased, pampered child with a roll of banknotes under her arm that she was.

It must be amusing to forgo duty and submit yourself only to silly pleasures, Valérie thought with quiet contempt.

"Luc Lémy is a godsend. Unless you were thinking to marry her to a Delafois back in Montipouret," she told her husband.

"Which one? They are already engaged or married. Cedric is widowed, but nearly fifty," Gaetan said.

Valérie knew this, and that was precisely why she had suggested it, guessing her husband would start panicking at the thought of his cousin remaining a spinster. Antonina was young enough that she could surely find herself a groom and take a bit of time doing so, but Valérie needed to create a sense of both urgency and opportunity.

"Luc Lémy is proposing an interesting business venture that would be sealed with a magnificent marriage. I do not understand what you have to lose."

"I was hoping she'd be married to a man she liked."

"Do you think she dislikes Luc Lémy?" Valérie asked.

"She has told me nothing of him."

"Maybe she is shy."

"She could hardly contain herself with Hector Auvray, speaking about every single visit they had together as soon as I walked in through the door."

"Maybe she's learned to be more decorous," Valérie said, her voice rising.

"They seemed well matched. I wonder what happened," Gaetan said.

Valérie stood up and opened her wardrobe's door, pretending she was looking for an item in there while taking a quiet breath.

"What happened is he was obviously of a different category than your cousin and did not mean to take her seriously. We should thank the stars we have not been saddled with a changeable man."

"You may be right," Gaetan conceded.

Valérie slid hangers to the side, her hands drifting across silks, lace, brocade.

"He did not even have the decency to speak to you and retire his courtship proposal," Valérie added.

If he had shown up at her doorstep, Valérie wouldn't have allowed him in. Yet, it rankled her a bit that he had not attempted to see her one more time. Did he think about her? He must. She had been in his mind for a decade.

He would never be rid of her.

"Luc Lémy comes from a reputable family, he is one of us. Antonina will be received in every house in the city, invited to every single ball, her name splashed over all the papers," Valérie said, closing the wardrobe's doors.

Her husband had moved to change behind a screen painted with white peacocks. Valérie pulled the sheets and reluctantly got in bed. They shared a massive four-poster bed wide enough that five people might fit in it, but certain nights Valérie felt it was not wide enough. Certain nights she wanted him to sleep at the other end of the world.

Had he gone to the party by himself, he would probably have done her the courtesy of going to sleep in one of the guest rooms, the hour being late and he not wanting to wake her.

Inconsiderate oaf, she thought, but she made an effort to candy-coat her words.

"You must think carefully of Antonina. You yourself told me how difficult it was to find her a proper suitor in Montipouret. All that talk about her talent . . . and that was before she smashed those windows at Oldhouse. *Everyone* was talking about it. Remember how even at Jacot's they'd heard of it?"

"People have always talked nonsense about Nina. She's an energetic child," Gaetan protested from behind the screen.

"We know that. But what do others think? They probably imagine she is difficult, even mercurial."

He did not answer but she knew what he was thinking. Montipouret would be no good for a husband. Not that anyone would have seriously considered it before—Antonina had been sent to the city for a reason the previous spring. A suitor from Montipouret was now a dimmer possibility. And it would look lowly for Gaetan if they had to resort to this. It would stain his pride, going back to the source he had discarded.

"Antonina made a mistake. She should not have pushed for us to accept Mr. Auvray as a suitor. Then again, what does a young girl know about picking a husband? Should we not counsel her?"

Gaetan emerged from behind the screen in his silk pajamas, no slippers on his feet. He was not old, he was Hector's age, but it seemed to Valérie as if he was aging fast. He was rather paunchy and his looks, which had never been especially good, were quickly fading.

Hector Auvray had a chiseled face, and time had made him harder but more distinctive. There was nothing distinctive about her husband.

And Gaetan's breath was sour. His teeth were bad. He had a peasant's mouth.

At least Antonina would marry a handsome boy.

Maybe he won't even count the seed pearls he gifts her, Valérie thought bitterly.

But let her have that blond youth, what did Valérie care? It was her family's position that mattered, the fortune they might snag that tantalized her. Was this not what she had been meant to do? They'd sent Valérie out in the world to battle in their name, and like a conquering general, she would deliver them a new kingdom.

Gaetan turned off the lights. "He does bear a reputable name," Gaetan said, now pulling up the covers and lying down, propping two pillows behind himself.

"It's crucial that we support his efforts," Valérie advised him. "You might have a word with Antonina in his behalf."

"If you think it necessary."

"Certainly," Valérie said with a vigorous nod.

"Then I will."

Victory assured, Valérie allowed herself to smile in the dark and laid her head against the pillow. Gaetan was soon fast asleep.

She did not have an easy time slipping into dreams. She'd accomplished much, yet she turned, restless. It was because Gaetan was there when she had wanted to be alone, she thought.

It was because of this.

But she kept thinking of Hector Auvray. It was as if by mentioning his name, Gaetan had conjured a demon, and Valérie could not order that linen be ironed and windows be washed to assuage herself. She could not walk to her garden and gaze proudly at her roses. She could not run her hands over her jewels, admiring the magnificent pearls Gaetan kept speaking about.

All she could do in the dark was remember what he looked like when she'd last seen him, when he'd leaned down to kiss her. A single kiss after many years.

And when they'd been younger and he'd curled his arm around her, brushing his lips against her hair. The way his voice sounded when he'd whispered against her ear. "Would you wait for me?"

She hadn't.

He had.

He'd wait forever, she thought. He *must*.

At least she had this satisfaction.

In her bitterness, in that oppressive bed, she thought Antonina Beaulieu would not know this devotion. She had all the wealth Valérie had ever hungered for and she'd have that pretty boy, but no devotion.

Had I been given her wealth, I would have done as I pleased, Valérie thought. *I would have waited*.

She turned her head and closed her eyes.

She ought to have gone to the party, a place where there were lights and champagne, and she might admire herself in the mirror and think herself satisfied.

Chapter 7

THE HADUIERS' HOUSE WAS TOO large, too bold to be considered genteel, and to make matters worse, Agnes had wallpapered it in a ghastly yellow that made visitors wince. But the Haduiers had a garden, which made up for their gaffes and served as a magnificent space for dancing under the open night sky. Many of the guests wandered around, glasses in hand, admiring the topiary, while the most adventurous sneaked into the hedge maze where a kiss or two would be exchanged.

Nina lingered in the sitting room, with its paintings of fruits and flowers on the walls—nothing matched here. Agnes had no taste, and where she should have opted for modern views of the city, she instead placed pedestrian compositions of bread and cheeses.

Four girls gathered around Nina, all of them in prim dresses, gloves on their hands. Nina had taken off her gloves because the business of manipulating objects with her talent was more difficult with them on.

Nina made the fan floating before her spin in slow concentric circles. It resembled a bird in its movements, rather than an inanimate object, and one of the girls squealed in delight at the sight of it. Nina reached out and the fan stopped, sliding into her hand. Nina smiled at the girls.

"How odd!" one of the girls said. "How interesting!"

"Fascinating," Luc chimed in.

He was standing next to her, looking keen. He'd danced two dances with Nina. Yet Nina had not failed to notice that he had filled out his dance card with many other names not five minutes after his arrival.

"That's probably enough," Luc told her, leaning down to whisper in her ear. "People are staring at you."

He was right. Two women were giving her an icy look, their fans pressed against their skirts. One of them spoke to the other, staring at Nina all the while. The girls smiled at Nina and stepped back, retreating, returning to the shadow of their mothers.

This party was on the smaller side and everyone was well acquainted, which left Nina in a bit of a cumbersome situation. Luc had been solicitous, taking her to and from the refreshment room, introducing her to several people, yet she felt a stranger. And now she'd made a grievous mistake.

"What is wrong?" she asked.

"It's not done," was his reply.

"But they asked me to," Nina protested.

"Yes. Best not make tongues wag, shall we?"

A man laughed loudly and she looked at him. He was glancing in their direction and she wondered if he was laughing at her or if it was a mere coincidence.

"Don't be upset, I say this for your sake. You don't want those old hens to be talking about you," Luc said.

"If they are old hens, then what does it matter?" she said, pushing back. She was tired of everyone judging her harshly.

"You are a lady, not a member of a circus troupe." His voice had a splinter of steel in it.

Nina looked down at her fingers. Luc handed her back her gloves and she clutched them but did not put them on. The fan dangled from a cord around her wrist.

"Nina, don't be upset."

She ran her hand along the mother-of-pearl handle of the fan. She had wanted to have fun, and the evening was souring.

Luc pressed a finger against her chin and tilted it up. He smiled at her and his eyes were soft, whatever slight unpleasantness had passed between them nothing but lightning streaking the sky, a moment there and then gone.

He was quick to forget, she thought. If ever they did quarrel in the morning, all would be amended by the evening.

"You look beautiful tonight. Did I say that already?" he told her.

She had woven hairpins that resembled orange blossoms into her black hair. Her dress was saffron taffeta with a ruched and pleated waistband, pretty and sunny and modish.

"Yes," she said.

"Did I tell you I want to touch you?" he said. The timbre of his voice made her drop a glove.

He picked it up and handed it back to her, and Nina gripped it tight.

Luc lifted his head and smiled. He was amused. She guessed he'd wanted to make her blush, and he had accomplished it. Yet a second later, he was distracted.

"What is it?" she asked.

"I see Guillem is here. I must talk business with him. Ah, my luck."

"Talk to him, then." Luc hesitated and Nina chuckled. "I'll be fine. It's a party, Luc. We are supposed to chat with other people."

"Perhaps we can dance again later. I've not bothered penciling anyone after the faster dances. Or, there's always a walk in the maze," he told her. "You'll be well? On your own?"

"Yes, go," she said, shooing him away.

She saw him walking through the crowd of revelers, greeting a man with an expansive chuckle. Two ladies, who stood next to the man, smiled and held their fans in their left hands, half-hiding their faces and looking at Luc. Luc was exaggerated in his charms, taking their hands and bowing low. Nina was not filled with cleaving jealousy. He had not spoken of courtship. She thought he might, and she did not know if this pleased her or not.

Nina felt eyes on her again and turned her head, guessing it was the "old hens" Luc had warned her about.

She was wrong.

It was Hector Auvray. Their eyes met, his gaze weighty then withdrawn.

He drifted out, away, and before she could put much thought into it, she was following him into another section of the house, into another room.

He stood in the middle of the library, his back to the door and hands in his pockets. The space was outfitted in crimson velvet, both on the curtains and the furniture. It was a small room, and the dark velvet made it seem even smaller.

And he seemed to fill up the space entirely.

"Do you always hide during parties?" she asked.

He turned around, looking surprised, but the surprise morphed quickly into composure.

"I don't do too well at them, no," he replied.

"A man of the stage and he cannot mingle at a party?"

"Being onstage does not require any conversational skills. I speak with my actions. At a party like this, though, everyone talks a secret language."

"Yes. They do," she said, remembering the women who'd glared at her.

Now that they were face-to-face, she did not know why she'd followed him. It had been a reflex, action before thought. She eyed the door and considered stepping out.

"I saw you out there, with the fan. You were good," he said tentatively.

"You are saying that to please me," she replied.

"No," he said. "I mean it."

She thought he did. His praise had always been measured and doled out slowly. It was hard earned.

"You lacked a proper flourish, though," he said, unable to leave a compliment be. "The ending. You can't put your arms down and walk off a stage. You must give them a proper ending. It's the most important part of the whole performance."

"How would you have done it?"

"May I?" he asked, pointing to the fan.

The door beckoned. A clean exit without another word, she owed him nothing. But her interest had been piqued.

She removed the fan from her wrist and handed it to him. Hector let it rest on his left hand, then tossed it up in the air. As it fell, he opened it with the movement of two fingers and flung it to the right with great strength, but the fan then came recoiling back, snapped itself shut, and he caught it with his left hand.

He bowed, presenting her with the fan.

"If it's moving that fast, how can you keep control of it?" she asked. The object had whipped by him rather ferociously. "And you were not looking at it."

She moved her right hand, imitating his gesture, but he shook his head.

"No, not like that. Let it go, stop it at the last second, and *don't think* that it will stop until that second. You don't need to see, you don't need to move your hands to know where an object is. If I tossed a coin behind you, you'd realize the sound came from behind. Most of all, *believe* you can stop it."

Nina flung the fan to the right three times, trying to catch it with her left hand as he'd done. She failed each time, but at the fourth she managed to grasp the basic mechanics of it even if she was clumsy in the execution.

He had manipulated the fan like it meant nothing, with the careless-ness that can come only from years and years of practice. Despite her crude handling of the fan, he seemed almost to be admiring her in his own fashion.

She stopped, holding the fan tight in her hands. "I miss this," she said softly. "The way you taught me things."

He looked sad at her words and Nina bit her lip, wishing she had not mentioned it. How odd it was to be in his presence now, like drifting next to jagged edges and knives.

And yet.

"I should be heading out now," he said quietly. "I hope I was not a bother."

Hector inclined his head toward her, ever the polite gentleman, and she imitated him, not sure what she was doing. He'd be gone in another second. When she last saw him, it had been simpler to part, the memory of her misery giving her strength. But now she remembered the things that she enjoyed about him.

She didn't think, just as she didn't think when she climbed atop the Devil's Throne and her sister chided her.

"Three Bridges Quarter is not far from your home. You could es-cort me to my great-aunts' house," she said abruptly.

Nina should not have said that, and yet as soon as the words were out of her mouth, she felt she could not have told him anything different.

"But you came here without an escort?" Hector asked, looking surprised for the second time that night.

"My great-aunts are supposed to chaperone me, but as usual, they are lax in their obligations. I am here alone."

Gaetan was going to be in attendance at the party, so the matter had not been really dire, but he had failed to make an appearance. Nina did not mourn his absence. If he'd come, she would have had to talk with Valérie.

"We did not arrive together, I am not escorting you to this party. If we leave now, it might be thought improper. They could gossip about you," Hector warned her.

"They are already gossiping about me because of the business with the fan," she said, shaking her head. "I must leave or suffocate Can you see me home, or should I fetch my own carriage?"

There was a curiously cautious air about him, he who was at other times incredibly sure of himself.

"I'll take you home, in that case," he said.

They did not speak once they boarded the carriage. He sat in front of her, looking melancholic, his eyes lost, and she kept her gaze on the pretty fan upon her lap. She felt she would burst in that silence and finally did, laughing.

"What is funny?" he asked.

"Nothing. I got into this carriage so I could speak with you, and now I don't know what we should talk about."

"Anything you want to talk about is fine with me," he said sympathetically.

"I do not understand how people are supposed to behave when they meet again. Considering the circumstances."

Hector drew a deep sigh. "I don't either. But back in the library, we spoke without impediments."

"Back there, I could have left any second I wanted."

"I can get out if I offend you," he offered.

"It's not necessary."

She examined him critically, like a painter ready to sketch a model. The shape of his mouth, the thick eyebrows, the strong hands encased in gloves.

"I wanted you to accompany me . . . to ride the same carriage, to prove that I could do it," she said, thinking out loud. "That I could sit still and in control of myself. From now on, if I bump into you, I can ignore you or speak to you or do whatever I wish."

"I see."

"Not that . . . not that I want to particularly ignore you. You must not think me cruel. But it's strange. I'm not mad at you. I don't see how people . . . I look to books for advice, you see, but they don't write these scenes."

What a mess, what nonsense. She ought to have stayed at the party. She frowned, her fingers dancing over the fan.

"Perhaps we can figure it out. Would you ever consider seeing me again?" he asked.

"Because you still want to make amends," she said, her voice almost cracking, to her annoyance. After she'd told him she was in control.

"Because your absence is noticeable."

"What is that suppo—?"

"I miss you, too," he said. "You also taught me."

The exasperation that had gathered at the tip of her tongue dissipated and she stared at him, baffled. They had arrived in front of her great-aunts' house and he exited the carriage, holding out a hand to help her down.

"Miss Beaulieu, I would like to see you again, but I won't pressure you to say yes," he concluded. "Thank you for your company."

If he'd been Luc Lémy, he might have punctuated their conversation by reminding her once again how pretty she looked, declaring that her hair was as dark as midnight. Hector was not Luc, and he'd say no such words.

She looked at him carefully, and saw a man. Not the romantic notion of a man she'd glimpsed before, her vision colored with memories of books and plays. A man, flawed and sad, who'd hurt her once, but whom she nonetheless esteemed. She saw, too, his genuine regret and the honest emotion lurking in his eyes.

"Have you been to the aquarium?" she asked.

"I had to fetch a shark from it at one point," he replied cautiously.

"Did you look around it?"

"Not on that occasion."

"I am headed there tomorrow morning. I should be arriving around eleven. I wouldn't think to demand that you escort me, and I imagine you are busy. But should you find yourself in the vicinity—"

"I will be there," he said at once.

He kissed her hand and she did not know whether to smile or not.

What kind of fool am I? she wondered. Because she could feel it there, in her chest, that flutter of affection, the thrill racing down her spine. She disliked it somewhat, how easily it came, and yet she lingered at his side for one more moment.

Chapter 8

HECTOR WOKE UP RATHER EARLY and he dedicated himself to his reading before finally heading to the bathroom for a hot shower and a shave. He always dressed well, knowing the kind of outfit that befitted a gentleman—he was studious, had learned to copy others—therefore, he should not have lingered before the mirror as he did, contemplating his reflection.

When it came to breakfast, he had no appetite and could hardly make himself drink his coffee.

It was because he had not slept well, he thought. He had not returned from the party at an untimely hour, but he'd had a fitful sleep.

It was too warm in the city. It felt more like summer than spring, and even if he left the window open, it did not help. There was no breeze to cool his bed.

That explained it, then, the restlessness, he told himself.

He boarded a carriage two streets from his home and arrived at the aquarium at the appointed time.

He saw Nina standing by the entrance and was relieved.

He had wondered if she might desert him. He offered her his arm and she took it.

The aquarium's ceilings were high, of cast iron and glass, allowing the light to flood the interior of the building. The floor was decorated with bright mosaics featuring mermaids and sea lions. There were many tanks filled with water and sea life, bright fish beckoning at every corner. Several tanks were shrouded with velvet curtains, and an attendant would pull them apart, giving people a chance to peruse the sea creatures, creating a sense of drama. Nina stood before each one of the tanks, whispering to him about the animals they were looking at.

Sometimes she'd stop, her back too straight, as if she'd remembered an important detail, and the smile that was blooming on her lips died. But it was not as painful as he'd imagined it, even if, for an instant, it might feel like his palm was sliding upon a piece of broken glass. Because she would also look eager and forget whatever worries plagued her, and her voice would rise and dip as they watched the animals.

When they were done observing the fish, they went to a seat by the fountain that guarded the entrance of the building, a stone mermaid spilling water from a conch. Nina had done most of the talking during their visit, but now, outside the aquarium, she grew quiet.

Even when he was young, he had not been terribly eloquent with women, and now the endeavor was doubly difficult, but Hector decided there was no point in sitting there in silence.

"May I ask you what may seem an indelicate question?"

"What is it?" she replied.

"Is Luc Lémy courting you?"

The idea had been buzzing through his head all morning long. When he'd caught sight of her at the party, they had been together and he'd thought that was the case, but then she said he had not escorted her.

"He flirts with me but he has said nothing of the sort yet. He might. It's difficult to know."

"He's not a bad man," Hector said.

"An underwhelming endorsement," she said.

He wanted to be fair in his assessment. He thought Luc Lémy volatile, movable, and perhaps lacking in imagination, but he had his positive qualities. When he wanted to, he could be a pleasant chap. To pretend otherwise would have been a lie.

"May I ask you a question that may seem indelicate this time?" she told him.

"You may."

"You and Valérie—"

"I have no interest in discussing Valérie," he said, cutting her off.

She grew serious, a frown upon her brow. "If there is a chance that we might be friends again, then we must be honest with each other. If you do not wish to tell me the truth, then I might as well leave now," she said, sitting firm and straight.

"What truth do you want?"

"You love her still?" Her tone was neutral; she might have been asking about the weather or the time a shop opened.

"No," he said with a similar coolness.

"She said you came back for her."

"I did everything for her."

"And yet she has vanished from your heart this effortlessly?" Nina asked. A flicker of emotion flashed in her eyes before she angled her head and he was not able to look at her.

The fountain behind them murmured in the language of water as he tried to find the right words. He spoke slowly.

"I have always loved artifice more than anything in the world. The painted backdrops and the lights on the stage, transforming the ordinary into a land of wonder. And it was like that with her. I met her in Frotnac, one summer. I had never seen anyone that lovely, of noble family, with fine manners, and I thought surely an exquisite woman would bring with her an exquisite love."

He did not wish to elaborate any more, but Nina had asked for the truth and he had the feeling anything in half measure would not satisfy. He pressed on, certain he would sound like an idiot by the end of the conversation.

"She loved me, but I was penniless and we couldn't marry. I left, determined to make my fortune. I gave her an engagement ring, and for a few months we wrote to each other. The letters grew scarce and then she told me she'd married someone else, a wealthy man."

"Gaetan," Nina said.

"Yes. It was like I lost my mind. I couldn't sleep, I couldn't think. One evening in Zhude, I made the draperies in my room catch on fire and they tossed me out. It was cold."

He could almost see himself, snowflakes in his hair and eyes shiny with tears, half-drunk with cheap wine, stumbling through the snow, his cap pulled down low.

"I got to the end of a street and I was near the sea and I stared at it. I thought 'What is to stop me from sinking in it?'"

"What stopped you?" she asked quietly.

"I thought . . . I thought, 'I'll show her. I'll get her back.' And insanely, this thought kept me alive. That thought became *me*."

He wondered if she judged him an absolute fool, but having begun his tale, he supposed he should finish it.

"She did not love me as I loved her, she never did. I did not understand that then, too lost in flights of fancy, but I see it now. I was enamored of an illusion for years on end, living on memories half-remembered and half-fabricated. At Oldhouse, something gave away. Even a sleepwalker must open his eyes at one point."

So many wasted days spent pining after a phantom. When he considered it now, he could hardly believe it. It had been madness, he thought. Like those men who would one day open the front door of their homes and step out and simply walk away for miles on end until they could walk no more, overtaken by a mysterious impulse that could not be explained. A "fugue," they called it. Pathological.

"It was not effortlessly. It tore me apart, but the poison has bled out," he concluded.

Hector felt her heavy gaze upon him, though he could not discern its essence. He stared back at her.

"You do not believe me."

"It is difficult to do so, considering the circumstances," she replied.

He recalled the way Nina had found them in the library, locked in an embrace, and he understood how it might seem somewhat improbable.

"There was a desperation in me last summer," Hector muttered. "I think I was trying to avoid the end of my old dreams because I could feel their demise dancing in the air. But they have ended. I was afraid of losing myself, of changing, and here I am and it's done."

"I'm sorry."

She meant it and her kindness as she spoke; it was beautiful and terrible because he realized how little he had appreciated it, how foolishly he had squandered his days staring across the table at Valérie. And Nina was there now, and despite it all, she had space enough for kindness. One more quality to admire—he had not lied when he told her that—he liked her intelligence, her humor, and her pluck.

"Thank you," he said.

Nina nodded, looking down. She dipped her fingers in the water of the fountain and the cuff of her dress was getting soaked, but she did not seem to mind.

"I have a gift for you," he said, reaching into his jacket.

He gave her the black box and she took off the lid, admiring the contents. The insect gleamed like gold.

"You said I shouldn't send the rest of them, but I did buy twenty. I thought you might want this one. It's like the one I saw you catch by that stream, and you were pleased with it."

"A water diving beetle. You remembered that," she said.

"Not at first. I told them to get me twenty beetles, but then there was one that looked like this and I recalled the one you caught. Do you want it? If you don't—"

"Yes," she said quickly.

She held the insect up to the light, and when she did, it seemed to change color depending on the angle, now growing brighter or duller. She placed it back in the box and secured the lid on.

"I did like the other beetles you sent," she said.

He chuckled at this only because the way she spoke it made it seem like a shameful secret.

"What amuses you?" she asked.

"Nothing," he replied.

Nina was peeved, blushing at his words even though once again he did not think he'd done or said anything that could cause any shame. He chuckled again, which, if he'd pause to consider it, was a feat since he tended to silences and a bit of starchiness.

"Thank you for the gift," she said once the color had faded from her cheeks.

"You are welcome."

"Twenty, you say?"

"One for each of your years."

"Whom did you buy them from?" she asked, sounding genuinely curious.

"Ferrier and Ferrier."

"You've been had. I wager you could have bought them at Theo's for a fraction of the cost," she replied cheekily.

"Next time I require twenty beetles, I'll ask you to accompany me to the shop."

Her eyes swept over him. Under the bright sun, her hair was so black, it seemed almost blue; it glinted, like a raven's wing. She dipped her hand in the water again, tracing circles with her fingers.

"Perhaps we might meet again if you'd like," he told her.

Nina did not speak and he could not begrudge her the caution in her face. There would be no leaps and bounds between them.

He did not wish to assume that she'd care about him anymore, even if she had at Oldhouse. A year had passed. And Hector himself was not sure where all this might lead; he'd had scant practice at the sport of affection. He'd seldom wanted it, preferring to dwell in the pits of melancholy. He was, in short, a jumble of thoughts and feelings, uncomfortably raw for a man his age.

"We could attempt to become friends once more, as you said," he proposed nevertheless, for he did need her to realize this was on his mind.

Her body was tense, her fingers stilling in the water. She looked at him and he thought it might all come to naught, because she'd suddenly drifted far, her thoughts no doubt wary. But then Nina smiled. It was like looking down and finding the first green sprouts rising from the frozen, black earth. Almost invisible and yet there, heralding spring.

"Perhaps," she said.

"Perhaps," he repeated.

Her hazy smile grew more obvious.

It was something. It was something indeed.

Chapter 9

AGNES HADUIER WAS OLDER THAN Valérie and as ugly as a worn sow, but she attempted to compensate for her inadequacies by purchasing the most expensive, fabulous dresses and sporting an array of highly elaborate hats. Though they moved in the same social circles and had known each other for years, they were not friends. Valérie couldn't truly trust anyone who was not a member of her family. She reserved her devotion for the Véries, the importance of blood kin and duty to her own imprinted on her since an early age.

"How are your beloved roses doing, Valérie?" Agnes asked.

"Blooming beautifully," Valérie replied. Agnes had a large garden, but it was tacky and disorganized compared to Valérie's perfect rose ensemble.

Agnes smiled while Valérie looked at her with a face of flawless alabaster, hiding the indifference that assaulted her in the presence of this woman. Agnes wore a blue hat with a feather sprouting from the back, which Valérie found ostentatious and off-putting.

"I was sorry you could not make it to my party."

"Yes, I apologize for that," Valérie said dryly. She had sent the woman a note promptly the morning after the party. She always minded her courtesies—what else could Agnes want now?

"My dear, if you had gone . . . well, perhaps . . . This is hard for me to say, but I feel it is my duty to inform you that your cousin Antonina behaved poorly."

"How poorly?"

"There was some small matter about her doing a few levitation tricks. Very *common,* I'm afraid. No, but the real issue, and the reason why I come here today, is to warn you about that other matter."

Agnes paused dramatically, as she was wont to do when she was spreading her poison. Nothing delighted her more than gossip. She had a barbed tongue.

"She was seen leaving the party in the company of a man, my dear. That performer, Hector Auvray. Everyone speaks about him these days, but he's too quiet in person. I wouldn't have invited him to the party, but my husband insisted. You know how he is about these sorts of people. Can't get enough of them."

It was a testament to Valérie's self-control that she did not begin screaming at the top of her lungs, for that was exactly what she wished to do. Instead, she managed to stay sitting in her chair and stare at Agnes with cool eyes.

"Did you see them?" Valérie asked.

"No. My friend Bertrand Roge did. Antonina, leaving with that man, and you can be sure he was *not* her escort to the party, not at all. And he is essentially a theater performer! Dear me, there will be talk of this."

Yes, there would. Which was precisely why Agnes had come. Not to warn Valérie, but to relish her discomfort knowing how embarrassing the incident could be. They'd say Antonina knew nothing of deportment; they'd gossip about the Beaulieus.

And Hector. Hector, why was he doing this?

I shall kill that girl, Valérie thought. *She provides me nothing but woe.*

"I am glad you have brought this to my attention. You must understand I would be grateful if you could do anything to mitigate such talk," Valérie said.

"I will speak to Mr. Roge, but one can't predict how these matters will go."

In Loisail, certain things were not said out loud. Secrets were written in the movement of a fan or the gestures with a glove. Innocent words hid the sharpness of knives. Now Agnes and Valérie were speaking in this code.

"I would be eternally grateful for your assistance."

"I shall try. In the meantime, will you be supping with us next week? My husband was dearly hoping you and Gaetan would come to our Thursday soirée, a last-minute reunion I've organized. Gaetan is a busy man, hard to talk to these days."

Yes. That was it. Tit for tat. Valérie didn't like Agnes, but now she'd have to make an appearance at her stupid get-together while Gaetan would be whisked away to the smoking room to discuss money matters. The Haduiers were not paupers, but everyone knew they spent more than they should and their extravagant lifestyle was funded with generous loans, which they repaid haphazardly. They owed Gaetan money and would try to defer payment.

Vipers and scorpions, she thought.

"I believe we can make it," Valérie said.

"Thank you. I have taken up too much of your time. It has been lovely speaking with you."

"Thank you, dearest Agnes. You will forgive me if I do not rise and escort you out. I suddenly feel rather tired," Valérie said.

It was undeniably rude not to stand and kiss the woman on the cheek, but then Valérie was trying to make a point. Agnes gave her a stiff nod.

When the perfumed cow had exited the room, Valérie allowed herself to dig her nails into the arms of her chair.

Antonina. That stupid whore. What else could be expected of her? But most important, what was Hector thinking?

They are on speaking terms, but that means nothing, she thought. But, no, it was bad. It could ruin all her plans. Say, for example, that he was merely being polite. That still meant a possible distraction, Antonina's head turned away from Luc Lémy. And at worst, he was a true rival for her affection.

Valérie needed Antonina to marry Luc. Hector was a wedge between them.

Without meaning to, she also thought about him in other terms. Hector was hers. He was always hers, and even if she wouldn't have him, he should remain so.

Valérie rose and went to the office, where she wrote a quick, stern missive. She instructed a servant to arrange for it to be delivered right away to the home of Luc Lémy.

Luc did not take too long to arrive, though the minutes were like sandpaper against Valérie's skin. She gave word that he should be brought to the conservatory, where she paced among her flowers, and there he greeted her with that charming smile of his and a bow.

"You are, as usual, utterly lovely," he said, and though he spoke with ease, the tone of her message had impressed the urgency of this meeting upon him: his eyes were anxious.

"Thank you," she said tartly.

She needed him to understand the gravity of the situation—rather than trying to delicately explain the matter, she decided to be blunt.

"Tell me, Mr. Lémy, exactly how difficult is it to seduce a naive country girl?"

"Pardon me?" Luc replied. He had opened his cigarette case and froze in astonishment.

"Antonina. She should be head over heels in love with you by now. You've had many days to reel her in, and yet what happens? I hear Auvray may be interested in her again."

"What exactly did you hear?" Luc asked.

"He escorted her home after Haduier's party."

"I was there. I had no idea Hector was there, too," Luc said, flustered.

"Did you even realize she was gone?"

The guilt tattooed across his face would have been sufficient proof for her, but then he babbled a few words. "No, I did—"

"Of course not. What were you doing exactly?" Valérie asked.

"Talking to friends. Dancing."

"Dancing. Not with Antonina, I would think, or else she would have been in your arms and it would have been difficult for Hector to extract her from them."

She imagined how it had gone. Luc had talked to his "friends," and after a bit of drinking and a bit of dancing, he'd forgotten all about her. Perhaps he had even left the party with these "friends," looking for other sport, and had imagined that Antonina was still at the Haduiers' home, safe and sound. He could not have predicted she would meet Hector or leave with him, but he should have been paying more attention. Now who knew what this would cost them.

"In my defense, I had not received approval from your husband to

court Antonina until a couple of days ago. It would have been improper—"

"Save your talk of manners. Do not pretend you have not lured a
woman before. A kiss or two, a bit of fumbling with each other is all it
should take."

He blushed like an idiot. As if the first thought in the mind of a man
of his ilk was not how to lift a woman's skirts and rut between her legs.
Valérie had asked about him; she knew about a dancer a year prior and a
painter's model the year before that, and the countless strings of nobod-
ies he carried behind him.

"Antonina is a lady," Luc said. "You can't be suggesting I attempt to
compromise her."

"You'll compromise her, whether on your wedding night or sooner
than that. Sooner would be better if it would help our cause. Don't stare
at me like that, boy. I speak from common sense. If you won't, I'm sure
Hector Auvray can volunteer to do the honor, then toss her at your feet."

She did not truly think Hector would commit such an impudent act;
he was too taken with the idea of being a gentleman. Valérie recalled
how sweet he had been, his infinite devotion.

But Luc need not know that. Luc needed fear, not reassurances.

"Surely you jest—"

"Mr. Auvray is not like you and me. He's a performer, and theater is
not exactly a temple of virtue, as I'm sure you have discovered in your
dalliances with actresses and dancers. How did you ply those? Champagne and a few choice words of romance? Is that not enough for her?"

"I am attempting to do right with Miss Beaulieu. As I said, she is a
lady," he stammered.

Valérie felt almost like laughing at that comment. Why, a dissolute
cad like this was developing fine morals? What was the world coming
to? Did he not wish to win this game? Valérie *did* want to win, and she
was going to ensure the pieces moved across the board as she'd planned.

"Not for long, if you let her dangle from the arm of another man,"
Valérie told him.

She caught the spark of anger in his eyes. There it was, what she
needed. Not fine, clean sentiments but hurt pride and common jealousy.

"Do you truly want Antonina and her money?"

"I want her for more than her money," he replied, his voice vehement.

Greed was good, but Valérie thought it was not greed speaking. It was his covetous heart, which now had focused on Antonina and aimed to consume her.

Fine. Even better. Whatever would stir this young man's blood and make him leap into the fray, no more cautious steps.

Chapter 10

Hector and Étienne were supping at the Crimson Fox again, only luckily they'd gone earlier and it was not so packed as the last time. All the tables outside, with their red parasols, were taken. Étienne and Hector had managed to wedge themselves near the door that led to the patio, but even the air blowing in was warm. It had rained the night before, briefly, and the temperature had not dropped.

Étienne held a glass of water next to his forehead in an effort to cool himself. Hector was hungry, but their waiter had yet to drop by to take their order. They were short-staffed that day.

"If I could carry a bucket with ice all day long, I would," Étienne said.

"I think I'll spend the rest of my evening in the bathtub," Hector replied.

"That's no fun."

"I can read even if I'm in the bathtub."

"I know you'd read, that's exactly the problem."

Hector raised his head, spotting Luc Lémy, who'd stomped into the establishment. He had a determined look as he moved toward their table.

"There comes your brother," Hector said.

"Really?" Étienne replied. "He didn't say he was joining us."

Luc sat down next to Étienne and across from Hector. He immediately reached for his cigarette case, all eager fingers and a scowl on his face. Hector wondered what had brought on one of his moods. When Luc didn't have money or couldn't get his hands on a new toy, he sulked, although this time he appeared a bit worse than usual.

"Hello to you," Étienne said.

"Hello," Luc grumbled.

Luc snapped his case shut.

"We were—" Étienne began, but his brother shushed him.

"You spirited Nina away from Haduier's party the other night," Luc said, his eyes fixed on Hector.

Hector suddenly understood the cause and extent of Luc's irritation.

"Yes. She wanted to leave," Hector said.

"Do you realize the kind of talk that leads to? A gentleman and a lady, alone at night?" Luc asked. "You did not escort her to the party, you had no business taking her home."

"We are friends and well acquainted. We spent plenty of time alone at Oldhouse."

"It doesn't matter and you know that."

"I did not withdraw my courtship request, thus if anyone dares to say anything, Nina can tell them Gaetan approves of me."

"That is nonsense. No one will ask her what is going on between you and her, they'll whisper behind her back. It aggravates me."

"It aggravates *you*?" Hector said. If any man had a cause to be upset with him, it might have been Gaetan, since Nina was his cousin.

Luc's face changed from angry to petulant. He looked now not like a sulking child but a boy who has scarfed down a whole cake, but does not care if he will have a stomachache. It absolutely rankled Hector.

"I have spoken with Gaetan Beaulieu, and he has agreed I may court Nina. I would like to marry her sooner rather than later."

"Has she been informed of this?" Hector replied, unable to suppress a chuckle. "I'm not sure she knows."

"Are you making fun of me?" Luc turned to Étienne. "He is making fun of me."

"I don't think he's making fun of anyone," Étienne replied. "Luc, let's get you a drink."

"I don't want a drink. I want him to stay away from my bride."

As if to emphasize his point, Luc slammed his hand against the table;

then he lit his cigarette and leaned back in his chair, challenging Hector with his gaze.

"She's not yours," Hector replied.

"Pardon me?" Luc said.

"She's not yours. She's not mine. She's nobody's. Stop behaving like a brat."

Hector spoke sternly, and for a moment he thought Luc might regain the use of his senses and see how utterly peevish he was being, but instead the young man grew more stupid.

"Now, listen to me, Hector. You had your chance. You didn't take it. This is my time now, and I'll be damned if I'm going to have you weaseling your way back into her life."

"What do you want?" Hector asked quietly. "Do you want a fight? Will that make you feel better? I've done you no wrong. She wished to go home, I took her in my carriage."

"You shouldn't have."

"I will offer no apologies to you."

Luc tossed his cigarette at Hector. It was headed toward his lap, but Hector stopped it midair, his talent at work, then flicked it away, crushing it under the sole of his shoe.

Luc did not seem happy with this display, having thought he could pelt him with the cigarette. "I want no apologies, but if I even think you've spoken to her again, I'll break your jaw."

"Try it now," Hector shot back.

Luc rose from his seat, ready to put the threat into action. Hector was not one for fistfights, but he had not shied away from physical confrontation when it was necessary. The company he kept had not been the most gentle one in his youth. And though normally the thrill of a fight held little appeal, he was angry and he wanted to throw a few well-placed punches.

Étienne reached out and grabbed his brother by the arm, speaking quickly. "Stop it, the both of you."

Luc shoved his brother away and straightened himself up. He did not bid either of them good-bye, instead preferring to glare at Hector before stomping off.

For a moment Hector considered tossing the remains of the damn cigarette at the back of Luc's head.

"That was jolly," Étienne said, drumming his fingers against the sides of his glass. "You didn't tell me you were speaking with Nina again."

"Only recently. You didn't tell me Luc was pursuing her," he replied.

"I had no idea. I thought he had a new fancy, but he didn't say it was her."

A fancy. Yes, no doubt it was hard to keep track of the women who danced in and out of Luc Lémy's life, but he did not think this "a fancy." As far as Hector knew, Luc Lémy had not courted a lady. He'd flirted with a good number of them and even enticed a few into his bed. Étienne had told Hector that one time, Luc had gotten himself into a whole lot of trouble over Mie Karlson, a diplomat's wife. But then, Luc collected women like other men collected coins or stamps, and ladies—much less marriage—were beyond his interest.

"What now?" Étienne asked, frowning.

"Do you think he is serious?" Hector asked.

"About what, breaking your jaw?"

"Her. Marriage."

"How am I supposed to know?" Étienne replied.

"He seems serious to me," Hector asserted.

He recalled what Nina had said, that Luc flirted with her. Gaetan might not have spoken with her about the matter already, but surely he would soon. At this moment, he could be summoning his cousin to let her know that Luc Lémy was interested in her. How would the conversation end?

He thought back to the party and how they'd looked together. They had been at ease, Luc acting his charming self and she interested in the performance. And at Oldhouse, he tried to remember what they'd been like. Nina had spent most of her time with Hector, but they all gathered for games and conversation. They got along well enough, he thought.

They'd make a pretty pair, a study in contrasts, Luc with his blond good looks and Nina with her black hair.

Antonina Lémy, he thought.

It sounded awful.

Étienne, attuned to Hector's moods, picked up on that thread. He narrowed his eyes at his friend. "Hector, please tell me I'm wrong, please tell me you're not—"

"I'm heading home," Hector said. "Suddenly the bathtub seems more appealing."

"Hector, don't start with a new madness."

"Have a good evening, Étienne," he said, his voice clipped.

As he walked toward a busy avenue, hoping he might find a carriage to take him home, Hector considered paying Nina a visit. He quickly discarded the idea. What would he say? That he and Luc Lémy had almost come to blows over her? And exactly over what?

Hector knew he and Nina were standing on ever-shifting sands. He was unsure where they were headed, too. It was strange because he was always sure of his actions, proceeding with the certainty of an arrow. It had been like that when he romanced Valérie, as he tried to fashion a career for himself, and in a myriad of business matters. The doubt that often clouded him when it came to Nina was odd, like listening to a tune and not knowing the steps of the dance.

At this point, Hector felt he could say nothing. Nina was a young lady in her second Grand Season, and she would be expected to catch the attention of suitors. Luc Lémy was a man of superior breeding, ripe for marriage, and that he should have turned his eyes toward Nina could not be faulted.

As Luc had pointed out, Hector threw away his chance. Hector's pitiful gifts, the attempts at establishing new ties with Nina, colored only more vehemently that truth.

He managed to attract the attention of a coachman and boarded the carriage.

"Boniface, please," he said.

The carriage moved under the shade of the light green linden trees, trotting quietly.

"Antonina Lémy," he whispered, and the words left him with a sour taste in his mouth.

Chapter 11

NINA'S GREAT-AUNTS ALWAYS TOOK A long time to go out. That day, they had spent nearly an hour bickering with one another even though they were paying only one visit, and that was to Penelope Ferse, who lived three streets away. Penelope was a pigeon fancier, and both Lise and Linette, given their interest in birds, found this hobby an exciting topic of conversation.

Once her great-aunts had left with many good-byes and a kiss on her cheek, Nina went to sit on the steps behind the house, reading by the canal. It was a hot day and the house felt stuffy even with all its windows open.

"Miss, Mr. Lémy is here to see you," Roslyn, her great-aunts' maid, said.

Nina's hair was in a long braid down her back, her head protected by a straw hat, and she wore a thin muslin dress, rather informal, but then she had not thought she'd have company. She paused before the mirror outside the parlor to make sure her hair was not, as her sister put it, a wasp's nest; then she grabbed the green wrapper the maid had brought down for her and greeted Luc.

"Antonina. It is gracious of you to meet with me," he said.

"It is always good to see you," she replied.

She gestured to the maid, who was waiting for orders from Nina, and quietly asked her to bring a pitcher of lemonade. Luc and Nina sat down, he in an overstuffed chair and she on the sofa.

"I have come with good news," he said.

"What kind?"

"I have spoken to your cousin, and he has given me permission to court you. I imagine he will be sharing the news with you himself soon, but I asked him that I be allowed to speak to you first. I hope you are pleased."

Pleased? When Gaetan had told her Hector was interested in courting her, she could hardly contain herself, feeling as if she would burst into a million pieces. The news of Luc's proposed courtship startled Nina somewhat, and she did feel her breath catch in her throat—despite the fact that she had imagined this day might come—yet she was not elated.

"I am flattered," Nina said.

"I want you to know I think you are pretty." He smiled, bright as sunshine.

She looked down, toying with the fringe of her shawl.

Luc rose and sat next to Nina, his hands falling over hers, holding them still. "It would not be objectionable if we kissed," he said.

"It would be too strange at this point," she replied.

He sighed but did not remove his hands from her own, shaking his head. "What is it that I am doing wrong?"

"You are doing nothing wrong. You are a lovely young man."

"But?"

Nina did not say anything. She did not know what to say. A year before, she might have been thrilled at this opportunity. He was like the prince from a fairy tale, the hero from a cheap novel—tattered pages and all—she'd read. She had learned about romance on the printed page but the realities of heartache had matured her; she could not look at him with the naive eyes of a child.

"Do not tell me it is that ruffian, Hector Auvray, who has you like this!" Luc exclaimed.

"No," she replied. "It is not so."

Luc stood up and paced in front of her. "He makes my blood boil. I should have beat him bloody today."

"Today?"

"He was with my brother at the Crimson Fox."

"You did not harm him, did you?" she asked, clutching the shawl.

"No! I should have. It might have given me satisfaction. He's a wretch from the gutters."

Nina sighed. "You should not be unkind. He is a friend of your family's."

"My brother's friend, not mine. And you speak to him! You left a party with him!"

Someone had seen them. She recalled what Luc had said about old hens.

"You speak to many ladies, Luc," she said in a matter-of-fact tone.

Oddly enough, Luc blushed a bit and he looked ashamed, suddenly running a hand down the lapel of his coat, as if he were cleaning away crumbs.

"You must not be jealous. I talk to a lot of people," he said.

"I am not jealous. I am pointing out how silly it is for you to complain that I speak with one man when you speak to many women. Why is it men can do as they please?"

"Come, now, I'll speak to no other girls from now on."

"I didn't say you should stop. I merely made a point that it seems unfair you should be jealous."

"I can't help it." He stepped forward and pulled her to her feet. "I want you to think of me and me alone," he said. "When you wake up each morning and when you go to sleep, and as you lie in bed each night, I want you to think of me."

Now he'd pulled her closer to him, and she felt paper-thin. It was hot inside and growing warmer, and the maid, she had not returned with the pitcher of lemonade. Perhaps she thought she ought to leave them alone.

"Luc, please," she said.

He kissed the corner of her mouth. "Please, what?" he asked, but then he did not allow her to reply.

He leisurely kissed her, a hand sneaking up to toy with a strand of her hair, the other at her waist. It was pleasant, the feel of his mouth and the elation she could now recognize as desire. She had demurred a few moments before, but she was young, infused with passion that often sought an escape and which at this moment had found him.

When he paused in his ministrations, he looked proud of himself. He was eager and he was admirable at that sport, she could tell. It might have embarrassed her if Nina had not been more intrigued than offended. Curiosity was her fault.

She initiated a kiss, attempting to imitate what he'd done, her hands in his hair this time. It was pleasant. The priest back home forbade such a thing, to be sure, but the church where they prayed was old. In the rafters lived beetles that bored into the wood, and Nina had spent more time trying to listen to their tapping sounds than to the priest. When the sun shone through the colored windows, painting martyrs upon the floor, all she could think about was the moment she might go outside and chase dragonflies by the river.

Nina had never had much appreciation for talks of damnation and sins. She existed, and had always existed, in a rather untamed state, which was facilitated by her family, who confused her intellectual inclinations with a wholesome disposition. They saw her explosions, when they took place, as a child's tantrums and could not imagine she was like the rivers and streams and forests she loved, riotous and luxuriant.

"See? It will be a delightful courtship," Luc told her. "You'll want to marry me in a fortnight. Like the moon in the sky, I can already feel you magnetized by my orbit."

Nina chuckled at his high-flown words. How silly he was, but it was all right. She did not mind.

"It'll take more than a fortnight, and the moon cannot be magnetized. It is gravity that attracts a celestial object to another," she said.

"Place a wager? Let us kiss again."

"No," she said, but she smiled at him.

"To a wager or a kiss?"

"To both."

"You'll rethink those words soon enough."

She rolled her eyes at him. The maid came back at last and set the tray with the pitcher on a table. Nina poured the lemonade herself, willing the pitcher to rise and tilt with the movement of two fingers on her right hand. She did not spill a single drop.

Nina then grabbed the glass and handed it to Luc. He frowned. Roslyn asked them if they needed anything else, and when Nina said no, she bowed her head politely and exited the room.

Luc was still frowning, staring at Nina.

"What?" she asked.

"The movement, with the pitcher and the glass," he said. "The maid saw you."

"Roslyn? She's seen me do that plenty of times. I can pour tea, lemonade, and any spirit you fancy. I haven't figured out how to uncork a bottle of champagne."

"Nina, if you want to play these games in the privacy of your room, I will not chide you, but in the presence of others, you should restrain yourself," he replied.

"You'll chide me only when others look at me, then," she said.

"With your family, you may do as you please, but outsiders are another matter entirely."

Nina crossed her arms against her chest and scowled.

"Look, you mustn't take it badly. Surely people have explained this to you. Your cousin Valérie must have—"

He could not have said a worse thing. Nina snapped her head up, furious at the mention of the woman's name. "I don't care what Valérie thinks of me. What is objectionable about it?"

"It is not normal. It is a performance at a fair, like the freaks they display for a few coins," he said.

"The freaks?"

"I don't mean *you*. I mean, in general, these are carnival games, these are things unfit for ladies." He stepped forward, wrapped his arms around her, and tipped her head up.

Her cheeks flared at the thought of his lips against hers, but she shook her head regardless of it and would not allow it.

"Nina, Nina—"

"No! You can't kiss me and make everything better anytime I am upset," she said, freeing herself from his grasp.

"But it is a ridiculous thing to be upset about!"

"This is me, Luc Lémy. Like my eye color and my hair, like the mole on my wrist, this is *me*. Why is it so difficult for everyone to see that?" she asked him.

"You have lovely hair and lovely eyes. We should not fight," he said.

He meant to take her in his arms once more, but then came the voices of her great-aunts as they returned home, and Nina was grateful for the interruption. She was both flustered and annoyed. The old ladies were pleased to see Luc Lémy, and he diligently greeted them, tossing them many choice compliments.

When he bade all of them good-bye, he held Nina's hand tight and she blushed, but she was upset.

During dinner she considered the matter more evenly. He meant well and his comment was not uncommon. Her family had said similar things to her, her mother fretting over the ability. She knew that they'd sent her to the city because the youths nearby, like the Meinard boy, viewed her with suspicion.

And yet!

She stood in her room, by the window, contemplating the canal as she twirled a card in the air.

Chapter 12

Nina Beaulieu stood admiring the great papier-mâché horse's head resting in his dressing room. It reached above her waist and had been damaged a bit during a recent performance: an ear had fallen off. Hector had plenty of people who could repair it for him, but he liked to do these things himself when he had the chance. He'd handled all his props and costumes by necessity when he was starting in the business, and could even mend trousers and shirts.

"How do you like the reality behind the spectacle?" he asked.

She'd insisted in taking a look inside the theater, although he had meant to meet her outside of it and head for a walk. He'd offered her a tour of the whole building, Dufren walking with them as a sort of impromptu chaperone, and Hector showed her the inner workings of his show. She seemed pleased looking at the backdrops and ropes, but he saw no harm in asking.

"It's wonderful," she said. "Did you always know you wanted to do this?"

"I didn't have a choice, seeing as both my parents performed—but, yes. I enjoy it."

"You could have done something else, I'm sure."

"Possibly. But why waste my talent?" he asked.

"True enough. It's not as if every man you pass on the street can lift an elephant with his mind."

She patted the horse's head. She was guarded. He did not ask what was wrong, feeling no need to rush the conversation. She'd asked to see him, and they were both slowly stumbling along a path, trying to determine whether they could become friends again. He was glad to be silent and let her speak her mind when she felt like it.

"Did you ever wish you could be normal?" she asked. "Did you ever wish your talent away?"

"And miss the chance to lift those pesky elephants?"

She smiled at that and turned around to look at him. "No doubts, then?"

"Maybe when I was young. I suppose you've considered it. I didn't realize that."

"At times. I . . . I want to control it, but sometimes I want it gone."

"You or others?" he asked.

"Does it matter?"

"It's an important distinction."

Nina sighed. "Certain days I believe that it might be easier to be like any other, ordinary lady."

Hector held both her hands between his and smiled down at her. "Nina, you can never be ordinary."

The warmth of his gesture was both genuine and unexpected, and it startled them both. There was a distance, a bracketing of their emotions, that held them at bay. When either of them breached the line that separated them, it was uncomfortable.

They could speak now, they could even smile at each other, but the wounds were there. These were not old battle scars, but fresh lines upon the flesh. They might mend, one day.

"It seems I also can't be a lady," she said, sounding nervous. She turned away from him, and her eyes alighted on the boxes of insects he'd left strewn across his desk. She drifted toward them, picking one up and examining its contents. "More beetles," she said.

"I did say I bought twenty," he replied, standing next to the desk and glancing down at the boxes, then back at her.

"But there are so many here. Your numbers don't add up."

"I bought a few more," he admitted.

He'd bought a few books, too, trying to determine exactly what he was looking at.

"Are you purchasing them in bulk now?"

"I'm starting to appreciate the beauty of insects."

"You say that to make me happy."

"I do not say things merely to please you," he replied, rather serious.

"But you didn't care about them before," she countered.

"A man may change his mind."

Again she appeared guarded, silence stretching between them. The discomfort of neither knowing their place, or proper role.

"I won't ask you why you've come to see me today, but you may always tell me what you are thinking," he told her.

Her eyes flicked to him but they were interrupted before she could speak.

"Hector, a word with you?" Mr. Dufren asked. He was standing at the entrance with papers in his hands. Hector had left the door wide open, thinking it would be less unseemly that way. Nina was an unmarried lady, after all. Appearances mattered. The open door, however, invited conversation from others, like now, Dufren awaiting him.

"I'll be back soon," Hector told her.

"Soon" turned out to be closer to fifteen minutes. When he returned and walked in, he saw Nina had moved behind his desk and was looking at his books, her fingers drifting across the spines, like a musician teasing the strings of a guitar.

She stepped back and made a book drift toward her, opening it as if it were a fan, the pages making a soft rustling sound.

There was something about Nina, something he struggled to name. It had to do with her hair like blackbird feathers and the way her hands fluttered when she was excited and how she bit her lips when she thought no one was looking.

Hector was focused. He looked at details. And nothing made him nervous; he could tame a crowd of hundreds with ease.

Yet he was nervous now, staring stupidly at her, and the force of that something held him in thrall.

She must have felt the weight of his gaze because she suddenly caught the book between her hands and pressed it against her chest. "Practice makes perfect," she said, sounding unsure of herself. She placed the book on his desk and pointed across the room, her voice cheerful yet strained. "What is that? I can't figure it out," she said. "Is that an ostrich feather?"

"That's a pirate's hat," he said, glancing at the corner where he kept the changing screen and his clothing.

"No."

"Do you want to try it on?"

He pushed the screen aside to reveal the mirror and a wardrobe. It was a tattered old screen, faded golden lions against black. He'd had it for a long time. The wardrobe was also a humble piece of furniture, scratched and battered, but big enough to contain an array of clothes.

The mirror was grander. Gilded, tall, allowing Hector to see himself entirely. He'd had to do with a cracked hand mirror when he was young, enduring costume changes in the back of patched-up tents.

Back when he thought only of Valérie.

That had been long, long ago.

He'd taught himself how to dress properly, how to speak properly, what items to order from a menu, and the fashionable dances. All for that one woman.

What good had it done him?

None.

And now, *this* woman, nothing of what he knew could help with her. That was the crux of the matter. He'd learned so much and yet so little.

"Come on," Hector said, setting the hat atop her head. "There's a coat to go with it."

"When did you dress as a pirate?"

"Two years ago, maybe. I despise costumes, but Dufren says it can't always be me in a black jacket. Here."

He pulled out a coat of rich, crimson brocade from the wardrobe and set it on Nina's shoulders. It was far too large for her, but the color was pleasing. It gave her an impish quality.

"If you ever compete against me, dress in brocade," he told her. "Though maybe you'll leave me without any business if you do."

He had meant to rest a hand on her shoulder, but at the last second, he stilled himself and his hand hovered but did not touch her.

He caught her gaze in the mirror and froze.

He was not used to this.

Everything about Valérie had been violent, hasty. There wasn't any time for them. The minutes of the day escaped them, and they suffered each lost second. Swift excesses and even swifter emotions.

He'd been young. Now that he was older, wiser, he ought to comport himself better.

He was a man grown, self-assured and seasoned.

He was behaving worse than when he'd been a boy. At least back then, he understood what he wanted, he could string a sentence together.

Now it was like stumbling in the dark, like stuffing thorns in his mouth.

He shoved his hands in his pockets, feeling ridiculous.

What he wanted to say, what he should say, was *I keep thinking about you, it frightens me.*

He might have said it, but then she slid the coat from her lean shoulders, straightened herself up, and took off the hat. "Luc Lémy courts me now," she said in a small voice. "I thought I should say this."

He finally understood why she'd been nervous and those uncomfortable pauses between them. He understood why she'd come to see him. It was Luc Lémy.

The invisible thorn, it bit into his tongue, and yet he found he could speak at last and his voice was cool.

"You must be pleased."

"He's fun," she said, and luckily Hector did not wince.

"I'm sure he is."

Hector went behind his desk. His papers were all in their place, but he pretended to look for an envelope so he could keep his eyes down and away from her. He was irritated and he did not want her to notice.

"He said you fought the other day," she told him.

"We had a misunderstanding."

"About me."

"He's hotheaded."

"Hector, Luc is—"

He did look up at her now, and his gaze was flat. "Very fond of you. I know. It makes me happy to see you happy."

Nina looked confused and also relieved and who the hell knew what else. He could not tell. He also had no idea if he meant what he had said, and that was deeply troubling.

No, he had. He wanted to see her happy. It was, if it hadn't . . . but . . .

Luc Lémy. But Hector had no reason to voice an opinion when he had not been asked to give one, and no reason to be upset after the way he had behaved the previous summer. As Luc had cheekily put it, he'd had his chance. It was Luc who was courting Nina now, Luc who would attempt to win her affections. For a gentleman, it would have been unseemly to interfere.

For the man who had broken Nina's heart, it would be even more unseemly.

Hector had no right to whisper a word or think an ill thought of Luc.

He swallowed the thorns and smiled at her.

She smiled back tremulously, like a butterfly testing her wings, and he thought, *She does like Luc.*

"I should go. My great-aunts complain that I miss mealtimes and then the maid must warm my supper," Nina said.

"It's been a pleasure seeing you again."

"I'll stop by another time," she promised. "I'll send a note."

After she'd left, he wondered when that would be and shook his head.

Chapter 13

THERE WERE NO PINES AT Pine Lake Park, which rendered the origin of its name a mystery. There was a lake, and one could rent boats and row across it. Unlike most of the other parks of the city, which exhibited a symmetrical arrangement of trees and garden beds with a fountain or an important monument at its heart, Pine Lake Park was a chaotic assemblage of well-trodden paths and clumps of trees.

"And then he confiscated the motorcar," Luc concluded dramatically as they approached one of those clumps.

"Can it be really 'confiscated' when it belongs to your brother?" Nina asked.

"You do not understand. It's the heartlessness of the matter."

From atop the hill, one had a lovely view of the lake, and the trees provided needed shelter from the sun, making it the perfect spot to linger.

"How heartless, yes, to deprive you of your toys," she said.

"You mock me."

Nina reached above her head, holding on to an overhanging branch with her left arm while she pointed with her free one at the lake. "We should rent a boat and row across the water."

"I'm afraid I'm not a man fit for manual labor," Luc replied.

"I'll row you if you can't," Nina said with a chuckle.

"That would not be gentlemanly."

"It would be fun."

Luc looked up, frowning. "It's sunny. I'll burn."

"A few freckles never killed anyone."

"I didn't say they'd kill me. I don't like them."

"You are the vainest man in the world."

Perhaps he had earned his vanity. The light filtered through the leaves, making his hair golden, like a halo, and his eyes were of a magnificent blue.

Luc moved closer to her and pressed her back gently against a tree, bending down for a kiss. She rested a palm against the trunk of the tree, tracing the rough texture of the bark, while her other hand rose to touch his cheek.

She had forgiven him for their tiff the other day, and quickly at that. He was an expert at begging for forgiveness, contrite words slipping easily from his tongue. Though she accepted the words and the peace offering in the shape of this walk through the park, she felt sad.

"Someone will see," she said, turning her head, her eyes on the lake.

"No one can see us here."

He was right. The grove was shady and cool, a wall of leaves and tree trunks shielding them from passersby. Not that there were passersby. No path led by the grove. They were alone. He had, perhaps, chosen this location strategically, knowing they would not be bothered.

"Maybe," she conceded. She tried to slide away from him, her eyes on the lake. "We must hurry if we are going to rent a boat, or they'll all be taken."

"There's time enough for that," he replied.

She parted her lips and Luc kissed her again, and this time he was too eager. He pressed her more firmly against the tree; the bark bit into her back, and his hands rested on her waist.

They'd warned her of men who took liberties with women. Both her mother and Valérie, and her cousins back at Oldhouse. They had *not* warned her that sometimes she might *want* to have certain liberties taken. They had also not explained what might happen when her body thrummed, electric, yet her heart remained subdued.

The books she'd read were of no help either—the heroines in them fainted whenever a man kissed them.

She did not feel like fainting. Her pulse did quicken, but it was not the same—she did not want to think it, but it wasn't the same as it was with Hector. When he'd walked into a room, she could not help but smile, and when he stood in front of her, she'd been very alive, heart hammering in her chest. Sometimes she had held her breath in anticipation, thinking he might kiss her, and that day at the tower, he had.

Luc's fingers traced her neck now.

She caught his hand and looked at him. "Luc, stop."

"Hmm?"

She shoved him back, only a smidgen of her talent on display, and he stumbled, frowning. "Luc, I would not want to mislead you," she said, glad she had the presence of mind to speak firmly.

"How so?" he asked.

"I enjoy your company and you are one of the most charming men that I've ever met, but I do not want you to think we are sweethearts. Or that anything may come of this."

He chuckled, but it was not a merry sound. Even so, he tried to maintain a mask of good humor. "You sound like me. I didn't think a woman would ever tell me this."

The memory of Hector's words, when they'd first met, echoed in her mind. *Do you talk to all men in this manner?*

"I am sorry," she replied. "You'll judge me a flirt and a poor example of a lady now."

"Nonsense," he said. "Nina, Nina, I don't understand why you must look somber and begin to overthink—"

"I do not overthink anything, but when I see you looking at me like that, I don't want you to imagine—"

"When you see me looking at you like what? Like I want you? By God, I do want you, but there's nothing I can do about it. I can cross my arms and keep a decorous distance, and perhaps that would make you happy, but that doesn't change the fact that I want you."

His good humor had evaporated, and the naked anger beneath the mask of courtesy made him ugly, which was a feat for someone that handsome. But he was not made for rage, and his lips should not be mouthing words as he did, the teeth tearing at each one.

She felt the warmth in her cheeks and knew she, in turn, must look a sight, trembling with embarrassment and also excitement that had not yet dissipated. Because she wanted him in turn, but that was not enough. Her intellect told her this, that it would be ruinous to be guided merely by the drum of the flesh.

She needed more.

"Do you wish it were him, here, with you?" Luc asked abruptly.

Nina pressed her lips together and turned her head, but he caught her face and made her look at him.

"Nina, don't be evasive."

"No, I don't wish it were him with me now," she said. "But that does not make everything better."

"Why not?"

"I do not know if we would be right together."

"What? We'd be fine together! You'd certainly be better off with me than with that bitter fool, he has the personality of dried codfish. I know him better than you do—three days married to him and you'd slit your wrists."

"Luc, be serious," she chided him.

"I am serious! I am absolutely serious! Why is he special?" Luc asked, sounding as if he was being denied a particularly tasty treat.

"I can't speak with you when you are like this."

"How the devil should I be?"

Nina began making her way toward the lake, ducking under a low tree branch, but he caught hold of her again and pulled her to him, her wrists trapped between his fingers.

"I'm sorry," he said. "I'm sorry." Luc smiled at her and pressed a kiss on her knuckles. One moment he was a raging storm; the next he had quieted and spoke gently.

"I'll row you around that lake, how about that?"

She nodded at him. The trip around the lake, however, was not fine. She felt miserable, he looked terrible, and by the time they were walking out of the park, Nina could not make heads or tails of her thoughts. They took a carriage, and she did her best to avoid conversation by looking out the window. He did the same.

"Nina, I truly am sorry," he told her when they arrived back at her great-aunts' home and before she could step out of the carriage. "I'm not used to . . . Girls, they usually—"

"Fall in love with you within the hour?" she replied.

He chuckled and was embarrassed as he nodded his head. Their good-bye was friendly and light.

When she'd spent her evenings flipping through the pages of romantic books, she'd always been enthralled by the heroes who declaimed their passion at the top of their lungs. Shouldn't she be happy, then? Luc was eager to play the part of her hero.

She ought to write to Madelena and ask for her counsel, although she worried her sister might share her letter with her mother, and everyone would make a fuss of the matter. Until now she had avoided mentioning Luc in her letters, preferring to be discreet until she had a firmer foothold on the situation. But by now, Gaetan must have informed the family at Oldhouse that Luc Lémy courted her.

She went up to her room and wrote a long letter to Madelena. It rambled, but overall she was happy with the final result. When she was done, she opened her desk drawer to look for an envelope and found the first box Hector had sent her in there. She'd placed the others all together in a chest at the foot of her bed, but this one she had left there.

"A man may change his mind," she whispered, echoing his words in the dressing room.

What about a woman? Could a woman change her mind, her heart?

The answer did not come easily, certainly not in her sister's reply, which set forth good-meaning sentences and questions that did not assist Nina. *Come back home, if you need to,* her sister said, and Nina was beginning to think that might be the best course.

NINA AND LUC SAT BEHIND the house, by the canal. She was reading a book; he had stretched himself on the grass next to her, his hat shadowing him from the sun's rays, a hand clasped behind his head. The afternoon held them in a perfect, quiet spell.

"Do you ever want to get away?" she asked him.

"From Loisail? All the time," he said, and managed to surprise her with his answer. If there was someone she thought belonged in the city, it was he.

"I have thought to go to Treviste, up north. I want to build a hotel. I think I mentioned this at one point," he continued. "No one thinks I can do anything, but they don't know me. I want to build the most fashionable establishment you've ever seen, by the sea. It'll be utterly modern, luxurious, and every night, there will be a party in the ballroom and we'll drink champagne. Wouldn't you like that? To drink and be merry every day."

"Surely you can't drink and be merry every day if you're busy running a hotel," she replied, but with a smile.

"Bah! I'll hire someone to run it for me, but we," he said, rising to his feet and helping Nina up, "you and I, we can have fun."

"One day, in Treviste."

"This summer," he said, and his aloof face grew serious. "Nina, I wish to speak to your cousin."

"Luc, please don't. Please wait," she said, knowing he meant to ask for her hand in marriage. Gaetan would in turn ask her what she thought of the matter, and Nina did not know what she would say.

He had slipped an arm around her waist and bent down, breathing against her neck. "Wait why?"

"Please wait."

"I'll die if I wait," he told her.

He sounded like the men in her books, but she grasped his hands and held them tight. "I want to think," she said.

Nina knew this wasn't right, that they kept pressing back and forth, like the current, and one of these days, she was going to be swept away, but she didn't know what else to do. She wavered and she considered, and Madelena in her letter asked, *But do you love him?* and Nina could not say. She could not.

Chapter 14

NINA HAD SENT HECTOR A short, polite missive, asking if he wouldn't be available to have tea. He almost wanted to say, *I'll cook you dinner instead,* but that was impossible—she could not visit him in his home, her journey to the theater had been bold enough already. It was not that he disliked tea, but it had occurred to him that it would have been nice if it were the both of them tangled in conversation, as in Oldhouse, when they went by the stream and gathered insects. The world had felt small, and he thought of what she'd looked like in the tower with her hair cascading down her shoulders.

He dismissed that memory, the kiss they'd shared. He did not wish to overstep boundaries. He also didn't like the way his pulse stirred when he remembered her.

Hector donned his overcoat with the black velvet collar and stepped outside. A light spring drizzle fell upon his shoulders, and by the time he reached the café, raindrops nestled in the folds of his coat. He ought to have taken his umbrella. He eschewed a hat, and when he walked into the tearoom, he ran a hand through his damp hair.

The tearoom was one of those narrow establishments found along Acadia Lane, right across from the river that divided Three Bridges Quarter. The tearoom occupied the ground level, a seamstress operated on the second one, and living quarters were found on the third and fourth levels. Hector made his way inside, past the gleaming counter show-casing scones and biscuits, and spotted Nina.

She had tucked herself in a large, comfortable chair and held up a book between her hands, absorbed in her reading. In front of her there was a low table, and on top of this a yellow teapot and two cups, slices of lemon, and sugar cubes set in blue-and-white dishes.

"Good day," he said.

"Hector," she said, and smiled at him. "You are never tardy, are you?"

"Should I be?"

"No, it's . . . Luc is always ten minutes late," she said. She blushed and put the book aside, gesturing to the teapot. "Do you fancy a cup?"

He nodded and he watched her hands, the slim wrist with a silver bracelet, as she poured the tea and then with a hint of mischief, made a sugar cube rise and roll into his cup with a tiny plop.

"You do it well now," he said.

"Sometimes," she said, "and sometimes the talent has a mind of its own, but less so these days."

She stirred her tea, looking melancholic, the splash of rain against the windowpanes amplifying the effect. *What's on your mind, Nina?* he wanted to ask, but he was afraid to know the answer. He raised his cup to his lips.

"I'm thinking of leaving Loisail," she said, as if she'd perceived his silent question.

"The Grand Season has not ended," he replied.

"I know. I may cut it short."

Hector nodded. "Is something wrong?"

"Nothing. Anyone, looking from the outside in, would say every-thing is perfect."

The rain made the street hazy; it distorted it. The shop was empty save for a man who was half-asleep in a corner and the employee behind the counter. In this cocoon of warmth, they sat close.

He took off his gloves. "I think I'd miss you if you were to disappear," he said in a low voice.

"I could write to you," she replied.

He realized they'd had the exact same conversation the previous spring, but their roles had been inverse. He chuckled, and likely notic-ing the irony, she laughed.

"Don't worry, Hector. I won't take off yet, and I wouldn't leave without saying my good-byes first."

"I'm grateful for that," he said, trying not to sound hurt, trying not to cringe, and he managed it.

She'd leave him.

It was to be expected.

Nina turned her head, in profile, to look out the window. Her hair was pinned up carefully in place, the collar of her pastel-colored dress high. He thought she was imitating another girl, a wealthy heiress out on society calls. She didn't look like Nina that day. But then, she *was* a wealthy girl, and he was, likely, *one* of her calls, even a charity case. By now, Luc Lémy must have taken her to the right parties, introduced her to all the Beautiful Ones in Loisail.

"I try to imagine sometimes, what it must have been, for you to leave for Iblevad. To take that leap, without knowing if you'd fail or succeed," she said. "Weren't you afraid?"

"I was terrified," he said. "But I couldn't have done anything differently."

The engine of his actions had been his belief in love, in happiness. The mention of his voyage obliquely included Valérie, and perhaps that was why Nina looked down at the slices of lemon, her brow furrowed.

"Nor would I have wanted to. I am glad of who I am now. You don't know that when you begin a journey, and looking back the picture is not always pretty, but I wouldn't take any of it back."

"Not even your heartbreak?" she asked, stirring sugar cubes with her mind.

"I doubt the tree complains about the arid seasons and the overwhelming rains as it counts its rings."

"You are wiser than I, then."

"A little older," he said. "Not much wiser."

She was looking outside again, did not seem able to remain with him even if they sat together. Her index finger slowly traced a sliding drop of water against the glass.

"I do not understand what I want. Do you think that changes as you get older?" she asked.

She had turned her face toward him again, expectantly. Hector, who was accustomed to being observed by multitudes, felt shy under the scrutiny of those hazel eyes. He demurred because he realized there was another question under the question, and he did not know what the hell to say.

"I think it is always difficult to determine that," he said. "And mistakes will be made."

"Yes," she said, sipping her tea.

If the day hadn't been gloomy, perhaps their conversation wouldn't be tinged with this pensiveness. And she'd been happy in Oldhouse, and he'd been happy, too, when she smiled. Although she was the one who provided their merriment, he decided it would fall upon him this time to distract them.

"Here, now, do you think we can build a house out of these sugar cubes?" he asked, and as he spoke, the blocks assembled themselves into a box.

"We wouldn't have enough."

"If you pilfer a few more from the table next to us, we might."

Nina reached toward the other table, with its matching porcelain jar full of sugar cubes. She set it down, and Hector made the lid slide off and the sugar cubes trailed out at his command, heaping themselves into place.

"I always find it harder to control small pieces," she said. "But you make it look easy."

"It is harder. But when I was about twelve, I was already earning my living doing things like this," he said, reshaping his creation, making a horse out of the cubes.

"When did you handle large props?"

"I was about fifteen. I joined a traveling show. The owner was an ogre. He overworked us and did not pay on time, but I honed my skills during that time."

"What is your favorite trick?" she asked, resting her chin on the back of her hand as she watched him.

"Chipping a block of ice until it acquires a specific shape. When they advertised it, on the posters, they said SPECTACULAR, twice. In big letters, so you'd get the point."

Nina smiled and then she blushed, although he had no idea how he'd caused that reaction. She had rested her free, ungloved hand against the table, and Hector thought of leaning forward and capturing that hand between his own. But like her, he did not know what he wanted, and he was afraid because he always knew what he desired, it was all atrociously simple, until now it wasn't.

"I have a busy day ahead of me," Hector said, lifting himself from his seat. "But it is always good to see you. Please, if you leave the city, let me know."

"I . . . Yes, I will let you know," Nina said.

It was still raining, but he stuffed his hands in his pockets and rushed off, mindless of the weather. She was leaving! And, why not? Why would she stay? Perhaps he might have asked . . . but he had already said he would miss her, and he did not believe there was anything else left to say.

Chapter 15

Luc Lémy stood rather dramatically with his back to her, an arm draped against the mantelpiece, as if posing for a painting. Valérie scrutinized the young man with a raised eyebrow and a dash of contempt.

"No, I *have* been hard at work. Three potential investors lined up for the project, and Gaetan seems to like me," Luc protested. "I think Nina finds me attractive."

"Then, what is the problem?"

"When I am with her, sometimes I feel as though she is not fully there. I don't think I've managed to capture her soul," he said, turning around and sounding so earnest, it almost made Valérie want to laugh.

"My dear Mr. Lémy, souls are flimsy. I wouldn't think you'd be the kind of man who bothers about capturing that specific item."

Luc did not seem amused by her comment. Valérie shook her head.

"Why is she reticent?" Valérie asked, pausing to rearrange the lush roses in a porcelain vase on the table next to her.

"She won't say it in so many words, but it's that damn Hector Auvray," Luc affirmed. "Why in heavens should she be fixated on him?"

"First loves tend to dig deep into one's heart," Valérie said, unable to suppress a rawness in her voice, which made Luc give her an odd look. Valérie composed herself quickly, rising from her chair with a rustle of silk, standing cool and firm. "There's a remedy to every malady, Mr. Lémy, and I think I have the tonic that may cure this patient."

"Will you speak to her? Attempt to sway her to my side? She says she wants time to think about me, but I fear she'll turn me away."

"You can trust me," she replied.

"I shall be forever grateful," he said.

Perhaps the elusiveness of Luc's prey had burnished Antonina, making her appear more glorious than she was. Or perhaps it was nothing but the novelty of a conquest, but whatever it was, Valérie was aware Luc's vehemence only increased by the day. Some of that *must* reach the girl's heart, surely, rendering her pliable.

Valérie was not one to leave things to chance. It could well be that Antonina might be driven into Luc's arms with a modicum of time. However, the matter of Hector Auvray remained troubling. If he was there, distracting her, Antonina might not do as they wanted.

Since her chat with Agnes Haduier, Valérie had been paying a man to keep watch on Nina. He had mostly reported about her meetings with Luc Lémy, but there had also been occasions when she had been in Hector's company: a visit to the theater, a tearoom. Each one of those encounters could have been disastrous.

Valérie knew enough was enough. The Grand Season was not slowing down, and they needed to secure an alliance before the arrival of the summer. Wait too long, and Antonina might drift toward another suitor. Spring was the time to settle this matter.

Hector Auvray must be dealt with, now.

The matter decided, there was nothing else to do than to head to the Royal. Valérie took care to wear a white hat with a veil in case she should be recognized. She did not want anyone to know she'd gone there.

Once she arrived, she was quickly ushered into Hector's dressing room. She noted the profusion of objects in there. Props, books, and the large desk dominating the space. Behind it sat Hector. She closed the door and he rose as she walked in. His smile turned into a frown.

"You expected someone else, I suppose," she said as she took off her hat. This, along with the veil, would shield her. They were not of the same height, but casual observers would assume it was Antonina Beaulieu, not Valérie, who had visited. After all, she'd given that name at the entrance.

"I did. What are you doing here?" he asked.

"I've come to talk about Antonina."

Valérie tossed her hat onto a chair upholstered in crimson velvet, a pattern of golden vines upon it. She ran a hand carelessly upon his desk, picking up a black box and looking at its contents. A beetle lay inside. This was so indicative of Antonina's taste that it immediately confirmed Luc's suspicions, and Valérie dropped the box as if she'd been scalded by boiling water.

She pressed her hands together.

"What about Antonina?" Hector said. His voice was hard as granite. But she'd expected this. She'd expected to meet his resistance. And she knew she could move him.

"She has a suitor. Luc Lémy. Young, handsome, charming, well connected. I think they'd make a lovely couple."

"What seems to be the problem, then?"

"The problem is you," Valérie said, her voice light, like crystal shining under a beam of sunlight.

Hector was leaning on his desk. In the privacy of his dressing room, he'd taken off his jacket; thus he stood in a gray vest and his white shirt, the top two buttons undone, no cravat. The casualness of his attire reminded her of their time in Frotnac when formalities were a distant consideration.

If Antonina had had a chance to see him like this . . . Valérie could understand her reluctance with Luc. Hector was terribly attractive.

"She's very young, you see. I think she's gotten it into her head that you might marry her one day, despite everything, and this holds her back from opening her heart to Luc," she said, measuring him with her gaze. "I am certain you'd want her to be happy. For that reason I'd ask that you cease speaking to her. It can't be that difficult, can it?"

"How do you know I've been speaking with her?"

"Hector," Valérie said, smiling, "do you take me for a fool?"

"If Nina does not want to see me anymore, she can let me know herself," Hector said, and he sat down again.

He began to scribble on a piece of paper, their meeting apparently at an end. His irritation only amused Valérie more. It always had. Like a match against the box, she'd caused the flame to bloom and enjoyed the ensuing fire.

"I understand your resistance. You'd be giving up a toy. But I'm sure you can find more amusing pursuits."

Valérie rounded his desk and took ahold of another black box with a beetle inside. This time the sight of it did not upset her. It was but a lifeless thing, devoid of any power.

Like Antonina.

"Last summer, you wanted me to run away with you. That option is out of the question, but I believe I could entertain your company a few times," she said.

Valérie let the box slide from her fingers onto the desk. It landed next to a silver letter opener.

Hector frowned, his attention focused on the box, his eyes narrowed. "You find yourself suddenly in need of a lover, Valérie?"

"I never find myself in need of anyone, Hector. I am merely offering certain terms."

A tryst or two should be enough, she thought. She did not intend for it to amount to more than that. Valérie saw no point in a long affair, not when it was weighed against the danger it entailed. But a meeting, perhaps a couple, if it might pry him off Antonina, seemed a fair exchange. There was much to gain with Antonina's marriage.

And there was also the personal satisfaction it would bring Valérie. Hector was hers. He had never belonged to another, nor would he ever. Whatever it took, he was hers.

"Do you think I am a dog to whom you can throw scraps?" he asked in a low voice.

He was attempting, she knew, to appear cool and distant. But it was an act, like his performances in the theater. The line his mouth traced was not born of irritation alone. She knew him better than he knew himself.

"I am Valérie Véries, and these are no scraps," she told him.

She extended a hand to touch his cheek and he allowed the gesture, turning his chair to look fully at her. Then he stood up, his gaze never leaving her face, and she tilted her face up, smiling.

"How foolish of me. I should get on my knees and thank the heavens that you would open your legs to me for five minutes."

The words hurt more than they should have, but more than that, it was the way he shook his head that made her want to dig her nails into his face. There was derision there.

Yes, yes, you should get on your knees, she thought.

"How dare you!" she said.

"How dare *you,* Valérie."

The quality of his anger surprised her, not the emotion itself. She had expected anger; they were no strangers to it. But this was black and ice cold, not the red-hot anger they had shared. It was dead, festering.

For the first time, she doubted herself, and this doubt made her sputter, her voice too shaky for her own liking. "Try to pretend all you want. You still want me. You want me and not her."

Hector scoffed and glanced down, as if examining the pattern of the rug beneath his feet.

Valérie's hands twitched at her side. Close to panic, she shivered. "We both know it," she told him.

Hector did not reply and she grasped his arm, maneuvering to ensure that he was looking down at her.

"You think me beautiful. Thrice as beautiful as she might ever be."

Valérie was indeed magnificent in that moment, anger making her eyes shine like a delicate glaze had been applied to them, every line in her body harmonious. He looked at her, appreciative, and she was aware he recognized this perfection, that he could not turn from it.

"You are beautiful, Valérie. I don't think you'll ever cease to be beautiful, and you'll continue to drive men crazy with your beauty. But there is no goodness in you, just poison," he said without malice, as if he were explaining a difficult arithmetic operation.

She faltered, astonished at how painful it was to speak, how her heart coiled and snagged. But she did find words aplenty after a minute, each one bathed in animosity.

"And there is goodness in your virgin girl? What do you hope to gain? Blood on your bedsheets, the clumsy caress of a child. She has no more wit than a fish snatched from water, and a face as enticing as a piece of blank paper. You'll be tired of her within a fortnight."

She looked at him in triumph, satisfied by her speech, her indignation neatly laid before him. Her experience told her now he would reply with equal fury, and that, being familiar territory, she could navigate with ease. She could guide him through the waters of rage.

But he looked more confused than angry, and then he didn't look angry at all.

"You know what is wrong with you, Valérie? You think everyone has the same low opinion of the world that you have. You simply cannot imagine anything else, stuck in the muck as you are. But I can at least hope for something *better.*"

Pity.

He was looking at her with pity, the look one might spare a beggar holding up a grubby, shaking hand.

Her palm collided with his cheek. He stood unmoving. Caught in his cold stare, it was she who was forced to retreat, to blink away the salt from her eyes.

"You'll regret crossing me," she whispered.

"I am sure of it."

Valérie snatched her hat from the chair and put it on, rushing toward the door. She stopped by the entrance to give him one last look. "Best forget about the girl, Hector. I won't let you have her. Ever."

She was dazed by the weight of their conversation, and when she found herself back in her home, she stumbled into the conservatory. She stood there, the sun shining through the glass, the scent of roses invading her nostrils.

She took in a mouthful of air and pressed her hands against her face.

The cloying scent of the roses made her turn and look at the precious white blooms that she'd carefully reared. Yet, now that she leaned down, she saw one of them was blighted. One of her roses was slightly imperfect.

She took the shears the gardener used to trim the plants, carefully snipping off the offending bloom.

She stepped back, surveying her work, and cut off another rose. The flower landed on her feet, petals as pale as a new moon.

A madness struck her then, and unthinking, Valérie began to hack at all the roses. She cut and cut and cut until not a single rose remained upon its stalk.

When she had finished, her arms bore the traceries of thorns.

Chapter 16

GAETAN PACED BY THE TALL windows of his office as he read the letter.

His office was considerably larger than Valérie's, though decorated in the same style. On one wall he had set up several hunting trophies, memories of his visits to the woods near Oldhouse. A deer's head with a magnificent set of antlers was the central piece, commanding attention.

Gaetan had commissioned a portrait of Valérie to decorate the other wall, and she sat in it in a pale rose dress, with a fan in her hand. The painting should have been in a more visible space, atop the stairs perhaps, but he said he wanted to look at her at all times.

She thought he wished to display her, like the deer's head. The artist, in an act of perversion, had painted her eyes as flat as those of the taxidermied creatures on the opposite wall, as if to enhance the resemblance.

"How did you come into possession of this?" Gaetan asked.

"I chanced upon Antonina while strolling in the park and offered her a ride home. The letter must have slipped from her purse because I found it on the seat after she stepped out," Valérie said, the lie coming effortlessly.

He ran a hand through his hair, nodding, and folded the letter. Gaetan knew Nina's handwriting; there could be no doubt in his mind that it was an authentic piece of correspondence. As for its provenance, he was credulous. She doubted he'd ask more than what he already had. If he spoke to Nina and she contradicted Valérie's story, Valérie would simply say the girl was being deceitful.

"Gaetan, I had not wanted to tell you this, because I simply did not believe it. But I heard gossip that she left Haduier's party with Hector Auvray. Such talk, and then this . . . she will ruin herself."

"At Haduier's? Who said that?"

"I'm afraid it was Agnes Haduier herself. Darling, I blame myself. We should have gone to the party and chaperoned her."

He sat down in one of the white wing chairs placed in front of the windows. "I cannot believe Nina would behave improperly," Gaetan said. "She is a sweet girl."

"Yes, but a girl nevertheless, a girl who may be easily swayed by talk of love and kisses and throw her whole future away in an instant. Think what might happen, think what they might say."

Gaetan gave Valérie a worried look. She could see the scenarios dancing in his head. Their names in the papers, the talk of the city. Antonina Beaulieu of Montipouret in a sordid liaison with that man, the entertainer, the talent. Yes, she'd always been odd, and now her bad character was confirmed.

They'd say that, they'd say worse, and poor Gaetan was hearing every word in his head.

"Antonina does not realize that he toys with her. She is like a puppet. He entices her, then discards her at Oldhouse. And now he is back. To finish what he started and stain her name."

"I should speak to Auvray immediately," Gaetan said.

Valérie adjusted the long shawl she was wearing, an expensive present Gaetan had bought her three years before. Its vivid greens, golds, and turquoise blues contrasted nicely with her pale face and the whiteness of her dress. Underneath the vibrant cloth, her arms bore the faint traces of the scratches from the roses. She could have explained them away. The shawl was more for her own benefit. She did not want to be reminded.

"Gaetan, no. Do you think that wretch can be spoken with?" Valérie asked.

"Something must be done," Gaetan protested, looking confused.

"I agree. But I think you should be speaking with Luc Lémy."

"With Luc?"

"He would be delighted to marry Antonina. He has told me that he loves the dear girl. Gaetan, Nina enjoys his company. Once she is married, she will come to her senses and forget that theater performer."

Gaetan was relieved at the thought, but only for a second. "I told Nina she might choose her groom. I am not certain she would want to marry Luc," he said cautiously. "Perhaps he loves her, but she has not told me she loves him. I'd think she would have hinted at it, if she were inclined—"

"'Choose.' What does a young girl know about choosing?" Valérie said.

"I wouldn't want her to be unhappy."

Unhappy. Women had no grounds for happiness, bartered as they were like hunks of meat. Why should Antonina be granted happiness? Why should a single thought be spared for her feelings?

Valérie's feelings had not been consulted. She had been told she should marry Gaetan, and she'd followed her marching orders, as all women did.

"If you let her choose, she'll end up that man's mistress," she said. "Are we to raise Hector Auvray's bastard child?"

There. Gaetan blanched. Her choice of words was perhaps extreme, but Valérie was feeling snappish.

"Surely not."

"You've read her own words. Nina does not understand what is the best for her. It is your duty to guide her as the head of the family. If you do not approve of Luc Lémy, by all means, propose another candidate, but we must act swiftly."

"I cannot proceed without the consent of her mother."

"That is but a matter of form. Ultimately it is your approval that reigns supreme, is it not?"

"I could telegram Camille, I suppose, to obtain her blessing," Gaetan said.

"I'm sure she won't object."

"If Luc is disposed toward her, I think we might speak candidly and make the proper arrangements. I will still ask for Nina's opinion, though. Her sister had a choice in the matter, and I won't deny Nina her say."

Valérie gritted her teeth, wishing she could speak a tart word or two about Antonina's precious opinion, but instead she smiled.

"I'm sure she will agree once you've spoken to her and Luc has made a formal proposal."

Gaetan nodded and rose, taking her hand between his and kissing it. "You are clever, my darling," he said. "Nina is lucky to have you watching over her."

Valérie gently pushed her husband's hands away. His physical displays of affection never failed to irritate her. Hector, on the other hand—she had not been able to have enough of his embraces. He knew how to hold her, how to speak to her, soothing and comforting her and planting kisses on her mouth.

The wretch, she thought, and her fury was such that she had to turn from Gaetan and pretend to look out the window, clutching the curtain tightly with one hand.

"We must have the engagement party before the Grand Season concludes—the sooner, the better," she said. Her voice sounded as if she were chewing broken glass, but her husband was oblivious to it or perhaps imagined she was overcome with emotion over Nina.

"It takes time, Valérie," her husband said, put off by the thought. "We can't possibly throw a proper party that soon."

"A small affair, close friends and family. We can have a grander party in the summer, at Oldhouse, and I think you would agree a winter wedding may be the best choice. But as far as formalities go, this one is a necessary one."

A most necessary one. An engagement was a serious thing, but engagements behind closed doors could be more easily dissolved. Once the city was informed of the situation, it was another matter. No one wanted to be singled out in the papers as the party who broke an engagement. There were also the financial penalties incurred if the engagement was broken, the bride-price, which must be forfeited—but it was the scorn of the community that would terrify Gaetan.

"It's not unheard of. Dellerière had the same arrangement for his two daughters, remember?"

"Yes, I know."

She released the curtain and turned to look at her husband. "Gaetan, it would quiet any gossip and it would rein her in. With an engagement ring upon her finger, Antonina will abandon whatever silly notions she has acquired. In the end, she will do what is proper."

"She will. I am sure of it. It is not malice that moves her. She is an innocent child."

Valérie did not say anything to this. Innocent child. Ha. That girl would be at a whorehouse if she did not have a disgusting amount of money in her coffers; indecency resided in every fiber of her being.

Valérie closed her eyes, recalling exactly what she had proposed to Hector and, more than that, the sting of his refusal.

"I shall write to Luc and explain we must meet with him," she said, needing an excuse, needing to get away from Gaetan.

"Of course."

Valérie might ordinarily have retreated to her conservatory, to walk among her flowers, but the violence she had inflicted upon the roses the day before was fresh on her mind. That space had been corrupted. Antonina had ruined even that. She was a poisonous creature.

She chose instead to go to her room.

Paper in hand, she scrawled a few sentences for Lémy.

> *Dear Mr. Lémy,*
> *I have impressed upon Gaetan the need of arranging a betrothal between you and Antonina. It is of the utmost importance that you act swiftly. I believe Hector Auvray may otherwise ask for her hand in marriage before you do, rendering your efforts null. You must meet with Gaetan at once and be at your most charming with Antonina. You may be married before the end of the year, as you wanted.*

He should be pleased about this, she thought as she signed the letter.

She was pleased, too, knowing the venture that they were pursuing could proceed. Nevertheless, she wished she could have married off Antonina to a repulsive codger instead of that golden boy.

She doesn't deserve anything, she thought.

At least Antonina wouldn't have Hector Auvray, and perhaps most important, Hector Auvray could see whatever notions of happiness he was attempting to thread together undone between his fingers. Valérie assumed that after the wedding, Luc Lémy would want to oversee the construction of the hotel. Valérie would recommend that he take Antonina with him to ensure she would not cross paths with Hector. Newlyweds should not be apart.

That would be the end of that tale, an aborted romance. In years to come, Antonina could look back and wonder about lost opportunities.

Valérie folded the letter and slid it into an envelope. The motion caused the shawl to slip from her pale shoulders, and she saw in the mirror her arms, the marks from the roses.

Chapter 17

SHE HAD NOT STEPPED INSIDE Gaetan's house since the past spring and now to be back, with Valérie sitting next to her cousin, was excruciating, especially considering the topic of their conversation. Nina had already suggested this matter might be discussed between Gaetan and her alone, but he had brushed the comment away. Valérie remained with them.

"I asked Mr. Lémy for time," Nina said, unable to disguise the irritation in her voice.

"It is not Luc who has called for this meeting," Gaetan told her firmly. "It is I."

Nina sat in the armchair, quiet. The drawing room was brightly lit, but there was no warmth in this place. Even her cousin acted coldly.

"I have written to your mother, and she agrees with me that Luc Lémy is a suitable, well-bred young man. I see no reason to deny him your hand in marriage. However, I shan't force the matter. Suffice it to say we have spoken and he is enthused with the idea. If you'd like to speak to him first, if it would help, I can call for him. He awaits in the library."

"Cousin, in my heart I do not know whether marriage to Luc Lémy is the best for me," she replied.

"Nina, your mother and I agree this marriage would suit you fine."

"If the matter has been thus resolved, why even bother asking me?" she said, her voice rising.

Gaetan looked most displeased. Her cousin was of a rather positive disposition. Nina had no idea what could have him in this state and why he looked at her harshly. Did he think her spoiled? It was her second Grand Season and he had been sure she'd be engaged during her first one, but that could not possibly be it.

"I realize now I have been too indulgent with you," Gaetan said. "I should have made you a match from the beginning."

"Cousin—"

"Why don't you fetch Luc?" Valérie suggested, turning to her husband and interrupting Nina. "Formalities may be formalities, but perhaps these matters are best discussed by the youths themselves."

"Yes, yes, indeed," Gaetan agreed with an exasperated sigh.

He stepped out, leaving Valérie and Nina alone. Gaetan had never spoken to her like this. They'd had disagreements, but her cousin was kind, generous. Nina was wounded by his attitude. But was she the one in the wrong? Wasn't Nina supposed to do the bidding of her elders, of the head of the family?

"That went poorly," Valérie said.

The woman was more than pleased. She was practically purring. Nina did not look at Valérie, but she felt her sardonic gaze all the same like a suffocating mantle.

"You are waiting for a man who will never set his eyes on you, Antonina. Don't be foolish and toss away a first-rate offer," Valérie told her, sounding casual.

To utter a word would be like baiting a hungry bear, but Nina's silence and her stillness betrayed her all the same, poignant with fear.

"I know Hector Auvray does not love you," Valérie said in a whisper.

Nothing more, speak no more, Nina thought.

"I have seen him," Valérie said.

Nina did not wish to ask the question, but she found it escaping her lips before she could prevent it. "You've seen Hector?"

"Yes. We are on speaking terms once more. He has expressed his utter, undying devotion to me. Poor man, he cannot live without me."

"You lie. He wouldn't speak to you. He does not want to see you again," Nina said.

Valérie raised her head, her eyes bright. Her smile deepened and her voice was silk and honey over Nina's reopening wounds. "In his dressing room, on his desk, he keeps those beetles. I'll have them tossed out, I dislike them."

Nina was unable, for the life of her, to form a reply. The words withered in her mouth; it was as if she'd been struck. She felt herself shrinking in her seat, her head bowing to evade the triumphant sneer on Valérie's face.

"No, why would he do that? He wouldn't do that, he wouldn't lie, he—"

"He lied once, easily enough," Valérie said with a shrug. "You must not take it too hard. He was trying to put me out of his mind. But those times you've met, it's been *me* he wished to be with, as always. And then, the last time, when you spoke at the tearoom, afterward he came to—"

It took every ounce of effort in Nina's body to keep herself from flinging Valérie across the room, and the older woman must have noticed this, the way Nina pressed her palms against her forehead and then her sharp, angry voice.

"Stop! Stop speaking to me!"

"I have nothing more to say," Valérie told her.

No. No need at all to add another word. Hector had told Valérie about the beetles, he'd told her about their talk in the tearoom, he had probably divulged all Nina's secrets. They must have laughed at her. Silly child! Trusting and silly and ever forgiving.

The door opened and Luc Lémy walked in. Valérie greeted him on her way out, her voice courteous, beautiful.

Nina sat with a closed fist nestled against her bodice, her breath burning in her throat. She had not ever fainted in her life, and whenever she'd seen a lady roll upon a divan, she'd thought it funny, people fanning her and bringing smelling salts.

She felt she could faint now.

"Miss Beaulieu," Luc said.

"Mr. Lémy," she replied.

There were tears in her eyes. She felt like an idiot, forcing herself to blink them away. Madness! She was mad and stupid for having ever thought that Hector . . . that they . . . What a fool!

"What is wrong?" he asked.

"Nothing. My nerves," she lied. Nina pressed her hands together, against her skirts, to keep them from shaking.

Luc, seemingly concerned a second before, must have judged this was the behavior of a silly, blushing girl overcome with emotion, because he smiled broadly and was pleased. "You should not be nervous. This is not an arithmetic test."

"I'm not bad at arithmetic," she said.

Luc stood with aplomb. He was dressed finely as usual, but there was a special vehemence to him that evening, the strut of a conqueror as he began to speak to her. "Miss Beaulieu, we both know exactly what I'm going to ask, as I can see by your beautiful face. I must therefore cut to the chase, as it may be, and inform you I find you most pleasant and would be delighted if you'd agree to be my wife."

"Thank you. It is sweet of you. I—"

"You will agree to it?" he replied.

His eagerness was almost grating. She did not wish to converse with him. She did not wish to discuss this, not now. Every nerve in her body hurt, and she wanted only to rush back to her room and to be alone.

"I cannot . . . I cannot say whether I should accept your proposal."

Her answer did not seem to dent his resolve, and he looked only mildly curious, not offended by her reply. "Why would you refuse a marriage proposal from a man as charming as myself?"

"Some might say you are conceited, too," she remarked.

"Some might be right. Is that a terrible impediment?"

He sank suddenly to his knees and clasped her hands in a display of exaggerated romanticism, kissing them both. He resembled the illustrations of sentimental novels she had read, but in real life, it was too theatrical and she shook her head.

"Please stand up," she told him.

"Nina, I would make you perfectly happy. If you marry me, you'd never have a sad day in your life ever again," he said. "You'll never cry another tear."

"You cannot possibly promise that."

"I am promising it."

He might promise her the moon and the stars, and not care for a moment that he couldn't pluck them from heaven. He might do that before the clock struck nine.

"That is the problem," she said, spreading her hands and rising from the armchair. "I'm not sure you ever take anything seriously, and you spout all these pronouncements, but have you truly considered what life with me really means?"

"It means kisses in the morning and at nights, and a mighty number of embraces. I don't think you are ill-disposed to my embraces." He stood up quickly and, as if to demonstrate his point, placed his hands on her waist, pulling her close.

"I'd lie if I said I was," she said, sliding his hands off her, "yet I'd lie if I didn't say there's more to life than kisses and embraces."

She walked toward a window, away from him. Distance at this moment was necessary; she was all raw nerves and raging emotions. She did not even know how she was able to summon the willpower to speak to him, though the conversation was helping to calm her down.

"Like what?" he asked.

"You hate my talent, for one."

"I do not hate it," he clarified. "I don't see a need to have you juggling apples in the air for the enjoyment of the servants."

"You are a ladies' man, and do not try to protest the point. Would you be satisfied with one woman alone when there's a city full of them, awaiting your attentions?"

"Dear Nina, when that one woman is as pretty as you are, yes."

"Don't 'pretty' me," she muttered. "It's the only thing you ever say. How pretty I look and what a fine dress I'm wearing."

"I'm sure you are very fine without your clothes on, too."

She could do nothing but blush at that, and he took it as a point in his favor, immediately moving to her side.

"I'll buy you a most extravagant engagement ring," he promised. "I've already spotted a couple at Duveras, both with enticing emeralds, to match those enticing eyes of yours. We can go try them on tomorrow. You'll be the envy of the city with that ring on your finger. Marry me for the jewelry if it pleases you."

She smiled at that. "I don't like jewelry."

"Nonsense, all women do. I'll buy you a horse. There."

Only a man like Luc Lémy would think to bribe her with a horse and a ring. She turned on her heels, away from him, but then he wrapped his arms around her from behind and she felt his lips against her hair, his chest pressed against her back.

"Why won't you marry me? It'll be fun," he whispered.

"I always thought I'd marry for love," she whispered back.

"I love you," he said so effortlessly, she thought it could not be true.

If it was a lie, was it so bad? If love was the terrible misery coursing through her veins and nothing but vain longing, perhaps it was not so wonderful as she had presumed. And whatever it was, with Luc, he was there, with her, with smiles and jokes and embraces.

And her family wanted this, Gaetan was pushing the point, and Hector had made a fool of her once more.

She closed her eyes and the tears returned. She recalled Oldhouse and her tricks with cards and the trips to the Devil's Throne, and how hard she'd tried to scorch Hector Auvray from her mind. It had not worked, and there she was again, like standing atop the rocks, ready to shatter once more.

Luc Lémy turned her around, and she was weak, she felt like she might fall, but he held her up. "Don't cry," he said.

"I'm not . . . It's . . . If you'll give me a moment," she said in a paper-thin voice.

He gave her a kiss instead. He constantly did that, ambushing her with caresses, and she realized he'd always be like this, that he'd attempt to wash away any hurt and any sin with a kiss on her lips, but it didn't matter now.

He said he loved her, and it had sounded pretty.

And when he kissed her she didn't think, she simply felt, and it was better than to have to deal with the anger, the sadness, the despair.

She buried her face in his chest.

"Let me make you happy," Luc said. "Let me take you away."

It almost did not matter that Hector did not love her. Except it did. It absolutely did. But to heap on top of heartbreak the humiliation of having been twice passed over for Valérie, twice fooled. Loisail was poisonous; it made her sick. She wished to be far from it, and when Luc spoke, she listened. She really listened this time.

"You asked me if I ever wanted to get away. If you want us to go, we can go."

"I do want to go away," she told him. "Far from everyone, until I remember nothing from this city."

She thought that for all his swagger and his posturing, Luc could be kind, and perhaps he was right, he could make her happy. And she wanted, more than anything in that moment, for someone to come and save her. For a hero to vanquish her fears and set the world right, and he looked the part of a knight in a book, he spoke the part.

"Then that is what we shall do," he said.

Nina nodded.

"You'll marry me, then?" His hand rose, coming to rest lightly against her cheek, and he smiled.

"I'll marry you," she said.

Chapter 18

HE CUT HIMSELF SHAVING AND uttered a loud blasphemy at the mirror, sending his razor spinning against the tiles with a flicker of his eyes.

Hector enjoyed certainty. He followed a rigorous schedule; he paid attention to the tick of the clock, marking the proper hours for appointments and activities. Lately, though, he found himself terribly uncertain, and the feeling was not improving. That morning he felt as if he were sinking into quicksand.

More than a week had passed since Valérie visited him at the Royal, plunging him into a miasma. He had wondered what he might feel if he ever spoke with her again. He had not imagined it would be disgust. But that was exactly what he had experienced. He could not help but believe that his past, his youthful love, was tarnished by her actions.

She had broken so many of his dreams, and it seemed to him that now she burned the last, sweet remains of his affection.

However, there was something liberating in the moment. He was like the man who is given a reprieve by the executioner.

And then she had swung the ax again, threatening to snatch Nina away.

Not that he could claim Nina was his in any way; it was ridiculous to imagine she might be carried off like a stolen brooch.

It was Thursday, and Hector had to go to the Royal. He was scrupulous in his punctuality. Mornings were not to be wasted. Yet he'd risen late.

Which was why he was in a bad mood that day. He made the blade spin in a whirl of silver and then stilled it. He leaned down to pick it up, washed it, finished shaving.

He concluded his preparations but stopped at the door.

Nina had not sent a letter, and the sensation that all was amiss, that Valérie had said or performed a new act of cruelty, was intensifying.

She is under no obligation to see me, he thought. *And I cannot saunter into her home.*

Perhaps he could send her a note. A simple, pleasant greeting. It would not be too bold. This thought revived him, and he set off to work, penned the note, and asked a boy at the theater to deliver it.

Unfortunately, the boy returned within the hour, looking mortified. "The lady said you should have your note back," he told Hector.

"She said what?" Hector asked.

"She sent it back."

He wanted to barge into her home, beg for an explanation, and he forced himself to remain calm. It would have been unseemly, and she would be put off by such rudeness. He sent another note the week after, and the answer was the same. Miss Beaulieu was not accepting his correspondence. What on earth had happened?

One day later, although it was a morning when Hector should have ventured toward the theater, he grabbed his coat and had a carriage take him to Three Bridges Quarter. There he waited in front of Nina's address, though not for long.

He was relieved to see her walking out of the house on her own. It would have been awkward to have to pry her from a chaperone, perhaps impossible.

He quickly crossed the street and approached her, speaking before she had even caught sight of him.

"What has Valérie told you that you refuse to converse with me?" he asked, seeing no reason to waste time with pleasantries. His imperturbability had gone missing, he was near panic, and that more than anything pushed him forward, forgetting the politeness and conventions he upheld, which kept him safe.

"Mr. Auvray, I have an important appointment today and I cannot be tardy," she replied, and though she looked surprised, she managed to sound utterly firm in her intent.

"Not until you explain what has brought about this change in you. I thought we were friends again," he replied.

Nina stopped in her tracks and looked up at him. She sounded more hurt than angry. "Can you truly be this brazen?" she asked.

"If by brazen, you mean I enjoy knowing what kind of wrong I've committed, yes," he said. And he was being ill-mannered and she'd think him vulgar, but he could not let her leave without an answer.

"You lied to me, again."

"I do not understand."

She walked as quickly as she spoke, her eyes fixed resolutely ahead of herself. "Valérie has told me how you have pledged your love to her, after you told me she no longer held a place in your heart. Well, the both of you can be happy, knotted in each other's embrace, like the pair of snakes you are, for I refuse to play whatever sick game you wish to play with me."

Nina attempted to cross the street, but he caught her arm and pulled her back.

"I play no games. Whatever Valérie said is a lie."

"I will not believe you this time," she said, shoving him away with a push of her talent.

He was not prepared for this, and it forced him to step back three paces. If their conversation had not been blistering, he might have congratulated her on the honing of her skills.

Undeterred, he followed her, his voice growing more gruff. "You must, I speak the truth. Valérie came to see me two weeks ago, demanding that I stop speaking to you—and when I refused, she left in a rage. Whatever poison she has poured into your veins is born of spite."

She stopped and leaned against a tree, turning her head and looking at him.

"She wants to set you against me. Don't you see that?" he told her, and he despised the anxiety that made him sound like a dunce.

"Why is she doing this?" Nina asked.

She was uncertain and young. He'd never realized how young she was. He knew the number of her years plainly, but it was not that; it was the inherent naivety that came with youth. He realized she had not stood a chance in Valérie's presence and chided himself for not having spoken to her sooner.

"She wants you to marry Luc Lémy. She . . . sees me as an impediment toward that aim," he said.

"Luc."

Nina looked utterly frail, and he moved to her side, offering her his arm that she might steady herself. Her fingers tangled with his sleeve, and she had a breathless look, as if she'd been running.

"She has nothing to gain from my marriage," Nina protested.

"I do not know why she is fixated on the idea, but I assure you it is what she wants. Nina—"

"I was not lying when I said I had an important appointment. I must go," Nina declared, her voice low; he had to lean down close to hear the words.

His hand fell upon hers, and he clutched it tightly. "Nina, you mustn't listen to her," he insisted.

"It's a terribly important appointment."

"Nina."

She raised her head and stared at him. Her lips wavered, but only for a moment. She had a solemn look about her. "I have accepted Luc Lémy's marriage proposal," she said.

It was odd. Hector felt little when she said this—perhaps he had already imagined this might be the case. He stood, expressionless, before her and wanted to tell her, *Say no more, I understand.*

"He has bought an emerald ring for me, and there is to be a party at Gaetan's home in two days' time," she said, and she was a lady, and she now addressed him with a sober voice. Not a girl, not at all. She'd found herself, found her place in Loisail. "I am supposed to go for the final fitting of my dress today. Now. My mother and sister are here from Old-house for the party."

He drew his hand back, his fingers sliding away from her own.

He could picture it already: Luc Lémy in his finest clothes, looking triumphant as everyone raised a glass for a toast. Nina, demure and pretty in an evening gown, blushing as her fiancé placed a kiss on her cheek for all to see. And the ring, it would no doubt be ostentatious, a heavy stone that would allow Luc Lémy to congratulate himself, which would let the world know that she was his own.

She who wanted beetles instead of rings, because Hector was convinced Luc Lémy knew *nothing* about Nina.

"Congratulations are in order, then," he said mildly.

"Congratulations," she repeated.

He averted his eyes. "I am sorry I troubled you. You have an important appointment, as you've said."

"Yes, I need to go."

She did. He did not even watch her walk away. Hands in his pockets, he stared down at the tufts of grass growing by the tree.

He'd wasted a morning on this silly business, and he had to make up for it; he decided he must head to the theater immediately. There were many matters to attend to. But when Hector slipped into a carriage, he felt so utterly exhausted, as if he'd performed two shows in a row, all the energy in his body drained, that he could do nothing but sit back and close his eyes.

"Boniface," he told the driver.

When he got home, he peeled off his coat, his jacket, and tossed them on a chair.

He had not had a proper breakfast in his haste. That was what was amiss. He thought to go to the kitchen and fetch himself food, but halfway there he stopped and it hit him, like a knife thrust in his back.

It was despair. Despair he had not thought he could ever feel.

He placed both hands on his long table and pressed down on the wood until it began to splinter under his fingers.

He turned his head and caught sight of himself in a round mirror hanging on the wall, this beautiful gilded creation with a wreath of flowers serving as its frame. He gritted his teeth and made it shatter, pieces of glass tumbling to the floor because he could not abide his reflection.

The man in the mirror was not him. It could not be him because that man looked like a fool, hunched over in pain, and years ago he had decided, in the quiet of a bare, cold room, that this could never, ever be him. That he was the great Hector Auvray, performer extraordinaire, and it was wonderful being that Hector Auvray who loved Valérie Véries because as long as he was that man, he was safe.

There was certainty there.

He raised his hands from the table.

I am too old for this nonsense, he thought.

This, this, whatever *this* was. He did not even dare to *think* the word.

Chapter 19

IT WAS THE SEASON OF Valérie's delight. Like an industrious bee, she made preparations for Nina's engagement party, which would be held at her house. This was supposed to be a joint mission between Valérie and Gaetan, but he naturally relegated these matters to his wife, and was happy to see the pleasure she derived from these activities. He ascribed the smile on Valérie's face to her fondness for Antonina and did not suspect Valérie's good cheer stemmed from a dark portion of her heart.

The preparations were, to Valérie, like beautiful bricks upon a rising wall that would enclose Antonina. Flowers had been bought, invitations were distributed, the reporter and photographer from the leading newspaper in the city were summoned. Each detail that was taken care of assured the girl could not retreat.

Valérie, astute as always, guessed that idle minds could wander into unwanted waters, and arranged to keep Antonina busy during this time, the precious few weeks it would take to seal her fate. There was first of all the matter of the selection and fitting of the engagement ring, which was followed by a quick, light toast at a restaurant, Gaetan and Valérie smiling kindly at the young couple from across the table. Then there was a dress that must be ordered and adjusted, the arrival of Nina's mother and her sister from the countryside so that Nina and Luc were advised to meet them at the train station, the lunch between the parents of the groom and the mother of the bride, and a myriad of other items.

Gaetan told the couple to begin considering the items they might want to place on their wedding registry, since the registry must be opened immediately after the engagement was announced. Country bumpkins might exhibit *any* gift that came in a week before the wedding in their parlor, but the elites had taken with gusto to the new custom of having all their purchases picked from one appropriate venue; nobody wanted to end up with an inferior silver epergne or gaudy porcelain for their friends to chuckle at. That meant not one, but two days perusing the department stores downtown. The result was that Nina was caught in a whirlwind of activity, and more often than not, Luc Lémy kept perpetual guard at her side. Only on the matter of the dress was he absent; it would not have been fitting for a man to accompany a lady while she had measuring tape wrapped around her bosom.

Astute Valérie, engineering teas and distractions and business that must be handled forthwith. And the girl, she was dazzled as any young woman is dazzled, intoxicated with the attention and the praise.

Luc pranced around like a peacock, and his natural charm augmented by the scent of victory. Never had the young man's fair hair appeared fairer, never did his smile gleam more brightly, his clothes fitting him with an elegant sleekness that could make any lady blush.

That afternoon, Gaetan had summoned Luc and Nina to reveal his engagement gifts: a diamond hair comb for the girl; a heavy, gold cigarette lighter for the boy. These presents were too expensive—decorum dictated any engagement gift must be plain—and might have instead been better suited for the wedding registry. But Gaetan's generosity with his cousin was on display.

This might ordinarily have irritated Valérie, who took each one of Gaetan's gifts and attentions toward his family as an attack against herself, possessive creature that she was. But she did not mind this time. She imagined the diamond comb weighing the girl down, like an anchor, tying her to Luc.

In this pleasant mood, Valérie was able to appreciate the adorable picture the both of them presented as they stood in the drawing room, cooing and holding the boxes bearing their gifts, showing them to Camille and Madelena, who made appreciative comments. Luc's hand rested on the small of Nina's back, and when she raised her head, his blue eyes monopolized her. Silly Nina smiled tremulously back at her husband-to-be, whispering a word to him.

They set the boxes down on a table, and Gaetan gave Nina a hug, Luc a pat on the back. More smiles, more cooing, but as Valérie sat there, resting lazily against the sofa, she saw the box with the diamond head comb slide slightly to the left.

Nina's gaze had been lowered, and she was staring at her hands, pensive, with a mystifying stillness that irritated Valérie because it hinted at hidden depths, secrets, and more than that, when she used her talent, it reminded Valérie of Hector.

Was she thinking of him?

Valérie had thought of Hector before her own wedding when, instead of throwing away the ring he gave her as she'd promised herself, she had instead secreted it off, assuring it would remain with her for the rest of her life.

Antonina's eyes, did they look haunted? Did they look sad? Had Valérie ever glimpsed that same expression in her own mirror?

She hated thinking she had anything in common with Antonina, but they both did share a past with Hector.

Valérie mentally corrected herself—*she* shared a past with Hector. Antonina had experienced nothing except an illusion.

Camille spoke to her daughter, and the girl smiled again.

Valérie's chin quivered, but she told herself not to indulge in paranoia. The engagement was imminent. A little more, a precious handful of days and Nina would be as good as married to Luc Lémy.

It was her fate, her only path, as once it had been Valérie's fate to marry Gaetan, that dull, sorry, and wealthy man her family had fawned upon. Valérie had marched forward like a soldier, dressed in white, clutching a bouquet in her hands. She'd said her vows and danced at her wedding party, and never once did she let the satisfied mask she wore slip. Nina would, must, do the same.

Chapter 20

THE MIRROR DID NOT ORDINARILY tell Nina she was beautiful. She knew herself—and most people reaffirmed this—passably pretty when she was at her best. Considerable effort, however, had been put toward her hair and dress that day.

The couturier at first had been ready to throw a fit, saying a dress for such an occasion could not be finished in a short time frame, but the item had been delivered with a day to spare. Her evening gown was aquamarine chiffon with a printed floral pattern, embroidered with glass beads, a sash at her waist. It bared her shoulders, made her look airy, and had been strategically calculated to contrast with her emerald engagement ring. Ordinarily the ring would have been bestowed at the end of the party, but Luc wanted all of Loisail to see her wearing his gift and had insisted that she put it on the moment she went downstairs.

She looked beautiful, then, with pearls in her ears—her mother's gift—a diamond hair comb from Gaetan, and her emerald ring upon her finger. She was the princess in storybooks, the embodiment of every girlish fantasy she'd ever had.

She felt, however, as if she were drowning, thrashing her legs in a futile attempt to remain afloat. She reproached herself for this—she had no business feeling like that when she should be laughing.

The door to the room opened, and Madelena peeked her head inside. "Nina? The guests are starting to arrive. Luc needs you downstairs with him to receive them."

It was supposed to be a small party, but the guest list kept growing and it had been quickly decided—Gaetan and Valérie were doing the planning—it must be hosted at Gaetan's home since they needed to accommodate Luc's parents, his brothers and their wives, and a number of friends and associates whose names Nina did not recognize but who were deemed essential. A newspaper writer and a photographer from *The Courier* were even in attendance, to report on the event and take a picture of the groom- and bride-to-be. Gaetan had told her this gathering would be the golden brooch that would close the Grand Season.

"The costume ball of the Sertis' won't have that honor this year," her cousin opined, and though Nina had tried to tell them she would have preferred an intimate gathering, Luc sided with Gaetan and Valérie. A larger party it was.

"How nice you look," Madelena said, walking in and setting her hands on Nina's shoulders. "Are you ready?"

Nina had been ready for nearly half an hour. She had arrived early with her great-aunts and rushed upstairs to one of Gaetan's guest rooms to change. The lady's maid had helped her into her dress, fussed with her hair, and Nina had spent many minutes staring at her reflection.

"One more minute."

"Luc will be beside himself when he sees you. And Mother is incredibly proud."

"I'm sure," Nina muttered.

Everyone was gushing with praise for Luc. He looked incredibly fine! His family was well connected!

"Such a nice match," her sister said.

"Yes," Nina replied, standing up. There could be no more dallying.

When Nina entered the ballroom, Luc hurried to her side and took her arm, kissing her on the cheek. They stood like that together, smiling as the guests streamed in, costly flowers arranged behind them for best effect. She had difficulty placing names and faces, but Luc knew everyone and could recall a detail about each person. Nina had to extend her hand many times to show off her ring and intone its provenance. Duveras, naturally, Luc would say, and Nina smiled.

Luc looked more than handsome, nearly perfect. He wore a black jacket and a blue watered-silk waistcoat, lavishly embroidered. He also wore a proud expression, his blond head raised high. And why shouldn't he be proud? Nina could see flashes of admiration, even jealousy, in the attendees' eyes, and for once the ladies and gentlemen whispering to each other were not pointing out something Nina had done wrong, but everything she'd done right.

After the bulk of the guests had arrived, they set to walking around the room, milling with strangers. Nina wanted to dance. When she'd pictured this moment as a girl—and she'd pictured it often, the whirlwind romance, the engagement party with exquisite music and distinguished guests—she'd focused on the dance.

"Not now," Luc told her. "We must speak to a number of people."

"We have already spoken to a number of people as they arrived," she replied.

"Nina, no one dances at their engagement party."

Having learned most of the things she knew from books, she did not recall this detail. In her romances, in her imagination, there had been dancing.

Nina stared at Luc, but he smiled and dragged her to talk to another couple, then another. Luc knew exactly what he wanted to say to each person and monopolized every conversation, steering it in the direction of his choice. She was left standing silently at his side.

She had a panicked feeling, as if splinters were digging into the palms of her hands. She wanted to draw herself into a corner and take a deep breath, but there was a terrible amount of activity, dozens of people smiling at her. She gripped Luc's arm.

She felt he was the only element keeping her afloat, and why, why was there such tightness in her chest?

"Could we sit down for a moment? Perhaps go outside for a breath of fresh air?" she asked. "I do not feel too well."

"Darling, do you see that man over there?" Luc said. "That is Flavio Odem, and I am hoping he will help finance a crucial business venture of mine. We have to talk to him."

"Five minutes, Luc."

"Nina, we must take advantage of this opportunity. It is difficult to obtain a meeting with a number of people in this room."

"Luc, please."

He was looking in the direction of Odem and only threw her a quick, irritated glance.

"He is heading toward the smoking room. Nina . . . fine, you go outside for a minute. I can't take you into the smoking room with the men, anyway."

"Luc."

"Be a good girl," he said, and now he granted her a sweet smile.

He left with that. Nina somehow managed to slide out of the house. She took a deep breath.

The full moon smiled above her, and Nina tipped her head up to look at it.

How much better and quieter it was outside, the voices of the party muffled, the lights of the chandeliers not blinding her. She'd wanted this, had she not? She'd come to Loisail for this, and the city had been cruel, but now it had granted her the childhood dream she'd built from scraps of books. And soon they'd be away from the metropolis; Luc had promised her a long honeymoon, and they would settle in another city. This suited her well.

Something buzzed against her cheek, and Nina turned her head and saw a nocturnal beetle flutter and land on her hand.

It was a blue lightning bug, with luminous spots, a creature meant for warmer climates and summer days. How odd it should fly around Loisail! Then again, it had been a warm spring.

I must tell Hector of this find, she thought, and had to mentally correct herself because it was Luc. She ought to tell *Luc* about the beetle. She turned her head, ready to slip back into the party, and then did not move.

Because Luc would not care. He was in the smoking room, speaking to his friends.

The beetle flashed blue in a blinking, cycling pattern, then suddenly took off, fluttering away.

She followed it, drawn by its light, with slow steps, then faster, then so fast, she was running, almost tripping over her dress. Three blocks from the house, she lost sight of the insect.

Nina stood there, stunned, uncertain, not knowing what she was doing or why.

It came to her then, a single thought so overwhelming, it erased everything: the discomfort of the evening and the rational voice in her head pleading for her to turn back ceased. The thought was simply that she wanted Hector.

She ran toward the nearest avenue where she might catch a carriage, almost stumbling into the path of a horse. The driver yelled a curse and reined in his mount, the carriage stopping right in front of her.

"Are you mad, girl?!" he exclaimed.

Yes, she thought. Yes and no, for she had not been this clearheaded in days.

"Take me to Boniface," she told the driver, and when he looked at her skeptically, she removed her pearl earrings and held them up. "You can have these if you do."

He muttered under his breath but snatched the earrings all the same, and she hurried inside. The wheels did not turn fast enough for her taste, nor could she rush out of the vehicle fast enough as the carriage pulled up in front of Hector's building. She forced the entrance open with her power, not even thinking to use it; the door simply sprang open, obeying her desire more than her mind. She ran up the stairs and knocked three times.

Hector opened the door in his lounging robe and stared at her, looking surprised.

She stood breathless before him and managed to speak in a low voice. "You will forgive me, but I had to see you," she said.

She walked past him, and he was too startled to impede her path. An army might not have been able to hold her back at this point.

"Are you unwell? Is something amiss?" he asked, sounding worried.

"It was my engagement party tonight," she replied.

She felt as if she were sinking into the deepest of waters and appropriately took a deep breath, a swimmer ready to dive under the waves. She was not sure he'd save her, he might let her dash against the rocks, but she must speak, she must attempt this.

"Hector, I cannot marry Luc Lémy. I do not love him, and I do not believe I could find true happiness with him."

Now that she had started speaking, it all became easier. She was nervous but determined. She had broken to the surface. She was not drowning but living, everything inside her eager and awake.

"I am in love with another man. Since Oldhouse and before that.

He is intelligent and dedicated and kind. He understands me, and I believe I understand him. I like the way he talks and the way he smiles. I
like many things about him, I cannot ever remember all of them."

She approached him and did not know what to do with her hands,
she was too nervous. She settled for clutching them together, and her
voice dipped.

"I love you," she concluded.

The minutes went by in a dense silence. He looked more wearied
than pleased. Then again, she was unsure how men should take declarations of love. This did not appear in any of her books.

"You have nothing to say to me?" she asked.

"Nina," he said with a sigh, "Nina we must get you back to your
party."

He extended a hand, as if to point her to the door, and she tensed at
once.

"No," she said, brushing his hand away. "No, did you not hear me?
I do not want to go back. I won't marry him."

He gave her an odd, brittle look. His shoulders were hunched.

Anger licked her skin.

"What is wrong with you? I am here, baring my heart to you, and
you can hardly look at me."

"Decisions made in the haste of the moment are often regretted.
Come morning, you might see matters in a different light," he replied.

"Different light?"

"Yes. What do you think will happen to your reputation? There will
be a scandal if you break this engagement, doubly compounded if you
break it for me."

"I know exactly what I am doing. I have finally regained my senses
and realize I cannot walk a path of lies," she told him.

He ran a hand through his hair and let out a low "no."

If she'd been wiser, she might have chosen this moment to leave him,
mortified by the whole sorry chain of events that had led her to his home.
Instead, Nina dug her heels in and she stared at him. It was the folly of
youth that gave her courage.

"You are a coward," she said.

He snapped up straight, tall and firm again, his shoulders stiff.

"Yes," she pressed on. "I see it now. You can act the part of a secure man onstage, but you are nothing but a coward. You fear what they'll say about *you*."

"No, I fear for you," he said vehemently.

He looked scared to death, and she felt like calling him every terrible name she'd ever heard because she could see him receding inward, his head falling. She thought, *He intends to leave it at this.*

Nina shook all over in disbelief.

"I fear for my heart, too," he said, raising his head and piercing her with his eyes.

Hector made a noise—it sounded like he was chuckling, she could not be sure. His thick eyebrows were furrowed, and he raised his hands, then dropped them heavily at his side, his fingers curled tight.

"You have no idea, Nina, what it is like to love someone so much, it tears you apart, that you think you will die when you lose them. And after experiencing such awful pain, you never want to feel it again any more than a man wants another limb hacked off."

"I have some idea," she whispered.

He did not reply, but she noticed how his jaw clenched at that.

Hector walked away from her, moving along the table, to the other end of the vast room, which served as parlor and dining area alike, this odd home he filled with its jumble of eclectic objects.

"You *are* a coward."

"Nina—" he began, and she bridged the distance between them as quickly as he had established it, reaching his side.

"Do you think you can put your heart in a box of iron and throw away the key? Do you think that is the best way to live? Keep your damn heart in a box and let nothing touch it!" she exclaimed.

Ready to depart, now that she had said her piece, she whirled away from him. Her chest burned with ardent sorrow, but at least she was glad she was not weeping.

"No, I do not think it is possible, because you are in there already!" he yelled back.

She gasped but remained afraid that if she said or did a single thing, he'd stop speaking.

"You are everywhere in my life. I did not want that," he confessed.

She turned around. Hector was severe and the look in his eyes was that of a man in pain, not one declaring his love, but there was a sincerity that had been lacking when Luc promised her eternal happiness.

Nina slid closer to him. "Then why won't you let me beside you instead of keeping me in a solitary corner of that box?"

"What happens when you stop loving me?" he asked tersely.

That was the crux of the matter, the invisible dividing line on the floor.

"Why should I?" she replied. "Because Valérie stopped loving you?"

She looked at him, straight in the eye. There was no room for coyness.

"I am not Valérie," she said.

"I've noticed."

"Then?"

"Then," he muttered. "You were speaking of leaving the city a few days ago, of Luc Lémy, and I—"

"And you said nothing."

He replied with a speechless stare, looking humbled. He was older than she, but one would have thought her the senior if they'd seen them then and noticed her carefully crafted boldness. "What would you have had me say? It would have been improper . . . and I thought you liked him, I thought—"

"I've thought silly things, too," Nina said. "It doesn't matter. But now? What will you do now? For a man who once gave me a pack of playing cards, I don't think you've ever learned one must gamble in order to win. And despite all your talk of teaching me, that's one lesson I can give you."

She extended a hand and smoothed the cuff of his faded lounging robe, wanting to touch his fingers and not daring, because he looked like he might bolt out of sight, as he had bolted when they were in the tower at Oldhouse.

"Will you kiss me now, or shall I let you be?" she asked, and couldn't help the fragility in her voice though she was attempting to sound resolute.

Hector pulled Nina to him, bending down to kiss her. She gripped his shoulders and kissed him back, her fingers dipping under the fabric of the robe, touching his skin.

He lifted his face and looked at her.

She thought if he pulled away from her this time, she might collapse in tears, but he smiled gently. Slowly, hesitantly, he caressed her cheek.

"You'll stay with me?" he asked in a hushed tone.

"Yes," she said, knowing he didn't mean for a while, that she could not possibly go back after this, and he was right, there'd be a scandal. "I'll stay."

Nina removed the diamond comb from her hair, drew several pins from it, too, and shook her head, letting the heavy mass of hair spill down her shoulders.

She raised her hand and took off the engagement ring, setting the precious emerald everyone had fawned over on the table, next to his papers and books and a bright, painted wooden box.

Then she pressed the same hand against his chest. His heart leapt up, like a wave, drawn by her touch.

Chapter 21

NO ONE KNEW WHAT TO say or what to do in the wake of the colossal disaster. Instead they sat together in the drawing room, in a mute stupor laced with horror. Antonina's mother and her sister were on a couch; Étienne Lémy sat on a chair while his brother paced in circles, a glass of wine in his hands. Valérie had lost count of how many glasses that made.

Luc was not sure at what point in the evening Antonina had stepped out for a breath of fresh air, but by the time the photographer from *The Courier* asked that they take the official portrait of the bride- and groom-to-be for the paper, she was nowhere in sight. When she was not found in her room, Valérie manufactured a lie and told everyone that the girl was a bit sick—this had a basis in reality, as Luc had explained she had not been feeling well.

"Nerves," she had told the guests.

They had to endure another hour of the party, Luc gripping his glass, his favorite brother standing at his right while Valérie smiled at everyone, pretending all was well. As soon as the last guests were dispatched, the inquiries and recriminations began. Why hadn't Luc stayed with her? Where could she be?

Gaetan walked in, and they all turned their heads. "She is not at our great-aunts' home," he announced.

"We must find her, wherever she is," Madelena said. "She took nothing and could not have gone far."

"We know where she is," Valérie said, unable to contain herself any longer. "If there was any doubt, it has been erased. She has run off with Hector Auvray."

Luc Lémy looked like he was about to hurl his glass at the wall, while Camille and Madelena clutched each other's hands.

"It is late. We do not want to cause a scene, knocking on someone's door at this hour," Gaetan said, composing himself, ever tactful. "Come morning, we must head to Auvray's home and see if she has indeed taken shelter in his abode."

"Hector is my friend, and I can stop by his home tomorrow," Étienne offered. "It may be best this way—it could be embarrassing if all of us burst in and Antonina is not there at all. For all we know, she might be halfway to Montipouret by now."

"Yes, undoubtedly," Gaetan muttered. "Let me show you to your rooms, gentlemen. Valérie, can you accompany my aunt and my cousin to their rooms?"

Valérie obeyed, courtesy making her muscles move, though she wished nothing more than to go to bed at once, her nerves frayed, her bones tense enough, they might split in two. A few minutes later, Gaetan joined her in their room.

"What shall we do tomorrow?" she asked as soon as he placed a hand on the covers.

Gaetan sounded resigned rather than upset. "If it turns out she is indeed there, I'm sure Étienne will bring them to us and we'll have to make quick arrangements at the courthouse for a wedding."

"You don't mean to marry her to Hector Auvray?"

"What else do you expect me to do at this point?" he replied.

"Punish her!"

"She is not a child for me to spank," Gaetan said.

"Our name, Gaetan," Valérie said. "Do you think nothing of our name? What will people say when she is suddenly wed to Hector Auvray after we said she was engaged to Luc Lémy? You think no one will piece it together? That the servants will not talk?"

"I expect there might be gossip, even if I do my best to mute it," he said. "That should be enough punishment."

"You will have me walk around Loisail, people murmuring I am related to a common whore?"

"You will mind your mouth, Valérie," he said, raising his voice. "I am tired and so are you. Save any words for the morning, and make sure they are more measured."

Valérie lay back, her body feeling as if it were encased in iron. If she'd had the means, she would have stabbed the girl in the heart a thousand times. She'd thrice wronged Valérie: the business venture was spoiled, they'd be the laughingstock of the city, and Antonina would marry Hector.

She was stealing everything from Valérie, even the ground beneath her feet.

It will not go unpunished, she thought, furious. If Gaetan expected to reward that monster with a quiet courthouse wedding to Hector Auvray, he was wrong.

Once Gaetan snored away, Valérie grabbed her robe and went in search of Luc Lémy.

At the first knock, he opened the door, obviously as awake as she was. "What do you want?" he asked, his manners forgotten. His breath was heavy with alcohol and the scent of tobacco.

"I want to know if you are bold enough to finish what you started," she replied.

"I don't understand," he said.

"Do you desire that hotel of yours? It is within your grasp. We told everyone Antonina was sick, and there is no reason why we cannot keep telling that tale, then have you marry her as quickly as we can. I'm sure you'll profit even more. Gaetan will give you all the money you may want, both to placate you and in a gesture of gratitude."

There was no doubt in her mind this would be the case. Gaetan was soft, weak. A man with more mettle might have dragged Antonina out of Hector's house by her hair and beat her bloody before disowning her. But dear Gaetan, he could not even do this right. He could not even muster sufficient outrage.

Luc could, infused with the bravado of youth. She saw the fire in his eyes, that naked hatred swimming there. He was a ready ax, and all Valérie had to do was swing it.

"Even if I thought this a good plan, I doubt Auvray is going to happily allow me to wed her," Luc said.

"He can't wed her without her mother's consent. She is not yet twenty-one. The law is clear on this point."

"Consent that she is sure to grant. It is but a trifle, a signature on a piece of paper."

"Which means your problem is Hector Auvray."

Luc had been holding the door open a fraction, but now he opened it wider and stepped into the hallway as if to get closer to her, perhaps fearing their voices might be heard.

He whispered to her. "What are you suggesting?"

"Kill him," she said.

The words were sweet, they dissolved like sugar in her mouth, and she savored them. Nourished with hate, she continued speaking.

"Challenge him to a duel in the morning, do not let your brother broker a peace between you, as I am sure he intends," she said.

"And risk getting shot?"

"I know you to be a huntsman. Is your aim adequate?"

"Excellent."

"Then you have nothing to fear. Aim for the heart. With Hector Auvray dead, Gaetan will want to put this whole mess behind us, and you will have yourself a bride."

She could see her words were having the intended effect on Luc. His rage was now laced with greed, a powerful combination. And he was foolhardy. The fuse had been lit. He would explode.

"If she repulses you now in her soiled state, you need not touch her. Except to put a couple of children in her womb, that might be advisable. Otherwise, you may do as you please," Valérie said, thinking perhaps this point was holding him back. But he hardly seemed to listen to her when she mentioned it.

Perhaps the silly boy had cared for her. In his mind, this might well be a rescue, Antonina playing the role of the poor maiden who is held in the claws of an ogre.

"He has dishonored her and dishonored you. He wants to make a fool out of all of us. Do not let him," she said.

"I warned him to stay away from her," Luc said.

"By all means you did. But this upstart man thinks he can do what he wants, that he can stomp on all of Loisail."

"You will assure me Gaetan's support?"

"Money was made to wash away sins. He'll give it, more than you expected."

"I think I might kill him even if I did not stand to profit from it," Luc said, his voice a low, harsh tone. "I might kill him so he cannot have her."

"We understand each other, Mr. Lémy," Valérie said. "Make sure it happens soon, and make sure to be discreet. A duel in the front page of *The Courier* will do us no good."

"Come morning, I'll tell that bastard what awaits him."

He closed the door, leaving Valérie standing in the hallway.

She took a deep breath.

There was no other way. Besides, she wanted blood. She wanted a sacrifice. She needed to witness Hector and Antonina's destruction.

In acknowledging the depths of her hatred, Valérie was simultaneously able to, perhaps for the first time in her entire life, admit the extent of her love for him. That she had loved him like no other man. That she had been able to exist, to breathe and talk and greet people on the street, because she knew he loved her. He nourished her in that way.

It was as if she had willed a part of her soul into his body, concealed it there. The best part of her, the part that was young and happy. There it had remained, safe. But now it was gone: she had been exorcised and that part of her was lost.

He had killed her, in his own way.

Satisfaction could be found only in vengeance, in his death.

Chapter 22

IT WAS THE SINGING THAT woke him up, not the sound itself but the strangeness of hearing it. For a moment Hector wondered if he were dreaming.

But, no: singing coming from his bathroom.

He had never expected to hear such a sound, it was a domestic detail and it was misplaced, causing him to lie under the sheets with his eyebrows furrowed for several minutes.

He had shared his bed with a number of women over the years, but it had not been something so intimate and cordial that one of them would have wound up in his bathroom, singing, in the morning. Moreover, if he had ever pictured a woman he might fancy living with, that woman had inevitably been Valérie, and not once had he thought Valérie capable of indulging in song.

Hector grabbed his lounging robe and followed the singing, standing at the doorway, his hands in his pockets, his fingers nervously rubbing against one another.

One of the most important considerations when he had taken this apartment was the bathroom. Hector could do without a number of things, but he demanded a first-class bathroom. When he started out in Iblevad, he'd been forced to content himself with water that was often icy cold and a landlady who begrudged him every single bath he dared to take.

This bathroom was generous and had green and white tiles, with the usual brass fittings, the added luxury of a fireplace and a claw-foot tub. Nina had climbed into the tub and piled her hair upon her head, and she was humming a tune he'd once heard when he was younger, a rhyme about a sailor who'd gone off to sea.

He saw her from behind, saw the curve of her neck, and extended a hand to brush a stray lock that fell down her back.

She jumped at his touch, splashing water, and turned her head over her shoulder in surprise.

"I should have announced myself," he said quickly, realizing this was likely an embarrassing moment for her. He did not want to seem like a lecher. "I'll let you be."

"It is fine," Nina replied, and stretched out an arm toward him.

He took her hand and planted a kiss on the back of it and she smiled prettily. He scratched his head, not knowing what one should say in this situation. He'd learned etiquette from a manual, but there had been no chapter on the matter of women.

"Do you always sing when you bathe?" he asked.

"The place an intelligent person sings is in the bathroom. One sounds better. Did I wake you?"

"Yes. It does not matter. I'll make you breakfast, come."

Nina slid down under the water, until only her head was showing, and bit her lower lip. "Hector, do you think you might lend me a bath-robe?" she asked.

"A bathrobe?"

"I could fashion myself one out of your bedsheets if you can't bear to part with it."

"I guess I need to buy you proper clothes," he said. "I suppose it's not what people mean when they say a trousseau, but things are what they are."

Nina gave him a look of displeasure, and it confused him. He was attempting to be considerate.

"You do realize I am going to marry you," he said, as it suddenly occurred to him that he had not mentioned the legalities before.

"It's customary to ask rather than assuming a positive answer."

"Well . . . one would think," he mumbled.

"One would."

She shook a hand, sprinkling his feet with water, and looked up at him.

"You might propose," she said.

That was what was bothering her.

A proposal, yes. Did he have to kneel? In his robe, by the tub? He decided he'd look less ridiculous if he stood and clasped his hands behind his back, not wanting to accidentally send the green and blue bottles sitting on a shelf stumbling to the floor due to a careless expression of his talent. He ordinarily did not lack self-control, but then again, he *was* nervous.

"I have money, you shan't be concerned about our finances. No name to speak of, but I'm certain you know that already," he said. "I am not the easiest man to live with, and I am sure more than one person might say I am rather bothersome, but I will try to be the best man I can be for you.

"With that taken into account, perhaps you'd marry me?" he asked her.

Young women expected flowers and florid speeches, or so he had been told, and thus he feared it was not enough. But when he looked at her, he could tell she was content, even if her eyes were downcast in an odd gesture of demureness.

"I suppose I could spare your reputation," she said.

"My reputation is dear to me. Now, let me lend you my bathrobe so you can get out of the water and give me a good-morning kiss."

Nina held on to the edge of the bathtub and pulled herself up. She blushed but looked distinctly pleased as she stood before him, naked, sliding a hand up his neck. He bent down to kiss her.

"Good morning," she said.

She did not have the ease of the consummate flirt, but there was something rather endearing about her, and he laughed and kissed her a second time, feeling terribly happy. Each word she had spoken to him since they met, he thought, had been like kindling, until in wonder, he had to admit he was on fire, and now that he looked at her in the morning light, he could not understand why he had not realized this truth sooner.

He found and handed her his bathrobe and went to the kitchen, wondering if he could possibly purchase a ready-made wedding dress for Nina or if she'd have to do with a common gown.

There came a heavy knocking, and he steered toward the entrance of his apartment instead, sighing at the knowledge that whoever was on the other side would be displeased.

It turned out to be Étienne, a small miracle.

"I am not going to ask whether Antonina Beaulieu is with you. I can see by the stupid look on your face it must be the case. You never smile before twelve o'clock, and you do not smile at all if you can help it," he said, taking off his hat.

"I am not smiling."

"It's in your eyes, you fool. Let me in."

Hector stepped aside, and Étienne sat on an old bench against a bare wall.

"Her family is beside themselves, and you do not want to know what Luc was muttering about you last night," Étienne told him.

"I can imagine."

"You could not, perhaps, have run off with her last summer? It would have been a lot more courteous."

"I could not have fallen in love with her last summer."

"And I thought I wouldn't get to hear you utter those three words before I died. Several miracles this morning."

Étienne flipped his hat between his hands and bent forward, looking rather tired.

"You need to go see Gaetan Beaulieu at once, if you do love her. He needs assurances."

"I'll marry her this instant if he wants me to," Hector said.

"And my brother—"

"Hector Auvray, open this door or I will break it down!" came a loud, gruff voice, making both men turn in the direction of the sound.

"Speaking of the devil," Étienne said. "Let me do the talking."

Étienne straightened himself up and opened the door. Perhaps Étienne meant to launch into a greeting, but Luc Lémy rushed in with such fury, shoving his brother aside, that no words were exchanged.

The young man stood before Hector, face aflame. It was not easy for

Luc to conceal his emotions; he had the transparency of glass, and it was obvious that he was currently infested with rage. For once, Hector could not blame him for being swayed by his baser instincts.

"I want to know at once if you have my fiancée with you," he said.

"I'm afraid Nina is my fiancée now," Hector replied, his voice calm.

"You son of a whore, how dare you look me in the eye?"

Luc stank of cigarettes and alcohol, and appeared as disheveled as a common drunkard outside a tavern who is having a hard time stumbling home.

"Throw a punch, Luc. I won't begrudge you that," Hector said, feeling sorry for him.

"Throw a punch?" Luc said. "I am not throwing a punch. I'll have a duel, you bastard." Luc Lémy laughed a boiling, forced laugh, which echoed around the apartment.

"Luc, you are drunk. We need to go home," Étienne said, grabbing his brother by the arm.

Luc shook him off and pointed at Hector, his face a mask of ferocity.

"Listen to your brother," Hector cautioned him.

"No, you listen to me, Auvray. You will accept my challenge or I swear by all that is holy, the next time you open this door, you shall see the barrel of my gun, for I intend to kill you on the field or off it, and I will not be satisfied until there is a bullet in your chest. Die a coward's death or die a man, I do not care, but die you will in two days' time."

Both men stared at each other, their gaze steady. When Hector performed, there was always a moment before the curtain rose when he paused to prepare himself for the act, and likewise he now paused, knowing he was standing at the beginning of an inevitable moment.

"Choose your second and we shall set terms, if you must," Hector said. "But I'd rather that you reconsider."

Luc did not reply, deciding instead to spit at the floor. He left without another word, and Étienne hurried behind him, yelling his name, his hat tight in his hands.

Hector slammed the door shut with a vague movement of his left hand and stared at the ceiling, drawing a deep breath.

"You won't do it," Nina said.

He turned around and saw her standing at the other end of the room, in his bathrobe, droplets of water dripping down from the tips of her hair upon the floorboards.

"I said I would."

"Then take it back."

"It can't be taken back."

"Then do not show up for the duel."

"You heard him. He will not desist and I would rather not spend the rest of my life fearing a gun suddenly pressed against the back of my head."

He knew how it went with men like Luc Lémy, and he would not become one of those haunted fellows perpetually looking over his shoulder; he'd consumed enough time running already. Besides, there was the basic question of honor. Hector did everything properly, and he would not cede to cowardice when it came to matters of violence and spite.

"That is ridiculous!" she yelled.

A heavy bookcase groaned and slid across the floor, driven by her thoughts. He moved toward her and seized her hands, but she slipped from his grip and slapped his chest in anger.

"No! You are not going to do something that stupid!"

"Come here," he said, wrapping her in his arms. "Come here."

She did not really want to be held, and squirmed in his embrace, but he planted a kiss on her forehead, which calmed her somewhat.

"You might die."

"Most men don't die in duels," he told her.

It depends on the conditions and one's opponent, he thought, but did not want to dwell on that point.

"Then you'll be injured! As if that makes it better."

"It makes it somewhat better, doesn't it? Give me a kiss, I need it."

Nina frowned, but after a few seconds stood on her tiptoes and kissed him. He swept her hair away so that he might touch her neck, and her eyes fluttered closed. He placed a soft kiss on the corner of her mouth.

"I have letters to write, to your cousin and to others, and there is breakfast to be had, but if you give me an hour, I'll take you to the dressmaker and we can have you looking like a proper fiancée of mine. We won't let this spoil everything, will we?"

She shook her head, but only a little, as if uncertain.

"Put your dress on. I'll get to these letters at once."

She was not thoroughly convinced, despite the calm in his voice, but she retreated in the end. Alone, he sat at the table and rested his elbows against its surface, lacing his hands together and pressing his forehead against them.

Chapter 23

Hector took her to one of the new shops on Winter Hill, where he instructed her to buy whatever she pleased, then make her way back to
his apartment. He had people to meet, he told her, and it was necessary
that he proceed alone. He would join her for supper, he promised.

"Make sure you have a nice trousseau," he told her. "And we can
worry about a bridal gown later."

It was not considered proper for a groom to provide his bride with
her trousseau, as it would undermine the lady's pride: a trousseau indicated a woman's wealth and social standing. It took time and care to
assemble one.

Nina did not have time, she knew this plainly. Her family would want
her married forthwith, and since Hector had made no mention of
having her return to her great-aunts' home—and sending for her trunk
might have caused the poor old ladies to faint or irritate her kin even
further—it stood to reason she needed new clothes.

She tried to be as practical as she could about the matter; truth be
told, she had not paid attention to her sister's arrangements when it came
to her trousseau. She settled for a handful of nightdresses, drawers, corset-
covers, and petticoats. She stumbled as she had to consider how many
pairs of gloves she required, because she often lost them and when she

wanted to manipulate objects, she did not use them anyway. She also had a way of misplacing collars.

When it came to gowns, matters were simpler, and she acquired a couple of housedresses, tea gowns, visiting dresses. She did not want to seem like a simpleton who spent all her money on opera gowns in a display of frivolity when clearly what was required were everyday clothes, but she did acquire one evening gown.

Before she left the shop, Nina changed into a blue linen day dress with a narrow skirt and much lace and pin tucking. Dressed like this, she went to another shop, where she purchased necessities for the toilette, including a silver set of brushes.

She had the carriage driver help her up with her numerous parcels to the fifth floor, and once he'd stacked them by the door and departed, she made the lock open with a flick of her fingers—not even bothering with the keys Hector had pressed against her palm—and willed the packages to slide into her new home.

Nina stood in the middle of the living room and contemplated the space around her, a box in her arms. After setting the box on the table, she went to the window and looked outside, observing the clear sky and thinking this was the view she would see from now on. These trees below their windows, this street, that other building in front of their own.

Upon his return, Hector found her in the bedroom in front of the mirror, with one of the new dresses pressed against her body, trying to determine whether she ought to change into something else, doubting her original choice.

"You've succeeded in your venture," he said as he stood in the doorway.

"I return like a triumphant conqueror," she replied.

He nodded at her, a smile on his lips, before he removed his hat and began tugging at his cravat, his eyes unable to mask his worry.

"Where have you been?"

"I went to see your cousin, but he would not speak to me. I left a letter for him, but he sent a note back saying he is to be Luc Lémy's second and cannot converse at this time."

"Then I shall have to go see him."

Nina sat down at the edge of the bed. In her childish excitement over purchasing new clothes, she had forgotten all about her mother and her sister and her cousin. She should have written to them at once; it might have smoothed the proceedings. They must all be thinking ill of Hector and of her.

"No, let it be. He has made a choice. After the duel, we can try to speak to him together and secure your family's blessing."

The duel. That, too, had been pushed from her mind, eclipsed by her mundane errands. Now the fear clawing at her heart washed over her anew.

"Luc hunts," she declared.

"Yes, he does."

"I mean he is a skillful shot."

"I won't deny it."

"How good are you with a pistol?"

"I am a performer, not a hunter."

At Oldhouse, Luc had made a show of riding on his horse and slinging a rifle over his shoulder. He'd know how to shoot; it was a gentleman's pursuit. Hector had not been reared a gentleman, and even if he'd had a chance to toy with pistols at a later point in life, surely he could not overcome the edge Luc had.

"But then, what will you do?" she asked.

"I shall wait until tomorrow. Tomorrow he may have changed his tune," he said calmly, as if they'd invited Luc over for tea.

"And if he doesn't?"

"Then tomorrow my second is coming to see me, to relay and negotiate the conditions of the duel."

"If you can't shoot properly, we might as well call it an execution," she said, unable to soften the grim words.

Hector removed his jacket and set it on the back of a chair. "Let us not discuss my mortality right this instant, shall we?" he asked, trying to make light of the whole affair. "There are more important topics to discuss." He sat next to her on the bed.

"Like what?" she scoffed.

"Like you."

"Me?"

He leaned toward her, his voice dipping, almost secretive. "I have a delicate question to ask. It is about us. About us last night. I hope I did not frighten you."

Rather than feeling embarrassed, as might have been expected, she was incensed, guessing that he probably thought her a complete fool fresh from the countryside who could not say what went on in the marital chamber. They covered the genitals of statues with fig leaves, marble made modest in this manner, but not the drawings in anatomical books.

"Hector, I am a naturalist. I have read books discussing the mating habits of many species," she told him.

"It is somewhat different when you are talking of something other than beetles."

"It depends. Beetles have fascinating mating habits. When stag beetles emerge, all they want to do is mate, and the male encloses the female on the ground with its antlers."

"I'm wanting to ask whether you are fine. Whether it was fine," he said.

He ran a hand carelessly across the rumpled bedsheets, and it was that vague, intimate gesture that made her dip her head and blush.

"My cousin Cecily, all she'd say after she married Émile was that she wouldn't rise for a week, but she is a liar and was surely trying to scare me, though her point about having to speak to the druggist, to ensure one doesn't have a babe at the first opportunity, I think was true," Nina said, frowning. "I don't think I'd like to have a child now. But I didn't think it was too awful."

"Not too awful," he repeated.

"Don't take it like that. I hardly know what to say."

He put both hands on her face, and she looked up at him.

"You can say, 'Hector, you fool, you were too impatient' or too unkind or anything at all. It is the way it gets better, if you correct whatever inadequate notions I may have."

Nina considered this with care, her fingers twisting around a corner of the bedsheets.

"What?" he asked.

"We could try again, and I can keep better mental notes next time you seduce me and discuss the results of this experiment with you later."

He laughed loudly, where before he had been speaking almost in whispers. "What a lovely creature you are," he said.

She kissed him and undid the buttons of his vest.

"I think you seduced me and not the other way around," he said as she eased him from his shirt.

"You might be right."

He had not kissed her for a considerable length of time, but now he kissed her slowly, over and over. He wasn't greedy on this occasion—there had been a volatile impatience to him, as though he'd thought she'd vanish from his arms—and she thought it pleasant, the weight of him on her and even more pleasant later as she gripped his shoulders.

Nina had spent the previous night in the darkness of his room, feeling startled, her eyes wide open as he slept next to her, the thought that the priest from her church and the martyrs on the stained-glass windows would have been cross with her. In the morning, though, she had sneaked into his bathroom, and lying in the tub all that came to mind were the songs she sang whenever she went by the river, the water reaching her thighs. Then he'd walked in as she sat in the tub, and even though there was her immortal soul to consider and also the scandal, she'd shoved those concerns away. They didn't seem important anymore.

It wasn't dark this time. She could see him as he lay next to her, his chest rising and falling, and it was a substantially more attractive sight than the images of martyrs. Not that she was ever worried about damnation; it had always seemed an abstract concept.

Other, more practical matters did disquiet her.

Hector toyed lazily with her hair, wrapping a strand around his fingers, and Nina turned her head to look at him.

"We could run away," she said.

"From Luc Lémy?"

She folded her arms across her chest, and fear filled her, as water fills the lungs of the drowning swimmer. "Yes. We could get on a ship. He is not going to chase us all the way to Iblevad, is he?"

"Perhaps we'd evade him. And you'd spend the rest of your life as an exile."

Nina did not reply. It was heartbreaking having to picture her family lost, her mother and her sister and her cousin turned into a distant memory. But it was the logical choice.

"Never to set your eyes on Oldhouse again. You think I'd do that to you?" he asked.

She knew the answer even before he spoke, resolution sharp on his face. There was no convincing him. He would not relent. Matters of honor were paramount to gentlemen, and he was more stubborn than most.

"No," he said. "Besides, I accepted. I gave him my word. A man is his word."

Nina nodded and squeezed his hand.

"But I appreciate your generosity," he said, his voice growing softer, "and know myself lucky that you'd give up everything you treasure for me."

His gaze pinned her down against the pillows, steady and true.

"I love you, Nina Beaulieu."

He had not said this yet, and his proposal had been almost an afterthought. It was perhaps silly how her breath caught in her throat when he spoke, given how obvious it was that he cared for her, but it was wonderful to hear it. The fears that, perhaps unreasonably, still dangled in a corner of her soul, were lifted with those few words.

"Would you say it back?" he asked rather timidly.

She bit her lip and then smiled.

"I love you," Nina said, laying her hands on his chest, and she giggled when he spun her around, making her rest above him, her hair falling like a curtain over his face.

Chapter 24

VALÉRIE HAD A DREAM THAT they were in Frotnac, in the intoxicating summer of their youth, when the nights were almost nonexistent and the days stretched on beyond the limits of the possible.

He wore that neat gray suit of his, cheap but carefully pressed, and they sat at a table in the café they used to visit. He was young, with a sheen about his eyes and a lightness in his limbs, and beautiful in the way only a boy can be beautiful.

In real life, the café had been bursting with customers, but in the dream it was the two of them sitting at a table. He held her hand and looked at her, and Valérie realized that their solitude was due to his gaze: he saw nothing but her. To him, the servers and the patrons and the people walking by the window did not exist. She existed, and she alone.

She was everything.

As though she were a goddess, he built a temple to her every morning and knelt before her, supplicating. She rewarded him, once in a while, with a smile or a touch of her hand, a kiss on the lips. But even when she gave nothing, he was happy because she was everything.

A clock struck in the plaza across the street, and he rose, silently bidding her good-bye.

Too soon, she thought.

She followed him outside, down the crooked streets. He was always ahead of her, and she could not catch up with him, but she managed to follow even when he disappeared around the corners or dashed sharply to the left.

He entered a building.

The stairs stretched up too high. This could not be a normal building. It must be a tower.

Up she went, up the winding staircase, and she stopped periodically to explore a hallway, open a door.

She pushed open many doors, but he was not there, until finally she shoved one last door of iron, stepping into a dark room lit by moonlight.

He slept upon the naked stones in this chamber, Hector, but not the young Hector. The Hector of the now, with stubble upon his cheeks and a face that had grown harder, more exact, as if a jeweler had chipped off bits of precious stone to reveal a faceted diamond.

She whispered his name, as she'd done in Frotnac, the exact same inflection, but he did not stir.

She extended a hand, as if to touch his shoulder, but then she noticed the woman at his side. Valérie couldn't see her face, because it was nestled in the crook of his neck, but she had hair so black, it was almost blue.

Valérie yelled his name this time, and it bounced around the room, but he did not wake.

She noticed then that there was no furniture around them. No mirrors, no paintings, no chairs, no wardrobe. Just the naked stones on which they slept and the moon watching them shyly from the window.

It was because she was everything, and he needed nothing else.

But she's no goddess, Valere thought furiously. A creature made of earth and water cannot hope for divinity.

It occurred to her then that if she were divine, he could not hope to hold her as he did.

The girl turned her head. Valérie might see her face now, but she raised a hand to shield her eyes.

She stepped back, and the door closed behind her.

Valérie woke early and was glad to find Gaetan was not at her side. If he'd been there, she might have cried. The dream clung to her like a poisonous cloud, it threatened to reduce her to hysterics, and her whole body trembled.

Valérie snatched her robe and sat in front of her looking glass, a hand at her throat, like a claw, until she grew still.

Slowly she examined her fingers, as if trying to find an imperfection that was not visible. She took the golden band from the bottom of her jewelry box, and it was cool against the palm of her hand.

This angered her. She thought it should burn, it should scald her, as if to punish her for her wickedness. It was nothing but a thin piece of metal, a trinket given to her by a boy who had loved her and thought of her no longer.

Again she looked at her fingers, but they were as they always had been, pale and perfect.

"This spring is giving me an ulcer," her husband said as he walked in, interrupting her reverie. "Luc Lémy came back from Boniface to tell me he's challenged Hector Auvray to a duel and he wants me to be his second."

Valérie ran a hand across her hair. It was happening so fast.

It had been fast in Frotnac, too, hadn't it? They'd had scarcely one season together. But it had been enough. And love could not bloom again the way first love had, it could not scorch as it did, a fever and a curse.

"Then she's with him," Valérie said.

But she knew the answer already. She had spoken because it was a reflex, not conscious thought.

"Étienne is also downstairs. He didn't see her, but he spoke with Auvray, and he says yes, she is with him and he wants to marry her. And it was as he was telling me that Luc interrupted him to say he was going to fight Auvray and he wanted me to be his second. I think I ought to remain impartial."

"Impartial?" Valérie asked.

"I'm not sure I should be his second. Maybe one of his brothers can do it—he has many."

Valérie thought quickly, furiously. The rules of duels established that the combatants could not communicate with each other. All matters were settled by their intermediaries. Only the seconds could speak to each other, write down terms, and determine proper conditions for the duel.

As Luc Lémy's second, Gaetan would not be able to speak directly to Hector, nor would he be able to discuss anything but terms of the duel with Hector's second. She did not want Hector and Gaetan chatting. The man was soft. With a bit of pressure from Auvray, he might feel compelled to intervene, even to bribe Luc Lémy to assure his precious cousin obtained what she wanted.

"He trusts you. That is why he's asked you. And what better show of faith than to act as his second? He is her fiancé, and the grievously offended party. Go downstairs and tell him you'll agree to it."

"Valérie, I am not fond of duels. If there was another way—"

"Look at what this man has done!" she exclaimed. "If Hector Auvray had a shred of honor, he wouldn't have placed us in this predicament. He has soiled your name."

This caused him discomfort. Gaetan frowned. God, how she hated him then. How weak and stupid he was, with his mouth slightly open like a fish. As if he had not thought the same thing himself, as if he did not realize that the violation of Antonina was a violation of all the Beaulieus.

Too soft, too stupid. If Valérie had been in his place, if she'd been a man, she would have put a bullet through Hector's brain herself.

"Étienne says they would marry."

"Yes, because Auvray is a reliable fellow. Last spring he came by each week, bringing flowers and sweet phrases, but come summer, Auvray disappeared with hardly a word. Do you think him incapable of doing the exact same thing again?"

"I don't know," Gaetan mumbled.

He was retreating now, a tortoise into its shell. That was the only thing poor Gaetan knew how to do. Again she was struck with the unfairness of the world, which had given a fortune to this man who did not deserve a single cent. Antonina did not deserve anything either, but the accident of her birth had awarded her with a future.

Valérie stood up and looked at Gaetan. Her harsh words were not having the effect she wanted; she decided to change her tune. She'd talk about romance, a topic Gaetan did not understand but that, with his lack of imagination, he revered as a special holy item.

"Luc loves her," Valérie said, clasping her husband's hand. "He clearly loves her. He is willing to fight for her, he is willing to take her back even after she has flung herself in the arms of another man. Love should be rewarded. Tell him you'll be his second."

This convinced him, and he nodded. She squeezed his hand tighter, feeling triumphant in her victory. She decided to press further, knowing that anything would be allowed to her now and it was the time to ask.

"Gaetan, when the duel takes place, I'd like to go with you."

He looked surprised. "I don't think the duelists' field is a place for a woman."

"I want to be by your side. To give you strength."

"It could be an awful sight."

She expected it to be. She wanted it. She wanted Hector's blood soaking the grass. She wanted Antonina's tears when they lowered him into his grave, with a marble headstone to mark his final resting place. She wanted to stroll one day by that cemetery where he lay and kneel by his grave. When the weeds grew upon his tomb and no one stopped to place flowers, she wanted to know he slept upon that narrow cage of earth.

She wanted, most of all, to watch his face as he lay dying. She wanted to be the last person he ever saw.

A curse upon him, yes.

"I know," she said firmly.

Chapter 25

THERE WAS A GENTLE KIND of pleasure in watching her move around the apartment, stopping to look at a book or to run her hand across the strings of the old violin that had belonged to Hector's mother. She was there and she need not go anywhere. She was there and they were together.

They had breakfast, and as Nina nibbled her toast, he performed several tricks to amuse her. Despite the sun shining outside, there was darkness lurking in the corners of their home, like a hungry beast ready to pounce. He would not let her worry.

And it scared him, too, to be honest. The beast hunted them both.

Hector toyed with cards, with a napkin. He performed that trick that always seemed impressive, where he spun a glass filled with water in the air quickly and did not spill a drop of liquid.

"How do you manage that?" Nina asked.

"It's control. But more than that, it is belief."

"Belief?"

"All we ultimately have to do is believe. We focus our mind on one single point, one single purpose, and we push. We grasp. We manipulate wood and glass and iron. However, the greatest trick is the belief. Belief is what makes it real.

"I've now told you all my secrets," he said. "You'd better not reveal them to my competitors."

"As if you had any."

"Hel de Grott seems to be getting nice press these days."

"He bends knives," she said, scoffing.

"I started my career juggling lemons above my head, my dear."

"He's not in *The Gazette for Physical Research*."

Nina looked down at her cup of coffee, gently tapping her spoon against its rim, a blush spreading across her cheeks.

"I read of you there first," she said. "I had this idea that you were an old, distinguished gentleman, I don't know why. But then I saw the posters across the city, and you were handsome and young.

"I think I stood in front of a wall near the Palace d'Ambelle for nearly five minutes, staring at your face. That is how I knew you at the party."

Hector smiled. It was sweet, this innocent confession, and yet her cheeks grew more flushed by the second.

"You realize this means you loved me before you met me?" he teased her.

"Don't be smug."

"I grant you I can be, maybe, a little smug," he said, and when she tried to slap his arm in mock chastisement, he pulled her to him, and she laughed.

Étienne arrived before noon. Although Hector had explained to Antonina that he was to be his second, she was still startled when the knock on the door came, her fingers gripping Hector's hand. Hector murmured an endearment and allowed Étienne in.

"Antonina, you look lovely," Étienne said, bowing low.

"It is gracious of you to say so," she replied. "Will you be having tea? I can fetch you a cup. Hector does not think I can boil water, but I'm determined to prove him wrong."

"That would be the utmost kindness."

Nina left for the kitchen. Étienne sat at the table, facing Hector. He was bare that morning, as if he was missing his usual polish.

"I have met with Luc's second, and I have basic terms to review with you," Étienne said. "A physician has been chosen to be present during the duel, Henri Davell. He is a friend of the Beaulieus' but if you would prefer to nominate another physician, they would be willing to consider a different name."

"I do not object to the choice."

"The pistols will be secured from Fabena's in the Third Quarter. He is reliable and I've suggested his name. If you are satisfied, we could examine the pistols today."

"Your choice is accurate, I am sure."

"Two important conditions of the duel. First, under no circumstances are you to use your talent to manipulate the outcome of this duel," Étienne said.

Hector nodded. He would not have thought to use his talent in any way, as it would have been patently unfair, but he supposed the details must be specified.

"Second, you may not shoot in the air or at the ground. You will face each other at a distance of twenty paces and discharge your weapons at each other."

Twenty paces was a rather standard measure, but it still sounded awful. Not so bad as six, which would have assured death for the contenders, but Hector knew that Luc could shoot straight and accurately at twenty. As for himself, Hector had handled a pistol on scarce occasions. He had a steady grip and counted himself cool and composed under pressure; he must trust that these two virtues would suffice.

"Luc would like to have the duel tomorrow at six in the morning on the Lawn behind Clocktower Hill."

"Will he shoot with the intent to kill?" Nina asked as she set down a tray with cups and a teapot on the table between them, the cutlery clattering because her hands were trembling.

Étienne smiled, his voice light, though he could not fool Hector. "I hope not—it is difficult for me to make new friends. What tea is this?"

Though deflected, the question hung in the air between them, and soon Hector told Nina that he needed to go with Étienne to take care of certain arrangements, promising he would return to sup with her. The dark fear that they had evaded that morning now rubbed itself against their legs, but Hector shooed it away, placing a kiss upon Nina's cheek.

Outside, there was a strong wind blowing, and Hector grabbed the brim of his hat to ensure it would not go flying away as they walked from the apartment building.

"Tell me the truth, now that she cannot hear us: Will he shoot to kill?" Hector asked gravely.

Étienne hesitated. "I tried to tell Luc this was silly and amends could be made, but my brother is stubborn."

"That is not what I asked."

"When we left your home together, that is the angriest I've ever seen him," Étienne said. "He has not only lost a woman, he seems to think he's lost a business proposition."

"You mean to say he wanted Nina for her money," Hector replied.

"Possibly. I am not sure. He did not tell me any details—it is all I could surmise, and it is not as if we are speaking now. Anything I've heard since yesterday has been communicated through Gaetan, since that is the role of seconds."

Hector felt offended. He could understand the irrevocable passion of youth and the rawness of anger, but the thought that all this was because Luc felt cheated out of a bank account made everything worse.

His shoulders tensed, and Étienne glanced at him, a crease forming between his brows. The day was bright and cheery, birds chirping in the trees, but it all felt chilly to Hector, as if winter had suddenly arrived and chased any possible warmth from the city.

"You must not judge him too harshly. He is brash, he always has been. He's also spoiled. It is our fault, we coddle and taunt him at turns. And he is the youngest of us, facing a more difficult path."

"For money, Étienne," Hector said.

Étienne stuffed his hands in his pockets. He sounded ashamed as he spoke. "Nothing matters more than money to us, the proper people who walk down these city streets in pristine gloves and silk-lined garments. You can give yourself the luxury of love because you are not one of us. That is why you are my friend: because despite everything, at heart you remain an innocent."

Étienne clasped Hector's shoulder, and they both stopped in the middle of the sidewalk, staring at each other's face.

"You will not shoot to kill, will you?" Étienne asked.

"You know I wouldn't," Hector said.

He had thought to shoot Luc in the leg or the arm, if he had the chance, though realistically that "if" was but a faint possibility that grew fainter in his mind with each passing minute. He felt like death was his shadow that day, lovingly licking each one of his steps.

"Accompany me to the notary public, then, and afterward you can select the pistols," Hector said. "I do not need to look at them. I know they will be fine, whatever you decide upon."

"What are we doing there?"

"You are witnessing my last will and testament."

"Hector, please."

"You are my friend, as you say. To you falls this grim business."

The matter of the will went smoothly. He left Dufren in charge of settling his business affairs, all accounts to be paid properly, and a fee for his services. To Étienne he gifted several of his paintings. To Nina went everything else.

After the will was notarized, he shook Étienne's hand and they agreed he would pick Hector up the next morning.

When they'd met, Hector would not have dreamed he would be facing the prospect of being murdered by the youngest brother of that careless youth he'd befriended during his travels. He could tell Étienne was thinking something similar, wondering how they'd arrived at this position.

On the way back, Hector bought fish, bread, and other ingredients at the market. He cooked dinner. To cheer Nina and to distract himself, he proposed they have a picnic inside their apartment, as she'd once suggested, one rainy day. He tossed a tablecloth on the floor, arranged the dishes upon it, poured wine into his finest glasses. She was amused by this, but the sun descended, and as the shadows stretched across the apartment, her anxiety returned.

She clutched her empty glass of wine between both hands, a desperate look in her eyes. "I should not have told Luc I would marry him," Nina said. "I was upset and I foolishly let myself be talked into an engagement I did not truly want. Then I came to see you, in the middle of the night, and I should not have done that either."

"I am glad you left the party and came to see me."

"You are fighting a duel for me. You cannot be glad," she protested.

He leaned forward; their foreheads almost touched. As he moved, his foot grazed the bottle of wine. It shook, but did not fall.

"When you knocked on my door, I was half-dead. I had spent days dragging my sorry carcass around my room, convinced I would not see you again and wishing I could tear the world apart for this injustice."

He clutched her, the weight of his mouth against her shoulder and his arms around her, and she poured himself against him, forgetting it all, but reality sneaked in at length. Nina drew apart. She raised a hand and pressed it against her neck, as if it might keep her voice from trembling. It did not.

"What are you going to do tomorrow?" she asked.

"I'm going to trust that Luc Lémy will inflict no lasting harm. Most duels don't end in death, I've told you that, and twenty paces gives me a fair chance. Tomorrow I might be back before breakfast with only a scratch for you to look at."

"You won't have me wait for you here, will you?" she asked.

"I can't have you with me."

"What, am I to stay in bed, in terror, praying that nothing happens?"

"You are to stay in bed, asleep. And when I return, I can wrap my arms around you and lie at your side," he said.

"Hector, don't treat me like a fool."

"I really need that. I need to know you are waiting for me at home. Please."

She wanted to cry, he could tell. He had been performing all day, all the tricks to distract her, and he would not let the illusion crumble at the last minute. He kissed her. She turned her head, he ran his hand along the side of her face and she sighed.

He shifted his legs and accidentally sent the bottle of wine tumbling down. It would leave a stain on the tablecloth.

Nina giggled as he tried to undo the buttons of her dress. "Here?" she asked. "But the bed—"

"Books detailing the mating habits of beetles don't explain everything, it seems."

Her brows lifted in challenge, and her voice slid low, scraping his skin. "Oh, really?"

She sat on his lap, and they kissed for a long time. In the end, it was the bed after all because he liked the way her hair fanned against the pillows, and he wanted to look at her like that.

If it is the last time I look at her, Hector thought, and panic shot through him. Nina must have noticed, because she pulled him closer to her with a knowing determination.

He'd been performing, he'd been misdirecting, to distract Nina and spare her feelings, but in the end it was she who was the superior artist, making him forget himself. It was the look of wordless wonder on her face, truly. It undid him. He spent the rest of the night awake, her head resting heavy against his chest, but he was unafraid.

Once the time was right, Hector snatched the clothes he'd left on a chair and dressed quickly, in the dark. When he walked the length of his living room, a faint light filtering through one of the windows illuminated the crimson stain upon the tablecloth.

He grabbed his hat and hurried down the stairs, down to meet Étienne, who was waiting in the carriage.

Their ride was conducted in silence—conversation would have been too difficult to endure, since it would surely turn to the only possible subject at hand, the duel, and Hector did not wish to speak a single word about pistols or bullets.

The Lawn was a patch of greenery that stretched next to Clocktower Hill, hiding behind a row of ancient elm trees. There was a clock tower nearby, a building of white stone with two hundred steps inside and five bells that chimed every hour.

The Lawn was a secluded place, with no road cutting through it. It served no particular purpose. It simply was. At one point, one city mayor or the other had tried to turn it into a rose garden, but the soil was poor and the funds ran dry. It had become, in the past couple of decades, a favorite spot for fighting duels after an edict had declared men were not to duel in the neglected Corners Cemetery, which had been the customary backdrop for these encounters.

Once they passed the curtain of elms, Hector saw that the other attendees had already arrived. There was a man with a bag, the physician he had never met. Luc stood with Gaetan. He was surprised to see Valérie was also present, her shoulders wrapped in a white shawl. She looked at him as he approached.

He had not thought what he might feel if he should see her again. It was nothing but a vague numbness, a whiff of sadness because her eyes were cruel and he could not help but feel sad for her, this woman he had once admired.

Hector fixed his eyes on Luc Lémy and nodded.

"I am here, gentlemen," Hector said in greeting.

"Good morning, Mr. Auvray," Gaetan said.

Luc stood straight and proud in a fine blue suit, his hair combed back, a cigarette in his mouth, as if he were headed to a party rather than a duel. He did not grant a single word to Hector.

"The pistols," Étienne said, opening the mahogany box and offering its contents up for a final inspection.

Gaetan checked the weapons and declared himself satisfied. He sounded disquieted.

Luc did not seem disquieted; instead, he looked slightly bored, his foot tapping impatiently against the ground, his eyes not bothering with Hector. No words and not even a glance. He had finished his cigarette and discarded it, crushing it under the weight of his patent leather shoes.

"Let us measure twenty paces," Gaetan said.

The seconds proceeded with this business, planting a sword on the ground at the appointed distance so that each man would know where to stand. Hector and Luc took their positions after the rules were explained. Each pistol was loaded with a single bullet. They were to shoot at the strike of the clock and not a second sooner.

Étienne handed Hector his pistol. "I have no idea what to say to you at this point," Étienne muttered.

"It's fine," Hector said.

Étienne nodded and stepped back.

The time was close now. The pistol felt heavy in Hector's grasp as he held it at his side, but his palms were not sweaty, and even if the blood was thumping rapidly through his veins, the fear of the previous morning did not manifest.

Luc now deigned to look at Hector with a scornful sweep of his head. Hector stared at the boy fixedly, but did not allow an expression to color his face. He felt a roaring fury inside his heart at the sight of his opponent's eyes, but he did not want to give the brat the satisfaction of catching him discomposed.

"Three minutes, gentlemen," Étienne declared.

"You must stop! Stop it, Gaetan!"

Hector turned his head sharply because that was Nina's voice. Nina stumbling toward her cousin.

Hector opened his mouth.

He wanted to rush to her, and had to close his eyes for a second to prevent himself from moving. He looked at Luc to force himself to stay firm. The weapons were loaded, they were in their places, the clock was about to strike.

Hector could not possibly speak to her now, could not clutch her for a single moment. It was too late.

God, in that instant how he hated Luc Lémy. He might have aimed for the heart right then, blinded by indignation. But then he thought of her, he thought of her only, and he found he could allow himself kindness.

The clock struck six.

Hector pulled the trigger.

He fell back, crashing against the ground, the strength of the blow robbing him of his breath.

It hurt.

Chapter 26

SHE WOKE WITH A START and discovered he was gone. She thought to weep, but there was no time for that, there was no time at all. She needed to find him. Now that it was morning, now that the day of the duel had arrived, she could not possibly allow him to walk onto that field.

Nina dressed as quickly as she could and did not even bother looking in the mirror, running down the stairs and onto the street. She found a carriage to take her to Clocktower Hill.

The tower rose, bone-white against the sky: a pale portent of disaster in the early-morning light. The Lawn could be accessed by foot only. She paid the man and rushed up the hill, the dew wetting her skirt.

It was not yet six. It wasn't. She dashed toward the Lawn, and she saw them there, the witnesses and the duelists. Hector and Luc were already in their positions, their pistols in hand.

"You must stop! Stop it, Gaetan!" she yelled, stumbling as she approached her cousin.

"Nina," he said. "Nina, I—"

"You must stop it!"

"It's a duel, dear child. He can't stop it," Valérie said.

Nina turned to look at the woman. For a moment she thought she could not possibly be real, that she had to be an apparition, but Valérie was there, solid, calmly glancing at the duelists as if it were another day at the park.

"Valérie, you must speak to my cousin. You must help me stop this," she pleaded.

"Must I?"

"Nina, for God's sake, shield your eyes," Gaetan said, taking hold of her and pulling her back.

She pushed Gaetan away, her hands slapping his chest for a second.

The clock struck the hour. The men raised their arms and fired their pistols.

She wanted to scream but could utter no sound, and her fingers curled against the palms of her hands, the nails digging into her skin.

She saw the shining pistols and she thought, *I love you.*

There was no time to say it, no time to utter a single syllable, but the word broke through and echoed in the space around them anyway, because her love was will.

And her will was an arrow, slamming both men with its strength and knocking them down; it made the grass waver in its path, the blades bending under an invisible wind for a second.

And her will was wind, but it was also iron. It clutched in its grip the bullets that had been destined one for the shoulder and one for the heart. The bullets stood in midair, as if they had been painted upon the landscape and had not been cutting through the air at an incredible speed a fraction of a second before.

She thought *no.*

The birds in the trees took flight, frightened by the noise.

Smoke rose in the air.

She opened her hands.

The bullets slid down onto the ground, rolling on the grass.

Nina ran toward Hector, who was lying on his back. She knelt at his side and touched his face. His eyes were closed.

"Hector," she said.

"What have you done?" Valérie yelled.

Nina looked at the woman, who was stomping toward her. Nina, her fingers shaking, did not bother answering. God, she hoped she had not hurt Hector.

Hector stirred and opened his eyes, wincing. Slowly he lifted his head and looked her full in the face. "Nina," he mumbled. "You are here."

"I couldn't let you do it," she said.

His hand reached up to her cheek, and Nina pressed a kiss against it, squeezing her eyes shut.

The physician was speaking excitedly to Gaetan, asking whether he needed to tend to the men and which one would he tend to first.

She heard Luc groaning. "What in seven hells was that?" he asked.

"It was her. The silly witch. You must load the pistols and proceed anew," Valérie replied.

It was the tone Valérie employed that cut most acutely. How neatly she spoke. It made Nina furious. She looked at the woman and noticed Valérie's face was as pale as bleached linen and her eyes were bright with pain, and yet she dared to speak those words.

"You are a viper," Nina told her.

"Call me what you want, you fool. Lémy issued a challenge, and it will be answered. There are rules to this game."

"It's no game."

Luc was now standing. He had picked up his revolver from the ground and held it between his hands.

"Step aside, Nina. Valérie is right. There are rules," Luc said.

Nina turned around. Luc had not raised his pistol again, but he was itching to load another bullet into the barrel and shoot. She might stop that second bullet, too, but there could be a third and a fourth. Her talent could not solve this conflict.

Hector's hand was on Nina's arm, and she gave it a light squeeze before stepping away from him.

Nina went toward Luc, slowly, without haste. Up close, he appeared as he always had, gilded, but also different, his luminosity tarnished.

He looked at her curiously, not knowing exactly what she intended to do. She pressed her hands together.

"Luc, you kept me company on many a day and we spoke of numerous things, in honesty and confidence. I want to think that we were friends," she said. "I think you meant what you said when you proposed to me about making me happy. I apologize if I hurt you, but you cannot make me happy, despite your best intentions."

He opened his mouth as if to utter a sharp word, but ended up observing her with eyes that were very blue, very confused.

"If you must be angry at someone, it should be me. Not him. I do not think you truly want to do this."

"You do not understand," Luc said.

"Luc, I want to believe . . . I *know* you are a good man. You are silly and impulsive, and you are a good man."

There had been a wild and unpleasant spirit inside Luc, but when she spoke, it died out, like cooling embers from an extinguished fire.

"Luc Lémy, do not be a coward now," Valérie said. "Will you allow this man to stomp over your honor and ruin your future? Remember why you are here."

"Will you let him be?" Nina exclaimed.

Valérie held her shawl with one hand and chuckled in indignation as she approached them. "They'll be laughing at you throughout the city, Lémy. Engaged for scarcely a day, and suddenly your bride is missing. And there are many *other* considerations one must not forget."

"Are you truly that desperate for blood that you must goad him?" Nina asked.

"Do not be weak now, Lémy," Valérie said, ignoring her. "Do not allow this silly child to take away what is rightfully yours."

Luc's eyes had been on the revolver, but when Valérie spoke, he raised his head and his eyes fell on Nina.

She knew he had loved her a little, just as she'd cared for him, the gentle love of friends. He had forgotten, and now remembered this detail and it was that memory that doused him.

"Nothing is rightfully mine, and it never was," Luc said slowly.

Valérie's body was as tense as a wire, her shoulders raised. As Luc spoke, she grew stiffer, her jaw twisted in its tightness.

"You are wrong to think me a good man. I have been terrible. I wanted to arrange a lucrative business deal using land owned by the Véries, but lacking the proper funds, I thought I could obtain the money by marrying you," he said. "When you went with Hector, Valérie and I decided the only way to ensure the marriage took place, the only way to obtain the money I needed, was to kill Hector in a duel."

The weight of her regard—it was leaden—hurt him. For a moment he was more boy than man. A boy who had been caught tearing the wings off insects and now faced his punishment with a quivering mouth.

"No. You can still prove me right," Nina told him. "Call it off."

Embarrassed, Luc lifted his eyes to the heavens and then looked down again at Nina, examining her face.

"Shots were exchanged today," Luc said, his voice broken. "I thus consider the terms of this duel satisfied."

"Fine words from a gutless coward!" Valérie said.

"Shoot him yourself if you desire blood," Luc replied sharply.

"If I had a revolver in my hand, dear Lémy, do not doubt I *would* shoot him myself and then shoot your former fiancée," Valérie said. "Hand me yours, and I will be happy to prove this point."

Valérie extended her hands, as if to take Luc's pistol.

"For heaven's sake, what is wrong with you?" Gaetan asked.

Nina remembered a groom who had been kicked by a horse and had to walk around all summer with his arm in a sling. Gaetan was like the groom when the horse had kicked him, startled and horrified and not sure if he had broken his arm.

"For heaven's sake!" he repeated, clutching his wife by the shoulders.

"Let go of me, you oaf."

Valérie was as sharp as glass then, as sharp and perhaps as fragile, for she moved back and stumbled. It was as if the veil she had worn each day had grown frayed, revealing the naked, desperate truth beneath. Her eyes darted ferociously; her fingers flew into her hair as she spoke.

"Are you happy now, Hector?" she asked him. "I hope you are happy, you faithless vermin."

Gaetan stared at his wife, and she stared at Hector. Valérie had the look of a woman who has spent many days in the desert and lies starving upon the sand.

"If you spoke but a word," Valérie said then, her tone changing, a note of warmth in her voice, as she took a step in Hector's direction.

But there was no warmth in him to mirror that change in her. There was only a chilling, polite inclination of the head, which stopped her from taking another step.

"No," Hector said.

Valérie's lips trembled, but she did not say anything else. She whipped her skirts up and began walking away, back toward the clock tower.

Nina pressed her hands together, holding them beneath her bosom. She felt Hector drifting to her side, his hand circling her waist. They both stood in front of Luc.

"I apologize for dragging you here," the younger man said.

Luc tossed his pistol to the ground with that. Not quite believing it was all over, Nina took a deep breath and exhaled. Her cousin seemed to have turned to stone, but now he lifted his head as they approached him.

Gaetan and Hector looked at each other.

"I will speak to you plainly, Mr. Beaulieu, for you deserve that," Hector said. "I came to your house without love for Nina in my heart. Had I been a wiser man, I would have loved her from the moment I met her, but I cannot claim this wisdom. I am sorry I have caused your family any strife, but I love Nina now, and I want to marry her."

Gaetan was somber, but he nodded his head. "I don't think I could stop her from marrying you even if I wanted to, Mr. Auvray," he said. "You must wed in Oldhouse. Her mother will want it."

Gaetan clasped Nina's hand and gave it a kiss, then he spoke to the others, and they walked off together, leaving Hector and Nina to stand alone under the shade of the elm trees.

He did not seem certain what to say, his brows lifted in surprise as he looked at her. "You stopped two bullets in the air."

"Yes," she replied, not knowing what to say either, drained and shaken as she was.

"How? It's the kind of trick one has to rehearse a hundred times before getting it right," he said, his analytical mind trying to put together the pieces of the puzzle.

A breeze was blowing, toying with her unwound hair and whispering against the branches.

"I am not sure."

"You are not sure," he repeated.

"You said to believe."

She looked up at him, and he gave her a dazzling smile before leaning down to kiss her breathless.

Chapter 27

VALÉRIE LOOKED IN THE MIRROR at the almost imperceptible lines of dissatis-
faction across her brow and bracketing her mouth. She ran a hand
down her neck.

She could not rid from her mind Hector's eyes when he'd spoken to
her. How cool they were. Not hard or cruel, but lacking in any pro-
found emotion for her and able only to reflect an odd clemency.

If he had hated her, she might have felt relieved.

She heard Gaetan walk in and did not bother looking at her husband.
She wished he'd let her be, but he began talking at once in a hurried,
anxious tone, as if he intended to vex her even more.

"I have spoken to Luc Lémy, and he has explained how you two con-
fabulated, how you plotted to have Nina married off to him and Hector
removed from the picture. You will explain yourself this instant, and do
not attempt to lie to me."

"Why? You said you've spoken to Luc," Valérie said, rubbing her
hands together.

"Because I want you to do it."

"So you can judge me?"

"You have tried to wrong my family."

Valérie stood up and faced her husband. Even in his anger, he had the quality of an insect, and she was not afraid to look him in the eye instead of feigning contrition. She was not going to crawl at the feet of this man.

"Your family. Always your family. The sacrosanct Beaulieus of Montipouret are the only thing that fills your mind. It has always been them. Camille and Madelena and most of all that worm, Antonina."

"I have given you everything, Valérie," he said, looking heartbroken, but she did not care.

Trinkets, she thought. Rings and necklaces and earrings, everything accounted for.

"No. Not at all," Valérie said. "You could have lifted my family from the muck, but you decided you'd only toss them crumbs. My cousin, you wouldn't buy him that post in the army, and my uncle—"

"I do not believe posts should be bought."

"Not merely that. Always, always the Beaulieus have been the most important concern in your life. Is it any wonder I would attempt to try to help my own kin? That when Luc spoke to me, I seized a business proposition that could benefit *my* family for a change?"

"At the expense of my cousin's happiness," Gaetan said dryly. "You have done nothing but manipulate and deceive me, and slander her."

Valérie curled her hands into fists against her skirts to keep herself from slapping him. "I was sacrificed. Why should she escape her fate?" Valérie asked. "I was forced to marry a man I did not care about, dragged to the altar by my elderly relatives, and told to repeat the words the priest said."

He looked more astonished than if she had hit him, and this filled her with a deep satisfaction. All the loathing, all the hate she had kept bottled inside was oozing out, and it was delightful. In her misery, she was able to find the beauty of spite and cling to it.

"I had nothing to gain from my marriage to you," Gaetan said. "You came to me without a dowry and the debts of your father, which had to be repaid."

"A fact you reminded me of every day."

"When?"

"In every look, Gaetan. Every word. Do you think I could not tell? How kind Gaetan Beaulieu is to have married her," Valérie said in singsong. "How kind, how generous, how marvelous of him to pick a piece of trash from the street, dust it off, and set it upon the mantelpiece."

"I did not think that," Gaetan said, pointing a finger at her. "You might have thought it, but I did not." He inclined his head slightly, every fiber of his being alight with sadness in that instant. "I have loved you," Gaetan said. "I have been a good husband."

"No, no, you never loved me. You loved Camille and Madelena and that stupid girl, Antonina," Valérie said. "I know what it is like to be loved, and *you* have never loved me."

Gaetan could not possibly deny it. All his tenderness had been intended for them. He did not smile at Valérie the way he smiled at Madelena or Antonina. He never was half so delighted with Valérie, even if Valérie was more accomplished, more learned, more beautiful than his silly cousins. Gaetan knew only the pull of blood, the bonds of familial duty.

"Only one man has loved me," Valérie insisted.

It hurt to admit this, and yet she had to. She was burning inside, consumed with a roaring pain, and if she did not speak this truth, she would be reduced to ashes. Hector had adored her. But even Hector had not been enough. Even his love had not been enough, and Valérie hated herself for it.

Her hands shook. She might have wept, humiliating herself in this man's presence, but then Gaetan spoke.

"At last I understand your indifference," Gaetan said.

His tone, the disappointment in his voice, made her snap up straight. She was the one who had a right to be disappointed! What could Gaetan complain about? How dare he look at her as if she were at fault.

She had been dutiful. *She* had been a proper wife.

"I would have his name," Gaetan said.

"Do you really want me to say it? Can't you guess it?" Valérie replied.

"I will have his name, damn you!"

He was angry. Finally true emotion coursed through him instead of the tepid affection he had always granted her, she who demanded a roaring fire and had been given but a tiny match to light her heart. No wonder he disgusted her.

"Hector Auvray," Valérie said. "We were engaged once. But I was forced to wed you and then he came back for me. From across the water, from Iblevad, as he said he would. He waited ten years for me."

A decade, she thought desperately. Despite everything, it meant something.

"He'll ask you for Antonina's hand in marriage. Can you possibly grant it, knowing this?" Valérie asked, a smile dancing on her lips.

"I have granted it. I will not rescind it."

"Even—"

"You are correct on one point, Valérie. And that is that I care for Antonina very much. I would like to see my cousin be happy, and she loves that man with all her heart, as was obvious today."

"And he loves her," Gaetan added.

She would have slapped him this time, but he moved across the room and opened the armoire, pulling dresses and tossing them on the bed as though they were old rags rather than precious silks and velvets.

"You will pack your bags tonight. You are leaving for Eli, near the northern border. There you will remain," Gaetan said.

"You will attempt to send me away from Loisail?" Valérie asked. "As if I'd go."

Loisail was as important as the air that she breathed. It was *her* city. She was in the society pages every other week, a constant fixture at the most lavish parties. The boulevards might as well have been named after her.

"You have no choice."

"Attempt to put me on a train, and tomorrow *The Courier* will have the most scandalous story printed on the front page, and it will concern Antonina Beaulieu. All a woman has is her reputation," she warned him.

He moved back toward her, clasping her arm with a force she did not know he possessed, his fingers tight.

"Attempt to say a word against my family, Valérie, and not only will I divorce you, I will see that you are left begging in the streets."

She tried to shove him off, but Gaetan only squeezed her arm tighter until at last he flung her away. Valérie landed by the bed, stumbling and almost tripping as her foot tangled in a dress that lay on the floor.

She heard the fabric rip as she straightened herself up.

"You wouldn't divorce me," Valérie said. "They'd blather all around the city about it."

"Yes, they would. Which is why I'm sending you to Eli. A separation of this sort is not unheard of and better for both of us. I'll give you an annuity. But my kindness has a price, and that price is that you stay far away from me and my kin, that you never speak of us."

"I am no fool, Gaetan. Kindness can run dry rather quickly."

"So can my patience. I want you out of this house by nightfall."

Nearly breathless and in shock, she tried to think of a solution, of a way to escape this maze she had trapped herself in.

"I'll speak to *The Courier* today," she said, and though she wanted to deny it, she was afraid. Gaetan's eyes had an edge she did not know.

"As you've said, all a woman has is her reputation. Take Antonina's, I'll take yours, and as I've explained to you, my kindness will cease. Trash on the streets, you said? Pray someone lifts you up then. Pray very hard," Gaetan told her.

He left her to sit at the edge of her bed, all her finery spread upon the floor. Valérie rubbed her hands desperately. For five minutes, she labored over a letter for the papers, then ended up tossing ink and paper upon the fine carpet when the futility of the situation hit her.

She rushed to her vanity and opened her jewelry box, thinking that she might sell the precious items in there and . . . and what? Return to her father's home? To do what?

She pulled out necklaces and bracelets, until she found that lonely, thin circle of gold Hector had given her.

She clutched it tight, and as she grasped it, everything bled away from her heart. The anger, the desperation, until she was left hollow and cold. She felt herself disappearing. If she looked in the mirror, she thought she would not be able to make out her own face.

A maid came to help her pack. Valérie did not resist.

She went into the carriage, then boarded the train. As it was leaving the station, her fury returned for a moment as she watched the city speed by. She took the ring, which she had been cradling for a long time now, and tossed it out the window.

Valérie regretted the gesture at once, pressing both hands against the glass.

"It is gone," she told a startled passenger who sat in front of her and surely thought her mad.

She looked down at her perfect hands, and she recalled how her grandmother had praised them. You can tell a lady by her hands, she had said. One day, she had promised, Valérie would marry a very wealthy man, she would bring glory to the family, and she would be very happy.

But Valérie hadn't known how to be happy.

She turned away from the window.

Chapter 28

I T WAS A RELATIVELY MODEST wedding, but then again it was put together with haste. The tradition of gifting silver items and exhibiting them upon a long table for a week before the couple wed was eschewed since there was no time to properly monogram the items. In any event, neighbors from all the nearby estates came to Oldhouse, as did assorted Beaulieus.

Nina wore a dress of rich yellow satin with a short train, the neckline and sleeves encrusted with crystal and mother-of-pearl. She shunned the veil. Instead, her hair was up, yellow flowers carefully woven into it. The priest made a bit of a fuss about this detail, since it really was not decent for a young woman to get married without a veil, but there was a precedent, since Madelena had gone without a veil as well.

Hector sported a gray suit and a yellow cravat and a single, yellow flower boutonniere, to better match his bride.

Had they been in the city, they would have journeyed to the photographer to have their official portrait taken, and their names would have been published in the newspaper three weeks in anticipation of the wedding, but in the countryside, such things did not matter so much, and, anyway, everyone in Montipouret knew Camille's youngest daughter was to wed.

The civil ceremony and the religious wedding were quick affairs. The magistrate handled all the paperwork in less than fifteen minutes, and then they went to the church. The fashion was for couples to write elaborate vows, but this couple was minimalist in their declarations because, as Nina had told Hector, no one could stomach to sit inside the church for more than half an hour during the summer months. With gold rings on their fingers, they soon exited the building, and everyone headed back to Oldhouse for the dinner reception.

Since the dining hall could not accommodate all guests and allow space for dancing, they set tables behind the house, the glass and silver gleaming under the afternoon sun. There were five courses, as befitted the occasion, and cakes for dessert.

When the sun went down, they lit the lanterns and it was time to dance. Nina partnered first with Hector, but they were allowed only one dance before she was whisked away by her cousin Gaetan. Then came Étienne Lémy's turn, who had acted as best man to the groom. It was tradition that the bride dance a total of seven dances with friends and family before she could partner again with her groom.

Hector, therefore, sat patiently and watched Nina twirl around while the guests made toasts to their health. Seven toasts were necessary; that, too, was tradition.

"I shall have to become used to this new outlook of yours," Étienne said as they held their glasses up for the seventh toast. "You look as happy as a clam."

"I would think clams cannot be happy, since they are mollusks who spend their days filtering water," Hector replied.

"It strikes me that your smile resembles one of those simple mollusks, placidly sitting on the ocean floor."

"I look forward to being a placid man."

Étienne chuckled at that. Then Nina came to clasp Hector's hand, and he let her lead him to another dance. It was a long day, but they did not proceed to their room until the moon was high in the sky, and then only after the guests had made half a dozen jokes about the couple because it would not have been a wedding in Montipouret if the young men had not launched into a series of colorful double entendres.

When they reached their room, Nina walked slowly around it, humming and running her hands over the wheat sheaves the younger girls had used to decorate the chamber.

"We have to kiss like this," she said, holding one of the sheaves between her hands.

He ran a hand down her neck and kissed her deeply, the wheat rustling as she pressed it against his chest and stood on her tiptoes to better reach him. She stayed there, stayed close, her breath hot against his neck.

She whirled away from him and set to undoing the chignon she wore, carefully removing each hairpin and the flowers, placing them upon a table, where she'd also set the sheaf of wheat, while she watched the night sky through an open window, one part coy and another part the coquette.

"Nina, I have yet to give you a wedding gift," he told her.

She turned around, a hairpin in her hand, which she quickly tucked away. He took out a case and offered it to her. Inside, there was a necklace made of the clearest amber. A web spinner, its wings spread, was nestled inside the largest stone.

"It's pretty," she said.

"It's from Iblevad. There are many of these in the jungles near Port Anselm. There are also mosquitoes—I feared I would be drained of all my blood during the nights when I was performing there."

"I shouldn't mind the mosquitoes if there are as many strange beetles as they say there are," Nina replied, her voice thick with delight. "We shall have to go there one day."

"It's far," he mused. "I don't know, how do you fare on a boat? Do you get seasick?"

"I fare fine on a skiff and have gone downriver many times, it's the way one is supposed to travel around here," she replied. "I would think a large ship would be no trouble."

Nina stood before a full-length mirror, admiring the necklace as she held it against her skin. Gently he took it from her and placed it around her neck, securing the clasp. He slid his hand down her shoulders.

"It's a bit different, a skiff and a boat. It can get somewhat monotonous, and the cabins are cramped," he declared.

"As long as I'm with you, I'm sure I'll be entertained."

"I hope you mean that, since we are boarding a ship to Port Anselm tomorrow."

She looked up at him in the mirror. "You said we could not honeymoon except for a couple of days in Bosegnan, at that summer house owned by Étienne's wife. You said that you had business in the city."

"I lied."

"You are terrible. I did not bring more than a couple of new dresses and you know it is bad luck to wear old clothes during a honeymoon," she said, but her eyes were merry.

"I'll buy you more clothes, three hundred gowns if you wish it. It's not as if you have a full trousseau, anyway."

She dipped her head, blushing, but then she raised an eyebrow at him, her eyes filled with mischief. "I jest. I don't need more than a couple of dresses," she said.

"I'll save a lot of money, then. And here I was told this business of having a wife was a great expense."

Nina walked a few paces, turned her back toward Hector, and proceeded to take out the rest of the pins from her hair. He saw her from behind and was mesmerized. When she spoke, he had to ask her to repeat herself.

"I asked how long we'll be gone," she said.

"A couple of months. We can't possibly see anything in less than that. It is a whole continent, and there is Port Anselm, but also Yehenn and Carivatoo."

"You performed there?"

"Everywhere."

"And now that we are going back, you won't do any shows?"

"It's not a business trip. But if you like, I'll make mirrors spin for you."

"Only if you show me how to do it. I don't think I understand the whole levitation trick where you are able to fly on them."

She undid the buttons of her dress, shedding the satin shell, until she stood only in her white linen chemise. Then she ran a hand through her hair, undoing a couple of knots with the motion.

He was struck with the incongruity of it all, wondering how he had arrived at this precious moment. So securely she had nestled in his heart, it was impossible to map his trajectory.

"How did I ever find you?" he asked as he moved to her side.

"You didn't. I found you. At the library of the De Villiers, at the party of the Haduiers, and that night I went to Boniface," she said lightly.

He thought that truly it had been so, but that he had also been drifting toward her since the beginning, magnetized, a compass that had spun wildly and then gently settled upon a true north. Not love at first sight, because those fancies were best left for books and songs, but she had extended her hand and invited him to follow her into a dance, and he had found after a few steps that though he had never danced it before, he did not want to stop.

"Keep finding me, then," he said.

One of her hands was resting on the windowsill and she was looking outside, her head tilted in the direction of the musicians who were still playing their merry tunes.

He knew that in the years to come, even when they were old and gray and their spines were bent by the weight of time, he would remember her as she was in that moment, with a couple of stray yellow flowers in her hair, her lips parted.

He stood still, holding the moment against his heart.

Then she turned her head and smiled at him.

Acknowledgments

Thanks to my agent, Eddie Schneider, to Quressa Robinson for acquiring this book, and to everyone else at Thomas Dunne/St. Martin's Press working behind the scenes. Thanks also to Orrin Grey, who read an early version of the manuscript and offered corrections. And finally, thanks to my husband. It's all for you, babe.

About the Author

SILVIA MORENO-GARCIA is the critically acclaimed author of the novels *Signal to Noise*—winner of a Copper Cylinder Award, finalist for the British Fantasy, Locus, Sunburst, and Aurora awards—and *Certain Dark Things,* which was selected as one of NPR's best books of 2016. She won a World Fantasy Award for her work as an editor and lives in Canada.